RUNNING
with
THE PROPHETS

FINDING INTIMACY IN
THE ARMS OF YAHWEH

TAFFY SPALOSS

CONTENTS

DEDICATION

To the love of my life, Jimmy, my best friend, my fellow
dreamer, my artist extraordinaire, my confidante,
my constant and faithful encourager, the one who like
Daddy, loves me always, always, always.

"For as a branch severed from the vine
will not bear fruit, so your life will be fruitless
unless you live intimately joined to me."
John 15:4 TPT

FOREWORD

God has a way of weaving people into our lives, and often we recognize that they are placed there for a reason. Every encounter carries the potential to shape us, to teach us, and to help us grow through the wisdom of another's experiences.

Stories are powerful. When we read about someone's journey, it feels as though we walk beside them—sharing in their struggles, triumphs, and discoveries. Sometimes a single story can spark an entire movement, birthing hope, courage, and faith in the hearts of those who encounter it.

Of all the stories ever written, one book stands above them all—the Bible. Within its pages we don't just find history; we find the living Word of God, full of real people whose encounters with Him continue to inspire, convict, and transform us today.

When Taffy Spaloss told me that God was giving her a book about the prophets, I became very excited. I knew that Taffy was not only going to write just a factual representation of the lives of these mouth pieces of God, but a more intimate look at their lives. I saw the excitement in her eyes as she began unpacking the assignment that Papa had given her.

I have known Taffy a short time in the natural but feel like I have known her all my life. She has a way of making you feel like you are the only person in the room even amid sitting among many. You not only feel seen, but the love she carries from the Father leaves an everlasting fingerprint on your heart. Hearing her share the adventures and conversations in heaven have helped me to see the gentle and tender way the Father teaches us to understand Him in deeper ways. Her ability to take you on a spiritual journey through her stories makes heaven come alive. The details of emotions and imagery leave you wondering did Jesus just come and have a conversation with me?

As soon as I began reading *Running with the Prophets, Finding Intimacy in the Arms of Yahweh* I knew this was not going to be just a book but a full-on encounter with the prophets of old. From the minute I began to read the great cloud of witnesses of the prophetic came forth revealing themselves to me. The tangible presence of Abba Father came rushing in as if He opened of a portal of His chosen mouth pieces where He would begin the introduction.

Let this book open something new in you. We all know the assignments and the stories of the lives of the prophets of God, but we have not seen their humanity, interaction, and their relationships. The ordinary man who was chosen by God to do the extraordinary. Called ones filled with doubt, fear, unworthiness, and never truly understanding their gifting. Those same doubts and fears that we deal with daily. Constantly disregarding our calling, running away from all that God has for us, for you.

Learning how the prophets walked in complete obedience to all that the Lord called them to do is a lesson you will uncover through the pages of *Running with the Prophets*. The clarion call of God for radical laid down lovers can be seen in all the prophets' lives, each calling unique for a time and a purpose just like today. It's time to learn from these voices that still speak to believers through their stories written in the Bible.

My prayer is that every person reading this book can relate to one of these powerful men who had destiny written into their DNA from the heavenly Father. That you can see through the life of Moses and Elijah the importance of intimacy and friendship with God. That through the story of Elisha you'll see how radical obedience to God will open the heavens to walk in signs, wonders, and miracles. Most importantly that each prophet knew that God, Jesus, and Holy Spirit all were connected to each other, preparing the way for the greatest prophet ever and His name is JESUS. May you know Jesus and know that He has a plan for you and in no time, you will start running with Him too.

Lisa Perna, Author, Minister, Speaker, and Host of
Touched by Prayer and Podcast Host of Crown Chats Daily

INTRODUCTION

I suppose this book is evidence that I have a severe case of FOMO. FOMO, of course, is fear of missing out. Don't just tell me your story—I need to jump into your story and understand what it feels like, what it looks like.

Just hearing about the burning bush wasn't enough. I wanted to ask Moses what it was like to stand before those flames, feel the heat on his body, and hear his name spoken out loud from the middle of the flames.

I wanted to weep with Elijah as he lay under the broom tree wanting to die. I needed to understand how it happened, how he went from the top of the world on Mt. Carmel to the depths of depression in the desert.

I could only imagine Elisha stepping through the walls of water as he tried to keep his focus on Elijah and not on the fish swimming next to his face. Then seeing his master Elijah pulled from the earth into a chariot of fire—I had to know, I had to step into the story and experience the wonder of encounter with Yahweh.

So that's what I did. I jumped into each character and tried to imagine living with them through the trials and victories, leaning deeper and deeper into Yahweh as the prophets needed desperately to do. And I discovered each writing episode was like sitting at Jesus' feet. I would disappear into my writing room and emerge five or six hours later with my heart full and even wondering if my face was glowing like Moses'.

So I invite you, dear readers, to imagine with me. Let's jump into God's Word and journey together with the prophets to that place of intimacy near to the Father's heart. Yahweh is saving a place for you!

PREFACE

"Yeshua?" I whispered.

He was sitting on his throne surrounded by countless saints. I could hear the exquisite multi-part harmony of the people and the angels singing, "Holy, holy, holy." Yet he turned at the sound of my whisper.

"Elijah, come." He stretched out his hand.

We both smiled then as our eyes met, and somehow, I knew we were both remembering a similar gesture when centuries earlier a king had stretched out a royal scepter to allow young Esther to enter the throne room of another kingdom.

"How amazing," I pondered, "that I should share an inside joke with the King of kings."

I accepted his outstretched hand and gasped as I felt the rough scars in the center of his palm. Then I heard in my spirit his gentle whisper, though his lips never moved. "I will never forget you, my son, Elijah. I have engraved you on the palms of my hands."[1]

I collapsed, weeping, my arms wrapped around his nail-scarred feet.

I don't know how long I lay at his feet, but I knew it didn't really matter. I had all of eternity to worship him. Finally, I rose. "Yeshua, I've been thinking."

He smiled.

"You already know what I'm going to tell you, don't you?"

I looked into his smiling eyes. "Yeshua, I want to speak your words again, like I did on the earth."

"So you want to return to the earth, Elijah?"

"Oh, no, my Lord. No one in their right mind would ever want to leave this place. No, I want to write down the words

---

[1] Isaiah 49:16

you gave me. I want to retell the stories of your goodness, your miracles on behalf of your people."

He nodded at me to continue.

"I know that many of your saints come through the portal expecting to know everything once they get here. But I have found that I discover something new every day here in heaven. I thought that maybe I could be part of their heavenly education by writing my story for your people to read."

Yeshua smiled. "Here's what I think," he said. "Write the vision, make it plain on a scroll, that they who read it may run with it. For the vision is for an appointed time, but at the end it will not lie. Tho it tarries, wait for it, for it will surely come."[2]

As I turned to head for a quiet place to begin my writing, Yeshua called out to me.

"Elijah."

"Yes, Rabbi?" I looked up into smiling eyes, crinkled at the corners as if he had a secret to share with me.

"Would you consider leading the Company of the Prophets yet again?"

What would it look like to be on assignment again? My eyes widened with anticipation. I shouted out my instant response. "Yes, oh yes! Count me in!"

Just then, out of the corner of my eye, I saw two others approach the throne. I turned and saw to my right my successor and son of my heart, Elisha, running to join us. He ran right into my arms, nearly knocking me over. We laughed as Yeshua watched, his face beaming with joy. Then we turned to my left and there stood Yahweh's friend, Moses, leaning on his staff. Elisha and I reached out to take his outstretched hands, but Moses would have none of that. He drew us both into his arms and hugged us close to his heart. Then Yeshua stepped down and joined our huddle. Oh, the hug of God!

We stayed in Yeshua's embrace for a long while, none of us willing to let go. Finally, he patted each of us on the back and sent us on our way.

---

[2] Habakkuk 2:2–3

"Go, write your stories, write the vision and make it plain, so that each one who reads your scrolls will receive the impartation you carry, and run with it."

ELIJAH THE TISHBITE

RUNNING WITH THE PROPHETS

My name is Elijah, and here's my story.

I was born in what is now known as 900 B.C., nine hundred years before Messiah arrived on the earth. My parents were God-fearing Jews. My abba, Savah, and my ima, Natanya, were residents of Tishbe, so I had the privilege of growing up in the rolling hills and mountain peaks of Gilead.

Some of my earliest memories were of quiet mornings assisting my abba tending our terrace gardens. Well-watered with rain from heaven and dew from the earth, our olive trees grew rapidly, producing some of the finest oil. Ima often prayed for me to grow tall and strong like an olive tree in the courts of Yahweh, our God. Abba sang over our family nearly every morning, "Your wife shall be like a fruitful vine within your house, your children like olive plants around your table."[3] Ima and I laughed and danced as he sang!

I learned many lessons from Abba and Ima, but none so great as when Abba took me away for a few days, camping outdoors near our vineyards.

"You are becoming a man, Elijah. And I want you to know who you are."

I laughed. "Oh, Abba, I know who I am. I am Elijah, son of Savah and Natanya, of the tribe of Benjamin!"

"Yes, my son, but there is more to your identity than your parents and your tribe."

I looked up at Abba and waited for him to say more.

"Elijah, your name means 'Yahweh is my God.' Do you understand what that means, for Yahweh to be your God?"

---

[3] Psalm 128:3

"I think so, Abba. It means that I worship the one true God. I don't worship idols or objects that I can see in front of me. But, Abba, I do wish I could see the God I worship!"

"Ah, but you do see, Elijah! You see the sun rise each morning and set each night. You see the vineyards bulging with the grape harvest, the olive branches heavy with fruit, the goats playing on the hills!"

"Yes, but I don't see him, I don't see Yahweh, and Moses taught us that 'You cannot see my face, for no one may see me and live.'"

"Ah, but do you remember what Moses prayed for? He asked Yahweh, 'Let me see your glory,' and what happened next?"

"I know! I know!" I stood up then and recited the words of Moses.

"'Then the LORD came down in the cloud and stood there with him and proclaimed his name, the LORD. And he passed in front of Moses, proclaiming, "The LORD, the LORD, the compassionate and gracious God, slow to anger, abounding in love and faithfulness, maintaining love to thousands, and forgiving wickedness, rebellion and sin. Yet he does not leave the guilty unpunished; he punishes the children and their children for the sin of the parents to the third and fourth generation."[4]

Abba's face beamed as he listened to me recite what he had taught me.

Then Abba continued. "My son, when Moses saw God's glory, what do you suppose it looked like?"

"Light brighter than the sun! A presence bigger than a giant!"

Abba laughed and pulled me close. "Elijah, Yahweh is my God. Today I challenge you to pray the prayer of Moses. For the rest of your life, ask and keep on asking Yahweh to show you his glory. Yes, it's a mystery, but one worth pursuing. It's a bit like when you play guess which hand with your ima. You know she's got something sweet in her hand, and you know

---

[4] Exodus 34:5–7

it's for you. She's not hiding it from you, but for you. For you to find. Yahweh is like that, my son. Search him out all your days. He's not hiding his mystery from you, but for you to find when you search for him with all your heart.

"And you, my son, will continue to speak the very words of Yahweh, both from the Torah which you have memorized, and also those mysteries you hear as you search for Yahweh with all of your heart. Your words will be weighty, life changing and lifesaving to kings and commoners in the days to come. I challenge you today, Elijah, to say what you hear, and speak what you see. The world needs to hear from Yahweh, and you will deliver the words he gives you at just the right time. Although it may be difficult, even dangerous at times, to deliver the messages Yahweh gives you, you can trust him to take care of you, because Yahweh is your God."

I felt Yahweh's presence that day, although I could not see him. And I fell more and more in love with this mysterious God for whom I was named, the one inviting me to search for him in all his mystery.

THE WORD TO AHAB

I spent the years of my youth in extended periods of time alone in the wilderness. There I learned to recognize Yahweh's voice, rarely audibly, sometimes through a natural occurrence or a sudden shift in the weather, but most often as a message within my spirit that grew in intensity until it was like a fire that had to be released. From time to time I would return home and share with my people the words Yahweh had put in my spirit.

Today is the first time Yahweh has asked me to speak his words before a king. I am excited, yet a little fearful.

Our king, Ahab, son of Omri, did not follow Yahweh, which grieved and angered Yahweh. Yahweh had often spoken with me about Ahab, and I felt his sadness at how Ahab directed the people to erect and worship idols.

I woke that morning when the sun touched my face through the tent entrance and immediately began to pray.

"Blessed are you, Lord our God, King of the Universe, who brings forth bread from the earth. Blessed are you, Lord our God, King of the Universe, who created the fruit of the trees. Blessed are you, Lord our God, King of the Universe, who made creation. Blessed are you, Lord our God, King of the Universe, who made the sea."

I felt the warmth of the sun on my face, and the pleasure of Yahweh in my heart as I blessed him that morning.

As I rose and went about my chores, King Ahab came into my thoughts, and I again felt Yahweh's sadness and rising anger over this man who had led our people far from the ways of Yahweh.

I sensed Yahweh had an assignment for me, and I turned my attention to him, seeking him with all my heart, so that I would find the mystery he had hidden for me that day. I stepped outside, lifting my face toward the heaven in anticipation.

Then I heard him speak clearly out loud! I was afraid at first, hearing his voice. But then I realized his voice was not intimidating at all. No, it was familiar, like the voice of my abba. I knew that voice—not the voice of a stranger, and he knew my name!

"Elijah."

I bowed low to the ground.

"Yes, Master."

"Speak all of the words I will give you to Ahab the king of Israel."

"I will speak your words, Lord. Give me your words to speak."

"You are to warn Ahab that drought is coming. As a result of the drought of righteousness in the land of Israel, I will send a drought in the natural world for seven years."

"Seven years without rain! Lord, that is terrible news! How will we grow food? How will we feed our livestock? How will we survive?"

Then Yahweh broke into my fearful rambling. "Elijah."

"Yes, Master?"

"Deliver my message to Ahab. Then trust me, for I will show you what to do."

I remembered the words of my abba, "Although it may be difficult, even dangerous at times, to deliver the messages Yahweh will give you, you can trust him to take care of you, because Yahweh is your God."

"I will speak all that you say, my Lord!"

I rose from the ground and prepared for my journey to Samaria to deliver Yahweh's message to the king. As I hiked down the mountain, I wondered how one obtained an audience with the king of Israel. Would he receive me in his courts dirty and dusty from days of travel? Would I have the chance to bathe and change my clothes before I went to see the king?

Just then I heard a crow cawing from the top of a gnarly tree. It sounded like laughter! And I began to laugh, too. I knew Yahweh was laughing with me over the foolishness of worrying how I would gain access to the king.

"If I give you the assignment," Yahweh spoke in my spirit, "I will arrange for you to complete it. Trust me."

So I smiled to myself and headed to the courts to speak to King Ahab.

The guard at the outer court spoke roughly to me, eyeing my well-traveled appearance.

"So, who are you, and why do you wish to see the king?"

"I am Elijah, son of Savah, of Tishbe in Gilead." The guard glanced at me and shook his head, dismissing me. Discouraged, I hung my head when suddenly the words Yahweh had spoken to me began to burn inside of me. I cleared my throat. "I bring a message for the king from Yahweh, God of Israel."

The guard looked me over again and stammered, "You are Elijah the Tishbite and you have a message from Yahweh?"

"Yes."

The guard's eyes widened as he gave me his full attention. He was silent at first, since he knew he needed a very good reason to disturb the king. Finally, he answered me. "Well, the king is busy in the court right now, so give me the message and I will tell him later when he's free."

"No, sir, this message is for the king's ears only. Yahweh has forbidden me to speak it to anyone but King Ahab. Please ask the king if he will receive me now, or if I may return at a more opportune time."

"Very well, wait here."

The guard left me at the outer court and quickly went to the king with my request, but I could hear every word of their conversation from where I stood at the end of the hallway. It seemed to me that instead of growing harder to hear in my older years, I discovered I could hear even subtle whispers in a miraculous way as if Yahweh himself amplified the sound

"Oh, King Ahab, live forever."

"Yes, what do you want? Don't you see I am busy?" The king sneered at the stammering guard.

"There is someone to see you, my lord. He says he has a message for you ... from Yahweh."

King Ahab's eyes opened wide, and he turned his attention to the guard.

"A message from Yahweh? Who is this messenger?"

"He is Elijah the Tishbite, son of Savah of Gilead, sir."

"I have never heard that name before! Who is this man and what is his 'message from Yahweh?'" the king mocked.

"That is all I know, my lord. He said that he would only deliver the message from Yahweh directly to you, so he is waiting your response."

"Who is this man who dares to come to my courts with a message from Yahweh! Tell him to come back tomorrow! I do not wish to see him today. I am busy with ... well, official business of Israel. Yes, tell him I do not wish to see him."

The guard nodded and turned to leave.

Suddenly King Ahab began to look uneasy and clutched his stomach. "Wait," he said to the guard.

"King, are you alright? You look pale. Can I get you anything?"

Before the king could respond to his guard, he heard my voice from the outer courts, calling out his name.

"King Ahab! I am Elijah, son of Savah, and I have a message for you from Yahweh that you need to hear!"

The king's voice trembled when he heard my words, as if I sounded to him like the voice of God. "Go and bring Elijah to me," he told his guard.

So I entered the inner court and approached the king. Then the word of the Lord became fully clear to me, as he had promised, and I spoke exactly what I heard.

"As the Lord, the God of Israel lives, whom I serve, there will be neither dew nor rain in the next few years except at my word."

I turned and left the court.

"Wait! What are you talking about? No rain? Why, what? Get back here, old man!"

But I had completed my assignment, and I left quickly and hid myself in a crowd of people.

"Now what, Lord!" I wondered aloud. "The king is not very happy with me. Will he send his soldiers after me? Will the God of Elijah take care of me as my abba told me?"

Then the word of the Lord came to me again: "Leave here, turn eastward and hide in the Kerith Ravine, east of the Jordan. You will drink from the brook, and I have ordered the ravens to feed you there."

KERITH RAVINE,
A PLACE OF SECLUSION
AND PROVISION

I fled the city as quickly as possible and headed east toward what I hoped was the location of Kerith Ravine. I had heard of the place but had never been there myself. Abba had described it as a beautiful, but secluded place, hidden by cliffs with the sparkling fresh water of the Wadi Al Yabis stream running through it. The words of the Lord continued to run through my mind, filling me with hope and purpose as I hiked through the wilderness. Although I didn't know the way, somehow, as if the Lord himself guided me to know when to turn to the right or the left, I stumbled into the ravine as evening approached.

I sat down, shrugged off my pack, and knelt by the stream to quench my thirst. Then sitting back, I suddenly realized that I couldn't remember the last time I had eaten. In my haste to flee the city, I had taken no provision. But what had the Lord said? Something about ravens ...

I heard them before I saw them, the coarse croaking call of the ravens as they appeared over the top of the cliff and headed straight for me! I covered my face as they dove at me and then I heard several thuds on the ground. When I looked up, the ravens were gone, leaving behind a perfectly baked loaf of bread and a large portion of meat.

"Blessed are you, Lord our God, King of the Universe, who has kept me alive and preserved me and enabled me to reach this season!"

I ate the bread and meat and drank again from the stream. Exhausted, I lay down and slept.

In the morning, the ravens woke me as they dropped my breakfast from the sky, more bread and meat. I spent the day exploring the caves surrounding the ravine until the ravens reminded me it was dinner time, and I ate again and then slept.

So my days continued in my secluded wilderness hideaway. I wasn't lonely, although I never heard a voice other than my own as I prayed and sang to my God. It was as if the ravens fed my physical being, while God himself fed my soul. I found myself taking silly delight in the tiny flowers that pushed right through the rock face of my cliff side home to bloom in the bright sunlight. I carried handfuls of water from the stream and watered them daily. I enjoyed watching the progression of the sun across the sky each day and the unveiling of the stars every night. I felt full in so many ways, so loved and cared for by Almighty God, El Shaddai himself.

After a time, I noticed the stream was drying up in the drought. The prophetic word I had proclaimed at God's direction was coming to pass. No rain had fallen in the land since I uttered God's decree. One day there was not even a handful of water left to water my flowers, and they died. The ravens came one last time, and I choked down a dry breakfast with none of the sparkling water to wash it down.

Although I had felt God's presence teaching my soul those weeks at the ravine, I had not heard his audible voice since the day he gave me the words to deliver to King Ahab. But that morning, as I sat by the dry stream bed he spoke again.

"Elijah. Don't linger here any longer. There is nothing here for you now."

He knew my heart. I had felt safe here. I felt his presence every evening as I returned to camp and every morning when I awoke, just as sure as the bread and meat that arrived by ravens twice each day. I did not want to leave this place of comfort and provision. I understood then that was precisely why there was no longer any water. It wasn't a safe place for me anymore, because God was leading me elsewhere. And I realized that any place God led me was where I wanted to be. He was my comfort. He was my provision. I had trusted him with my life when I agreed to speak his dreaded words to our king, and he had been so very trustworthy. I knew I would go anywhere he led me.

"Elijah, go at once to Zarephath of Sidon and stay there. I have commanded a widow in that place to supply you with food."

Go where? Stay where, Lord? Zarephath? But that's all the Lord said.

In response to his direction that I "go at once," I rose in confusion and left the safety of my secluded safe place. I wasn't confused about my destination—I knew the route to Zarephath, a well-traveled road going that way. But it was *well traveled*, meaning lots of people walked along the way, people who could tell King Ahab they had seen the man who brought this cursed drought to the land. Taking the main route could be dangerous for me. And who would welcome me in Zarephath, the hometown of King Ahab's wife, Jezebel? Didn't God know that?

"Forgive me, Lord, of course you know all things. You know Jezebel lives there, where you're sending me. And you've promised me food, this time not by raven delivery, but at the hands of a widow."

First ravens, now a widow. I wonder, will there be a place to sleep? And how was I going to make this long journey—nearly eighty-five miles in my estimation—from Kerith Ravine to Zarephath, without any water? I stopped and looked to heaven. Would Yahweh give any further direction? But in my spirit I only heard the urgency to "go at once," so I picked up my pace and tried to focus on the lessons I'd learned by the stream. My memories immediately returned to my boyhood and the words of my abba, Savah.

I remembered his strong voice, filled with love for me and for his God: "My son, although it may be difficult, even dangerous at times, to deliver the messages Yahweh will give you, you can trust him to take care of you, because Yahweh is your God."

Then I fell to my knees right there on the dusty road, bowed in shame, weeping for forgetting who I was and who my God is.

"Oh, my God, do you want to choose someone else to speak your words? I understand if you do."

I immediately heard God's response echoing in my chest, "Elijah, go at once!"

And I knew again he had chosen me once and chose me still! "Yes, I can trust him!" I declared out loud. I raised my head and shouted as loud as my parched lungs could muster, "I trust you, Yahweh! I trust you to take care of me, for you are my God." And I rose with renewed determination to do all that God had entrusted me to do.

The rest of the journey was somewhat of a blur for me. I don't know how I kept up my pace and walked for so long. I don't know why no one along the way recognized me or bothered with me. All I remember is that suddenly I saw the town gate of Zarephath in front of me and a young woman gathering sticks in the field.

"Is she the one, Lord?" I asked in my spirit. Then I turned to the woman and bowed low. "Dear woman, would you please bring me a little water in a jar so I may have a drink?"

She answered me not a word but immediately rose to do my bidding. Was she also the one who was to feed me while I stayed in this city?

"Dear Woman!" She turned and looked toward me. "Please, please, would you bring me a piece of bread as well?"

At this she hung her head. "As surely as the Lord your God lives," she replied, "I don't have any bread, only a handful of flour in a jar, and a little oil in a jug. I am here gathering a few sticks to take home and make a final meal for myself and my son, that we may eat it and die." Her eyes were red from weeping, and her shoulders drooped over with weariness. This was the widow chosen to provide my food?

But then God's words came pouring off my parched lips. "Don't be afraid, dear woman. Go home and do as you have said. But first make a small cake of bread for me from what you have and bring it to me, and then make something for yourself and your son. For this is what the Lord your God, the God of Israel says, 'This jar of flour will not be used up and the jug of oil will not run dry until the day the Lord gives rain on the land.'"[5]

At first the widow seemed confused by my words, as if she wondered how she could even do the first part, make a cake of bread for me, and then have enough to make something else to feed her son and herself. But as I watched her face, I saw her eyes light up and she turned, lifting up the hem of her skirt, and ran home to bake me some bread.

As she passed by me, I heard her singing her prayer to the Almighty, "Blessed are you, Lord our God, King of the Universe, who has kept me alive and preserved me and enabled me to reach this season!"

I followed the widow to her home and sat outside, sipping the water she had brought me. In a short while my stomach rumbled as I inhaled the fragrance of the bread baking over the coals. Not long after that she brought me a tiny loaf of bread which I eagerly received. She delivered my dinner, then skipped back into her home to make use of the full jars of flour and oil Yahweh had refilled to make a dinner for herself and her son.

And I remembered how I felt back at the ravine which seemed already a lifetime ago, so full and satisfied in so many ways, so loved and cared for by Almighty God, El Shaddai himself. And I worshiped the God of my fathers who promised to always take care of me, for he was not only the God of my father, but my God as well.

The widow fed me morning and night for many days, as faithful as God's ravens. Better than ravens, my widow was able to speak with me, and I enjoyed long talks with her little son, Joshua, while his ima baked for us both. She also provided lodging for me and my servant, Haniah, in a rooftop room above her home.

---

[5] 1 Kings 17:14

One morning I came down the outside staircase and approached the widow's door to wait for breakfast, but she did not come outside for quite some time.

Finally, toward noon, she called to me from the window, "Man of God!"

"Yes, I am here," I answered.

"My son is very sick. Come into the house and help yourself to some bread, but I cannot leave his side right now. He is burning up with fever!"

I quietly got my own breakfast and sat outside to be near the widow as she tended to her son.

Then I heard her scream. "He's not breathing! Man of God, come quickly! He's not breathing!"

I ran inside and stood helplessly watching the young boy whose chest no longer rose and fell with the breath of life.

Then she turned to me in her anguish and fell at my feet. "What do you have against me, man of God? Did you come to remind me of my sin, and kill my son?"

I turned my eyes toward heaven in desperation and prayed in my spirit, "No, that is not why I came, is it Lord?" His answer came suddenly and surely pouring out of my mouth.

"Give me your son!"

She did not stop me. I took the lifeless child out of her arms and carried him to the upper room where I was staying. I laid him on my bed and cried out to God, "O Lord my God, have you brought tragedy also upon this widow I am staying with, by causing her son to die?"

I have no idea why I did what I did next, except that my God directed me as he always does. I went to my bed and stretched out on top of the little boy. Then I rose and cried out, "O Lord my God, let this boy's life return to him!" Then I returned and lay over him again and got up again to cry out to God. I did this three times. The last time I lay on the child I began to feel warm breath on my face. I jumped up and saw his chest rise and fall. Then he sat up and, finding himself in a strange room, began to cry for his ima. I picked up the child and held him to my chest to comfort him, then carried him down the stairs. His ima sat against the wall of the house, weeping.

As I approached with the boy, he heard her weeping and cried out for her, "Ima, Ima, do not weep! I am alive!"

"Yes, look!" I said, "Your son is alive!" And stooping down, I placed the child in her arms, where she held him and wept and laughed and wept some more.

Then lifting her tear-streaked face, she called out to me, "Now I know that you are a man of God and that the word of the Lord from your mouth is the truth."

I could only bow my head in worship. "Blessed are you, Lord our God, King of the Universe, who has kept me alive and preserved me and enabled me to reach this season!"

I went off by myself for a short time after this incident, trying to understand how to navigate the utter depths of despair I had just encountered, followed by the experience of such exhilarating joy. I felt content but utterly exhausted from the events of this very trying day. I needed alone time with Abba God, just as I had needed alone time camping with my earthly abba. Yahweh did not speak with words during our time away, but I felt his nearness and that was enough to keep me going when I returned to the home and company of the widow and her son.

SECOND ENCOUNTER WITH AHAB

I didn't understand why during the time I lived in Zarephath I was never approached by King Ahab or any of his officers. It was as if the Lord kept me hidden away in that upper room. I later heard stories of how God had in fact hidden me away from the king's grasp.

I had been spotted numerous times by the king's servants. They would run back to Ahab with the news, "Elijah is down by the city gate!" Then the king's officers would rush to find me, but suddenly I found myself in another place. I couldn't remember why I had left the gate, or how I had gotten to where I now was, but now I understood the stories.

During this time of hiding, the Lord confided in me how grieved he was because of the evil practices of the king. Ahab had married Jezebel, daughter of Ethbaal, and began to serve and worship the false god, Baal, although the Lord, Yahweh, was the Lord of Israel. Ahab rebuilt the temple of Baal in Samaria and set up an altar to worship him. Perhaps the thing that grieved God the most was that Ahab stood by while young babies were killed as sacrifices to this false god. Ahab supervised the rebuilding of Jericho by Hiel of Bethel and condoned first the sacrifice of Hiel's firstborn son, Abiram during the laying of the city's foundation, and then the sacrifice of Hiel's younger son, Segub during the setting up of the city's gates. The Lord grieved for those children, just as his heart had grieved for young Joshua, the widow's son whom he had raised back to life.

Finally, in the third year of Ahab's reign, the Lord spoke to me again.

"Elijah."

"Yes, my Lord."

"Go now and present yourself to Ahab, and I will send rain on the land."

"Oh, thank you, Lord. This drought has been so terrible on us all."

Unbeknownst to me at the time, there was a man in charge of Ahab's palace, Obadiah, who somehow in those terrible conditions remained a devout believer in the one true God, Yahweh.

One day King Ahab approached Obadiah and sent him on an assignment to find some grass still alive so that the king's animals could eat and survive the drought. Obadiah journeyed to places where he knew there had been streams or creeks, hoping to find some grazing land for the animals. All of a sudden as Obadiah was walking along, there I was standing on the path in front of him!

Obadiah recognized me and bowed low to the ground in honor. "Is it really you, my lord, Elijah?" he asked.

"Yes," I answered. "Go and call the king, your master, and tell him I am here."

"What have I done wrong, my lord, that you would want me to die? As surely as the Lord your God lives, there is not a nation or kingdom where my master has not sent someone to look for you. And even if you were there, and my master's servants saw you there, they returned to the king and swore they had not seen you. For we had all heard how you would be in one place, and then when they blinked their eyes for a moment you disappeared! The Spirit of God had whisked you away somewhere else. My master, King Ahab, put servants to death for lying to him about you being someplace, since by the time the king arrived, you were gone and he blamed them for helping you to escape."

Obadiah paced as he spoke, wringing his hand in anguish.

"But now you tell me to go and tell Ahab you are here? I don't know where the Spirit of the Lord may carry you when I leave you. If I go and tell Ahab and he comes and doesn't find you, he will kill me. Yet I, your servant, have worshipped the Lord since my youth! Haven't you heard, my Lord, what I did while Jezebel was killing the prophets of the Lord? I hid fifty of God's prophets in one cave and fifty in another and supplied them with food and water, keeping them safe from the hands of Jezebel. And now you tell me to go to my master and say, 'Elijah is here.' He will kill me! Then who will feed those hidden prophets?"

I reached out my hand and laid it on Obadiah's arm. "Do not fear, my brother, as the Lord Almighty lives, whom I serve, and you serve, I will surely present myself to Ahab today. I will not disappear this time."

In a short while Ahab came to me. I actually heard him shouting at me before I saw him coming around the bend in the road. "Elijah! Is that really you, you troublemaker of Israel?"

"It's not me making trouble for Israel, King Ahab, but you and your father's family who have greatly harmed us all! You have abandoned the Lord's commands and have followed gods who are not gods at all, the Baals."

"Who are you to say that Baal is not a god?"

"Why don't we let the Lord answer that question, King Ahab? I suggest a contest to see who is really God over Israel."

"What sort of contest? Will there be a prize for the winner?" Ahab sneered at me.

"You will see what sort of contest this will be, and yes, there will be a prize for the winner. Now go and summon the people from all of Israel to come and meet me on Mount Carmel. Oh, and make sure that you also bring the four hundred and fifty prophets of Baal, you know, the ones that frequent your wife, Jezebel's table."

"And who will you bring, Elijah, being as you are the only prophet of God still living?"

As I turned and walked away, I heard the king laughing loudly. "How long, Lord?" I prayed. "How long until you avenge the death of your prophets?"

So Ahab sent word throughout all of Israel, gathered the four hundred and fifty prophets of Baal, and came to meet me on Mount Carmel. Once they arrived, I turned and addressed the people of Israel who had assembled for the contest, "How long will you waver between two opinions?" I shouted. "If the Lord is really God, follow him, but if Baal is God, then follow him. But you can't have it both ways."

The crowd did not answer me.

"Look," I continued. "I am the only one of the Lord's prophets here, but Baal has four hundred and fifty prophets. But today, O Israel, you will learn who your God is. Now bring me two large bulls for sacrifice, one for Baal, and one for Yahweh. King Ahab, you may choose which bull you like the best."

Ahab and his prophets inspected the two bulls carefully. I heard them whispering to each other as they considered which would be the more acceptable sacrifice.

"This bull is larger and more muscular."

"Ah, but this one is spotless. I don't like the blemishes on that one's shank."

Finally, Ahab pointed to the smaller bull with the unblemished coat. "This one is mine."

"Now cut your bull into pieces and put it on the wood for the sacrifice, but do not light the fire. I will prepare the other bull and put it on the Lord's altar but will not light the fire. Since there are so many of you, and only me manning the Lord's altar, I will allow you the honor of going first in this contest."

"Now, are you ready? The bull is all arranged on your god's altar, yes?"

One of the false prophets answered, "Yes, we are ready." He added, with a sneer, "Now may we have your permission to light the fire?"

"No! No, now you must call on your god, if he is a true god, and ask him to light the fire to burn up your sacrifice. The god who answers by fire, he is God."

Immediately the prophets of Baal began to cry out to their god to send fire. From early morning to noon they prayed and sang and shouted to Baal. "Oh, answer us, Baal!" But there was no response. No one answered. The prophets began to dance around the altar. Perhaps that would get Baal's attention.

After a long while I looked up at the sky and saw that the sun was directly overhead. It was the noon hour and the prophets had been dancing and shouting for nearly three hours.

I glanced over at Baal's altar and remarked, "Maybe you should shout louder. Surely, he is a god! Perhaps he's deep in thought, or too busy to listen to you? Or maybe he is away on vacation? Or perhaps he is sleeping, and you need to scream to wake him up?"

The prophets, enraged by my taunts, shouted louder and slashed themselves with swords and spears, something they often did to appease their gods, letting their blood run onto the wood and the sacrifice. Their desperate attempts to rouse their god continued all afternoon until it was nearly time for the evening sacrifice, but there was no response. No one answered their cries. No one paid attention to their prophesying and prayers.

Then I stepped forward. "Enough! Now it is my turn." I turned to the Israelites. "Come here to me."

The people gathered around. They watched me as I reverently repaired the altar of the Lord, which was in ruins. Then I took twelve stones, one for each of the twelve tribes descended from Jacob, to whom the word of the Lord had come, changing his name from Jacob, deceiver, to Israel, triumphant with God. With the twelve stones, I built an altar in the name of Yahweh. Next, I dug a trench around the altar, deep enough to hold about thirteen quarts of seed, arranged the wood on the altar, and arranged the cut-up bull on the wood.

The crowd looked on with wonder. No one spoke, but I heard out loud, "What is the trench for?"

It was as if I could actually hear their thoughts! Although their lips were not moving, I heard what they were thinking. Is this hearing also from the Lord?

I turned to the people and said, "Now bring me four large jars filled with water."

Again, I heard voices from the crowd, though no one was speaking. "Doesn't he know that we are in a drought," the people wondered. "Four jars of precious water? What does he need water for?"

When the water jars arrived, I instructed the men, "Pour the water out over the sacrifice and the wood."

"What a waste, pouring this precious water over the sacrifice!" they murmured.

"Do it again!"

"What?" one of Baal's prophets shouted. "We are in a drought, Elijah! You cannot take our water supply for your games."

But several men from the crowd had already refilled the jars and poured them out over the soggy sacrifice and wood.

"Do it again!" I commanded, and the men once again obeyed me. The altar was so saturated that the water ran down the stones and completely filled up the trench around it.

The prophets and the people were on edge to see what God would do. How in the world could a fire be lit for the sacrifice now that the wood was soaking wet?

Then at the time of the evening sacrifice, filled with God's Spirit, I stepped forward and prayed aloud for all to hear: "O Yahweh, God of Abraham, Isaac and Israel, let it be known today that you are God in Israel and that I am your servant and have done all of these things at your command. Oh Yahweh, hear me and answer me with fire so these people will know that you are God and that you are turning their hearts back again to you!"

Immediately a fireball streaked down from the sky and landed on the bull, turning it into a blazing carcass. God's fire then consumed the wood, the stones, and the soil, and also sucked up all the water in the trench. We could hear the sound of the water boiling away and see the steam rising from the sacrifice as it was consumed.

When the people saw and heard what God did, they fell on the ground and cried out, "Yahweh, he is God! Yahweh, he is God!"

"Now that you remember who your God is, get up and seize these false prophets. Don't let any of them escape."

The men of Israel bound the wrists of the prophets of Baal, and I led the captives down into the Kishon Valley. The men lined up the prophets at my direction and looked to me for guidance.

"Yahweh demands that these false prophets of a god who is no god must perish. Draw your swords, men of Yahweh."

The people of Israel trembled uncontrollably, overwhelmed by the events of the day. One by one they hung their heads and stepped back unable or unwilling to draw their swords. I could see relief in the eyes of the prophets of Baal as they watched God's people still cowering in fear.

I stepped forward then and drew out a sword that was concealed in the folds of my robe. "In the name of Yahweh, I condemn you to death for following false gods and leading God's people astray!" Then I raised my sword and one by one plunged my blade into each and every follower of Baal.

Then I turned to Ahab, who stood trembling, watching the slaughter of all his false prophets.

"Ahab!"

He turned wide eyes on me, fearing for his very life in light of what had just happened to the prophets.

"Ahab, go now, eat and drink, for there is the sound of a heavy rain."

Ahab listened but heard no such sound. Still, he knew better than to doubt the words of this prophet of God who had called down fire from heaven right before his eyes. He hurried off to do as I instructed.

Still filled up with the words of the Lord, I left the valley and climbed again to the top of Mount Carmel. At the top I bent down to the ground and put my face between my knees.

My servant, Haniah, who had climbed the mountain with me, stood aside, waiting on my bidding. Without lifting my head from its bowed position, I called out to Haniah, "Go and look toward the sea."

"What am I looking for?" Haniah wondered aloud. But he obeyed my instructions, nonetheless, walked to the edge of the cliff, and gazed out over the sea. Returning, he called out to me, "There is nothing there."

"Go back!"

Haniah turned again to the sea, and answered as before, "There is nothing there."

Seven times I told Haniah "Go back!" The seventh time, he squinted and smiled. "A cloud! I see a tiny cloud, about the size of a man's hand, rising up from the sea."

I rose from the ground. "Go quickly now to Ahab. Tell him to hitch up his chariot and hurry for shelter before the rain stops him."

"Surely we have some time to prepare," Haniah protested. "The cloud is yet so far away, and so small."

Yet even as he turned to go to the king, the sky grew black with clouds, the wind began to whip the trees, bending them nearly to the ground, and the rain started with a vengeance. Haniah hurried then and delivered my instructions to Ahab. We watched as Ahab rushed away in his chariot towards Jezreel, leaving us alone on the mountain top. We were quickly drenched with the pelting rain.

As Haniah looked around for some sort of shelter for himself and me, I heard God speaking again to my spirit. Haniah stepped into a shallow cave and beckoned me to come and shelter with him. But God had given me another set of directions. He said "run!" So I grabbed my staff, tucked my cloak into my belt and raced down the mountain after Ahab's chariot.

"Master!" Haniah called after me. "Wait! I'll saddle a donkey for you. It's a long trip."

But by the time the words finished rolling off his tongue, I was but a dot on the horizon. I heard in my spirit Haniah talking to himself as I ran. "What? How can this old man run that fast?" I know he watched me as I caught up to Ahab's chariot and then passed it and disappeared from sight. I heard the tremble in Haniah's voice as the cold rain quickly soaked him head to foot. The last words I heard were filled with wonder. "Who is this man, Elijah? Who is this God of Elijah?"

As for me, I was filled with the power of the Lord and outran Ahab's chariot all the way to Jezreel. "There's nothing like this, O Lord, being filled up with your Holy Spirit!" my heart sang as I ran. I heard his response in my spirit but did not understand what he was saying.

"One day, Elijah, one day I will pour out my Spirit on all flesh ..."

I questioned in my mind what that would be like, for every one of the Lord's people to hear his voice, to be led in their steps which way to go, to be empowered to run faster than a chariot. Surely, if all flesh could hear your voice, Lord, all of life would be different, everyone would be changed from the inside out. I longed to hash this out with the Lord, but all that he said in response was "one day ..." and I knew the conversation was over, for today, as far as the Lord was concerned.

But I could go on dreaming about it, couldn't I? What would it look like if the king heard your correction on his own, because you had poured out your Spirit on him? One day, all the kings of the earth will rise up and give you thanks when they hear the living words that I have heard you speak.[6]

When Ahab reached Jezreel, he drove the chariot straight to his wife's palace. Jezebel heard him calling out to her as he jumped from the chariot. "Here I am!" she answered. "Come up and get out of the rain! Isn't it wonderful, all this rain? Curse that Elijah for all the drought we've suffered through."

When Ahab had dried off and was seated with his wife, he told her everything that had happened, how I had won the contest, and then slaughtered all of Baal's prophets with the sword.

"How could you let this happen, Ahab? Didn't you try to stop him? First, he curses our land for years with no rain, and

---

6 Psalm 138:4

now he kills all our prophets! May the gods deal with me, be it ever so severely, if by this time tomorrow I do not make Elijah's life like one of them." And she summoned a messenger to tell me her intentions.

I was exhausted, so tired and completely spent when the messenger found me near the palace and delivered Jezebel's murderous promise. Fear rose up in me. This evil woman certainly had the means to carry out what she had threatened. So I again tucked my cloak in my belt and ran, this time for my life.

When I reached Beersheba, I traveled for another day and night out into the desert. "I just can't, God!" I prayed as I trudged through the hot sand. "I can't do this anymore." At last, I spied a small broom tree in the distance and collapsed on the ground under its meager shade.

"Lord, where are you?" I called out, but I heard nothing. "I have had enough, Lord. Take my life. I am no better than my ancestors that perished in this desert."

Then I lay down under the tree and fell asleep.

I was awakened by the touch of someone's hand.

"Who's there? Haniah?"

In the dark I couldn't see who was standing over me, but somehow, I knew it was an angel of God. He spoke and said, "Get up and eat." Lying next to my head on the sand was a cake of bread, still warm from baking over hot coals, and a jug of water. I didn't have it in me to talk with the angel. But I ate and drank and lay back down and slept again.

After another nap, the angel returned once more and touched my shoulder. "Elijah, get up and eat, for the journey is too much for you." I sat up and ate and drank and felt strength returning to my legs. Then I stood up, strengthened by the angelic food, and took off running again. The days and nights passed as I ran in the strength of that meal, a total of forty days and forty nights until I reached Horeb, the mountain of God. There I discovered a cave where I entered and fell fast asleep.

No angel woke me the next morning. No, it was Yahweh's voice that had been silent for too long.

"Elijah, what are you doing here?"

"You know, O Lord," I answered. "I have been very zealous for the Lord God Almighty. Your people, the Israelites, have rejected your covenant, broken down your altars, and killed all your prophets. I am the only one left, and now they are trying to kill me, too!"

The Lord spoke again. "Go out and stand on the mountain in the presence of the Lord, for I am about to pass by."

My mind returned to the conversation I had with my abba so many years ago, when I had told him that I wished I could see the God I worship.

"What are you saying, Lord? Like Moses, am I going to see your glory?"

As I waited for the Lord's response, a great and terrible windstorm arose out of nowhere. I heard rocks tumbling off the mountain, splitting apart, and shattering on the cliffs below. But somehow, I knew in my spirit that God was not in that wind. I remained in the cave.

When the wind had died down, an earthquake hit the mountain, causing a huge landslide. But the Lord was not in the earthquake, so I remained in the cave.

Next, I saw out of the mouth of the cave a huge fire burning up everything in sight. The trees and the desert shrubs all turned to ash before my eyes. But the Lord was not in the fire.

After the fire I heard a gentle whisper, so subtle that I would have missed it if I weren't listening so intently. I knew it was him! It was God's presence, and I rose up, covered my face with my cloak and stood at the mouth of the cave.

Then I heard God speak. "Elijah, what are you doing here?"

"Lord, you know," I cried. "I'm the only one left, and now they are trying to kill me, too!"

Part of me wanted to judge myself. I had been on top of the world. I had heard God's voice. I had bested the evil king by calling fire from heaven to burn up a soaking wet sacrifice. I had somehow had the strength to swing a sword four hundred and fifty times and kill all the false prophets. I had outrun a chariot over thirty-one miles from Mt. Carmel to Jezreel. And now all I wanted to do was die.

"Lord, please give up on me as I have given up on myself! I am a poor excuse for a prophet. I can't do this anymore, God. Take my life."

Memories flooded my anxious mind as I stood at the mouth of the cave. First, I remembered my abba's words: "You can trust him to take care of you, because Yahweh is your God." Next came the memory of God's promise to me when I wondered how I would gain access to the king to deliver God's message: "If I give you the assignment, I will arrange for you to complete it. Trust me." My final memory came as I heard again the coarse croaking of a raven. Is that my raven, Lord, coming back to remind me that you, Lord, were and are Jehovah Jireh, my provider?

"O Lord, you have done such amazing miracles for me, and yet here I am so broken that all I want to do is die! I'm all used up, God. All alone with no heart to go on, in spite of your promises and all you have done for me." I hung my head and wept in God's presence.

Then I heard his voice strong and clear. "Elijah, my son, I am not finished with you. There is more for you. Now go back the way you came. The queen will not find you. Go to the Desert of Damascus. When you get there, anoint Hazael king over Aram. Also anoint Jehu, son of Nimshi, king over Israel, and anoint Elisha, son of Shaphat, from Abel Meholah to succeed you as prophet. Jehu will put to death any who escape the sword of Hazael, and Elisha will put to death any who escape the sword of Jehu."

It was as if God had ignored my death wish. Instead, in that gentle whisper, he gave me a new assignment. Was this good or bad, when all I wanted to do was die?

I rose to follow God's instructions, but he was not yet finished speaking with me. "Elijah." I could feel his breath on my face. He was so near as he whispered to me. "Elijah, you are not alone. You are not the only one still alive. I have kept seven thousand faithful ones in Israel, all whose knees have not bowed down to Baal and all whose mouths have not kissed him."

What happened next is something hard to explain. It was as if I was held, embraced by Yahweh. I felt him all around me. I felt the pressure on my body, over my chest, as I was surrounded by his strong presence. I felt held, held by God.

Not only held but also understood. God Almighty looked at me and saw me as I was, a tired servant, and he did not condemn me for my failure. No, instead he kissed the top of my head, just like my abba used to do, and thanked me for following him all my life. Then he acknowledged my frailty, and asked me to anoint my own successor, Elisha. I guess I could have felt that was a punishment, like Yahweh saying he was finished with me after hearing the depths of my depression. But the way he spoke to me, it was as if he was honoring me, and honoring Elisha to receive his commission through my hands.

"Lord, why are you not disappointed in me? I am disappointed in myself for how I've behaved, for not trusting you, for wanting to escape this life."

I did not hear his voice but again felt it in my spirit. "Well done, my son. I am not disappointed in you. I know your frame, that you are but flesh and blood, and I know that you have loved me with all your heart and soul and strength. You gave up your life for me. How could I be disappointed in you, my son? This is not a demotion, but a call to come up higher."

"Come up higher?" I mused. "Is there anything higher than I feel right now, enveloped in your embrace?"

I felt, though I did not see, his smile. "You will see ..."

I wept then at the kindness of the Lord, and the Spirit of the Lord filled me once again, lifted me up off the ground, and sent me on my next assignment.

ELIJAH AND ELISHA

A strange peace surrounded me as I journeyed down the mountain in the coolness of the early morning, this time walking, not running for my life. Not far along I saw a young man in a nearby field. It was the man I was looking for, right in front of me! Elisha, son of Shaphat, was there in his father's field, plowing with twelve yoke of oxen.

I approached Elisha with a determination that must have shown on my face. Elisha's eyes widened at my presence, but he said nothing. It was as if Yahweh had prepared him for my message before I spoke a word. So I took my cloak and wrapped it around his shoulders for a few minutes. Then I turned and began to walk away.

Elisha seemed momentarily stunned by my actions, but then he left his oxen and ran after me. "Elijah!" he called out, and I stopped to allow him to catch up with me. "Let me kiss my abba and ima goodbye, and then I will follow you."

Elisha then ran back to the oxen and drove them with haste out of the field toward his home. There he slaughtered his oxen and used the plowing equipment to build a roaring fire. He cooked the meat and gave it to his family and friends who had gathered. Not one of his relatives objected to my intrusion in his life, not even his elderly father who wept as he held tightly to his son. No one attempted to dissuade Elisha from following me. Again, it was as if Yahweh had prepared Elisha and his family to recognize and accept Elisha's invitation to follow me as if Yahweh himself had spoken.

I looked on with awe watching Elisha literally burning up his current life -there was no coming back - to pursue a life of uncertainty following an old man who heard from God.

"How, why, Lord," I asked? "Why would this young man abandon all his earthly means of provision to follow me? Am I not just a man?"

Then I heard my abba, no, it was not my abba's voice; it was Yahweh's voice this time speaking my abba's words over me, "And you, my son, will continue to speak the very words of Yahweh, both from the Torah which you have memorized, and also those mysteries you hear as you search for Yahweh with all of your heart. Your words will be weighty, life changing, and lifesaving to kings and commoners in the days to come. "

My tears flowed freely as I worshiped and walked on from that place of sacrifice, with Elisha following close behind me.

ELISHA

MEETING ELIJAH

Only a few short months had passed since I turned around in the field that day to find out whose shadow was blocking the sun and giving me a brief respite from the heat of the day.

That day I met Papa Elijah for the first time. Oh, I had heard stories about the man, some of the seemingly crazy things he did, the risks he took with kings and officials, telling them what God thought about what they were doing. He was somewhat of a superhero in my mind, a legend, larger than life, and then he shows up behind me in the field!

He said nothing, just stood there looking me in the eye. Then he took off his cloak and tossed it over my shoulders. I found myself shaking as I felt the weightiness of the cloak on my back. Not that it was heavy, no, it was more like what it meant to me that was a weight I'd never carried before.

I knew that if I accepted the weight of that cloak, life would never be the same. In the few seconds that followed as we both stood still and quiet, I realized that Yahweh had been preparing me for this very minute.

I had always loved the fields, loved watching the furrows turn brown under the plow, loved inhaling the fragrance of the freshly turned earth. I loved when the young plants miraculously poked out of the soil and eagerly turned upwards seeking out the sunshine. But lately, I'd felt a yearning, a dissatisfaction in my soul, as if, there was something more. There had to be something more.

And now that something more was standing in front of me, the sun streaming through his graying, disheveled hair as he locked eyes with me. Then he removed the cloak from my shoulders and began to walk away.

"Father!" I called after him. "Wait for me. I'm coming! Let me go home and kiss my parents goodbye."

Elijah, still silent, followed behind me, almost nonchalant, as if our encounter meant nothing to him at all. Looking back at that first encounter with the man of God I realized that Elijah was not a man of many words, especially when he was on assignment. It seemed he had learned to only speak the words given to him by God, and not add any of his own, a lesson desperately needed by an impulsive young man like me.

When I reached home, I immediately slaughtered my twelve oxen. Using my plow for firewood, I prepared a feast for my family, my own farewell party.

We sat around the fire afterwards, laughing and enjoying what would be our last family gathering. Then Elijah rose without a word and swiftly walked away. Without hesitation I was up and running after him, and I've never looked back!

CHARIOTS AND HORSES OF FIRE

Alive! That's all I can think to describe how it feels to follow Elijah. I love my life. I'm learning to hear Yahweh's voice. This morning, however, I awoke with an urgency that was strangely both disturbing, yet exciting.

I heard Yahweh speak to my spirit, "Today, my son, today is the day."

"What day is this, my Lord?" I asked.

"Today is the day when you will wear your master Elijah's cloak and never take it off again."

"What? What do you mean? What will my master wear if I take his cloak, Lord?"

Yahweh chose not to respond to my questions, but he gave me this instruction. "Do not take your eyes off of Elijah today." And that was all he said.

I made breakfast for Elijah then and tended to his needs. Elijah began packing up his meager belongings and I knew we were getting ready to move on as God directed. We shouldered our packs, and I got ready to follow him when Elijah turned to me and put his hand up as if to block my path. "Stay here!" he said sternly. "The Lord has sent me to Bethel."

I was confused. I had heard God's direction for me to keep Elijah in my sight at all times today. But now Elijah was telling me to stay behind and not go with him. How was I to obey both my master, and my God, when they were sending me in opposite directions?

Only seconds passed before I knew that it was God's voice that I must obey. I must obey God over man at all times, even when the man is my earthly master, the one I look up to above all others, the man I've entrusted my life and future to.

"Father Elijah?" I began almost timidly, but then the words bubbled up inside me, and I spoke fervently. "As surely as the Lord lives and as you live, I will not leave you." It was then that I first experienced what I like to call "the smile of Yahweh." I felt Yahweh's pleasure like warm sunshine on my face. I knew he was pleased with me for hearing his voice and obeying his voice above all others. As I matched my steps with my master's I caught sight of a slight uplifting at the corners of his mouth, and though he spoke not a word, I knew he was pleased, too.

Not long afterwards we reached Bethel, and a company of prophets came out to greet us. The prophets then allowed Elijah to walk ahead of us, and they whispered to me, "Do you know that the Lord is going to take your master away from you today?"

Did I know? Maybe not a second before they spoke, but now suddenly I knew that was exactly what was going on.

"Yes, I know!" I shushed the eager prophets. "But do not speak of it."

As if on cue, Elijah then turned to me with another stern command. "Stay here, Elisha, the Lord has sent me to Jericho."

Without hesitation I replied, "As surely as the Lord lives and as you live, I will not leave you."

Together we traveled on to Jericho where another group of prophets asked me if I knew today was the day the Lord would take my master away from me.

"Shhh! Yes, I know," I told them as before. "But do not speak of it."

The contest with Elijah continued next as he told me "Stay here, the Lord has sent me to the Jordan Riv—"

I interrupted him before he even finished speaking. "As surely as the Lord lives, and you live, I will not leave you."

So together we walked on until we reached the banks of the Jordan. There a group of fifty prophets approached us and then stopped a short distance away to see what we would do.

My heart was pounding in my chest as we stood for what felt like an hour with the Jordan lapping quietly at our feet. I received no further messages from the Lord, so held fast to what he had said to me. My only assignment that day was to keep my eyes on my master so that is what I did, not turning to the right or left, or looking at the prophets gathered behind us. My heart cried out to God, "Yes, Lord Yahweh, I will not let my master out of my sight!"

Elijah then took off his cloak. He rolled it up tightly and struck the water with it. Before my eyes, the water divided in two, and I followed Elijah into the exposed riverbed.

We walked silently in between the walls of water. I was tempted to examine the water on either side of me as we crossed through. How can this be that water can stand up like a column of rock? My peripheral vision showed movement in the water, even as it stood at attention on either side of me, and I desperately wanted to turn my head to take a closer look. But today was the day! The Lord had spoken! And I was not going to miss a thing by diverting my attention off my master.

As we climbed out of the riverbed, Elijah turned to face me. "My son." He spoke tenderly to me, like my own abba. "Elisha, what can I do for you before I am taken away?"

There it was! Now out in the open, Elijah was finally admitting that today he would be leaving me. He knew it, his prophets knew it, and I knew it in my spirit! And now, Elijah was offering me a parting gift, a gift of my own choice. At first, I was overwhelmed by his offer. What should I ask for? What is in his power to give me? I was taken back to a memory, as a young boy, dreaming with my friends. We had sneaked out of our homes one night and lay on the ground in a nearby field watching the night sky together. Stretched out in a circle, with our heads touching, we gazed upward and marveled over Yahweh's magnificence in arranging every star in its place. We challenged each other to dream with Yahweh about our own futures. If we really believed that we were the chosen people of God, the God who created the universe, the God of unlimited power, the God who owns the cattle on a thousand hills, then what amazing things will we do when we grow up?

"I'll be rich!" my friend, Oni said. "I'll own thousands of cattle, sheep, goats and camels."

I laughed with him, thinking of the tiny flock of goats his father owned and required Oni to look after.

Susa followed right behind Oni, "I will own a city. All the people will work for me and build me a wonderful palace." Susa and his family lived in a goat hair tent at that time.

Then my friends turned to me. "What about you, Elisha? What will you do, what do you want from Yahweh?"

What do I want? The thought was overwhelming to me! If I could have anything, do anything, because my God is so amazing, what do I want?

"Elisha!" Elijah's insistent voice called me back from my daydreaming. "Tell me, what do you want me to give you as a parting gift, from the unlimited resources of Yahweh?"

Then I knew, or maybe it was Yahweh himself who decided for me. "Let me inherit a double portion of what you carry, Elijah!" I cried.

Elijah seemed taken aback and actually stepped backwards as if my request had stunned him. "You have asked a difficult thing, my son. Yet if you see me when I am taken from you, it will be yours. Otherwise not."

Suddenly, more than anything I had ever dreamed of with my friends, possessions, property, fame, nothing mattered except that I receive this thing that I asked of my master. I barely blinked my eyes as we walked along, determined that nothing would take my gaze off him. My final challenge came when right in front of us, a chariot on fire, no, not on fire, but made of fire appeared, pulled by fiery horses! Just as when I had wanted to examine the walls of water, I never allowed my eyes to leave my master. I saw Elijah climb into the chariot. How was he not burned up?!? I saw Elijah's cloak fall from his shoulders and float toward the ground, but still my eyes stayed on my master, not watching to see where the cloak would fall. Elijah picked up the flaming reigns! Then the whole chariot began to spin as a tornado erupted in the sky, and I watched Elijah ride that burning vehicle in a whirlwind right into heaven! Then he was gone.

I stood there for some time, my heart nearly beating out of my chest, gazing into the now empty sky. "My master, Elijah," I whispered.

What had happened? My master was gone. First it began as a trickle, then I wept as waves of grief overtook my body. I grabbed my tunic with both hands and tore it apart. I was expressing my grief at losing my master, yes, but more than my own personal grief I realized that I was experiencing the grief of my people, my nation over the loss of this prophet who had served them his entire life. At first, I could not understand what I was feeling. It was as if I was somehow responsible for my people, Yahweh's people. It must be how my own father felt when he proudly released me to follow Elijah.

This was new for me, and I realized I had received the first of many impartations from my master. Though I had no children of my own, all at once I was father to a nation, entrusted to my care by the impartation I received from my master.

I realized another truth after the weeping had subsided. I knew that my master was not dead. I saw him alive and well, driving horses of fire into heaven! I marveled at what I could not understand. My master, still alive, had gone into heaven before my very eyes. And I had fulfilled my final assignment from Yahweh while under Elijah's instruction. My eyes had never left my master. Therefore ... therefore ...

"What else?" I wondered aloud. "What does a double portion of the spirit of Elijah look like, besides instantly becoming a father to a nation?"

I looked down then and spotted Elijah's cloak lying on the ground where it had fallen. I walked back to the bank of the Jordan river, rolled the cloak as I had seen my master do a short time ago, and struck the water.

"Where now is the God of Elijah?" I spoke aloud.

At once the waters parted as before, and I crossed through the walls of water. This time I walked slowly, examining the watery columns as I passed by. I could see the water flowing as it stood up and even saw fish bumping into the boundary I had created with my words and Elijah's cloak. I marveled and worshiped the God of Elijah, now the God of Elisha.

On the other side of the river the company of the prophets were waiting for me, watching what had happened. I heard them speaking to one another, "The spirit of Elijah is resting on Elisha!" Then they approached me and bowed low to the ground. "Master," they said. "We want to honor Elijah with a proper burial. Where is his body? We will cross the river and find it."

"There is no body," I told them. But they would not, could not believe what I was saying.

"What do you mean there is no body? Perhaps the Spirit of the Lord has picked him up and set him down on some mountain, or in a valley somewhere. We are willing to send a company of fifty men to find him."

"No, I replied. Do not send them. There is no body."

But the prophets persisted, as if they thought I was so full of myself that I didn't want the body of my master to be found. So at last, I relented and allowed them to search for a body they would never find, since Elijah, my master, was not dead at all.

For the next three days the fifty men searched for Elijah's body but did not find him. Did they believe me now?

"I told you not to go," I said. I hoped they would begin to believe what I knew in my heart, that their master was alive, and now saw Yahweh face to face.

The men left without a word, and I was left alone with my thoughts. I realized then that I was truly alone. There was no one who understood me like my master, Elijah. He had experienced hearing the voice of Yahweh. He had lived his life in obedience to the sometimes quirky commands of the Most High. Under Elijah's sometimes unspoken tutelage I had learned to lift my face toward heaven for direction over the choices of life. But I had usually also turned to the one shadowing me, my master, for confirmation over my decisions. All at once the loneliness of my life hit me like a millstone, and my body was wracked with sobbing.

"Lord, how will I know, who will confirm to me that I have heard your voice correctly? A whole nation is depending on me now to hear from God on their behalf! Where is the God of Elijah?"

Suddenly out of nowhere a strong wind nearly blew me off my feet. Obliging, I got on the ground face down as a sandstorm blew all around me. I closed my eyes to keep the sand from blinding me. Then as suddenly as it had started, the wind ceased and the air was silent, even eerily still. I felt the warm sun on my body. It felt to me like the smile of my father as he sent me off in service of my master, Elijah. It felt like the smile of Elijah as I learned to hear God's voice. But I knew it was again the smile of Yahweh! And once more I was overcome with weeping, this time with joy. I would never again be alone as I lived my life under the smile of Yahweh.

After a time, I rose from the ground, shook off the sand that covered my head and clothing, and traveled into the city. As I walked, I prayed. "Lord Yahweh, what does it look like to wear a double portion of Elijah's spirit?" I waited for Yahweh to speak, but only heard God's gentle whisper in my spirit, "You will see."

I had barely entered the city limits when a company of community leaders approached me. Just as I had seen them look to Elijah for guidance, now they were coming to me. I silently asked Yahweh to give me the answer the leaders needed for whatever was on their minds.

"Look, Lord Elisha," one of the leaders called out as they came near. Lord Elisha? It must be the mantle, I thought, as I pulled Elijah's cloak more tightly over my shoulders.

"This town is in a great location as you can see, with a water source flowing right through our territory. But we have discovered that the water is contaminated, and we cannot use it for irrigation, nor for drinking water. Can you help us, Lord Elisha?"

I heard in my spirit and merely recited what I knew I was hearing from God. "Bring me a new bowl. A bowl that has never been used for any other purpose. Put some salt in the bowl and bring it to me."

Without hesitation the bowl of salt was brought to me. I walked over to a spring of water bubbling out of the sandy earth and threw the salt into the water. I watched as the crystals of salt scattered over the surface of the stream. The men around me looked on in wonder.

Again, I spoke the words I was hearing in my spirit. "This is what the Lord Yahweh says, 'I have healed this water. Never again,' Yahweh has spoken. Never again will this cause death or cause the land to be unproductive."

A shout of praise erupted from the men around me.

"Blessed are you, Jehovah Jireh, our provider! Jireh! Jireh!" they chanted as one voice.

Then these grown men stepped into the spring and began to jump like children in the cool water. They bent down and drank from the water that had been deadly only minutes before but now was completely safe for them and their families, their crops and their livestock.

I marveled at their trust, how they received my words and immediately acted on them, drinking the water that they knew had been poisonous. They trusted me as I trusted Yahweh. And that, I was learning, was a formula for success in the life of a prophet.

THE POWER OF A PROPHET'S WORDS

I left the city and went up towards Bethel, still marveling over the miraculous healing of the waters.

Lost in my thoughts, I barely noticed as a crowd of young boys came around the bend in the road, laughing and joking among themselves. Then they turned their joking toward me.

"Look at that guy!"

They were pointing, staring at me.

"He's so bald the glare of the sun off of his head is blinding me," said one boy, covering his eyes and moaning as if in pain, as the other boys roared in a laughter.

"Go up, Baldhead!" they jeered. "Go up and get out of here, like Elijah! We don't need you around, Old Man!" And they approached me with bravado, hoping to scare me off as I traveled seemingly alone on the road.

I was filled with anger, and yes, with shame over my baldness. Though I was still a young prophet, this baldness made me look and feel like an old man. I hated the baldness, hated having to keep my head covered in the heat of the day to protect myself, never getting to feel the wind in my hair that I had enjoyed as a child running in the fields with my friends. But I was feeling something else, something more than my own selfish anger. These young men were not only mocking me as a prematurely bald man. No, they were also mocking my master, Elijah, and shouting their unbelief about his translation to heaven. They may as well had said "go to hades" as "go to heaven with Elijah." They didn't believe what God had done either way.

I turned and faced the boys, my face stern and without even the hint of jest. "You are cursed by Yahweh. Because of your words. your mocking of me, the servant of the Most High

God, and the mocking of my master, Yahweh's prophet, Elijah, you are today cursed by God."

I watched as the boys abruptly stopped walking toward me and their faces filled with fear. Not a word of jeering or laughter was heard among them. All at once two growling she bears ran out of the woods and fell upon the young men, killing them all, then lumbered off into the woods without a glance in my direction.

I fell to the ground, lay with my face in the road and cried out to Yahweh.

"Lord, what just happened?" I cried as I thought of the boys and their soon to be grieving families.

And I heard the Lord's reply, stern and without apology. "I will not allow my anointed ones to be mocked. And I will not allow my words spoken through my prophets to fall to the ground. So shall my word be that goes forth from my mouth, it shall not return to me empty, but it shall accomplish what I please and fulfill my purposes."[7]

He went on, less sternly than before. "My people must learn to listen to the words of my prophets. Anyone who welcomes a prophet and honors him as my messenger will receive a prophet's reward."

"My Lord," I whispered. "I have never heard of this before. What is a prophet's reward?"

"I reward the one who receives the words that you speak on my behalf with the fulfillment of what I have spoken."

"Yes, Lord, but how does a man receive your words?"

"Just like you do, my son. The one who hears the prophetic word receives it into his heart as if he had heard it directly from me, although he did not hear me speak it as you did. And he demonstrates he has received it by doing what I have directed him to do, just like you turn to the right or left at my direction. In such a way, that man or women receives a prophet's reward."

I was stunned by what Yahweh said to me that day as I lay in the dirt. I realized that I had better be very careful with

_____

[7] Isaiah 55:11

every word of God that came out of my mouth and only speak what he said. Apparently, my words were very powerful. They carried both the power of life, and death. I determined I would never take that truth lightly.

ELISHA AND THREE KINGS

My heart grieved that another of the wicked king, Ahab's descendants, his son, Jehoram had succeeded him as King of Israel in Samaria. Jehoram wasn't quite as evil as his father, but he didn't follow Yahweh. Since he did not particularly want to hear from God, he also did not consult with his prophets. I had not yet been summoned to his court for any reason since he began his reign.

During the reign of King Ahab the kingdom of Moab was subservient to Israel. As a sheepherder, Meesha, King of Moab was required to supply the king of Israel with a hundred thousand lambs, and the wool of a hundred thousand rams, which cut deeply into Moab's economy. When Ahab passed away, Meesha, king of Moab decided it was time to throw off Israeli rule, and he abruptly cut off the flow of livestock and wool to Israel.

Jehoram knew he had to work quickly to end Moab's rebellion or lose the benefit of their labor. So he set out from Samaria and mobilized the troops of Israel. Next, he sent messengers to the King of Edom and the King of Judah. "The King of Moab has rebelled against me," he wrote. "Will you go with me to fight against Moab?"

Edom's king was immediately on board, but Jehoram wondered if Jehoshaphat, king of Judah would come along as well, since their two nations had parted ways shortly after the last of David's sons had ruled the combined areas of Israel and Judah. However, Jehoshaphat replied warmly to Jehoram, "I will go with you. I am as you are. We are both sons of Israel, both followers of Yahweh. My people are as yours, my horses are as yours. We will crush this rebellion together!"

Since Jehoshaphat was more experienced in battle than Jehoram, the kings deferred to Jehoshaphat to decide the best route into Moab. "Let's come at them from the south," Jehoshaphat advised. "They won't be expecting us to come through the wilderness of Edom."

Early the next morning, the kings and their troops set out and traveled seven days through the desert. They were still far from Moab, but had already used up their entire water supply, with no replenishment in sight.

When King Jehoram learned of their predicament, he became very angry. "What do you mean there's no water? Has the Lord called us three kings together only to hand us over to Moab?"

Jehoshaphat came quickly to Jehoram's side to try to calm him down. "Jehoram, remember, we are not alone here in the wilderness. Yahweh is still with us. Isn't there a prophet of God around here that can inquire of the Lord for direction for us?"

Since becoming king Jehoram hadn't sought the Lord yet for any guidance. "Would the Lord even hear my prayer if I asked him?" he wondered. But before he could respond one of the officers came forward.

"Yes, there is a prophet nearby!" he called out. "Elisha, son of Shaphat is here. He's the one who served under Elijah, and now it has been said of him that he carries a double portion of the spirit of Elijah."

"Well said, my son," Jehoshaphat congratulated his officer. "Elisha surely speaks the words he hears from God. He will help us determine the next steps we must take."

So the three kings traveled to the city where I was staying.

I was waiting outside my home as they approached. "Why are you here, King Jehoram? What do you and I have to do with each other? You have never come to me before. Why don't you go inquire of your father, Ahab's prophets, or your mother, Jezebel's prophets, since you have had no use for a prophet of the Most High God?"

Jehoshaphat turned to Jehoram. "Is this true, Jehoram? You have a prophet who speaks the very words of Yahweh, and you have not asked his guidance for Israel?" Jehoshaphat shook his head in disbelief.

"I am here now, my Lord!" Jehoram cried out. "I am here because the Lord called us three kings together and it appears we are destined to die of thirst in the desert or become slaves of Moab!"

I wanted nothing to do with Jehoram, who was to me but a poor image of his father, Ahab. I prayed in my spirit, "God, do you really want me to help this evil man?" I knew right away God's response.

"As surely as the Lord lives and whom I serve, King Jehoram, if I did not have regard for the presence of King Jehoshaphat of Judah, I would not even glance your way or give you the honor of a response. But because of Jehoshaphat and his respect for me and my God, I will inquire of the Lord on your behalf. Now bring me a harpist."

A young harpist was quickly summoned and began to play. I sat down on the bench outside my home and closed my eyes. "Yahweh," I prayed silently. "Forgive me for not wanting to help King Jehoram, when I perceive now that you have decided to rescue him."

At once I heard it before I felt it, a strong wind rushing up over the parched grasses. Empowered by the wind of God's presence I stood up and faced the kings.

"This is what the Lord says: Make this valley full of ditches."

"Ditches?" I heard the unspoken thoughts of the kings and the people as if with one voice.

"Gather your farming tools, hoes, axes, and shovels and dig ditches across the land. For this is what the Lord says: You will see neither wind nor rain, yet this valley will be filled with water, and you, and your livestock will drink and be refreshed!"

King Jehoram and Edom's king both turned to King Jehoshaphat to see his reaction to this impossible thing that Elisha was speaking. "Is this possible? How will water fill the ditches if it doesn't rain?"

Jehoshaphat was grinning. "If Yahweh says it, it will come to pass. Don't give up hope. Our God is for us still!"

Elisha heard the kings whispering to each other and was smiling as he continued. "And since this feat Yahweh will perform is such a simple task for him, filling up dry ditches with water when there is no rain, Yahweh has decided that he will hand over Moab and it's king to you as well. You will overthrow every fortified city and every major town. You will cut down every good tree, stop up all of Moab's springs and ruin every good field with stones."

I could see the faces of the soldiers brightening as they heard Yahweh's promises to them. Many nodded and smiled as they began to believe that there was still hope. It helped that Jehoshaphat was nearly jumping up and down with excitement over the words of Yahweh on their behalf. If King Jehoshaphat could accept that God truly cared for his people and had come to their aid, then they could, too.

Jehoshaphat wondered again how the king of Israel could go so long without taking advantage of such an amazing prophet living right in his community. He hurried to me and knelt at my feet. "Thank you, Elisha! Your words have brought hope and life to me and our men this evening. May Yahweh bless you!"

As I entered my home for the night, I heard the men of Israel, Edom and Judah digging ditches in the hard earth. After several hours of digging, the men lay down with their packs and settled in for the night to wait for the word of Yahweh to be fulfilled. I was asleep the moment I lay down, filled with the warmth of Yahweh's words that had filled my heart and poured out of my mouth that day.

The next morning, I awoke and began to recite my morning prayers. "Blessed are you, Lord our God, King of the Universe!" As I glanced out the open window, there it was ... water flowing from the direction of Edom, from the desert wilderness, and it flowed through the land and filled up every ditch the men had dug at the Lord's direction. I watched as the men laughed with joy, splashing the water over their dry faces, drinking handfuls and filling bowls and troughs for their livestock. "Yes! Blessed are you, Lord our God, King of the

Universe, who has kept us alive and preserved us and enabled us to reach this season!"

While the kings and their men were enjoying the refreshment the Lord had provided, the King of Moab was preparing for battle. He had heard that the three kings had joined together to fight against him, so he called every man, young and old alike to take up arms. They were encamped at the border of Moab, waiting for the king's instructions. When the troops awoke early that morning the sun was shining on the water that had covered the land in the direction of Edom. Reflecting the rising sun, the water appeared red, like blood.

"Look, that's blood," they shouted to one another. "Those kings must have turned on one another and slaughtered each other. Now to the plunder!"

When the Moabites approached the camp of the three kings near the home of Elisha, they discovered the soldiers were very much alive. The Israelites rose up and fought the Moabites until they fled. In accordance with the words of the prophet, the Israelites invaded the land and slaughtered the Moabites. They destroyed the cities. Then each man threw a stone on every good field until the fields were covered. They stopped up the springs of water and cut down every good tree.

I heard the stories as the Israelites returned from battle. I heard specifically how each word Yahweh had given me to speak came to pass. The ones who had come to destroy God's people had themselves been destroyed. And I bowed my head to the ground and worshiped the God whose words never fell to the ground.

"Thank you, My Lord and my God. Every word of God proves true. By your words shall men live. Blessed are you, Lord our God, King of the Universe, who has kept us alive and preserved us and enabled us to reach this season."

THE COMPANY
OF THE PROPHETS

There's nothing so wonderful as doing life with a prophetic community, a group of people whose mutual heart's desire was to hear from God and speak what he said. I had the privilege of living among such a company. We continually challenged each other to listen well to the Holy Spirit, to learn what his voice sounded like. The young prophets looked up to the mature ones, and the mature ones were intent on preserving their legacy by teaching their students to begin to build their own history with God.

There was no rule book when it came to the prophetic. We could not instruct each other by saying, "This is how God always moves!" When God's direction seemed too harsh to declare, like when the bears killed those young boys who had taunted me, God would caution us saying, "Do not be more merciful with your enemies than I am." Sometimes evil just had to be called out and dealt with, on the spot.

Other times, we were personally offended by the evil around us. My master, Elijah, had explained to me how he had reacted when King Ahab repented at the end of his life. There was never a man like Ahab who sold himself to do evil in Yahweh's eyes, urged on by his conniving wife, Jezebel. Ahab had a good man, Naboth murdered at Jezebel's suggestion, just so he could take over ownership of Naboth's vineyard.

Then Elijah had pronounced God's judgment on Ahab. "Everyone in your family will die!" he told Ahab. "Thus says the Lord: I will consume your descendants and cut off from you every last male in Israel, slave or free. You have not only provoked me to anger, but you have caused an entire nation, my people Israel, to sin."

Elijah described to me how he had watched Ahab sink to the ground under the weight of his words. Still Elijah had continued to speak what Yahweh commanded: "You and your descendants will all be cut down, young and old. Dogs will eat the dead bodies of you and your family living in the city, and the birds of the air will feed on the flesh of your descendants in the country."

When Ahab heard Elijah's words, he tore his clothes, put on sackcloth and sat in a pile of ashes in the palace. It was reported that he also fasted from food for days on end.

But Elijah had not been fooled by his charade. "Too little, too late!" he had thought. "This evil ruler must die for what he has done."

But Yahweh had other plans. Elijah shared with me what Yahweh spoke into his spirit as he raged inside over this evil man. His words stopped me in my tracks! Here I was ready to call fire down from heaven to immediately devour this man and his entire family! But instead, I heard God's whisper, "Elijah, have you noticed how Ahab has humbled himself before me?"

"He doesn't fool me, my Lord!" Elijah had said.

"Oh, is that so, Elijah? So I am fooled?"

Elijah had fallen to the ground then in repentance for challenging the words of Yahweh.

"Here is what Yahweh taught me, my son," Elijah had instructed. "Yahweh looks inside a man. He doesn't judge by what you or I can see. He must have seen some small spark of repentance in Ahab's heart. In my anger I had already judged the man and condemned him to die, as if the mighty Elijah was judge and jury, instead of leaving those roles to Almighty God."

I had listened intently to Elijah's instructions but now bowed my head to my chest as I recognized in myself that I, too, was quick to judge by appearances.

Elijah had somehow known my thoughts. "I know my son, that you have, as do I, a strong sense of justice. And that is a good thing. Your spirit rises up inside when you see someone getting away with evil, when you see someone suffering under the hands of an evil man or woman. But I share this story of my own failure to see as God sees, so that you will learn with me yet another lesson about this God we serve. This is what Yahweh says: 'I do not judge by outward appearance. I judge by what I see in a man's heart. Sometimes you will think I am too harsh. Sometimes you will think I am too lenient. So each time you don't agree with me, I want you to get alone with me and we will talk about it. I want you to tell me when you're upset, or confused, or angry.'"

I had interrupted my master then. "But Elijah, God knows already every word on my tongue before I open my mouth. Why does he want me to talk to him about what is in my heart when he already knows?"

"My son, Yahweh wants you to know him. He is not only interested in having you speak for him, as if being a prophet of God was merely a job to do. Yahweh is after your heart, Elisha. The Creator God wants relationship with you. He wants to be a father and a mentor to you, as I have been. If you don't believe that you can speak freely with him, share the things on your heart, good and bad, then you will not be able to clearly hear what is on God's heart. Is that something you want, my son?"

I had not answered Elijah for some time as I pondered that question in my heart. Do I want to hear God's heart? What would that be like? I remembered playing with my friend, Oni, as a child. Once when Oni and I were skipping stones at the river's edge, I noticed that he was unusually silent, and I knew something was wrong. I wanted to be there for my friend, so I asked him what was troubling him. He hesitated at first, not wanting to "air his dirty laundry" outside his family home. But he must have seen in my face that I loved him and wanted to help if I could, so he told me the story of a dishonoring that had taken place between a young man, and Oni's older sister.

"Nothing happened, really," Oni had said. "It was just words spoken, but my poor sister was so crushed with shame that she has not gone out of the house for weeks now, and she did nothing wrong to begin with! What can I do to help her, Eli?"

"'I'm so sorry, my friend,' I had told Oni. 'I feel your anger against that young man for hurting your sister. I am angry, too.

But it's not true what he said, so any shame your sister is feeling is based on a lie. Oni, you must speak the truth over your sister and help her to lift up her head again.'"

Oni had been so grateful to have someone to talk to about the problem his family was dealing with. "You won't tell anyone about this, right?" he had asked.

"No, I'll never bring it up again, unless or until you want to talk about it again."

It had been such an honor that Oni confided in me. I knew then that our friendship had gone to another level.

And now here I was, being invited to move into another level of friendship ... this time friendship with God!

Elijah interrupted my thoughts and asked again softly, "My son, the Lord confides in those who fear him. Do you want to be God's friend? Do you want to be one that Yahweh confides in?"[8]

I blurted out, "This is what friendship with God looks like? Sharing my secrets with him, although he knows them already, and having Almighty God bare his heart to me? Yes? Then yes, I want to be that one, that ear that hears the very heart of Yahweh, even when, especially when, I don't understand why he would change his mind about an evil man like Ahab."

I fell to the ground, weeping. "Yes, Yahweh!" I cried out. "I accept your invitation to hear your heart, to love who and what you love, to hate all that you hate, to honor the secrets of your heart and to share those secrets when you tell me you are ready, and not a moment before."

Elijah had joined me on the ground, also weeping. Through his tears I heard him singing a little song to Yahweh, "The Sovereign Lord has given me an instructed tongue to know the words that sustain the weary. Morning my morning he awakens me, awakens my ears to listen like one being taught."[9]

"Yes, Lord, yes. Give me always ears to listen like one being taught!" my heart sang.

---

[8] Psalm 25:14
[9] Isaiah 50:4

OIL FOR THE WIDOW

One of my fellow prophets from our company of the prophets had passed away, leaving a widow and two young sons. She had kept to herself after that, grieving and trying to care for her boys. I hadn't seen her or even thought about her for months when she showed up at my door one morning. At first, I heard a timid knocking, rousing me from my sleep. The sun was barely up, so I tried to ignore the knocking. It was way too early for visitors!

But the knocking continued. This early morning visitor was not going away. Next, I heard her voice calling out, "Elisha! Elisha! Wake up! I need your help!"

I rose and wrapping my cloak about me, I stumbled to the door. As I opened the door, she nearly fell inside. Her face was wet and her eyes swollen and red from a night of weeping, and months of mourning.

"Mother, what is wrong?" I asked, leading her to sit at my table.

"You know, Master Elisha!" she cried. "You know my husband is dead, and you know how he worshiped the Lord and served you. I am alone now, with no source of income except for what I can earn from cleaning or mending for our neighbors from time to time."

I felt embarrassed. Why of course I knew what was wrong. Why had I not tended to the family of one of my own prophets after he passed? Yes, his widow had not made her needs known as she isolated in her home, but as a leader over this company, it was my role to shepherd these people. "I should have known," I chastised myself.

As the weeping widow sat with her face bowed down on my table, I felt Yahweh's compassion rise up in me, and I heard him speak.

First, he addressed me. "Elisha, stop making this about you. I am El Roi, the God who sees. I knew about the widow and her plight, and I am not chastising you for not being aware of her troubles. She was not ready to hear from me, or you. Don't ever try to give my words to someone who is not ready to receive them. Always wait on me, wait on my timing. Don't go running ahead of me or lagging behind."

I bowed my head and humbly received God's instructions to me.

He continued, "The widow hid from the company of the prophets because she was so angry about losing her husband. But I always watched over her, always made sure there was bread on her table until today when her heart is finally ready to look to me and receive from my hand. Now speak to her all the words you hear from me."

"How can I help you, Mother?" I asked gently.

"I've tried to make it on my own, but I just learned that my dead husband's creditors are coming to my home to take my sons as slaves in payment for their father's debt! What can I do?" She slipped off the chair and fell sobbing to her knees before me. "They're my sons, Elisha! They're all I have!"

"Woman, what do you have in your house?"

"I have nothing at all." She sobbed. "Except a little oil in a jar."

"Go around and borrow empty jars from your neighbors. And don't just ask for four or five jars. Borrow as many as you can. Take the boys with you. They can help you carry the jars to your house."

The widow lifted her tear-stained face to me and listened. The tears stopped flowing. "Yes, my Lord," she answered.

I was filled with the joy that comes from speaking the words of Yahweh, and seeing those words received. I continued sharing Yahweh's instructions: "Then go inside your home, you and your sons, and shut the door. Take your little jar of oil and pour it into the borrowed jars. As soon as one jar is full, put it to the side and take the next." That was all Yahweh spoke, so I stopped speaking.

The widow then rose from the floor, wiped her face off with her apron and hurried from my house to do God's bidding.

When she reached home, her boys were just waking up. "Ima, where were you? Is it time for breakfast yet?"

"Quickly, up and wash your faces. We have a job to do!" she told them with a smile.

It had been many months since they had seen their ima smile like that, and they quickly obeyed her, dressed and washed their faces and stood at attention waiting for her instruction.

"Come, my sons." She led them out the front door where she began knocking on the neighbor's door. "Good morning, Sarah and Joseph!" she called out. "May we borrow a few empty jars from you?"

"Certainly, my friend." Sarah called out. "Come in. We have missed your visits. Can you come and sit with us for a minute? Oh, the boys are with you? Welcome Jacob and Andrew, come and share a piece of bread and jam with Uncle Joseph and Aunt Sarah."

The hungry boys eagerly accepted the bread and jam. Then, the widow placed two borrowed jars in the pockets of her apron, and put one jar each in her boys' hands, allowing them to have one hand to hold their bread and jam.

"We can't stay, Aunt Sarah," said Andrew, the younger child.

"No? Perhaps another time? We have missed the sound of children in our home."

The boys turned to their mother. "Ima?"

"Yes." She smiled. "We will be back soon to visit. But right now, we are on an assignment from Elisha."

"We are, Ima?" the boys whispered as they followed their mother outside. "On assignment from Elisha just like Abba used to do?"

"Yes, we are!" the widow replied, walking confidently up to the next house. "Miriam! Are you home? Yes? It's just me and the boys. Could we borrow some empty jars from you? Come on, boys."

By the time the widow and her sons returned home about noon their hands and pockets were filled with clinking jars, and the widow's cupped apron held a dozen more. They walked slowly not wanting to chip or break any of the borrowed jars.

"Now what, Ima?" Jacob asked. "What's next? What does Elisha want us to do with all these jars?"

"I will need your help, my sons. Now each of you bring me the biggest jar you can carry."

The boys scrambled to the pile of jars lined up on a blanket on the floor of their home. They each chose a large jar and hurried back to their ima. The widow then took the nearly empty jar of oil from her kitchen shelf and the jar that her firstborn, Jacob had carried to her. The boys watched wide-eyed as their ima began to pour the oil from the little jar into the larger one. They watched the golden oil fill up only an inch or so of the larger jar and then drip, drip, drip as the oil ran out.

After about twenty drops fell one by one from the little jar into the larger one, the boys tired of watching and turned away. Then they suddenly heard a new sound, not the drip, drip of tiny drops of oil, but now it was more of a glug, glug of an abundance of oil pouring. They turned back quickly to see golden oil cascading rapidly from the small jar until the larger jar was filled to the top.

"Quick, Andrew, give me your jar!" And the widow continued pouring until the second jar was full. "Another jar, my son," the widow sang out.

The children laughed. What a wonderful game this was, Elisha's assignment! And they danced about as they carried one after another of the borrowed jars which their ima filled to the top with the golden oil.

"Another jar, Jacob! Andrew! This one is almost full."

"Ima!" they cried out together. "There are no more jars!"

They turned back to their ima and saw the flow of oil from the small jar suddenly cease flowing until there was not even one drop left. The widow placed the empty jar next to all the others on the table and suddenly it too was filled. The sunshine coming through the open doorway shone on each jar, making the oil glisten like gold.

"Come, my sons."

Jacob and Andrew followed their ima out of the house and ran to keep up with her as she made her way once again to the house of Master Elisha.

I was waiting for them at my door. The boys rushed to me and wrapped their arms around my legs. "Master Elisha! We did it! We did your assignment!"

Once again, I was filled with remorse for not keeping in touch with the widow and her sons. They needed an abba, and I had not been there for them. Yahweh interrupted my thoughts.

"No regrets," he said. "My timing," he reminded me. "These young men, and their ima needed to see my provision, not yours. They forgot who they are, my chosen people, and thought they had to do life on their own, without their abba. I needed to show them that I am their Abba. And now you can be their abba as well. Always, only, follow my lead."

The widow and her sons excitedly recited how their "empty" jar had filled up over twenty jars with oil.

I lifted my eyes toward heaven in thanksgiving for Jehovah Jireh's provision. "Now, Mother, sell the oil and pay your husband's debts. Then you and your sons can live on what is left."

I hugged the boys close to me and began to worship. "Blessed are you, Lord our God, King of the Universe!" I heard the young voices of Jacob, and then Andrew, joining me as I prayed. "Blessed are you, Lord our God, King of the Universe, who has kept us alive and preserved us and enabled us to reach this season!"

I watched then and the boys and their ima, hand in hand, skipped away from my front door. As for me, I closed my door and laid down on the floor to wait for what I knew Yahweh wanted to say to me.

A ray of sun shone through the open window and warmed my head as I lay waiting for his voice. But he came and held me instead, wrapped me in arms that I could almost feel.

"Abba! Abba!" I wept.

He just held me and smiled. And I knew that he was promising me that he would always be my Abba, and the widow's Abba, and the Abba for these two young princes, Jacob and Andrew who had seen golden provision flowing from an empty jar.

THE SHUNAMMITE WOMAN

Being a prophet, I usually draw either an overtly positive or overtly negative reaction from the people I encounter. I'm either well received or avoided like a contagious disease. Bethany of Shunem was one who immediately became like family to me. I met Bethany when God sent me to Shunem to meet with the prophets under my ministry there. The journey from Carmel to Shunem took me from four to six hours, depending on weather conditions, so I often had to find a place to spend the night, or run the risk of traveling at night.

One afternoon on my way out of the city back to my home at Carmel, I heard my name called out. "Elisha, Man of God!"

I turned and saw the Shunammite woman who had regularly waved to me and called out "shalom!" each time I passed by her house on the edge of the city. This time the woman, Bethany and her husband, Zachariah, were standing outside their door as if they were watching for me. "Please, Man of God," they called out. "Honor us by sharing a meal with us on your way home to Carmel."

"You're always providing for me, Abba!" I whispered to Yahweh as I followed the Shunammite couple into their house. I noticed the furnishings and tapestries hanging in their home and understood that poverty was not an issue for this family. Their food was abundant and freely shared.

Thereafter, they set an extra plate at their table anytime they saw me passing by. I so enjoyed sitting with them, sharing a meal, talking together, and getting to know this amazing couple. What happened next was so unexpected. One night, after another warm and filling dinner with my Shunammite friends, Bethany turned to me with a big smile. "Dear Man of God, my husband and I have a surprise for you!"

"A surprise? You already honor me so well, welcoming me into your home anytime, day or night. What is this surprise?"

Bethany rose excitedly and I followed her out the front door, and up a staircase I'd not noticed before, on the side of the house. Her husband followed behind me. When we reached the roof, she hurried over to a newly constructed room on the rooftop and threw open the door. "Welcome home, Man of God!" she laughed. "This will be your room, anytime you are here in Shunem."

I was speechless as I entered the small room. There was a bed, a table, chair, desk and lamp. "You are too kind!" I exclaimed, tears in my eyes. "Did she put you up to this, Zachariah?"

"Well, yes." Zachariah smiled. "But the honor is ours to have you under our roof, Elisha."

"Yes, dear Man of God," Bethany added. "We are blessed to have you here. And you can come and stay here anytime, whether or not we are home, since you have your own staircase and entrance to your room. Even if you arrive in the middle of the night, you will always have a place here at our home."

Sometime later my servant, Gehazi, and I arrived at the Shunammites' home late one evening and quietly made our way up the staircase to the rooftop. We entered my room and found the lamp full of oil. Gehazi lit the lamp and there on the table was a pitcher of wine and a bowl filled with dried fruit, bread, and cheese. Gehazi served me as I sat on the edge of my bed.

The next morning, we awoke to the smell of freshly baked bread wafting from the dwelling below. Shortly afterwards there was a soft knock at the door, and there stood Bethany with a platter of bread and figs and a pitcher of spring water.

"Good morning, my friends!" She smiled and quickly left down the staircase to her home.

After we gave thanks and ate our fill, I turned to my servant. "Gehazi, go and deliver this message to the Shunammite woman: You have gone to all this trouble for us. Now what can be done for you? Can we speak on your behalf to the king, or the commander of the army?"

Gehazi returned a short time later shaking his head. "She says she wants nothing. She owns her own home, and her husband runs a thriving business. Her exact words were that she 'seeks nothing but the honor of having you in her home'."

"What can be done for her?" I wondered aloud. "She gives and gives but seems to be less adept at receiving."

"Well," Gehazi said. "The couple are alone. They have no children, no son to carry on their family name. And her husband is much older than she is."

"Yes! Gehazi, call the Shunammite at once."

A few minutes later, Bethany stood in my doorway, framed by the light of the morning sun shining behind her. "Yes, my lord? What do you need? Gehazi acted as if it were urgent."

"This time it is I who have a surprise for you, dear woman."

"I need nothing, my lord."

"No, dear woman, Yahweh says otherwise. About this time next year, you will hold a son in your arms."

Bethany's face fell, and she actually stepped back from my door. "No, my lord," she objected. "Don't mislead your servant, oh Man of God!" And she hurried down the staircase.

I heard her as she walked away. "I don't need this. No, I can't get my hopes up again. Just when I was learning to be content without children."

I heard her weeping softly the rest of the afternoon until her husband returned home from the fields. "Yahweh, did I hear you wrong?" I asked. "Didn't you tell me that you will bless Zachariah and Bethany with a son?"

I heard Yahweh whisper his assurance to me that I had indeed spoken his words. So I laid down on my bed, on top of the quilt sewn for me by my generous benefactor and drew near to God to see if he would reveal to me what was going on in the heart of my friend, Bethany. "Why did she reject your blessing, Yahweh? Doesn't she want to bless her husband with a son in his old age?"

"Have you ever hoped for something, my son?" Yahweh asked.

"Yes, of course."

"This woman, Bethany, has given up on hope."

"Yes, I see that, my Lord," I replied. "But why?"

"She's been pregnant with hope five times already."

"I am sorry, Lord. Pregnant with hope? What is that?

Then he spoke plainly to me. "Elisha, Bethany has been with child five times, and each time has lost the child before birth. For the past six years she has poured herself into learning to live without the hope of having children. She won't even discuss the topic with Zachariah, although they are very close. Instead, she blesses others with the abundance of her house, as she does for you, gives away what she has to others in need. But for herself, she closes off her heart from hope as she keeps herself so busy serving others. I see her at night sometimes, crying softly into her pillow as Zachariah sleeps beside her, oblivious to her suffering. And if he does awake, he pretends not to hear, for he knows her too well, knows she is hurting, but also knows that she will not discuss the issue with him anymore.

"Elisha, she cannot receive my blessing, because she does not trust my goodness anymore. So she busies herself with what she can see."

"Yahweh," I whispered. "How can you help Bethany to hope in you again when all she sees are the tiny graves of her dead children?"

"My son, will you trust me?"

"Yes, Abba, I trust you with all of my heart, my soul and my mind, even when I don't understand I choose to trust you."

I felt his smile as he drew closer. "Elisha, let me teach you about hope."

I waited silently for him to continue.

"Hope means that we must trust and wait for what is still unseen. For why would we need to hope for something we already have in our possession?"

"Yes, I understand," I answered.

"So because our hope is set on what is yet to be seen, we patiently keep on waiting for its fulfillment."

"That is hard to do sometimes, my Lord," I said. "You are unseen, Yahweh, and I so want to see you face to face someday!"

"Exactly, my son. It is not easy for you to hope for what is still unseen. Sometimes, when your hopes have been dashed as many times as my daughter, Bethany, you don't know what to put your hope in anymore."

"So how can I help her, Lord, when I am of the same frail spirit, hoping in unseen things?"

"No, Elisha, you are not the one to help Bethany."

"Who then? I don't doubt that you have brought her and Zachariah into my life for a reason."

"My Spirit will help Bethany. This is what my Holy Spirit does for each of my children. He takes hold of you in your human frailty to empower you in your weakness. For example, sometimes you don't even know how to pray, or know the best things to ask or even hope for. But my Holy Spirit rises up within you to intercede on your behalf, pleading to God with emotional sighs, tears, and groanings too deep for words.[10]

"I have heard Bethany's tears, like liquid prayers, rising up to my throne room. I have not forgotten her and Zachariah. God, the searcher of the heart, knows fully the longings of his people, and when my people cannot even form words to cry out to me, the Holy Spirit passionately pleads before me for you, for Bethany, for all my people, in perfect harmony with my plans and your destiny.

"Elisha, will you trust me with Bethany, no matter what happens?"

"What could happen? What do you mean no matter what happens?"

"Elisha!" he interrupted. "Will you trust me?"

"Yes, I choose to trust you, Abba. Yes, no matter what happens."

"One day, my son, you will be convinced of this truth, that every detail of your lives is continually woven together, like one of those beautiful tapestries Bethany has collected in her

---

[10] Romans 8:26 TPT

home, designed to fit into my perfect plan of bringing good into your lives, for you are my lovers, called to fulfill my designed purposes. I know all about you, Elisha, what makes you fulfilled and joyful. And I know my daughter, Bethany. I will teach her, as I am teaching you, that she can trust me, trust my perfect plans for her, that it is safe for her to trust in Yahweh. She struggles with the shame of childlessness, but I will show her that those who look to me are radiant! They will never be put to shame."

It was nearly seven months before I traveled again to Shunem. After meeting with the local prophets, I headed to my rooftop lodging. Bethany met me at the bottom of the staircase, and I saw that she was evidently pregnant. She handed me a bowl of bread and fruit and apologized.

"As you can see"—she smiled—"I am not able to climb up such a steep staircase at this time. So here are some provisions for you, my lord." And she bowed and returned to her home.

Gehazi told me a few months later that Bethany had indeed given birth to a son. I got to meet the little boy the next time I visited Shunem.

"Dear Man of God! Come and see our blessing, little Zachariah!" She thrust the child into my arms.

As I rocked the little boy, I thought to myself, "Is this what hope looks like?"

The years passed by, and little Zachariah became such a delight to me each time I visited. He liked to help his mother serving me, tidying up my room and bringing treats upstairs for me and Gehazi. He seemed to enjoy just hanging out with me in my room and I loved hearing him recite the passages from Torah that his abba had taught him.

Then one day, the young boy went with his abba out to the fields during the harvest season. Little Zachariah had been following the reapers when he suddenly ran to his father. "My head, my head!" he cried out in obvious distress. His father instructed one of the servants "Quickly, carry him to his mother!"

Bethany saw the servant approaching the house and ran out to meet him. "What happened?" she cried, taking the boy into her arms.

"He complained earlier to my master about his head hurting," the servant replied. "But as I carried him home, he just lay there in my arms and hasn't said a word all the way back from the fields."

"He's burning up with fever!" Bethany cried. She carried her son into the house and held him on her lap the rest of the morning. She stroked his forehead with a cold, wet cloth to try to bring down the fever. Again and again, she tried to force him to drink some water, but he became unresponsive. About noon she realized he was no longer breathing.

"No!" she cried. "This cannot be happening! Yahweh gave me this child! Elisha promised to bless me!"

At last, she wiped her tears and stood up. She carried the child up the outside staircase, into Elisha's room, and laid him on Elisha's bed. Then she quietly closed the door and hurried downstairs. Her husband's servant was still there awaiting her instructions. "Take me to my husband in the field, please," she said.

When she reached her husband, she told him she needed to go to Elisha right away. "Please get the donkey saddled for me and give me one of your servants to accompany me so I can go to the man of God and return."

"Now? Why do you need to go today? It's not the New Moon or Sabbath," Zachariah asked. "Is everything alright?"

"Yes. It's alright. This is just something I need to do."

Zachariah knew that look of determination on Bethany's face and chose not to press her further. He helped his wife up onto the donkey and sent her on her way to meet Elisha at Carmel. "God be with you!" he said.

Once out of sight of her husband, Bethany instructed the servant, "Lead on! Don't stop or slow down for me unless I tell you." Several hours later she approached my home in Carmel.

I was outside with Gehazi, and we saw Bethany as she came through the fields. "Look! There's the Shunammite woman, Bethany, and she seems to be in great hurry to reach us. Gehazi, run out to meet her and ask if she's alright, if her husband is alright, and her son."

Gehazi ran to meet Bethany. Her servant helped her off the donkey and she hurried toward me. Gehazi fell into step beside her. "Dear woman, is everything alright? You seem to be in distress."

Bethany did not turn to look at Gehazi but answered quickly, "Everything is alright!" and pressed on, nearly running now.

As she reached me, Bethany fell to the ground, weeping, and wrapped her arms around my feet.

Gehazi rushed in to push her away, but I told him to stop. "Leave her alone, Gehazi. Her heart is full of bitter distress. Something terrible has happened, but the Lord has hidden it from me and not told me why."

For several minutes, Bethany just clung to my feet, sobbing. Finally, she spoke.

"Did I ask you for a son? Didn't I tell you, don't raise my hopes?" She resumed weeping bitterly.

"Quickly, Gehazi. Take my staff and run to Shunem. Go and lay my staff on the boy."

Then Bethany held tighter to my feet. "No!" she cried. "It must be you, Lord Elisha, not your servant. I will not let go of you until you agree to come with me to help my son."

"I will go with you, Mother." I pulled Bethany to her feet.

Gehazi met us as we entered Shunem. "The boy has not awakened, my lord."

I climbed the stairs and opening the door, saw the boy lying dead on my couch. I heard Bethany gasp when she saw him, and another wave of sobbing erupted from her chest.

"Gehazi, take the Shunammite downstairs to her home. I must be alone with the child." I shut my door on Gehazi and Bethany and began to pray.

Although I did not hear his voice, my body seemed to be obeying unspoken instructions from Yahweh, bypassing my brain. I climbed on my bed and lay upon the boy, my mouth over his, my eyes over his lifeless eyes, my hands on his now cold hands. I don't know how long I lay over the child, but after a time I began to feel the cold leaving his body. I got up then, still obeying Yahweh's unspoken commands and walked back and forth in the room praying in my spirit. Then I turned back to the child. I climbed back onto the bed and once more stretched out my body over his. Then I sprung off him as I heard and felt him gasp for air. Suddenly his body jolted and he sneezed violently, seven times, sat up, and opened his eyes.

When his frightened eyes reached mine, young Zachariah smiled and ran to me, wrapping his little arms around my legs. "Abba Elisha! You are here! I was so sick." And he began to share with me the story of being so ill a short time ago. "I was so scared," he told me. "But now you are here, and I am all better."

"Come, Zachariah. Mother is worried about you." As I opened the door of my room, Gehazi practically fell inside as he had heard our voices and had his ear pressed to the door. I clapped him on the back as he stared in wonder at the smiling child standing beside me. "Quickly, Gehazi! Call the Shunammite."

A moment later Bethany came running. She stopped in her tracks when she saw the smiling boy by my side.

"Ima, Abba Elisha said you were worried," Zachariah called out to his mother. "Don't worry, about me, Ima. I am here with the Prophet."

"Dear woman." I turned to Bethany. "Here is your son." Bethany, still weeping, stepped into the room, fell at my feet and bowed to the ground.

I heard Yahweh whisper, "This is what hope looks like." I knew his words were not just for me as they burned inside my chest.

"Dear woman." I took her hand and pulling her to her feet, placed her hand on the head of that beautiful boy who stood beside us. The glow of his smile seemed to light up the room.

I whispered as I had heard Yahweh whisper. "This is what hope looks like."

She turned then and stared into my eyes as I continued.

"Never be afraid to place your hope in the goodness of God. Now take your son and go celebrate God's goodness."

A short time later I heard the celebration beginning, and I heard the child's father, Zachariah, call out for Gehazi and me to join the party. I sent Gehazi down ahead of me and waited for Yahweh. I knew he had words for me to hear, and I was eager to hear them.

"Elisha!"

"Yes, Lord, I am here."

"Elisha, do you remember when I asked you to trust me no matter what happened with my daughter, Bethany?"

"Yes, my Lord."

"Do you see the tapestry now? Tell me, what do you see?"

"I see that you are the master artist, skillfully weaving every detail of Bethany's life into a beautiful tapestry. Well done, Master!"

"And do you see that I have woven some Elisha into her tapestry, and some Bethany and big and little Zachariah into your own tapestry?"

"My tapestry?" I bowed low before him. "You are making a tapestry for me?"

"Of course! You will see when you join me and Elijah. It's already a beautiful work of art with so many colors, and golden threads of my goodness woven throughout. And you, my son are weaving right alongside me, weaving my golden goodness into so many others' lives."

I sat for a while, trying to grasp what God was teaching me. I've never considered myself an artist, a creator, but God says otherwise. "You are weaving right alongside me," he told me.

I felt like a boy again, excited when my abba would take me with him to work in the fields or tend our flocks. Then when we returned home, he would brag to Ima about all *we* had accomplished, as if my childish efforts had actually made a difference.

"Yes!" Yahweh interrupted my thoughts as if he had heard them out loud. "Exactly! You and I working together to weave my goodness into the lives of my people."

"But, Lord," I countered. "Couldn't you just do it all yourself? Why did you choose me to work alongside the Almighty? I am humbled! It's like my abba calling the crops we harvested *my* harvest. You are weaving a magnificent tapestry, letting me move the shuttle, and telling me to sign my name alongside of yours on the finished work of art.

"Who am I, Lord, that you would choose me for this honor of weaving your likeness, your goodness into the beautiful masterpieces you are creating?" I wept in amazement.

"Blessed is the man who trusts in the Lord, whose confidence is in him. Your trust qualifies you to join me, my son. Never be afraid to place your hope in the goodness of God."

He held me close, just as I had held the boy, Zachariah, a short time earlier.

"Now go and join the party!"

FEEDING THE PROPHETS

"Generations." Tho I had no children of my own, I had heard Yahweh speaking that word to my spirit from time to time.

This morning as I awoke, I heard it again.

"Elisha, it's all about generations."

I lay still on my couch and waited to hear more.

"Your life, your words, your work. It's not just for today, my son."

"I know you spoke about tapestries, Lord. Is that what you mean, that I am helping to weave what you teach me into the tapestries of other lives than my own?"

"Yes, that, and more. Elisha, do you remember when our friend, Bethany, was pregnant with little Zachariah?"

"Yes, Lord!" I smiled. "She was very fearful at first, afraid to stop and enjoy the blessing because she had lost five babies before this one. But those last months she seemed almost to glow with joy and anticipation."

I could almost imagine Yahweh's face as we sat talking together. Oh, what a wonderful privilege I had as a prophet to just dialogue with Almighty God, to hear his thoughts, sense his emotions.

"Elisha." He broke into my thoughts. "I so enjoy our chats together."

I gasped as the weight of his words caused my heart to leap. He enjoys spending time with me?!?

He continued. "Did you know that I confide in you? I have shared the secrets of my heart with very few, and only with those who are in reverent awe of me."

I was overcome then, and I slipped from my couch onto the floor and lay face down before him.

"Oh, God!" I wept before him. "I do not take it lightly that you, God of the Universe, would share the secrets of your heart with me."

"It's not just for you, my son. Each word I speak to you is a seed. Sometimes men eat my seeds, and the seeds die with them. Some men plant my seeds and feed many. I have called you to plant my seeds, just as you planted seeds of hope into my daughter, Bethany. Today you will sow among my prophets, and we will talk again later about the harvest."

I lay there for a while, letting the warmth of his breath wash over me. Then I rose and prepared to journey to Gilgal to meet the company of the prophets there.

When I approached Gilgal later that day, I heard the Lord say, "Elisha, they are hungry."

There was a famine going on in that region so I already knew the men must be hungry. "Am I to feed them, Lord?"

As the prophets were gathering, I called my servant and told him to start cooking some stew for the hungry men. One of the men overheard me and went into the nearby fields to find some herbs to add to the stew. He picked some gourds he found growing on a wild vine, and chopping them up finely, he added them to the stew.

It was difficult for the prophets to listen to my teaching when they began to smell the spicy aroma coming from the stew pot some hours later. So I had my servant dish out the stew to the hungry men. They began to eat, but within a few minutes, several men were holding their stomachs in pain.

"Oh, Man of God! There's something poisonous in this stew! There's death in this pot!"

Somehow, I knew what to do. "Get some flour!"

I sprinkled the flour into the stew and stirred it in. "Now, serve the stew to the men."

I watched as the prophets tentatively received the stew and began to eat. They ate slowly at first, and then I saw big smiles begin to erupt on every face. "This is delicious! What's the secret ingredient, Elisha?"

There was no longer anything harmful in the pot. Was it the flour? The men had watched me stir in the flour. Was it the stirring? Or was it hearing God's voice and obeying his instructions no matter how difficult or in this case, how simple.

"This is the recipe," I told the prophets. "Trust Yahweh. Don't rely on yourself or wait until you understand what he is teaching you. Let him be your counselor in every area of your life. Even"—I smiled—"even in your cooking."

I dismissed my followers and heard their chatter as they started off toward their homes.

One prophet, large around the middle laughed. "Does God have a will regarding our cooking? Wait until I tell my wife that we have to pray before we cook!"

Another shook his head. "Surely we don't have to consult Yahweh about everything, do we?"

"Well, we might have died today unless Elisha heard from God about adding flour to the pot."

As for me, I had my servant pack up the leftovers from our wonderful, harmless stew for a midnight snack, and I set off toward home.

The very next day, my servant wakened me with more good news of provision for my hungry followers. "Master, a man from Baal Shalishah is here with a gift for you, twenty loaves of barley bread baked from the first ripe grain as an offering to Yahweh."

"Wonderful, Gehazi. Call the Company of the Prophets to assemble again today."

"But Lord, they're small loaves, not enough to feed one hundred men."

"Call the people, and hand out the bread," I answered. "For this is what the Lord says: they will eat, all one hundred of them, and have some bread left over."

At the end of the day, I sat with Yahweh outside my home as the sun was setting over the plain. I felt satisfied, well fed in my stomach and nourished in my spirit, in the midst of a famine.

"Elisha."

"Yes, Lord."

"Have you planted any seeds today?"

"You know, my Lord."

"You can give a man a fish and he will be fed. Or you can teach a man to fish, and he will feed his family. Today, you have taught men how to feed a village. You have taught them to look to Jehovah Jireh, The God who Provides."

"Blessed are you, Lord our God, King of the Universe, Jehovah Jireh, who brings forth bread from the earth," I prayed.

"And stew!" Yahweh reminded me.

"And stew!" I smiled. "And has kept me alive and preserved me and enabled me to reach this season!"

THERE IS A PROPHET IN SAMARIA

It's always tragic during times of war, but when children are affected, the whole community weeps and grieves. After a raid by the army of the Ben-Hadad II, King of Aram, a young Israeli girl was discovered missing. Her devastated family never knew whether their daughter was killed or kidnapped.

I visited the grieving family soon after their daughter was reported missing.

"We taught her to keep Yahweh's commandments from the time she was a little girl," her father told me. "She learned to read the words of the Torah alongside her brothers and even memorized his promises," her mother added. "I would often hear her singing the words of Yahweh as she went about her chores."

Her father spoke again. "We named her Lela, meaning loyal and faithful, and she was just that, a daughter we could trust and rely on. And now we don't know if she is living as a slave in our enemy's camp, if she is mistreated and abused, or if she was killed."

I could only sit and weep with the grieving parents and pray with them that wherever their daughter Lela was, if she was still alive, that Yahweh was watching over her and keeping her close to his heart.

I learned sometime later how Yahweh had done just that.

The commander of the army of Aram, Naaman had found little Lela cowering among a group of children who had been kidnapped from Israel. Lela was a beautiful child with dark curls framing her terrified face. Yet in her distress, she was holding the hand of a younger child, a little boy, and trying to keep him calm and quiet so he wouldn't draw unwelcome attention from their captors. Knowing that many of the young children would be violated and enslaved, Naaman stepped forward and claimed Lela and the young boy as his own spoils of war.

"Don't worry," he whispered to Lela and the boy she had taken under her care. "I will not hurt you. You are safe with me." And he had kept his word, not touching the young lady as another man might have done, but giving Lela to his wife, Sarona, to be her personal servant, and letting Lela continue to take care of the young boy until he was old enough to serve as well.

Just as she had served her own family, Lela now served her new masters, Naaman and Sarona, with kindness and dedication. She stood silently when they worshiped their gods, gods of wood or stone. But from time to time, Naaman and Sarona would find their new servant girl praying to a god they could not see, a god she called Yahweh. They heard her sweet voice singing songs of thanksgiving, praising the goodness of a god who had allowed her to be kidnapped from her family and exiled in a strange land.

"How could that god be good?" they wondered to each other after Lela had finished her chores and gone off to her sleeping mat. "And how can Lela be such a sweet child, so kind to us, her captors, and to the little servant boy she calls Samuel?"

Naaman was not only the commander of Aram's army, but also his most valiant and trusted soldier. So King Ben-Hadad II was devastated when he learned that Naaman had begun to exhibit symptoms of leprosy. Sarona also wept bitterly, knowing that there was no cure for the disease and she would lose her husband.

Hearing her weeping, little Lela came quietly and sat down beside her distraught mistress. "How can I help, dear lady?" Lela whispered. Sarona pulled the girl into her arms and wept on her tiny shoulders for some time. Then Sarona told Lela about Naaman's leprosy.

"Is there nothing we can do to help my master?" Lela asked.

Sarona shook her head silently.

"Mistress? I may be able to help you and my master."

Sarona held the girl's face in her hands and kissed her forehead. "Dear Lela, you're such a sweet child, always trying to help. But you're just a little girl, a captive in a foreign land. What would you know about leprosy?"

"If only my master could meet the prophet who is in my homeland, in Samaria! He would cure my master of that awful leprosy! I know it!" Lela spoke excitedly.

"In Samaria, you say ..."

Later that evening when Naaman came home to rest, Sarona told him about what little Lela had said.

Naaman was skeptical at first. "What does she know, Sarona! She's just a child. And even if this 'prophet' could heal me, I'd have to go into enemy territory to find him. Do you think he would take kindly to healing a soldier who kidnapped the children from his community? Perhaps Lela wants me to go there and be captured by my enemies!"

Sarona shook her head. "Forgive me, my husband, but no, you are wrong! Lela cares about you, Naaman! She knows that she is safe and alive and unharmed because you rescued her from the rest of the slave children. Lela is so thankful to live with our family. She tells me so frequently. It's because she cares so much for you that she is telling us about the prophet. What have you got to lose? We don't have any other options, do we?"

The next day Naaman went to his master, King Ben-Hadad II and told him what the girl from Israel had said.

"By all means go!" said the king. "I will send gifts and an official letter to Jehoram, king of Israel and see what he can do for you."

So Naaman departed for Samaria, taking with him a letter sealed with the King's official seal, along with ten thousand talents of silver, six thousand shekels of gold, and ten sets of clothing as gifts.

Jehoram, king of Israel trembled when he heard that the commander of King Aram's army was in the outer court. After all, the nation of Israel was still recovering from Aram's previous attack. The king withdrew to his quarters, opened the letter and read aloud before his staff: "With this letter I am sending my servant Naaman to you so that you may cure him of his leprosy."

"What?!?" Jehoram tore his robe, dropped the letter and sunk to his knees. "Am I God? Can I kill and bring back to life? Why would the King of my enemy send someone to me to be cured of leprosy? Ben-Hadad II must be looking for a way to trap me!"

When the king's messengers reached me a short time later and told me what had happened, I sent back this message to King Jehoram: "Why have you torn your robes? Did you forget that there is a God in Israel? Have the man come to me, and he will know there is a prophet in Israel!"

So King Jehoram instructed Naaman along with his chariots and horses to go to my home in Samaria.

I heard the horses and the murmur from the soldiers as they approached my door. "Gehazi," I called out. Gehazi came and awaited my instructions. "Go and tell the soldier, Naaman what he must do to be healed."

"Yes, Master?" Gehazi stood ready to memorize my instructions to recite them to the soldier waiting outside my door.

"Tell him this: Go, wash yourself seven times in the Jordan River, and your flesh will be restored, and you will be clean."

Then I sat inside and listened as Gehazi delivered my message, word for word, to Naaman.

"Commander Naaman, go wash yourself seven times in the Jordan River, and your flesh will be restored and you will be clean."

I listened then for Naaman's response, but he said nothing. I heard his thoughts, however, as he turned away in anger to return to his land.

"Here I am, the head commander of the troops of Aram, the same army that just defeated Israel in battle. Yet this fool, this 'prophet' has no respect for me or my position. I thought he would surely come outside to me and stand and call on the name of Yahweh his God, wave his hand over the leprous spot and cure me of this disease. But no, instead he sends a servant to tell me to wash in the Jordan. That shallow, dirty river where people bathe and wash their clothes! Aren't the rivers of Damascus, Abana and Pharpar better than any of the waters of Israel? Couldn't I just wash in them and be cleansed, if just washing in a river would cure leprosy!"

So Naaman went off in a rage, and I sank to my knees to inquire of my God.

"Are some men too proud to receive healing, Lord?" I prayed. "Why did you have me send Gehazi to speak to him? I could have delivered the remedy, and maybe he would have listened to me. Don't you want Naaman to be healed, Lord."

"Have I any pleasure at all in the death of the wicked, Elisha? Would I not rather that they turn from their ways and live? Trust me and learn to expect my goodness, my son."[11]

Rebuked, I lay on the floor and listened as another conversation followed between Naaman and his servants.

"My father," said one servant.

I heard Yahweh's whisper, "Elisha!"

"Yes, Lord, I am listening."

"Did you hear the servant call his commander 'father'?"

"Yes, Lord."

"Not every man calls his military commander father, Elisha. I know this man, Naaman. I know that he is an obedient soldier, faithfully carrying out the commands of his king, Ben-Hadad II. So why do you suppose his troops call him 'father'?"

"I perceive that he has always been a fair and compassionate leader over them, providing for them, caring about them and their families, even while serving as their commander. It seems, Lord, that these men care about Naaman, not just respect him as their leader, but have grown fond of him because of how he has watched out for them. Is that what you're telling me, Lord?"

The servant continued, "My father, if the prophet had told you to do some great thing, like climb to the top of a mountain,

---

[11] Ezekiel 18:23

or dig a new well, or, whatever, would you not have done it? But the prophet has given you a simple command, maybe too simple, just to wash and be cleansed. Please, my lord, don't despise this simple command. We will all go with you, even wash with you in the river if that's what it takes. Please, my father!"

Naaman listened to his servant and traveled to the Jordan River. He took off his sandals and waded into the water, washing himself with his hands. Then he turned and nodded to his men who had encouraged him to do this simple thing.

He washed and then dunked under the water once, then again, and again and again, feeling life flooding into his body, as his men on the banks counted aloud "One, two, three, four, five six, seven!"

When he rose from the water the seventh and final time, the leprous spots were gone.

"Hurray! Our commander is healed!" they shouted, and some ran into the water to congratulate Naaman and help him back to shore.

"Let's return home, my Lord!" shouted one servant. "Wait until our king hears the good news!"

"No, not yet, my son." Naaman smiled. Naaman and his entire company returned to my house. This time I came out to meet him, and he bowed low before me, as did his servants, some of them weeping with gratitude for having their commander whole.

"Master Elisha." Naaman looked into my eyes. "Now I know that there is no God in all the world except in Israel. Please accept a gift from your servant. I've brought silver and gold and sets of new clothing as gifts."

"As surely as the Lord lives, whom I serve, I will not accept a thing."

Although Naaman urged me, I continued to refuse payment for what I had done at the Lord's command.

"You won't allow me to give you anything, dear Elisha, yet you have given me the greatest gift of all—you have given me back my life. Now my wife will not be a widow, nor my children orphans! My master King of Aram will continue to have his trusted commander. Even little Lela will dance with me when I return home clean and whole. Do you understand what you have done for me this day?"

Naaman wept as he knelt at my feet, overcome by the goodness of my God, as I have often found myself.

"If you will not accept my gift, please allow me, your servant, to be given as much earth as a pair of mules can carry, for your servant will never again make burnt offerings and sacrifices to any other god but Yahweh. But may the Lord forgive me this one thing, when my master enters the temple of Rimmon to bow down, and he is leaning on my arm and I bow there also, in the temple of Rimmon, to assist my master, may the Lord forgive your servant for this."

In my spirit I marveled at what had just happened. Yahweh had stepped outside his people, and healed a gentile soldier, a pagan man who led the enemy's army against his people, the nation of Israel. As strange as it seemed to me, I still knew in my spirit that I had heard the Lord rightly when I spoke God's words of healing over this man. I had no doubt that this was in fact Yahweh's intention, to so overwhelm this gentile man with his goodness, that he would forsake his false gods and choose to follow the God of Israel all the rest of his days. From this day forward there would be a tiny plot of land in Aram filled with Israeli soil, dedicated to the worship of Yahweh.

"Go in peace," I told Naaman.

I watched then as his servants dug from the ground and filled several bags of soil from the land of Israel to take with them back to their land. I knew that Naaman would build an altar to the God of Israel, on Israel's own soil, though in a foreign land, and would forever worship Yahweh who healed him.

After Naaman and his men had gone and I was resting on my bed, I heard Gehazi leave quietly. I heard his thoughts as he ran after Naaman.

"My master was way too easy on Naaman, this Aramean, not accepting any of the gifts he offered. As surely as the Lord lives, I will run after Naaman and get something from him."

Naaman, of course obliged Gehazi and gave him a talent of silver and two sets of clothing, thinking that I had changed my mind. Naaman's servants accompanied Gehazi almost all the way back to Samaria to carry the gifts. Then Gehazi dismissed them, took the gifts and hid them in the house.

"Where have you been, Gehazi?" I asked as he came and stood before me.

"Nowhere, my lord. I've been right here."

"Gehazi, was not my spirit with you when the man got down from his chariot to meet you? Is this the time to take money, or to accept clothes, olive groves, vineyards, flocks, herds, menservants and maidservants? Naaman's leprosy will now cling to you and to your descendants forever."

Gehazi gasped as white patches of skin appeared on his arms, then his legs, then his face. Then he left my presence leprous, as white as snow.

I lay on the floor then and wept again as I waited for the Lord to speak. I'd seen a stubborn man, one loved by men, and children for his fairness and kindness, miraculously healed once he humbled himself to do things God's way. And Naaman was not only healed physically, but his eyes were opened to follow the one true God and forsake all other gods. Then I saw another man receive the curse of leprosy when he chose to do things his own way.

"Oh, Yahweh, I love Gehazi!" I wept.

"I love him, too, my son. I love him, too."

"Sometimes a man will humble himself and receive my goodness. Naaman heard about me from my little one, Lela who carried the light of my presence into that dark house. But it was in that encounter of humility, washing in that dirty river, that Naaman discovered me for himself, and once he had found me, he chose to forsake any other gods."

"An encounter with you is worth everything, my Lord!" I cried. "How could Gehazi, after all he has experienced, choose riches above you?"

All at once heavy rain began to pelt the roof over my head. It was as if I heard Yahweh's weeping. "I take no pleasure in the death of the wicked, Elisha but would so much rather they turn from their ways and follow me."

Our tears mingled as I worshiped.[12]

---

[12] Ezekiel 18:23

BUILDING WITH ELISHA

The Company of the Prophets approached me one morning as I sat outside my door enjoying the morning sunshine.

"Where are you off to, my friends?" I called out to them.

"Our meeting place where you instruct your followers is too small to fit us all, so we are going to another place to build a new meeting house," they replied.

"Wonderful! Go and do what you are proposing."

"Elisha, would you please come with us as we build?"

I smiled to myself. How often had I made the same request to my abba as I built my little forts and play villages in the sand: "Come with me, Abba, come watch what I am building!"

"Yes, I will come!"

I packed some water for the day, and we set off.

The men went down to the Jordan River and began to cut down trees for the new meeting house. Suddenly I heard someone yell, and then a splash. One of the men had been cutting down a tree when the iron head of his ax came loose and quickly sank into the muddy river.

I hurried over to the place where the ax head had disappeared. The man who had lost it was feeling around in the mud desperately trying to find it under the water.

"My lord!" he said. "It was borrowed!"

"Show me where it fell," I said to the man. When he showed me the place, I cut a stick from a nearby tree and threw it into the water where the ax head had disappeared. As we watched, bubbles appeared in the water, and the iron ax head slowly floated to the surface.

"Go and get it!" I called to the man. He reached out in wonder, plucked the ax head from the water and secured it back onto the ax handle, this time more carefully.

So construction of the new meeting house continued all the rest of the day, with much joy. From time to time, I heard the men talking to one another. "Do you believe it? Elisha can make iron float!"

I smiled to myself as I listened to their banter and watched them build. The prophets thought it was so fortunate that they had asked their leader, me, to join them for the day. I glanced heavenward, knowing that there was another Abba that had chosen to come with us that day, and it was his presence that had made all the difference.

SPYING ON THE ENEMY

The nation of Aram continued their raids on Israel. One day as I was sitting in my home praying for Yahweh's protection over our nation I began hearing voices, as if there were conversations taking place outside my door. I rose and went outside, but no one was there.

Then I heard the Lord speak, "Elisha."

"Yes, I am here."

"Do you hear the voice of Ben-Hadad II speaking with his officers?"

I listened, now standing in the doorway of my home and again I heard a conversation, but saw no man. Then I heard the king tell his officers where he was going to set up his next secret encampment in hopes of attacking the Israelites in the vicinity of that town. Of course, I immediately sent word to Jehoram, King of Israel to avoid that area, since the Arameans were there.

Jehoram sent spies near the town I had told him about, and sure enough they located the enemy's camp. So the king sent his troops in another direction to avoid any confrontation.

Time and time again I would hear the whispers and send word to Jehoram to warn him about the plans of the enemy's troops.

I later heard the enraged voice of King Ben-Hadad II after the Israelites had avoided another one of Aram's ambushes yet again. The king had called together all his officers, Naaman included, and was accusing someone of spying on behalf of Israel.

"Will you not tell me which of us is on the side of the king of Israel?" he shouted.

"None of us, my lord the king!" said one of the officers. "But we have learned that Elisha, the prophet tells the king of Israel the very words you speak in your own bedroom!"

Furious, the king commanded, "Go and find out where this Elisha is hiding so I can send and capture him."

When the report came back that I was in Dothan, Ben-Hadad II lost no time in sending horses and chariots and a strong force of soldiers by night to surround the house where I was staying. I heard the commotion when I awoke and stepped outside to find myself surrounded in every direction by Aramean troops. My servant stumbled out the door after me and gasped in horror.

"My lord, what shall we do?" he stammered.

"Don't be afraid, son," I told him. "Those who are with us are more than those who are with our enemy."

"What?!? What do you mean, those who are with us? It's only just you and me, Elisha!"

Then I prayed, "Oh Lord, open up the eyes of my servant to see what I see."

At once the young man's eyes opened wide and his mouth fell open as he turned first one way, and then another and saw what I was already seeing—the hills full of horses and chariots of fire, surrounding both the troops, and me and my servant.

The Arameans, unaware of the heavenly force surrounding them began to advance toward me.

"Lord Yahweh, King of the Universe, just as you opened the eyes of my servant, now I ask you to blind the eyes of each and every soldier advancing against me!"

The entire company from the commanders in their chariots to the foot soldiers and armor bearers were immediately struck with blindness and began to stumble into one another in fear and confusion.

I then called out to the soldiers, "This is not the road, and this is not the city. Follow the sound of my voice and I will lead you to the man you are looking for."

The soldiers turned and followed my voice as I led them right into the city of Samaria, and stopped in front of the palace of Jehoram, King of Israel.

"Now, Lord, open their eyes!"

Then the Lord opened their eyes, and they found themselves in Samaria, surrounded by the troops of King Jehoram.

Jehoram grabbed a sword. "Elisha, shall I kill them, my father? Shall I kill them?"

"Do not kill them," I answered. "Would you kill men you have captured with your own bow and sword? No, this is what the Lord commands: Set food and water before them so they may eat and drink and then go back to their master."

At my words a great feast was prepared for the bewildered marauders. After they had eaten, they were escorted out of the city to return to their master, King Ben-Hadad II of Aram.

After that, Aram's soldiers stopped raiding our land. I never again discussed this military incident with King Jehoram. I did, however spend much time with King Yahweh, marveling in his presence about his battle plans that both fed and routed the army of our enemy without one soldier, or prophet, losing his life.

WHEN GOD FOUGHT FOR ISRAEL

Although Aram's soldiers remembered the kindness our people had shown to them when the king of Israel obeyed my words, and instead of slaughtering the enemy troops, fed them and sent them home to Aram, their king, Ben-Hadad did not. Ben-Hadad gathered the troops once again and decided to attack God's people in Samaria by another strategy, a siege.

The Aramean troops surrounded the walled city and allowed nothing and no one to pass in or out of the city. Within a few months, famine had set in for the Israelites. The poor were in great distress, while the wealthy managed to buy some meager provisions. A donkey's head, not a desirable cut of meat, but in such desperate times was selling for eighty shekels of silver! A half pint of seed pods which barely took the edge off a family's hunger was hard to find for even five shekels.

I spent much time on my face before the Lord during those difficult months. I, too, had lost much weight and was feeling the effects of the famine, but I knew that the Lord would provide for me as he had done time and time again. As a prophet to a nation, however, my heart was broken for my people who were starving to death before my eyes.

One day the Lord instructed me to listen just as the king, Jehoram, was walking along the top of the city wall. I was sitting with a group of elders in my home and whispered to them to be still. They just looked one to the other and wondered what I was hearing. They apparently heard nothing.

I closed my eyes to listen more attentively and found that not only could I hear the sound of the king's footsteps along the wall, but I could actually see Jehoram on his perch above the city. Then I heard a woman cry out, "Help me, my king!"

Jehoram shook his head and told the woman, "There's nothing I can do to help you. If Yahweh doesn't see fit to help you, how can I? Am I supposed to pull grain out of the bare threshing floor? Can I wring wine out of an empty vine press?"

Undaunted, the woman continued to wail before the king.

"Woman, what happened to bring you this anguish of heart?" the king asked.

"My neighbor said to me, 'Give up your son so we may eat him today, then tomorrow we'll eat my son.' So, we cooked my son, and both of our families ate him. The next day I said to my neighbor, now you give up your son as you promised, so we can eat him and not starve. But she refused! I pushed my way into her home, but she had hidden her son, sent him away to hide. Help me, my king! I demand justice! Make this woman live up to her word!"

"Oh, God!" I cried out and fell to my knees as the prophets stood by me in fear. "Oh, God, what have we become? Parents should be sacrificing to feed their children, not sacrificing their children so they can eat! And now this woman is appealing to the king for justice, when she should be wailing in repentance for murdering her son!"

The king was appalled and angry when he heard firsthand about the cannibalism taking place in his city, a mother sacrificing her son to feed herself. Then the king tore his royal robes in desperation, and there, underneath his robes, he was wearing sackcloth. Sackcloth was a symbol of sorrow and repentance!

"Look, Yahweh!" I prayed softly. "Perhaps my king, Jehoram, is finally ready to repent of his evil ways and seek God's help!"

But Jehoram's next angry outburst dismissed from my mind any hope that the king was ready to turn to Yahweh.

"This is Elisha's fault! This is God's fault! May God deal with me, be it ever so severely, if the head of Elisha, son of Shaphat remains on his shoulders today!"

I heard every word of the king's threat and turned to the confused elders gathered around me. "Quickly, close the door, shutter the windows! The king is sending a murderer to cut off my head! When the murderer arrives, you must hold the door shut against him!"

A short time later, my door began to shake as the messengers pounded on it. "Open this door in the name of Jehoram, king of Israel!"

I heard the king screaming behind his messenger, "God, you did this! This famine, this siege, it's all your fault! I'm taking matters into my own hands now!"

Then I heard Yahweh's unspoken instructions, and I opened the door to confront the king and his henchman.

"Hear the word of the Lord! This is what the Lord says: About this time tomorrow, seven quarts of flour and thirteen quarts of barley will sell for one shekel each at the gate of Samaria."

The messenger sneered and practically spit his words into my face. "You stupid old man! Look, even if Yahweh were to open the windows of heaven, how could this ever happen? Your words mean nothing! You can't help us! Your God can't help us! You know the cost of even a grain of barley, yet you tell me that thirteen quarts will sell for a shekel by tomorrow?"[13]

I felt the Lord restraining me even as I was filled with anger at this messenger who challenged the word of Yahweh, and whose mouth was practically touching my nose as he screamed in my face.

"You, messenger of Jehoram, hear God's word for you." I spoke softly, but firmly.

The messenger must have felt the weight of my words and backed away.

"You will see with your own eyes this miraculous provision from Yahweh to his people, but you will not eat any of it!"

Then the king and his messenger retreated, leaving me, and my head untouched.

---

[13] 2 Kings 7:1

I sat down again, the elders quite shaken sitting beside me. "Now watch and pray, and you will see that not one word that Yahweh has spoken will fall to the ground," I told them.

Now there were four lepers, also cut off from food and water during the siege. They were forbidden to enter the city, as required by the law due to their leprosy, so they huddled near the wall. One of the lepers spoke up. "Why are we just sitting here, starving to death? If we try to find food in the city, the people will stone us to keep us away, and we'll die. And there isn't any food there anyway. If we just stay here, we will die. I propose that we leave the city and go over to the camp of the Arameans."

The other lepers shook their heads in amazement at their companion's words. "What? Are you crazy? They're the ones causing us to starve in the first place!"

"What's the worst that can happen?" said the first leper. "If the Arameans spare us, we'll live, and if not we'll die, but perhaps faster than starving to death."

So the four lepers slipped out of the city gate and headed toward the camp of the Arameans. They reached the enemy encampment about dusk and huddled behind a cluster of rocks near the edge of the camp. As they peered around the rocks, they saw no one. They heard no sounds, though it was the time of day that the troops should be gathering to share a meal together.

Yahweh revealed to me later that what the lepers did not know at that time was that God had caused the Aramean army to hear the sound of chariots and horses and the rumbling sound of troops advancing in their direction. They had been confident that they outnumbered the Israelite army until they heard what sounded like a vast army approaching them.

One solder cried out "Look! The king of Israel has hired the Hittite and Egyptian kings to attack us!" The rumbling grew louder, closer as they listened in fear, the ground shaking from what they imagined were thousands of enemy troops entering the camp.

The next voice they heard was the voice of their commander: "Evacuate! Run for your lives!"

So all the soldiers ran from their tents and followed their commander out of the camp. They deserted the camp leaving behind their tents, horses and donkeys and all their belongings.

One of the bolder lepers cautiously tiptoed onto the now deserted field and lifted the flap of an Aramean tent. Gazing inside he saw someone's dinner set out on a cloth. His stomach rumbled at the sight of a fresh loaf of bread. Seeing no one in sight, the leper snatched the loaf and began to eat it. Then he turned back to his fellow lepers and shouted the good news. "Come and feast with me, my brothers! There's plenty of food!"

The other lepers wasted no time reaching the camp and went from tent to tent, grabbing food and drink, clothing, and even gold and silver left behind by the Aramean army. At first they gathered armloads of spoil and hid it, as there was way more than they could use at one time. But then one of the men spoke up, his mouth still filled with the soft bread. "Wait!"

The others looked around, thinking they had been discovered by the enemy army. "What? There's no one here. We're safe."

"No, wait. This isn't right. This is a day of good news, and we are keeping it all to ourselves while our people are trapped and starving. We must let the king know so all our people will share the plunder."

With their bellies full, the four lepers approached the walls of the now dark, sleeping city of Samaria. They stopped at the gate and called out to the gatekeeper on the wall, "Shalom! Shalom! We have news for the king!"

The gatekeeper stood to attention and looked toward the men on the ground. "Lepers!" he thought in disgust. "What do you want? You know you can't come in here!"

Undeterred, the lepers bellowed out their good news. "We went into the camp of the Arameans, and it was deserted! We heard no voices and saw not one person anywhere. But we did find plenty of food and drink, horses and donkeys still tethered near the camp, and the tents filled with much spoil, ours for the taking! We ate our fill, but then remembered our people, trapped inside the city with no food. We had to share the good news! This siege and famine is over!"

The gatekeepers passed the marvelous news one to another until it reached the king's palace. Roused from his sleep, the king was skeptical at first.

"Don't be fooled!" he warned his officers. "It's a trap! The Arameans know how desperate we are, that we are starving to death as they hold us captive in the city. They are hiding in the countryside, just waiting for us to come to their empty camp so they can surround us and take the city!"

"Oh, King, hear me out," said one of the king's officers. "We saw the four lepers outside the gate, wearing the Arameans' clothing, loaves of bread in their hands. What if it's true? What if Yahweh has truly delivered our enemies' spoils into our hands?"

"If we do nothing, we will all perish from starvation, oh king. Let us send a small party of soldiers to find out if what these lepers are saying is true."

So Jehoram chose two chariots and his last five horses and several officers to go to the Aramean camp. "Go and find out what happened, and bring us word," the king commanded.

Messengers followed behind the chariots as they headed toward the enemy camp. "What's that in the road?" one driver called out. The messengers ran ahead to clear the debris from the road, only to find the entire road strewn with clothing and equipment that the Arameans had thrown away in their haste to flee.

"It's true! Yahweh has fought for us and conquered our enemies yet again! Hallelujah! Praise God! Now on to the plunder!"

The troops ransacked the enemy tents, taking the food and drink, clothing, equipment, livestock, silver and gold back to Samaria.

The prophets stood in awe at the entrance to the city as the troops came running into the now open gates and began distributing bread and barley to the starving people.

"It's just as Elisha said it would be!" they marveled. "Seven quarts of flour and thirteen quarts of barley are selling for one shekel each at the gate of Samaria! Now where is that servant who scoffed at your words, Elisha?"

But the king's servant who had challenged me was nowhere to be found. "I put him in charge of the gate just before the soldiers returned," said the king. And he sent officers to search for the servant.

A short time later, as the crowds thinned and people returned to their homes with joy in their hearts, and their bodies filled with good food, the king's servant was found. The officers discovered his body in the gateway, crumpled against the wall where the crowds of hungry people had unwittingly trampled him to death. And they remembered the words of Yahweh I had spoken: "You will see with your own eyes this miraculous provision from Yahweh to his people, but you will not eat any of it!"

Not a word was spoken as the servant's body was removed and buried outside the camp.

Still gathered with the other prophets inside my home, I worshiped Jehovah Jireh, the provider. "Blessed are you, Lord our God, King of the Universe, Jehovah Jireh, who brings forth bread from the earth and has kept me alive and preserved me and enabled me to reach this season!"

After the prophets returned to their homes, I rehearsed with Yahweh all that had happened over the past few hours. It had been a somber day. I found myself grieving for the family of the trampled servant. But it was also a day of celebrating the end of a very long siege against the people of Israel. Yahweh had once again provided for his people and yet made it clear that his words held the power of life, and of death. And the word of the Lord was highly respected in Samaria that day.

NOT ONE AND DONE

My heart was encouraged when God provided miraculously for his people during the siege. I later learned of another example of Jehovah Jireh's provision for an old friend of mine.

When the siege was just beginning, I had urged my friends, Bethany and Zachariah, to leave the area with their little son, Zachariah. "Go away with your family and stay for a while wherever you can, anywhere but here!" I warned them. "God has revealed to me that a famine is coming that will last for seven years. Leave now, save yourselves and your son!"

Bethany knew the power of the word of the Lord, after the miracles she and her husband had witnessed firsthand, so she packed up their household, and they traveled to the land of the Philistines. After seven years, Bethany returned to the land of Israel, only to find that other people now lived in her beautiful home and had taken custody of her land.

"What shall we do?" she asked her husband.

Zachariah was so distraught over the situation that he simply hung his head in despair.

"These squatters must have thought we were never coming back. I never imagined that obeying the voice of God through his prophet would bring us to ruin!" Zachariah wept aloud.

"No!" Bethany thought to herself. "I've been down that road, and I won't go there again! I know what it's like to hope in God's word, to feel like my hopes have been canceled and give in to fear and bitterness. But I also know by personal experience that hope can rise from the dead, just as my son, Zachariah, rose from the dead at the word of Elisha."

She turned to her husband. "God's word is true, dear husband. Elisha would never have sent us away to save our lives, only to have us lose our home! Now stay here while I go and ask the king to restore our land and home to us, the rightful owners."

As Bethany was in route to the king's palace, my servant, Gehazi, was visiting with Jehoram, king of Israel. The king was finally able to relax now that the siege was over, and the people were no longer begging for food to survive. "Gehazi, tell me more about Elisha," Jehoram asked. "I want to hear about all the miracles Yahweh has done through your master's hands!"

Gehazi began to tell Jehoram story after story of God's goodness and provision, the iron ax floating in the water, the healing of the poisonous stew, and many more. He was just telling Jehoram about dear Bethany and how Yahweh brought her son, little Zachariah, back to life when Bethany came walking into the court.

"There she is, my lord the king! This is the woman I was telling you about, and this is her son, Zachariah who was raised from the dead!"

Jehoram's eyes lit up. "Come, dear woman. Tell me, is this true? Can a child die and be raised to life?"

Bethany approached the king and told him in great detail all that Yahweh had done for her family, the miracle of her son's birth, the second miracle of her son being raised back to life, and God's provision for her and her family during the seven-year siege.

"And that is why I am here, my lord king. My husband and I have just returned to Israel now that the famine has passed, only to find that others have taken over our home and our land. I have come to seek justice, oh king. We did not abandon our home but only left at the word of the prophet to save our lives during the years of famine."

Jehoram rose and called an official to come at once. "Give back everything that belonged to this woman!" he commanded. "Her land, her home, and all of the income from her land from the day she left the country until now—restore it all to her immediately!"

Back at my home later that evening I marveled at Yahweh's perfect timing and provision for my friends. "Yahweh, you didn't just bless them one time in return for their generosity to me and Gehazi. Now these three times you have blessed them! The blessing of their son, the blessing of his restoration to life, and now the restoration of their home! I am overwhelmed by your goodness, oh God."

I bowed low, overcome with weeping. Finally lifting my wet face toward heaven, I whispered my praise. "Blessed are you, Lord our God, King of the Universe, who brings forth bread from the earth and has kept me, and Bethany, and big and little Zachariah alive and preserved us all to reach this season!"

SORROW FOR THE PROPHET

I had traveled to Damascus at Yahweh's urging. Once there I learned that King Ben-Hadad of Aram was quite sick and feared for his life. When Ben-Hadad learned that I was in the area he called his servant, Hazael.

"Hazael! The man of God has come all the way up here. Now take a gift with you and go speak to Elisha on my behalf. Have him ask God if I will recover from this illness, or if I will die."

So Hazael came to meet me, bringing gifts of forty camel loads of the finest wares of Damascus. "Man of God," Hazael bowed low. "Your son, Ben-Hadad, king of Aram has sent me to ask you, will he recover from his illness?"

"Go and tell your master, 'You will certainly recover'," I told him. Then I paused and locked eyes with Hazael as I continued. "But I tell you this, the Lord has revealed to me that your master, Ben-Hadad will not live, but die."

I kept staring at Hazael for several minutes, until he began to feel ashamed. Finally, I averted my eyes and began to weep.

"My Lord, why are you weeping?" Hazael asked.

"Because I know what harm you are planning to do to the people of Israel! You will set fire to Israel's fortified places, kill their young men with the sword, beat their children to death, and rip open the wombs of their pregnant women!"

Hazael stood with his mouth hanging open. "Me?!? How could your servant, a mere dog, undertake such a feat?"

"The Lord has shown me what you will do, and that you will become king of Aram."

Hazael quickly left the court after that, and returned to his master, Ben-Hadad.

"Hazael, what did he say? What did Elisha say?"

"Oh King, Elisha says that you will certainly recover," Hazael replied. But he did not share any of the rest of my words.

The next day, as Ben-Hadad lay on his couch, Hazael took a thick cloth, soaked it in water and spread it over the king's face. Although he struggled, Ben-Hadad was weak from his illness, and it took little effort for Hazael to suffocate him.

Hazael waited until close to the noon hour when the servants would be bringing a meal to the king. Then he cried out to announce that the king had passed away from his illness.

Hazael was then appointed king in place of Ben-Hadad.

IT'S NEVER OVER, UNTIL GOD SAYS IT'S OVER

Gehazi here! Telling the account of what I thought was the last miracle of my master, Elisha.

Jehoash had become king of Israel and continued in the evil ways of his father. When Jehoash learned that Elisha was on his death bed, he remembered how his own father had reached out to Elisha for help. Jehoash had lived through the seven-year siege against Israel and had seen with his own eyes how God had miraculously provided for his people at the word of the man of God. So Jehoash decided to go and see the prophet before he died.

I brought the king into the room where Elisha lay sick on his couch.

"Elisha, here is King Jehoash to pay his respects."

"Oh, my father!" Jehoash wept when he saw the weakness of the prophet. "My father, the chariots and horsemen of Israel, defender of God's people!"

Elisha raised his head and told the king, "Get a bow and some arrows." With some effort, and my assistance, Elisha rose from his couch. "Take the bow in your hands," Elisha told the king. Jehoash placed an arrow in the bow. Then Elisha came behind the king and placed his hands over the king's hands.

"Now, open the east window," Elisha commanded. So Jehoash opened the east window. "Now shoot!" Jehoash and Elisha together pulled back the bow and shot an arrow out the window where it landed in an open field.

"That is the Lord's arrow of victory, the arrow of victory over Aram!" Elisha declared. "Israel will completely destroy the Arameans at Aphek."

By now Jehoash was excited and so pleased with himself for having the good sense to visit with Elisha before he was lost to him, and to Israel forever. "What is next, my lord?" he asked.

"Now," Elisha continued. "Set aside the bow. Take the arrows in your hand."

Jehoash picked up the arrows.

"Now, strike the ground with the arrows!"

Jehoash raised his arm and struck the ground once, twice, three times with great force, and then turned to Elisha for approval. Instead of approval, he saw Elisha's face filled with anger.

"You should have struck the ground five or six times! Now you will only defeat Aram in three battles!"

Jehoash left after that outburst, and I helped Elisha back to his couch, now quite weak.

"My father," I asked Elisha softly. "I don't understand. The king did everything you asked him to do, didn't he? Why wasn't it enough for Israel to completely conquer Aram?"

I didn't know if Elisha would have the strength to even answer me, but after several minutes, he opened his eyes. "Gehazi, you saw the prophetic act that Jehoash and I did together, shooting that arrow out the east window, yes?"

"Yes, I saw."

Elisha continued, "That symbolic act of shooting the arrow showed Jehoash what God was about to do. But Gehazi, I want you to take notice that I did not ask Jehoash to do that symbolic act on his own. We shot that arrow together. The next act, striking the arrows, I asked him to do on his own. Now Jehoash is not a godly man. He accepted my words about the first act, the victory shot, but not wholeheartedly. So when I asked him to strike the arrows, he obeyed my instructions but did not believe strongly enough to continue striking the arrows with all his might, and so received less than was in God's heart for him to receive."

I was silent before my master, replaying in my own mind when I myself hadn't believed God enough to receive all that he had for me. Like the time I sought provision from Naaman after Elisha healed his leprosy. I had thought my master foolish to not accept some of the gifts Naaman had brought along, when we could have really used some of the silver and those sets of fine clothing. I had lied to Naaman, telling him that Elisha changed his mind and wanted to accept some of the gifts after all. In return for my deception and greed, I contracted Naaman's leprosy.

Still by the kindness of God I was alive to hear my master's instructions, as he lay sick on his death bed, and hopefully to receive it this time with all my heart.

Not long after the meeting with the king, I found Elisha lying still and lifeless upon his couch. I called for the company of the prophets and together we buried and mourned our mentor and friend.

But I have one last story to share about my master.

It was a common event each spring that raiders from Moab would sneak into Israel to steal whatever they could get their hands on. Well, one day some Israelites were burying a man when they suddenly spied a group of Moabite raiders heading toward them. The Israelites did not bury the man but instead threw his body into Elisha's tomb which was near the burial site, and turned to flee their attackers. All at once they heard a loud gasp and cough, coming from the grave. When the dead man's body touched the decaying bones of Elisha, the dead man came back to life and stood up on his feet. Then both the raiders and the dead man's friends fled in terror!

Who is this man, my master, that one who received a double portion of the spirit of Elijah, who still performs miracles from the grave?

MOSES, FRIEND OF GOD

LIFE AND DEATH UNDER PHARAOH

My parents were born, grew up and lived all their lives in Egypt. They married not long after Pharaoh Ramses II became the ruler of Egypt. Here is their story, as they recited to me so many times:

"We've got to limit the rights of this people, these Jews among us!" Pharaoh complained to his officers. "They are becoming too numerous for us to control."

One elderly officer, Samoah, motioned to Pharaoh for permission to speak. Pharaoh nodded his head. "Yes, you may speak,"

Samoah bowed before Pharaoh. "My Lord, these Jews are sons of Joseph who ruled our economy under our great leader, Pharaoh Sesostris III. Our economy both grew and thrived under Joseph's guidance. Sesotris trusted him implicitly and made him ruler over all of Egypt, with no one ranking higher except for Pharaoh himself."

"Silence!" Pharaoh bellowed. "I don't know this man, Joseph. And I don't know this man, Sesostris III, although I respect his leadership during past years. But times have changed. The goods and services these Jews provide to us are invaluable now that we have made them all our slaves. They serve us well, but what if they continue to outnumber us? If our enemies attack us, they may side with our enemies, overpower us, and leave Egypt. Then what would happen to our economy, Samoah?"

Samoah, still bowed down, backed slowly away from Pharaoh, retreating into the shadows of the court.

A younger officer then gestured to Pharaoh for permission to speak.

Seeing Pharaoh's nod, the young man spoke nervously. "My Lord, we have already systematically placed slave masters over all these Jews. Under our command they have completed construction of the cities of Pithom and Ramses as store cities for your majesty."

Pharaoh smiled his approval.

"But may it please the king if I continue? We, me and my fellow officers, have discovered that the more we oppress these people, the more they multiply and spread! Even though we have increased the workload and made their lives bitter with hard labor in brick and mortar, and with all kinds of work in the fields, they still seem to flourish. There are more of them, strong and healthy every time we count!"

"This must stop!" Pharaoh rose from his throne. "Have the midwives brought to me!"

In a short while, two Egyptian midwives, Shiphrah and Puah, were brought trembling before the king.

"I give you this command. When you assist the Jewish mothers as they deliver their babies you are to kill every male child as he is born. If it is a girl, you may let her live. But no male Jewish children will be permitted to live and grow up to bring trouble to Egypt! Do you understand?"

"Y-y-yes, my Lord," they stammered and then fled the court.

Once they had escaped the palace grounds, Shiphrah and Puah stopped running and ducked behind a courtyard wall to catch their breath. They were still cowering there, whispering to each other when a breathless Jewish man came running up to them.

"My wife, my wife, Sharonne is about to give birth! Will you come?"

The midwives looked at each other and then followed the Jewish man back to his home where his wife, Sharonne was in hard labor, approaching the point of birth. "Yahweh be praised! You are here in time to help my wife!" And the man opened the door to his house and ushered the ladies inside. Shiphrah, the elder of the two midwives, snapped into action.

"Puah, you take her head and support her back so she can push. I will assist with the delivery."

Puah and Shiphrah each took their respective positions. Puah's training took over, despite the fear surrounding her heart after their encounter with Pharaoh. She found herself, as if by rote, tracking Sharonne's breathing and coaching her to keep on breathing and push with all her might at the beginning of each contraction. As a curly brown-haired head appeared at the end of the birth canal, Shiphrah gathered clean cloths and prepared to catch the infant.

Both midwives found themselves praying, "Please, God, let it be a girl!"

All at once the baby was free and began to cry. Puah looked to Shiphrah whose face had turned pale. Shiphrah quickly quieted and wrapped the baby in the cloths and called for the woman's husband to come into the room. Then she and Puah slipped out of the house, glancing around to see if any court officers were there, and fled the scene.

They did not speak to one another until they reached Puah's home. They went inside and Puah took Shiphrah's hands and faced her. "Was it, was it a boy?" she whispered.

"You know that it was," Shiphrah hissed back at her. "I could not do it! I could not bring forth life and then kill it. God himself has entrusted me with the gift of life. I cannot kill a child!" And she began to weep softly.

"Will you now report me to Pharaoh?" she continued. "I almost don't care if you do, Puah. I fear God more than I do Pharaoh, and killing these little boys is not what these hands were made for!"

"What are you talking about, Shiphrah?" Puah smiled. "You know how it is, Hebrew women are not like Egyptian women. They are vigorous and always give birth before we even get there, like today."

"Like today?" Puah stammered. "What are you saying? You know that the lady delivered ... delivered, oh, yes, you are correct. She clearly delivered that boy and was sitting with her family holding the infant when we arrived. There was nothing we could do but clean up and leave."

"Exactly!" Shiphrah smiled. And they parted ways until they were called again to bring forth life into Egyptian and Hebrew families.

Yahweh was smiling, too, upon the midwives and upon his people, the Jews. The Jews continued to multiply, and the midwives had many children of their own as well.

Pharaoh was furious when he saw that the Hebrew people were not decreasing. The midwives claimed innocence saying that the Hebrew mothers delivered on their own without the need for their services. Pharaoh called once again for his officers.

"Write a new decree. I hereby order that all Hebrew baby boys must be thrown into the river. The girls may live, but every baby boy must die!"

Such was the situation when my parents, Amram and Jochebed, married. What should have been a joyous time for them was fraught with anxiety.

"Children are supposed to be a reward and a blessing for our marriage," Jochebed worried. "But how can I look forward to the birth of children, if I may have to drown my own sons in the river?"

They were spared when their first child was a daughter, Miriam. But not long after Miriam's second birthday Jochebed's fears became real. She had missed her monthly cycle twice already, and her abdomen began to swell with new life. She and Amram held each other and wept softly at what should have been a time to rejoice.

"What will we do, Amram? I could never kill my baby!"

"No, me neither. All life comes from Yahweh. Only the pagans sacrifice their children."

And they clung to each as they wept.

After a short while, Amran lifted his wife's chin and looked into her eyes. "I'm reminded of a story."

"Could it be that we are both remembering the same story?" Jochebed whispered.

"A time when Yahweh," Amram began.

"When Yahweh provided an alternate sacrifice so our father, Abraham did not have to kill his son!" Jochebed finished.

"Yes!" Amram wrapped his arms around his weeping wife. "God himself will provide. That is what Abraham said. That is what we will believe. God himself will provide so our son will live."

INTO THE RIVER

All throughout my childhood my parents frequently told me the story of my birth. My father, Amram, had hurried in search of the Egyptian midwives early that morning, my birthday. When he approached Puah's home, it was evident no one was yet awake. The house was dark and silent. Amram had circled the house and finding an open window whispered anxiously, "Puah! Puah! My wife is in need of your services!"

Puah, already awake in her bed, heard the whisper and rose silently. "I am here. I will be out shortly."

A few minutes later, Puah cautiously opened the door of her home and looked around to see if any of Pharaoh's officers might be patrolling the area. Seeing no one but Amram, she slipped out the door, closing it silently behind her, and followed my father through the streets to my parents' tiny dwelling.

Puah found my mother, Jochebed, writhing in the pain of labor, biting fiercely on a piece of leather strap to keep from crying out.

After a brief examination, she instructed Amram. "Quickly, bring me some clean cloths to catch the child. It will not be long. And you, go stand guard outside."

Amram kissed his wife and slipped outside. It seemed only minutes later that he heard my mother groan loudly and then a tiny cry pierced the stillness of the dawn. He continued to listen, but no other sound was made. Fearing for the life of his wife and child, Amram hurried back inside.

"Shhh!" Puah hissed. "All is well."

Jochebed was lying on the couch, smiling, but exhausted. She gestured eagerly toward Puah who was holding a tightly wrapped bundle in her arms.

"My lord," Jochebed whispered. "Your son!"

Amram accepted the tiny bundle, and Puah silently slipped out the door. As I fidgeted in my father's arms, he put his little finger into my mouth for me to suckle and keep still.

Such was the story of my entry into this world, as my parents declared it to me so many times growing up. "You were such a fine child," my mother would say. "How could we cast you into the river?"

Nonetheless, those first few months of my life were difficult ones for my family. My big sister, Miriam, helped to care for me, and keep me quiet and unseen. Our Hebrew neighbors were often heard walking by our door or windows and hissing "Shhh!" in warning as Pharaoh's officers patrolled nearby. My parents managed to keep me at home unseen for three months.

One afternoon, Miram overheard our parents' whispering in their bed about how to continue to keep me hidden. The next day, Amram brought a large papyrus basket into the house. Jochebed coated the basket inside and out with tar and pitch to make it waterproof. Then she lined the basket with soft cloths.

"What is it, Ima?" Miriam asked.

"It is a boat, Miram," she replied.

"For me?"

"Well, yes and no. It is for you and your brother to share. Abba will teach you how to sail your little boat on the river."

When the tiny boat was deemed seaworthy, Abba and Miriam brought it down to the river. A long rope was tied to the boat and Miriam learned how to keep the basket afloat near the edge of the river, hiding it among the tall reeds. Some days she would take her little dolly that Ima had made for her out of sticks and cloth and place it in the little boat for a ride.

One evening, just after sunset, when Ima had nursed me to sleep, my abba stood and announced softly, "It's time."

Then he took me carefully from Ima's arms. She began to weep softly, and Miriam became alarmed. "Ima? Ima? Why are you crying?"

"Shh!" she whispered. "It's time to put Jekuthiel, your brother, into the river, my daughter."

"What? No! Not my little brother!" And Miriam began to weep.

"Shh, my child!" Abba whispered urgently. "Do not worry! Yahweh will keep Jekuthiel safe and dry in the tiny boat. In this way we will be obeying Pharaoh by putting our son into the river, yet also obeying our God, Yahweh, by treasuring the life of the son he has given us."

Miriam's eyes became wide. "You mean Jekuthiel will be in my boat, floating in the river?"

"Yes." Abba smiled. "I will stay with him tonight. In the morning, I want you to come to the river like you do nearly every day to sail your dolly in your boat. But this time and from now on, your little brother, Jekuthiel, will be in the boat. You have learned to sail so well, I know you and Ima can keep Baby Jekuthiel safe during the day while I am working. You can bring him to shore from time to time to change his nappy and feed him some milk. In the evenings I will take over and keep him safe during the night."

My ima and abba looked at each other, neither saying a word. Then Abba took me and the little boat and slipped out the door.

How did they know their little plan would work? They did not. But they remembered what Yahweh had whispered to each of their hearts that day months before I was born: "God himself will provide."

MIRIAM'S WATCH

The next morning, Miriam woke up and excitedly prepared for her turn to sail me in the tiny boat. She dressed and ate and hurried down to the river.

Abba smiled when he saw her coming. Miriam saw that he looked tired, in spite of the smile on his face. She looked around for the boat and finally spotted it among the reeds about fifteen feet away. Abba quietly pulled on the rope in his hands and brought the boat to shore. Miriam lifted the clothes and there was Jekuthial, cooing and smiling.

Just then they heard voices, people coming to the river to bathe or wash their clothes. "Here, Miriam," Abba said loudly. "Put dolly in the boat and give her a nice ride!"

Miriam told me that she had placed her dolly into the boat, where I grasped her tightly and began to suckle on the milk-soaked cloths wrapped around the dolly. Then she covered me, and her dolly, and let the river take us downstream. My father looked upward to Yahweh and left Miriam and me there at the river.

About mid-morning, a company of female servants approached the river near the place where Miriam stood sailing her boat. They cleared the shore, sending other bathers on their way, and Miriam saw a beautiful young women step down into the river. Miriam gasped as she recognized the woman. It was Pharaoh's daughter, Queen Bithiah!

The servants then approached my sister to make her leave like the others, but Bithiah stopped them. "It's just a little girl!" she scolded them. "She can stay. Leave her alone." So they backed away from Miriam.

Miriam breathed a sigh of relief. She knew she needed to keep a grasp on the rope to keep me from floating out to sea. But her relief was short lived. I was hungry and had learned that there was no real sustenance in the milk-soaked cloths

Miriam had left for me. I began to whimper, then wail as Miriam stood by helplessly in fear.

"I hear a baby!" Bithiah called out to her servant girls. "There, look, a tiny boat! Bring it to me!"

The servants waded down river to where the tiny boat rocked to and fro from my crying and thrashing about. Miriam had wisely let go of the rope, and the servants towed the boat to where their mistress stood in the shallows. Bithiah pulled back the basket cover and came eye to eye with a tiny, brown-eyed infant, who was wailing in distress.

"Oh, you poor thing!" she cried, and she lifted me from the basket and cradled me on her shoulder. "This must be one of the Hebrew babies. You must be so hungry, poor baby!"

Just then Miriam broke her silence. "Dear lady, would you like me to find a nursing mother from the Hebrews who can feed the child for you?"

"Yes, my child. Go and bring her to me at once."

Miriam arrived breathless at our home, nearly bumping into our mother who was on her way out the door to join us at the river.

"Miriam! Where is Jekuthiel?" she cried out in a fierce whisper. "Have you left him all alone?"

Miriam quickly told Ima what had happened as they ran together back to the river. Stopping suddenly, Ima smoothed out her dress, calmed her voice, and smiled at Miriam. Miriam nodded in understanding and also placed a big smile on her face as they confidently approached Bithiah and her servants on the bank of the river.

It was as if I knew my Ima was there. I began to wail and hold my breath, turning beet red, as Bithiah described the scene to me so many times. "Here!" she thrust me into my mother's arms. "The young Hebrew girl told me that you are nursing a child at home and can feed my baby. Please feed him at once! Then bring him back to me when he is calmer, and I will pay you for your services."

Ima bowed low to the ground, took me home and nursed me until I was sated, then returned me to Bithiah who was waiting at the river. Bithiah and her servant girls played with me, passing me around and cuddling me as my mother and sister stood nearby smiling.

As the afternoon drew on, and I once again needed nursing and changing, Bithiah returned me to my mother's arms. "Will you keep my son for me until he is weaned? I will come and visit him, and when he is weaned, he shall live with me and be my son."

Bithiah visited our home often after that, paying my mother handsomely for caring for me. Once I was weaned Ima brought me, now a toddler, to Bithiah and placed my hand into hers.

"Thank you, mother!" Bithiah smiled and placed a generous payment in my mother's hands.

I looked up at the queen, my new mother, and smiled. I could see that she loved me.

"What is your name, little man?" she whispered. "I will call you Moses, since I drew you out of the water!" And she took me into Pharaoh's palace where I was raised to be a ruler like my step-grandfather, Pharaoh.

MY IDENTITY

I knew Ima Bithiah, as I called her, was not my birth mother. She never hid that fact from me, nor the identity of my Hebrew mother and father, sister and brothers. In fact, she encouraged me to visit them on the Hebrew side of the city. Nevertheless, my home was with Ima Bithiah. I enjoyed the privileged lifestyle of living in a palace, receiving education from the wisest teachers, never having to be concerned about provision. It was not the same when I visited my birth family in their tiny home. I never visited without bringing some sort of gift from the kitchen at the palace, and it was always appreciated.

My mother, Jochebed, always welcomed me with a warm hug. And when I left, she always had tears in her eyes. She often sent me on my way home with a handmade gift for my adoptive mother, Queen Bithiah. Once it was a linen handkerchief with tiny crimson pomegranates embroidered along the edges. Another time it was olive wood beads whittled by my abba, then sanded to remove any roughness, that I had strung into a bracelet.

One morning Ima Bithiah dropped me off to share a meal with my birth family. They invited her to come in and eat with us, but she shook her head. "No, no, this is your time with little Moses. I'll be back before sunset."

In deference to my ima Bithiah, my birth family continued to call me by the name she had given me. But still, I knew my birth name, Jekuthiel, and I knew what it meant, Hope. And I knew that my parents had given me that name at a very hopeless time in their lives. I never tired of hearing them tell me the story of my birth and rescue from the river by Ima Bithiah.

"Are you ready for a story, young man?" Abba asked me after our meal together.

"Yes!" I said. "Tell me again about Baby Moses?"

Jochebed smiled. "I was hoping you wanted to hear that story again."

Miriam, sitting next to me, just laughed out loud. "You always ask for that story, Moses! And Ima, you always hope he will ask again!"

We all laughed together. I imagined, just for a minute, what it would have been like to only live in one home, instead of going back and forth from the palace to the Hebrew community, to live with Ima and Abba and Miriam, to share every meal with them, to have Ima tuck me into bed each night, and Abba take me with him to work each day.

Ima cleared her throat to begin the story, and I was pulled back out of my daydreams. "We saw that you were a special child, dear Moses. So we made the decision to disobey the rules of the government and not put you to death."

"But Ima, you could have been put to death, you and Abba, for your rebellion! Were you afraid?"

"Yes, Moses. We were terrified!" Abba responded this time. "We knew that if our baby turned out to be a boy, he could be sentenced to drowning for no other reason than being born as a son to Hebrew parents. And then you were born, a boy!"

Although I had heard the story many times before, each time they got to this point, I asked again, "What did you do? How did you have the courage to hope for my life?"

"It was Yahweh, my son," Abba said. "Yahweh gave us hope."

Abba continued. "One evening, before you were born, Ima and I were both crying as we held each other in our bed. But then Yahweh brought to our minds a story passed down from our ancestor, Abraham."

I smiled. I loved this part of the story!

Abba opened his mouth to speak but was quickly cut off by Ima's excited interruption. "We both remembered the same story at the exact same time, Moses! It was as if Yahweh himself was whispering into our ears."

"Yes," Abba agreed. "That is how we knew it was Yahweh telling us what to do. We both remembered the story of our ancestor, Abba Abraham, how Yahweh had told him to take his son, his only son, Isaac, and sacrifice him to God on the mountain."

"But Abba," I interrupted here. "I thought Yahweh was not like the other gods, that he hated human sacrifices, and never asked our people to sacrifice their children! I don't understand."

"Yes, you are right, my son." Abba gently laid his hand on my arm as if to calm me. "But listen, don't judge before you hear the end of the story. Please, Jochebed, continue."

"Now you must understand, son, that Abraham was as confused as you are with Yahweh's instructions. No, he was more confused, since Isaac was his only son, and not only that, Isaac was the son of promise. Abraham and Sarah had been barren. They had prayed for a child throughout their marriage, and finally when Abraham was ninety years old, and Sarah about eighty, both past the prime childbearing years, somehow ..." She paused and looked to Abba.

Abba nodded and smiled. He repeated, drawing it out into a very long word. "Sommmehowwww ..."

Abba always paused and winked at us when he got to that place in the story. We all knew that Yahweh was the reason behind the "somehow."

"Somehow, Sarah conceived and miraculously bore a son. Isaac was the fulfillment of their promise from Yahweh, a living symbol of the goodness of our God!"

Then Abba closed his eyes and recited the story as he had learned from his father, and his father from his grandfather and so on. "Then God said, 'Take your son, your only son, whom you love—Isaac—and go to the region of Moriah. Sacrifice him there as a burnt offering on a mountain I will show you.'

"Early the next morning Abraham got up and loaded his donkey. He did not tell Sarah where he was going, nor what Yahweh had told him to do. He took with him two of his servants and his son, Isaac. He cut wood for the burnt offering, and they set off for Moriah. On the third day Abraham looked up and his eyes were drawn to a grassy area on the side of the mountain and somehow ...

"Somehow ..." Abba winked again as Miriam and I laughed. "Somehow, Abraham knew that was the place where he was to sacrifice his son. So he told the servant to stay behind with the donkey while he and Isaac scaled the steep hillside. 'We will worship and then we will come back to you,' he told his servants.

"Then Abraham took the wood for the burnt offering and placed it on his son Isaac to carry, and he himself carried the fire and the knife. As the two of them went on together, Isaac spoke up."

"Oh, Abba!" It was my time to interrupt.

"Yes, my son?" Abba smiled as if it were the first time I had interrupted him at this point in the story.

"Oh, Abba, let me be Isaac!"

He nodded to me, and I continued in what I thought sounded like the voice of young Isaac. "Abba?"

Abba answered in the role of Abraham, "Yes, my son?"

"The fire and wood are here," I continued in my role, "but where is the lamb for the burnt offering?"

Abba, as Abraham answered, "'God himself will provide the lamb.' And the two of them went on together. When they reached the place God had pointed out to him, Abraham built an altar there and arranged the wood on it."

I rose and approached Abba. Abba turned me around and moved his hands as if he was removing the wood I had carried up the mountain on my back. Then he arranged the imaginary wood on the altar I could almost see at my feet. He bound my hands and feet with imaginary ropes and gently laid me down on the altar. By now I could hear Ima softly weeping as she imagined the agony of Abraham in that moment.

Still Abba, stone-faced, continued in our charade.

"Then Abraham took his knife and raised his arm to kill his son."

I lay there not realizing I was holding my breath as I watched Abba raise his arm as if ready to plunge a knife into my chest.

Now Ima burst into the narrative. "But the Angel of the Lord called out, 'Abraham! Abraham!'" And she grabbed the arm of my Abba holding the imaginary knife.

"Here I am," Abba answered.

"Don't hurt the child!" Now Ima was too emotional to continue, so Abba stepped up.

"Don't hurt the child, Abraham. Now I know that you fear God, because you have not withheld from me your son, your only son.

"Oh, can I finish?!?" I leapt off the altar. "Yahweh said, 'Look, Abraham!' Then Abraham looked up and there in a thicket he saw a ram caught by its horns in the underbrush. And he remembered Yahweh's words." I paused here and together, Ima, Abba, Miriam and I recited the words of Yahweh: "God himself will provide!"

"So Abraham took the ram and sacrificed it as a burnt offering instead of his son. And he named the place Yahweh Yireh, The LORD Will Provide. And to this day it is said, 'On the mountain of the LORD it will be provided.'"

I sighed. "Oh, Abba, one day will you take me there, to that place on the mountain where Yahweh provided the ram!"

"Yes, I would love to take you there one day, Moses. But for now, let us finish the story, as Yahweh was not done yet blessing Abraham. And you will see that you and me and Ima and Miriam and all the Hebrew people are part of this story!"

Now I perked up. I didn't remember there being another part to the story of Father Abraham, and that I was included in it.

"The angel of the LORD called to Abraham from heaven a second time and Abraham turned his eyes to the heavens and listened." Abba lifted his own eyes, looked up and continued. "I swear by myself, declares the LORD, that because you have done this and have not withheld from me your dearest possession, your only son, I will surely bless you and make your descendants as numerous as the stars in the sky and as the sand on the seashore. Your descendants will take possession of the cities of their enemies, and through your offspring all nations on earth will be blessed, because you have obeyed me."[14]

"That's us!" Abba said excitedly. "We're the descendants the angel was talking about!"

We all sat back, lost in our thoughts, until Ima whispered, "And that's the story that Yahweh spoke to us that night we were so frightened about what would happen when you were born. He told us both, in our hearts, at the same time, "Yahweh Yireh! God will provide.""

Then Ima looked toward the open door. "Come now, Moses. Ima Bithiah is already here to bring you home."

I saw Ima Bithiah's eyes light up as she came through the open door and spotted me standing by my abba. I quickly kissed Ima and Abba goodbye.

As Abba drew me close, he kissed the top of my head and then whispered in my ear, "I love you, my son. Never forget who you are."

I raised my head and whispered back. "I know, Abba. I know."

---

[14] Genesis 22:16–17

DREAMS

For thirty-five years I learned the ways of royalty as a grandson of Pharaoh. Although I was not a blood relative, still Pharaoh trained me to carry on his family legacy. I studied at the university in Heliopolis under the wisest of Egyptian scholars. My fellow students came from the nobility of several neighboring nations. I enjoyed debating with the other students, learning how their cultures differed from mine. They were often surprised to learn that I was a Hebrew.

Upon hearing about my Jewish roots, my fellow student, Ajaz from Greece cautioned me to keep my Hebrew identity a secret. "Stick with Pharaoh, Moses," Ajaz whispered. "What have the Hebrews ever contributed to society? They're just slaves, uneducated nobodies."

I thought it best not to respond to Ajaz, but I pondered in my mind what he had said as I traveled home to the palace at the end of the term. Approaching the city, I suddenly made a detour, sent my servants on ahead to unpack my luggage at the palace, and hurried on foot to the Hebrew quarter. I heard singing as I approached the home of my Hebrew family. "Ima, Abba!" I called out. "I'm home!"

The door flew open and my family poured out the door, Abba, Ima, my lovely sister, Miriam, and my young brother, Aaron. "Moses!" they cried out in unison. And I was soon surrounded and drawn into the house with many hugs and kisses.

"You're just in time for dinner, my son!" Ima beamed at me. "Quickly, Miriam, set another place at the table for your brother."

We ate in between my family plying me with questions about university, who I had met in Helopolis, what I had learned, and what was my favorite subject of study this term.

"Are you still stuck on mathematics? Ughh!" Miriam said with distaste.

"Have you tried out any other battle weaponry?" Aaron wanted to know. "That streamlined bow you showed us last visit was incredible!"

"Well, actually, yes, Aaron, and yes, Miriam, you're both right. I've been exploring this new device, I believe it's called a wedge, and it has mathematical properties and applications both in construction and on the battlefield."

Abba and Ima sat back and enjoyed my interaction with my siblings. After a time, my mother, brother, and sister kissed me goodbye and withdrew to finish their nightly chores. Abba walked with me part of the way back to the palace.

"Abba," I said, gazing up at the star filled sky above us. "I've learned the names of some of the stars. There, see that bright one, almost pulsating in the sky?"

"Yes, I see it."

"That's Polaris," I told Abba. "Did you know that you can find your way in the dark using the location of Polaris in the sky?"

"Well, that is a valuable life skill that I would like to learn, my son." Abba smiled proudly.

We walked on a little farther. I knew Abba would soon halt and return home as Hebrews were not welcome anywhere near the palace grounds.

"Abba?"

"Yes, my son?"

"Am I too old for stories?"

"You're never too old for stories!" Abba laughed. "Which story would you like to hear? Your rescue from the river? Abraham and Isaac on the mountain?"

"Well, since astronomy is my favorite subject this term, I would like to hear a story about the stars, Abba, the story about Yahweh's promise to Abraham."

"Ah, yes, that is one of my favorites, too."

We stopped walking and both of us looked up at the star-filled night sky.

Abba began. "Abraham and Yahweh were very close, you know, on speaking terms. Yahweh called Abraham his friend."

We both sighed at that point and then laughed. I knew Abba was thinking what I was thinking, about what it would be like to be Yahweh's friend.

"So one night, a clear night like tonight, Yahweh spoke to Abram. You do remember, Moses, that at this point in the story, Yahweh had not yet changed Abram's name to Abraham, yes? 'Do not be afraid, Abram,' he said. 'I am your shield to protect you, and I am your extravagant reward.'

"Abram was silent for a time, not willing to say what he was thinking. But Yahweh knew.

"'What's wrong, Abram? Why are you so quiet?'

"'You know, my Lord.' Abram bowed low. 'Lord, even if you reward me with all the treasures of the world, that means little to me. Since Sarai and I have no children of our own, any treasures you give me will not remain mine, but will go to Eliezer of Damascus. You have given me no children of my own, so a servant in my household will be my heir.'

"Abram heard the Lord's immediate response, reverberating in his chest: 'No, Abram, you are mistaken. That man will never be your heir, but a son who is your own flesh and blood, he will be your heir.'

"Then the Lord called Abram to come outside of his home. 'Look up, Abram! Look up and count the stars!' Abram turned his head to the right and to the left and then laughed out loud. 'I cannot count them all, Lord.'

"I imagine Yahweh chuckled, too," Abba said.

"Then Yahweh told Abram, 'so shall your offspring be, as numerous as the stars you see before you today, you will not be able to count them all!'

"Yahweh let that statement hang in the air a few minutes and then spoke again. 'Abram.'

"'Yes, my Lord?'

"'Do you believe me?'

"'Yes!' Abram answered. 'Although I cannot see my offspring, tonight I can see the stars that are too many to be counted, and I receive, and believe what you have said. For every word of Yahweh is true, like silver refined in a fire, purified seven times.'[15]

"And because Abram believed the Lord, he credited it to him as righteousness."

"What does that mean, Abba?" I asked. "Does that mean that forever from that moment in his life, Abram never sinned, never had an impure thought, or let his anger lead him to say or do evil ..."

"I'm still learning about that concept, my son, but no, Abram was not sinless after that encounter with God, that much I do know. He was a man, after all, so how could he not sin?"

"But Yahweh looked at Abram and saw a man who trusted the word of Yahweh more than what he could see right in front of him—a barren, childless wife—and Yahweh declared him righteous because of his faith."

Abba continued with the story. "Then the Lord went on to tell Abram, 'I am the Lord, the one who called you to leave Ur of the Chaldeans, to enter a new land and take possession of it.' Abram stood there, on soil owned by other nations, none of it his own. 'Are you again asking me to believe what I cannot yet see?' he asked Yahweh. 'How can I know that I will take possession of this promised land around me?'

"Yahweh did not answer Abram's question directly, but told him instead, 'Bring me a calf, a goat and a ram, each one three years old, along with a dove and a young pigeon.'

"So Abram brought all the requested animals before Yahweh, killed them, cut them in half, except for the birds, and arranged the halves into two lines, opposite each other, as the Lord commanded him. Then he watched over the sacrifices, driving away the vultures that tried to take the carcasses.

"That was the last thing Abram saw, for as the sun was going down behind the mountain, he fell into a deep sleep, surrounded by a darkness so thick you could feel it. But even in the darkness, and in his sleep, Abram heard Yahweh's voice

---

[15] Psalm 12:6

loud and clear. 'Abram! You can be sure that your descendants will be strangers in a country not their own for four hundred years. It will be a difficult time for my people, and they will be enslaved and mistreated during this dark time. You will not be alive to see this take place. No, my son, you will live a long life in peace. But in the fourth generation, your descendants will return to this land.'

"Then Abram awoke and saw that the sun was gone and the sky pitch dark. Suddenly a blazing torch appeared. Abram gasped and shuddered as the torch, not held by human hands passed between the two rows of the sacrifice pieces, burning them up.

"On that day," Abba brought the story to an ending that we both knew so well. "On that day, Yahweh made a covenant with Abram."

I closed my eyes and listened to Yahweh's promise.

"Look at the land before you, to the east and the west, to the north and to the south, as far as your eyes can see, and beyond what you can see. To you, Abram, and to your descendants I give this land. The land now owned by your enemies, the Kenites, Kenizzites, Kadmonites, Hittites, Perizzites, Rephaites, Amorites, Canaanites, Girgashites and Jebusites, I give it to you."

"Did Yahweh mean that he would give Abram the land in the future, Abba?" I asked. "Surely nearly four hundred years have already passed, and this land does not belong to Abraham, or to us, his descendants."

Abba answered softly. "That is a hard question, my son. I cannot answer it. Why don't you ask Yahweh, and see what he speaks to your heart?"

I hugged Abba then and he returned home, while I continued to the palace. I did not consciously ask Yahweh my question, but that night in my dreams I stood alongside Abram on the mountainside watching Yahweh's torch of fire burn up the covenant sacrifice. This time, in my dreams, the story ended differently. This time I stepped into the story, stepped right inside of Abram and spoke to Yahweh myself.

"How long?" I asked. "You made a promise, Yahweh, that you would give all this land, this land of promise, to our descendants. Yet here we are in Abraham's fourth generation, and it is indeed a very dark time. My family and my people are enslaved to the cruel taskmasters of Egypt, while I live in the palace of my enemies, caught between two worlds."

"Moses." Yahweh answered me as I stood in the form of Abram on the mountainside. "Moses, count the stars. You can see the stars! Abram believed, and I called him righteous. Believe me although you cannot see. When it is time, you will see what I will do."

I awoke with a start, no longer standing with Yahweh and Abram. It was just me, a very confused Moses who lived life in two different worlds, laying alone in my bed in the middle of the night. But somehow the room was no longer as dark as when I had laid down to sleep. I turned toward a bright light shining through the open window. There, in the night sky was Polaris, the navigation star, my favorite star.

"What are you saying, Yahweh?" Although I heard not a word, I silently slipped from my couch to lie face down on the floor in the streaming starlight.

JUSTICE?

One morning I awoke early to the rhythmic sound of hammers striking stone. It was very early, and Ima Bithiah and my grandfather, Pharaoh had not yet ventured from their chambers. As I listened from my bed, I imagined the Hebrew arms swinging those hammers in the low light of dawn, and the hopeless faces of the men forced to such hard labor from dawn to dusk, nearly every day. Slipping from my bed, I dressed, quietly left the palace, and headed in the direction of a nearby labor camp.

I stopped short of the camp and stood watching my people, the Hebrews, as they lifted arms glistening with sweat and brought their hammers down on the stubborn stones. One elderly man was obviously struggling. I saw him hit the stone he was shaping over and over without even a chip of stone breaking off. Just then one of the Egyptian guards turned toward the old man and saw that he was not keeping up with the other slaves.

"You, lazy old man!" he shouted, sneering at the trembling man. He grabbed the man by his ear and pulled him behind the shed on the side of the work yard. "I'll teach you what happens to lazy Jews!" And he raised the stick in his hand and lashed out at the elderly Hebrew, beating him until he fell moaning to the ground, unable to rise.

"Oh, God, he's going to kill that man!" I thought.

Then I realized that a few years from now, that man being beaten could be my own Abba. How could I allow this injustice to go on? First, I looked around to make sure no one was watching. Then, raising my own walking stick in my hand I rushed toward the guard and struck him over the head. He fell to the ground, where a pool of blood began leaking out into the sandy soil around him. I helped the elderly Hebrew slave to his feet and sent him on his way with a stern warning that he tell no one what had happened. Then I fled back to the palace by another route.

I knew I should lay low after what had happened, but I felt drawn to return to the Hebrew labor camp the very next day. The injustice of the labor camps was nothing new to me. I had witnessed the often cruel, forced labor of my people since the time I was a young boy. But it was somehow different now, seeing injustice as a man.

Maybe it was that dream last week where I spent what seemed like hours, begging Yahweh to deliver the Hebrew people as he had promised his servant, Abraham that he would do. In my dream I had cried out in desperation, "How long, Oh Lord? How long until you deliver your people from bondage and settle us in a land you described as 'flowing with milk and honey?'"

Just then I heard a man cry out in distress. "Oh, no!" I thought. "It's happening again! I shouldn't have come here!"

I hurried to the labor yard scanning the camp for the slave who needed assistance but saw no Egyptian task masters mistreating the Hebrews as before. Instead, there were two Hebrew slaves fighting each other.

"What are you doing, fighting your brother!" Enraged, I grabbed the sticks each man was holding and broke them across my knees.

One of the slaves shook his head in disgust and stared at me with disdain. "Who do you think you are? Who made you ruler and judge over us?" Then he drew closer to me and whispered harshly, "Are you planning to kill me like you did the Egyptian?"

I gasped in horror. How did this slave know what I had done? I thought I had made sure no one was around to see me. I turned toward the other slaves standing nearby and they nodded one by one, acknowledging that they all knew that I had murdered that Egyptian guard. Soon Pharaoh would hear, if he had not already heard, that I had betrayed him by choosing my people above his own.

Then my brother, Aaron, came running to me out of the crowd that had formed. "Moses, Moses! You must go right now! Pharaoh is coming with his guards to kill you for what you have done!"

There was no time to say goodbye to my Hebrew family, or my ima Bithiah who must have been so distraught by my actions to choose my people over hers. I covered my head with my cloak, turned and fled out of Egypt toward the mountains of Midian.

IN MIDIAN

I had nothing but the clothes on my back when I left Egypt. Fortunately, my brother, Aaron, came to meet me in the desert that first night, bringing a few supplies and a skin of fresh water. He also told me that my step-grandfather, Pharaoh, had put out a bounty on my head.

"Don't come back, Moses!" he warned. "Pharaoh promises a generous reward to anyone who can bring you back to Egypt, dead or alive. Ima and Abba love you very much, but they urged me to come to you. 'Tell Moses to stay away,' they said. Now I must go. I will return to Egypt by another route, in case anyone seeking your harm has followed me."

I embraced my brother, and we wept, not knowing if we would ever see each other again. Then he hurried away.

I knew I must also move on. It was dangerous for me to stay too long in any one place this near the Egyptian border.

After about a week, I approached the land of Midian. I was starting to see some flocks of goats and sheep on the surrounding hills and knew that a water source must be nearby. I stopped and turned around scanning the landscape for signs of water. "There! That must be it!" I thought. I spied a group of people clustered around a well on the next rise. My water skin was completely empty by then, so I hurried to the well and sat down to wait my turn to draw water.

Just then a group of young ladies, seven in all, each carrying an empty water jar, approached the well. They, too, stood in line, to wait their turn at the well. My ima had always insisted I honor my sister, Miriam, by allowing her to go first so when at last it was my turn, I gestured to the ladies to go ahead of me.

"Thank you, sir," said the oldest. "We are seven sisters, daughters of one father, drawing water to fill the troughs for our father's flock." She and her sisters bowed in thanks and began filling their jars.

"Not so fast, ladies!"

Another group of shepherds had approached the well while the girls were bent over the well. One rough man started to wrestle a jar right out of the hands of the smallest sister, nearly spilling its precious contents.

"Stand back and let the men go first!" he shouted harshly.

The girls quickly stepped back from the well and cowered a short distance away, too frightened to lift their eyes at the angry shepherds.

"No, sir!" I stood to my feet. "It is my turn. I was here long before you. Stand aside."

The young shepherds who had been eager to bully a group of women seemed to look me over to see what sort of threat I imposed.

"Now!" I raised my voice and my staff and stepped between the shepherds and the well.

"He's only one man." One of the shepherds reasoned with the one who had bullied the women. "He won't be long. Let him go first."

I stared sternly at each of the young men who then backed away from the anger they saw in my eyes. I then proceeded to draw water from the well. I filled my skin, then one by one, took the jars from each of the seven ladies and filled them all. I could see that the men were enraged, but no one dared to confront me as I angrily stared them down.

When all their jars were filled, the seven sisters shouldered their jars and hurried home to their father, Jethro.

Jethro smiled when he saw his daughters approaching. He knew that the women were often hindered for hours as the shepherds pushed ahead of them, but he had no sons to send in their stead.

"My daughters, how quickly you have returned today!" Jethro exclaimed. "Was there no one at the well today?"

"Oh no, Papa," the youngest daughter said. "There were many shepherds at the well, and that mean young one—I think his name is Raama—he grabbed my jar and started to pull it away from me!"

"So what happened?" Jethro stood to his feet in anger. "I regret that I have to send you into danger every day! Are you alright? Did Raama hurt you, my daughter?"

"No, Papa," the eldest daughter wrapped her arms around her father. "Please, Papa, calm down. We are all fine, thanks to an Egyptian man who stood up to those bullies."

The girls surrounded their father then and told him how the Egyptian stranger had not only kept the young shepherds from harassing them but had drawn armload after armload of water from the well until all seven of their jars were filled.

"Well, where is your Egyptian champion?" Jethro looked around. "Why did you leave him there? Go back and invite this man to share a meal with us!"

"Of course, Papa! We were all so scared that we fled after our jars were full. How thoughtless of us to leave our kind Egyptian at the well!"

They hurried back to the well where I sat in the shade of a nearby tree.

"Is everything alright?" I stood to my feet as the ladies hurried to meet me.

"Please, sir, forgive us! Our father, Jethro, requests that you come to our home for a meal. He is, and we are, so grateful for your kindness to our family today. Will you honor us by coming to our home?"

"A home cooked meal?" I thought and quickly gathered my things to follow the girls back to their father's house.

Jethro received me with tears of gratitude in his eyes. "Dear sir, thank you so much for not only protecting my daughters today from the rough men at the well, but also drawing water for all my flocks. I have no sons, only these seven daughters, princesses they are to me and my wife!" And he laughed as he gathered his daughters into his arms. "May Yahweh be praised for bringing you to our home this day! Please, stay with us. Our home is your home."

I agreed to at least spend that night in Jethro's home. We talked long into the night, and then he prepared a place for me to sleep.

"Yes!" I prayed silently as I lay back on my makeshift bed. "Yahweh be praised for leading me to this family and this home tonight."

I fell asleep quickly but was awakened a short time later by a bright light shining on my face through the open window. I sat up with a start, thinking that some disgruntled shepherds were outside the window with their lanterns, looking for revenge. I saw no one. Then I looked up. There was the navigation star, Polaris! Had it somehow followed me from Egypt to Midian?

"Yahweh, oh Yahweh!" I laid down again, this time on my face. "Did you lead me here?" I wept as I worshiped, remembering the words Yahweh had spoken to me in my dream what seemed like a lifetime ago, but was in reality only a few weeks earlier.

"Moses, count the stars. You can see the stars! Abram believed, and I called him righteous. Believe me although you cannot see. When it is time, you will see what I will do."

Through my tears I prayed. "I believe you, Yahweh! I believe!"

THE FIRE

After staying a few days Jethro's home, he invited me to become one of his shepherds. I was eager to work and earn my keep and served Jethro well.

Several months later, we sat together around the dinner table in Jethro's home. I watched as his eldest daughter Zipporah served up a savory stew of lamb from the herd, and vegetables from her well-tended garden. How blessed Jethro was to have seven daughters, each one more beautiful than the next. Jethro's wife had died before I came to live with them, but that Zipporah, she kept their household running like a queen. She honored her father and taught her sisters to do the same. I had once arrived early from the fields to overhear her scolding Jethrodiadah, the youngest, who was in tears.

"Don't ever talk about Abba like that! Do you see all he does for you, every day from morning to night, and how he looks for you when he comes in from the fields every night? You, little one, are the apple of his eye!" Then she dried her sister's tears with the edge of her apron. "And he named you, his last born, after himself, saying "Yahweh saved the best for last!" Then I watched through the window as Zipporah grabbed her sister's hands and danced with her around the kitchen singing over her, "Jethrodiadah, apple of his eye, apple of his eye." The tears were gone, replaced by rippling laughter as the other five sisters joined the dance.

That night, after the girls had gone to their beds, Jethro and I sat around the fire outside.

"Moses, I thank Yahweh for bringing you to me."

"Well, thank you for that, Jethro. And I too am grateful for how you have opened your home to me and loved me as a son. You've listened to me, you know my story, and you are both a compassionate listener, and a wise counselor to me."

Jethro's eyes were moist as he turned to face me. "Moses, you are like family to me, so I would like to invite you to become my son-in-law. Marry my daughter, Zipporah!"

I could hardly believe my ears! The lovely Zipporah, my wife? I could hardly keep my eyes off her when she served our meals and had sometimes caught her looking at me. We were married a few days later.

Zipporah was a lovely woman, and a great cook! I looked forward to returning from the fields each evening both to her company, and a delicious meal. In some ways Zipporah reminded me of my birth mother, Jochebed. She was beautiful, but also very wise. I enjoyed being able to sort out my thoughts with Zipporah, many of them involving Yahweh. She was a great listener but also knew how to ask questions to help me dig deeper.

Yahweh soon blessed us with a son. I was so happy! Now I had a family of my own, a home of my own. But even so, I knew something was missing from my life. I was home, but even saying the word "home" reminded me of my home, my two homes in Egypt. So I named my son, Gershom, which means stranger or alien. Although I had a home in Midian, a wife, and now a son, I somehow still felt like an outsider in a land not my own. Even so, I continued to raise my family and serve my father-in-law, Jethro, for the next forty years.

I heard very little during that time about my family in Egypt. One day a runaway Hebrew slave passing through Midian reported that my step-grandfather had died. A new king, a harsh man had picked up where my step-grandfather left off, tightening the grip on his slaves, my people. I wondered if my parents and siblings were still alive.

Thoughts of Egypt troubled me the rest of the day and into the night.

After I fell asleep, I slipped into a familiar dream. I found myself once again standing with Yahweh on the mountainside.

"Listen, Moses!"

I stood still and began to hear the agonizing sound of groaning and weeping.

"Lord, who is that? Someone is in great pain. Can you help them?"

Yahweh's response was immediate. "It is my people, your people, the Hebrews crying out to me!"

I began to weep, thinking of my family, my siblings, possibly their children, groaning, crying out for deliverance. Then I realized that Yahweh was also weeping. The mountain began to shake as his body heaved with sobbing. Then a strong wind passed over us, and he spoke again.

"I have heard their crying, Moses. I have not forgotten the covenant I made with your fathers, Abraham, Isaac, and Jacob."

And I heard his voice as he recited the words of the covenant as we stood together on the mountain.

"Look at the land before you, to the east and the west, to the north and to the south, as far as your eyes can see, and beyond what you can see. To you, Abram, and to your descendants I give this land. The land now owned by your enemies, the Kenites, Kenizzites, Kadmonites, Hittites, Perizzites, Rephaites, Amorites, Canaanites, Girgashites and Jebusites, I give it to you."

I stood in silence, my heart crying out for my people.

"Moses, I have not forgotten."

The next morning, I awoke before the first light, my heart still heavy over the plight of my people. I took my staff, slipped out of the house and began driving Jethro's flock toward the grassy hills to graze. As it was still in the coolest part of the day, I led the flock a little farther than they usually traveled, to the far side of the desert until we arrived at Mount Horeb.

Suddenly, out of the corner of my eye I saw a flash of light on the mountainside. I spun around to see what had happened. There on the side of the mountain I saw a bush on fire. It was one of the acacia bushes, dry and thorny. I watched it burning, fully expecting the flames to either jump to the other shrubs nearby or die down after the bush was fully consumed. Neither event happened. Maybe there was no breeze up there to cause the flame to jump, but why was the one bush still burning? Surely it should be completely burned up by now. I decided to climb up and get a closer look.

I climbed until I reached the ledge where the bush continued to burn. How could this be? Was I still dreaming? But no, my thigh muscles were feeling the burn of a real climb. I walked slowly closer to the bush. The flames were brilliant, the way a flame looks when it initially soars to life over dry wood. But this fire had been burning for nearly an hour by the time I came to stand in front of it. I watched the dancing flames and rubbed my eyes in disbelief as I saw what looked like a human-like form in the midst of the fire.

"Moses!"

I knew that voice! It was the same voice I had heard in my dreams, on this very same mountain. But this time I was not asleep.

"Moses! Moses!"

"Here I am, Lord."

"Do not come any closer. Now take off your sandals, for the place where you are standing is holy ground."

I removed my sandals and fell to the ground trembling. Had my eyes truly seen the form of Yahweh in the fire? Were my ears really hearing the audible voice of God as my ancestors had?

As if in response to my unspoken questions, Yahweh answered me.

"I Am the God of Abraham, the God of Isaac, and the God of Jacob."

I hid my face in my cloak, afraid to look at God.

"Moses, I have indeed seen the misery of my people in Egypt. I have heard them crying out because of their cruel slave drivers. I do care about their suffering, and I have come down to rescue them from the hand of the Egyptians and to bring them up out of that land into a good and gracious land, a land flowing with milk and honey, the home of the Canaanites, Hittites, Amorites, Perizzites, Hivites, and Jebusites. Now the cry of the Israelites has reached me and I have seen their oppression under the Egyptians. So now, go, for I am sending you, Moses, to Pharaoh to bring my people out of Egypt."

I opened my eyes. "Me? The one who fled from Egypt for my life, with only the clothes on my back? Who am I that I should go to Pharaoh and bring the Hebrew people out of Egypt?"

"I am not sending you alone, Moses. I will go with you."

I was trembling from head to toe. "How can this be happening?" I thought. "Surely I am hallucinating. This cannot be real!"

"I will show you how real this encounter is. I will show you how real I Am." Yahweh once again answered my unspoken questions. "And I will give you this proof to you that it is truly I who am sending you back to Egypt to rescue my people. When you have succeeded in this mission and have brought the Israelites out of Egypt, you will worship on this same mountain where I am meeting you today."

I lay on the ground trying to formulate in my mind how in the world I, Moses, a shepherd, one of the most despised trades among the Egyptian population, an outcast from my people, and a labeled murderer, could turn into a leader who could rescue God's people. Yahweh remained silent as I tried to imagine how I would even begin to do what he was asking of me.

"So, if I approach the Israelites and tell them that the God of their fathers has sent me to them, what if they ask me your name? What should I say?"

"I Am who I Am, with you. I have been, am now, and will be forever, and I have chosen to be present with you. Tell them that is my name. I Am the God of Abraham, Isaac, and Jacob, present with you today. That is my name forever, the name by which I am to be remembered from generation to generation."

It was amazing to me to hear Yahweh speak his own name, and to grasp the fact that he did not simply eternally exist, but that he existed with his people. So yes, that was amazing that the Creator God chose to be with his people but also staring me in the face was the fact that his people had been enslaved in a foreign nation for four hundred years. My own parents had feared for my life and theirs from the minute I was born! Where was Yahweh, the "I Am Present" God then?

My parents had told me their story, how his promise "the Lord will provide" came true for them. But what of the countless others who died in slavery, men cruelly murdered by their slave owners, women violated at a master's whim, all those male babies drowned in the Nile. Abba had taught me that Yahweh is good, but four hundred years of slavery in a foreign land did not seem so good. Yes, we remembered his promise, that there would be a promised land, and that we would bring the bones of Joseph up to this land when the promise came to pass, but what of all those others' bones that lay buried in the land of our slavery? Who will remember their bones? Why of all men should I, Moses, receive the promise?

My heart cried out, "Yahweh, where is your goodness?"

As I lay trembling on the ground before the Lord I began to weep over my people. The earth in response began to shake and a light rain followed. I remembered my dream when the whole mountain shook and knew that Yahweh was weeping with me, for me. In my sorrow I realized I was also confused, even angry over Yahweh's four-hundred-year delay in rescuing his people out of cruel slavery. Yet he was weeping with me? I wanted desperately to ask him if he cared so much, why did he wait so long to act.

I cowered before the blazing bush, knowing that Yahweh somehow heard my every thought. He knew that I was questioning his goodness in my very soul. How would he respond to me? Who was I to think I could hash out my doubts and questions with Almighty God?

"Moses, remember how you felt when you delivered justice to our people, by killing the Egyptian who was beating the Hebrew slave?"

"Yes, I remember."

"And then you were amazed when you found the Hebrew slaves fighting one another, remember?"

"Yes, it seemed to me that we Hebrews were just as messed up as our slave masters, almost like we all deserved the mess we were in."

"So it has been from the beginning, when your forefather, Adam who I made in my own image, chose to disobey me. There are consequences for sin, natural consequences and supernatural ones. I rescued my people from famine and certain death four hundred years ago through my servant, Joseph. I gave Joseph two sons born to him in Egypt, Manasseh and Ephraim." Yahweh paused from his history lesson. "Moses, do you know the meanings of these names?"

"Yes. Manasseh means to forget. The joy of having a son caused Joseph to forget all the hardship he had suffered to bring him to the place of his position of leadership in Egypt. And Ephraim means fruitfulness. You were blessing Joseph with fruitfulness in his new home."

"Yes, your parents taught you well. I blessed my people greatly in Egypt. They prospered, grew and supplied grain and livestock to all of Egypt. Just as I had promised Abraham, the people were being blessed through his seed. I remained who I AM. But my people began to stray from me, to adopt Egyptian practices, including the worship of Egyptian gods. They rejected me and my ways, and it has been disastrous for them."

I nodded in understanding.

"The very people who had been blessed by my people then enslaved them. What I had wanted for my people was to forget their trials, Manasseh, to leave behind the ordeal of the famine, and to be fruitful, Ephraim, in the land of Egypt. But my people rejected me and chose to try the lifestyle of the Egyptians instead of recognizing where their fruitfulness had come from. Then the greed of the Egyptians caused them to enslave my people. My people were now stuck, imprisoned in a lifestyle they chose, a prison of their own making. Moses, that was never my plan for them!

"That is why I made a promise to my servant, Abraham, a promise to deliver my people out of slavery. They could never get there on their own. They had forgotten who I AM. But I have never forgotten who I AM, and I have never forgotten my people and my promises to them. It is time. So get up, go now to the elders of Israel. Say to them 'The Lord, the God of your fathers, the God of Abraham, Isaac and Jacob appeared to me and said: I have watched over you and have seen what has been done to you in Egypt. I see you, Israel! And I remember my promise to you, to bring you up out of your misery in Egypt into a land flowing with milk and honey!'

"They will listen to you, Moses. Then you will go to the King of Egypt and give him this message: 'The Lord, the God of the Hebrews, has met with us. Let us take a three-day journey into the desert to offer sacrifices to the Lord our God.' But Moses, I know that the king will not let you go unless a mighty hand compels him. So I will stretch out my hand and smite the Egyptians with great and terrible wonders that could only come from God. After that, the king will let you leave.

"Not only will the king allow you to go, but the people of Egypt will have favor on you and allow you to borrow articles of silver and gold and clothing, which you will take with you when you leave their land, thereby plundering the Egyptians who enslaved you!"

"You say they will listen to me, but what if they don't? I've been gone for forty years. What if they say, 'Who do you think you are? Yahweh did not appear to you!'"

"Moses, what do you have in your hand?"

I wasn't aware I had anything in my hand until that moment. I pried my fingers from my shepherd's staff and held it aloft toward the bush.

'It's just my staff."

"Throw it on the ground!"

So I threw my staff. It landed several yards away and immediately began to shake, change form and curve in upon itself.

"It's a snake! A deadly one!" I ran some distance away and turned back to watch the snake curling and hissing as it moved along the rocks.

"Moses, don't be afraid! Now grab the snake by its tail."

"But Lord—" I began but was quickly cut off.

"Moses! Do as I say. Do not be afraid."

I softly walked up to the snake as it slithered away from me, and I reached out and grabbed it by the tail. Immediately the snake became rigid and lifeless in my hand, no longer a snake, but my familiar shepherd's rod.

"This will be a sign to my people that I have truly appeared to you."

I was still shaken from my interaction with a venomous snake. How would the Hebrews receive this trick?

But Yahweh was not done with my preparation.

"Moses! Put your hand inside your cloak."

I slipped my hand inside my cloak over my heart. A few minutes passed as I waited for more instruction, my hand held over my racing heart. I began to feel a tingling in my hand, then sharp pains. I pulled my hand out and saw that it had become shriveled, crusted with white, flaky skin.

"Leprosy!" I cried and I shook my hand as if I could shake away the leprosy.

"Moses."

I looked toward the bush again.

"Moses, put your hand back into your cloak again, and it will be restored."

I did not waste a second obeying God this time and sighed with relief as I pulled a fully restored hand out of my cloak.

"Now you are almost ready to go and bring my message to Pharaoh. If he doesn't believe you when you turn your staff into a snake, he may believe you when you cause your hand to become leprous and then restored."

"But what if he still doesn't believe your words and signs at that point?"

"Moses, then you shall dip a jug into the Nile, draw some water and pour it out on the ground in Pharaoh's presence. As he watches, the water will become a crimson pool of blood at Pharaoh's feet."

I was silent, anxious as I stood before the flaming bush. I had run from the danger of Egypt. Now Yahweh was asking me to go back and confront the King of Egypt. I shook inside at the thought of such an encounter.

"Yahweh, I've never been good with words, since childhood I've stuttered and struggled to know what to say and how to say it. It's no different now that I'm a man."

Even as I spoke, I could sense that Yahweh was becoming upset with me.

"Moses! I created man. I'm the one who created your mouth. Who do you think causes a man to be able to speak, or remain mute? It is me. I made your mouth, and I will help you speak and teach you what to say."

"O Lord, please, send someone else to speak to Pharaoh!"

The mountain shook fiercely at that point, and I fell to the ground. Surely Yahweh would either strike me dead for my words or leave me and find a more willing servant. I lay on my face until the shaking subsided, then lifted my face to see that the fire was still burning brighter than ever.

"Moses."

His voice was stern, but he apparently hadn't given up on me. "I will send your brother Aaron the Levite to go with you."

"Aaron? Is my brother Aaron still alive?" I began to feel hope creeping into my heart.

"Yes, he is most certainly alive! He can speak well."

Maybe I could do this thing that Yahweh was asking of me, if my brother would go with me.

"Moses, your brother is already on his way to find you."

What? I shook my head in wonder. Yahweh knew me so well! He knew I would need a burning bush to make me stop and hear him. He knew I would need a companion, a brother to go with me or I would be too afraid to go. He knew and had already started the plan in motion before I even agreed to it.

"Aaron will be so happy to see you, Moses! He, too, has wondered if you were still alive after not seeing you for over forty years. Just as you helped him as a young boy, teaching him what you had learned from your abba, now you will hear my words, and you will speak those words to Aaron. And

Aaron will be your mouth, speaking the words you give him, as if you were God to him."

I rose from the ground excited. My brother was on his way to me! Together we would return to Egypt and rescue God's people! I turned to go home to prepare for my journey.

"Moses, don't forget your staff! You will need it to perform the miraculous signs."

I took one last look at the fire, and the form of a face that flickered in the flames, and headed home.

It was late afternoon when I arrived at the home of my father-in-law, Jethro. He had just returned from the fields and was resting outside his door. "Moses, come sit with me. You have been gone all day."

As I drew near to Jethro's door, I wondered what he would think about my plans to suddenly leave my flocks, my family, his daughter and grandchildren, and return to the land where I was still considered a fugitive. Would he think I was crazy? Maybe this is a crazy plan.

"Moses? Your face! It's so red and raw. Didn't you keep your head covered from the sun today?"

I reached up and put my hands over my cheeks. I could feel the heat radiating from my face. But I had been in the shade of the mountainside most of the day, I thought. How could I have received such a harsh sunburn that felt so hot to the touch? But wait, it must have been the burning bush! I turned away from Jethro, tears springing to my eyes as I understood yet another of Yahweh's signs, a supernatural sunburn that reminded me that I had truly experienced his presence this day.

"Yahweh!" I prayed silently. "You know I needed this!" My flaming face spoke the truth louder than the words I was carrying in my heart! Yes, it really happened! Yes, it was really you in that bush, Yahweh! Yes, you are truly the one sending me on this assignment, and yes, I'm saying yes! I will go!

Then I turned my sunburned face to my father-in-law. "Jethro, I've been with Yahweh today."

Jethro looked first to heaven, and then to me. "Go on."

"Jethro, I need to return to Egypt, to my people, to see if any of them are still alive. Yahweh says it's time, it's time to set his people free from the slavery of Egypt, and he's sending me and my brother Aaron."

Jethro reached out and grasped both of my arms. There were tears in his eyes as he blessed me. "Go, and I wish you well."

Buoyed with confidence after Jethro's blessing I returned home to my wife, Zipporah.

"At last you are home, my husband! You left so early I thought for sure you would return hours ago." Zipporah then turned from the cooking pot to face me. "Moses! Your face! Here, let me put some goat-milk salve on your burns!"

I sat while she gently applied the cooling salve on my face.

"Zipporah, I've been with Yahweh," I began.

"Yahweh is always with you, Moses."

"Ah, but this time it was different. He appeared to me—"

"But you have said it yourself, no one can see his face and live!"

I told Zipporah about the burning bush, and the image I could see wavering in the flames. I told her about my assignment. Then I sat back and waited to hear what she would say.

"When are we leaving, my husband?"

"You will go with me?" I asked gently.

"I would follow you anywhere, Moses, especially if I know that you are following Yahweh."

I took Zipporah into my arms then, and thanked Yahweh for yet another sign of his leading, that my wife was willing to go with me.

The next day I put my wife and my two sons on a donkey, and we started back to Egypt. I carried my staff in my hands, which I now considered both a tool and a weapon. Our first night we set up camp in a hilly area near a spring. We ate and then lay down to sleep under the stars. Sleep evaded me for a time as I wrestled in my mind about my upcoming encounter with Pharaoh. As I drifted off to sleep, I found myself composing a script in my mind, the words and arguments I would say to Pharaoh to convince him that he should do as I ask and release the Hebrews. Then I found myself once again standing with Yahweh on the mountain of God.

"Moses!"

"I am here!"

"When you return to Egypt make sure that you only speak what I tell you. Don't try to explain what you are doing or use your university debating techniques to convince Pharaoh that he needs to release the Hebrews. You must tell Pharaoh that I have met with you and make sure that you perform before Pharaoh all the wonders I have given you. Tell him 'This is what the Lord says: Israel is my firstborn son. Now let my son go that he may worship me. If you refuse to let him go, I will kill your firstborn son.'"

As I slept, I began to moan softly. Zipporah, lying next to me, suddenly bolted upright and turned to me. "Moses, are you sick?"

I awoke and began to feel waves of pain cascading over my body. I doubled over on my mat, clutching my stomach.

"Moses! I saw you in my dreams tonight, so sick, and now here you are writhing in pain. It is Yahweh! He is killing you!"

I could not answer her in my distress, but I knew in my spirit that what she was saying was true.

"Yahweh told me, Moses! You knew his covenant! You knew that you must circumcise every male child coming from your loins. But you have not obeyed him."

The Zipporah opened her pack and removed a small flint cooking knife. She took her sleeping sons, uncovered them and cut off the foreskin of their penises. Then she comforted her wailing children and lay the bloodied foreskins at Moses' feet.

At once I felt as though a cool wind blew straight into my mouth and I gasped and sat upright. The pain instantly left my body.

After Zipporah had gotten our sons back to sleep she lay again beside me. As I drifted off to sleep, I heard her muttering under her breath.

"Surely you are a bridegroom of blood to me, Moses!"

But I heard no more, for I was standing again on the Mountain of God, hearing another voice.

"Moses!"

"I am here, my Lord!"

"No matter what, you must always keep my covenants that I have shown you. You will be safe within the covenant, you and your family."

"Yahweh, what is a covenant? You speak as if it is some sort of structure or building where I can shelter with my family."

"A covenant is a mutual promise, my son. I made a covenant with your father, Abraham. I promised him protection from his enemies and a land flowing with milk and honey for him and his descendants, and Abraham promised that he and his descendants would follow my ways. Then I commanded Abraham to perform the ritual of circumcision as a symbol of the covenant, a symbol that he could see first in his own body, and then in the bodies of his children, and grandchildren."

He was silent, allowing me to think through what he was telling me.

"Yahweh, please forgive me for not keeping the symbol of your covenant with my sons."

Then I looked at my wife, sleeping beside me, her face still moist from the tears she shed doing to my sons what I should have done as their father.

"Zipporah," I whispered. "Forgive me for leaving undone what I should have done to keep the symbol of the covenant in our family."

Yahweh then gathered me and Zipporah in his arms and held us to his heart on the mountain.

Then I heard Zipporah sigh. I looked down from where I stood on the mountain and saw her smile in her sleep. I laid back down next to her, and we slept until the sun woke us the next morning. We laughed out loud as we both opened our eyes at the same minute and took in deep breaths of the cool morning air. Then the boys woke up and needed our attention, so we did not speak of what had happened the night before. I didn't know if Zipporah had also encountered Yahweh on the mountain with me in her own dreams, or if she had heard my heartfelt apologies to her and to Yahweh. But I saw that her step was lighter, and her face was smiling as she built the fire to make breakfast, and in my heart I believed that she, too, had been with Yahweh.

BACK TO EGYPT

Because Yahweh had warned me that things would not go well at first when I approached Pharaoh, I decided it would be best, safest, if Zipporah and the children stayed behind in Midian for now. I escorted my family back to Jethro's home that very day. It was hard to say goodbye. There had been too many goodbyes already in my lifetime.

I knew I was obeying God by going back to Egypt to fulfill the assignment he had given me, but my first few miles alone after leaving my family behind were bittersweet. As I approached the mountain of God, I remembered my dreams and the sweetness of Yahweh's embrace and began to put the sadness behind me. Then I spied a lone man standing near the mountain. He raised his hand in greeting, and I realized it was my own brother Aaron! Yahweh had again fulfilled what he had promised and sent Aaron to meet me. Energized by God's goodness I ran toward Aaron and hugged and kissed him.

"Aaron, how did you know where to find me?" I asked him after I finally released him from my arms.

"Yahweh told me, I can't explain it." Aaron shook his head. "It was like I just felt this strong urging to see you, to somehow find you in this vast desert. My wife thought I was crazy. 'There are miles and miles of desert there. How will you know where to find him? What if you run out of water or food?' she warned me. But I had this dream. I saw you on this mountain enveloped in a cloud. Call me crazy, but I mapped out a route to Mt. Horeb, left a bewildered wife at home, and here you are!"

We both shook our heads in amazement, then raised our eyes to the mountain, both of us amazed at how Yahweh had been clearly leading us to this very moment in time and this very place.

"So tell me about this assignment from Yahweh," Aaron said.

I shared the story, starting with the burning bush. Aaron was amazed.

"A bush on fire but never burning up?" he asked. "Where is this bush?"

"Well, it's on the ledge, right over there ... Or maybe not. That bush is in the right location, but there's not a charred leaf on it!"

Aaron quickly scaled the hill and reached the ledge. "Moses! There are ashes all around this bush, but the bush is green and healthy. Maybe you were dreaming?"

"Yes! This is the bush, the very bush that was burning the entire time I was on the mountain. I swear, Aaron, this really happened! It was not a dream. In fact, the fire was so hot and brilliant that my face was burned from being so near the bush."

"Moses, I believe you. I can still see the remnants of your burned cheeks even now. And how else could there be ashes around the bush. There's no other signs of fire nearby? Moses, tell me what God said to you out of the fire."

I sighed, so happy that my brother believed me and needed no convincing. I told Aaron everything that had happened, the staff turning into a snake, my leprous hand, and the assignment God had given us.

"Yahweh remembers, Aaron! He has not forgotten the promise he made to Abraham, the promise of a land to call our own after four hundred years of slavery in Egypt. He is sending you and me on assignment to fulfill his promise and set the Hebrew people free."

Aaron jumped to his feet and grabbed his pack. "What are we waiting for, Moses? Let's go!"

The miles passed quickly as Aaron caught me up on the latest news about our family and our people. It was sad to hear of so many of my friends that had passed away and would not be leaving Egypt with us.

My heart cried out silently "Lord, if only they had held on a little longer they would have been able to enter the Land of Promise with me!"

Even so I remembered the Lord weeping with me over his people as he held me on the mountain. I knew the cries of the heart of Yahweh. Maybe that was what I was feeling, not my own grief, but the ache of his heart over the ones whose bones lay buried in the sands of captivity.

After several weeks we entered Pharaoh's territory. I was ready to find a place to sleep for the night, and start fresh with Pharaoh the next morning, but Aaron did not want to waste another minute before we started our assignment.

First, we went to the Hebrew encampment. We called the leaders together, and Aaron took the lead. He told them how Yahweh had appeared to me. He took my staff and showed them the miracle of the staff becoming a snake and then turning back into a staff again. He put his hand into his cloak to make it leprous and then clean again. I could see their level of fear rising as they watched Aaron perform the signs Yahweh had given us.

But then Aaron told them about what Yahweh had said. "Don't be afraid, dear ones! Yahweh has heard your crying and moaning over your enslavement. He remembers his promise to Abraham, and has sent me and my brother Moses to lead you out of Egypt into the Land of Promise!"

We began to see smiles on the faces of the Hebrew leaders. We heard them encouraging each other to believe what we had told them.

"He really cares about us!"

"Yahweh is concerned for us, his people!"

And one by one the leaders bowed to the ground and worshiped. Aaron and I fell face down to the ground alongside the Hebrew elders. We had passed our first hurdle—the Hebrew people believed us and were ready to follow us out of Egypt and into the Land of Promise!

Then I lifted my face and began to pray aloud that ancient blessing our fathers had taught us. "Blessed are you, Lord our God, King of the Universe."

The voices of my people then joined me, speaking the blessing together, as one:

"Blessed are you, Lord our God, King of the Universe, who has kept me alive and preserved me and enabled me to reach this season!"

Our elation was short lived. The next morning Aaron and I approached the next obstacle on our assignment, Pharaoh himself.

Would we even be permitted into Pharaoh's presence, two Hebrew goat herders?

We entered the palace grounds and were quickly confronted by Egyptian guards.

"Stop! Who are you and what are you doing here?" One of the guards pulled a long knife from its scabbard and held it aloft.

Aaron spoke with confidence. "We are Hebrews, brothers, Moses and Aaron, and we bring to Pharaoh a message from Yahweh, God of the Hebrews."

The guards seemed to recognize my name as they whispered to one another and gestured toward me.

The lead guard turned to me. "Are you the same Moses who was raised in this palace?"

"Yes, I am."

Another guard came alongside. "And the same Moses who killed an Egyptian man who was beating your fellow Hebrew?"

"Y-yes," I stammered.

"Wait here!"

The two lead guards turned and entered the palace, while the remaining guards surrounded us, keeping us from leaving the courtyard or from entering the palace doors.

Several anxious moments passed as Aaron and I stood encircled on the palace grounds.

Then the lead guards returned. "Pharaoh will see you. Do you have any weapons?"

"No weapons, only my brother's shepherd's staff," Aaron answered.

The guards led us inside the palace and into the meeting hall where Pharaoh presided.

Pharaoh received us with little acknowledgment. "What is your message from Yahweh?" He sneered.

I was so thankful for Aaron. My tongue was quite tied as I stood shaking before the successor of my step-grandfather, Pharaoh, in the very palace where I had grown up.

Aaron took a step closer to Pharaoh. "This is what the Lord, the God of Israel says, 'Let my people go, so that they may hold a festival to me in the desert.'"

"And just who is this god of yours? Who it the Lord that I should obey him and let Israel go? I do not know your Lord, and I will not let Israel go!"

I joined Aaron then as we delivered Yahweh's message to Pharaoh. "The God of the Hebrews has met with us. Now let the Hebrew people take a three-day journey into the desert to offer sacrifices to his name. If you do not allow us to go, the Lord may strike you with plagues or the sword."

Now Pharaoh rose from his throne in anger. "Get out of here, you worthless sheepherders! Why are you keeping your people from finishing their work, giving them pipe dreams about leaving Egypt?" He waved his hand to dismiss us and screamed, "Get back to work!"

The guards grabbed us from behind and dragged us out of the palace, across the grounds and tossed us out of the gate, slamming it shut behind us.

As we picked ourselves off the ground and dusted the dirt from our robes, we heard Pharaoh ranting from the inner hall.

"They have too much time on their hands, these Hebrews! Too much time left for daydreaming about a trip into the desert to worship their god! I'll take care of that right now. Guards! Call the slave masters and foremen at once."

A few minutes later we passed the foremen and slave drivers running toward the palace. Then we heard Pharaoh's screeching voice instructing the foremen.

"You are no longer to supply the Hebrews with straw for making bricks! Since they have so much free time on their hands, make them gather their own straw."

"But master." One of the foreman bowed and approached Pharaoh. "Surely brick production will suffer if the Hebrews must spend half of the day gathering the straw."

"No, you are to require them to produce the same quota of bricks as before. They are lazy. That is why they are crying out for time to go and sacrifice to their God! Make the work harder for the Hebrews so they have no time to listen to this nonsense about sacrificing to their god!"

Life became even more bitter for my people after that. Their workday had to start before the sun even came up so they had a chance to gather enough straw to make their full quota of bricks. A reduction in brick production was met with severe beatings from the Egyptian slave masters.

After several days of hard labor every waking hour, the Hebrew leaders sought out Moses and Aaron. "Look what you have done!" they shouted. "May the Lord look upon you and judge you! You have made us a stench to Pharaoh and his officials and have given them cause to kill us when we cannot meet their demands!"

Aaron's face fell. "Moses! What is going on? I thought you told me God was going to deliver the people out of Egypt and use us to do it! Now we are doing the opposite! Our action is causing the people to be more firmly entrenched in their slavery with not a moment of rest to catch their breaths!"

I could not answer my brother, nor the Hebrew people. I turned and ran off to be by myself. Then I tore my robe and turned in the direction of the Mountain of God, the place where I had encountered Yahweh before. Was he still there? Would he hear me from hundreds of miles away?

"Oh, Lord!" I wept with my face to the ground. "Oh Lord, why have you brought trouble on your people? Is this why you sent me? Ever since I obeyed your voice and spoke your words to Pharaoh, he has made your people's existence a living hell! You have not done what you said. You have not rescued your people at all!"

I heard no answer at first, but then a gentle whisper of a question. "Moses, why are you here?"

"Here as opposed to someplace else?" I thought.

"You didn't come to this place the last time you saw your people mistreated."

I stopped and thought back to that time now over forty years ago when I had seen my people mistreated and took the matter into my own hands. Then I continued my prayer to Yahweh.

"Now I know better than to try to fix this myself, Yahweh. That is why I am here. I don't know what to do, but I know who to run to this time. Don't let your people down, O Lord! Show me what to do!"

I began to feel a comforting warmth spreading across my shoulders as I lay on the ground. I lifted my head to see where the sun was in the sky but saw that it was quickly setting over the city. I knew then that the warmth I was feeling was the presence of Yahweh overshadowing me. I waited to hear what he would say.

"Moses, now you will see what I will do to Pharaoh. My mighty hand will cause him to let the Hebrews go, in fact he will drive them out of Egypt by his own hand."

"Oh, God, I have caused so much trauma for my people! Because of me the slave masters have exacted greater punishment on the Hebrews, and your people don't trust my words anymore."

"Moses, trust me. Although you and your people have broken my covenant over these past four hundred years, I Am the same. I never forget my covenant. I will set these people free from their captivity in Egypt as I have promised, and you will lead them. I am not a man, that I should lie, or change my mind. Every word I speak carries within it the authority to fulfill what I have spoken."

"I trust you, Yahweh. I have seen your presence in the burning bush. But my people have lost faith. They cannot see you. They only see their slavery, now harsher due to the new requirements to gather their own straw for the bricks. It's hard for them to trust a promise that stands in stark contrast to what is right in front of their eyes. How can I help them?"

"Moses, the best way for you to lead my people is by trusting me. You will show them what it's like to be a friend of God."

My eyes flew open. A friend of God? Me?

"Now go home with Aaron. Greet your family. Get some rest tonight, and tomorrow I will show you what to do."

MIRACLES BEFORE PHARAOH

The next morning, Yahweh sent Aaron and me back to the Hebrew people. We told them again about Yahweh's promise, and that it was time for Yahweh to deliver them from slavery. This time the Hebrews were so discouraged because of their increased workload that they turned and walked away.

As we watched our people walk away, I heard Yahweh's voice. "Go now and tell Pharaoh to let your people leave Egypt."

It was almost ridiculous to me. I just shook my head. "Yahweh, if my own people won't listen to me why should I expect Pharaoh to listen?"

"You must tell Pharaoh everything I speak to you, Moses."

I again shook my head in discouragement. "Surely Yahweh must be aware of my faltering speech," I thought. "Why does he ask me to speak to the king when he knows I will stutter and make an absolute fool of myself."

Yahweh responded to my thoughts as if I had said them aloud.

"Have I not sent your brother Aaron to speak for you? You are my prophet, Moses. I speak my words to you, and you make my voice known to the people. Now you will be as God to your brother, Aaron. You will speak my words to Aaron, and he will speak them to Pharaoh."

All the while during my conversation, spoken and unspoken, with Yahweh, Aaron stood by my side silently watching and waiting. Only I seemed to be hearing Yahweh's voice, but Aaron was able to hear my spoken responses.

Finally, I turned to Aaron and shared all that Yahweh had spoken, including his instruction about being as God to Aaron, and Aaron being my prophet. Not just any man would trust me that deeply to accept my words as the very words of Yahweh.

I paused then, trying to allow Aaron time to process what I was saying.

"Moses!" Aaron rose from where he had been sitting.

"I know, I know, my brother. It is hard to believe, especially when you cannot hear him speak to me," I began.

Aaron grasped my arms and looked into my eyes. "No, Moses. I believe you. I know you. You would never make up a story like this! You would never leave your family behind and go back to Egypt, taking your life in your hands to act on some whim or fantasy. Moses, I have always trusted you, looked up to you, and I believe you now. I saw the fear you lived in when you fled Egypt forty years ago. Now I see a greater determination in you that brings you back to Egypt, at the risk of losing your life. I believe that could only be a result of your encounter with Yahweh. If Yahweh is in this plan, then I am in it with you and Yahweh. What's next?"

I pulled my brother into my arms then and wept on his shoulder. "Thank you, Yahweh," I whispered. Then I looked into Aaron's eyes and told him, "I am so very proud of you, my brother. Although you have not heard Yahweh's voice, you trust his words. You are so precious to me! Now, here's what Yahweh told me ..."

We spent the rest of the day planning out how we would approach Pharaoh the next morning.

Aaron and I approached the palace grounds shortly after daybreak. At Yahweh's direction Aaron brought along his staff. After the way Pharaoh had us ejected from the palace the last time, I was uncertain we would gain access this morning.

Just then I heard Yahweh repeat what he had told me earlier, "Every word I speak carries within it the authority to fulfill what I have spoken."

I wasn't sure what that meant the last time Yahweh had said it, but I repeated Yahweh's words aloud so Aaron would know what he was saying.

"Yahweh says that every word he speaks carries within it the authority to fulfill that word."

"Moses! Do you know what that means?" Aaron said excitedly.

"No, Aaron, well not at first, but now I think I do. I think it means that if God says Pharaoh will let our people leave Egypt, it's going to happen. It means that we can trust Yahweh no matter that the Hebrews no longer believe us, and no matter how hard it gets for us to go before Pharaoh and demand that he free the Hebrew people. If he says it's going to happen, it will happen, and we will live to tell the story. Just as he promised, one day we will worship together on the Mountain of God!"

Aaron grabbed my hands and together we danced around laughing, like little children, me an eighty-six-year-old man and my brother not far behind me at eighty-three. We would need the joy of that moment, and the sweet reminder of Yahweh's promise to us, to carry us through our next encounter with Pharaoh, and many days of trials to come.

THE BEGINNING OF MIRACLES BEFORE PHARAOH

I am not sure why Pharaoh allowed us back into his presence the next morning, but somehow, we were permitted through the palace gates and brought to the table where Pharaoh sat finishing his morning meal.

We stood quietly by, waiting until Pharaoh had finished breakfast and pushed aside his plate. Then he looked up at us, rolled his eyes, and motioned for us to speak. Aaron repeated the same words we had said the last time we were in Pharaoh's presence. We had no new message.

"Moses has heard from Yahweh that he is to lead the Hebrew people into the wilderness to worship our God. Now allow us to leave Egypt so we may obey the voice of our God."

Pharaoh's eyes narrowed as if deep in thought. "What did his voice sound like, Moses?" he asked skeptically.

"It was like no other voice I have ever heard," I began. "Yahweh's voice, although not particularly loud, seemed to reverberate in my chest."

Pharaoh's face tightened into a scowl. "What about you, Aaron? What did you hear when your god spoke?"

"Well, I didn't actually hear Yahweh's voice. He spoke to Moses, and Moses told me what he said, and what we should do."

"And you believed your brother? You are an idiot! Why would your god speak to your brother and not to you? Why would he speak to either of you, you filthy shepherds! I don't believe a word of what you're saying!" And he rose and beckoned to his officers to take us into custody.

"Wait, Pharaoh!" Aaron spoke up. "We have proof! Yahweh gave us miracles that we can perform to show you that Moses truly heard from God."

"Miracles?" Pharaoh gestured for the officers to step back.

Aaron and I looked at each other and remembered the words Yahweh had spoken to us: "When Pharaoh says to you, 'perform a miracle,' then Aaron is to take his staff and throw it at Pharaoh's feet. It will become a snake right in front of him." We had waited only seconds when we heard Pharaoh's voice, dripping with sarcasm.

"Go ahead then! Perform a miracle for me!"

Aaron raised his staff, and the guards started to rush toward him thinking he would strike the king. Then he threw the staff to the ground. As soon as it hit the ground the staff transformed into a snake, hissing and curling up at Pharaoh's feet. The guards ran up and used their spears to keep the snake away from the king.

At first Pharaoh seemed shaken by the miracle, but then he looked up and called out loudly, "Send for the wise men, my sorcerers!"

Several men, Pharaoh's wise men, were quickly ushered into the court, each holding a staff.

"Look!" Pharaoh told them. "These lowly shepherds have performed a miracle by the power of their god. Now show them the power of the gods of the Egyptians!"

The sorcerers each raised their staffs, threw them to the ground, and their staffs also became writhing snakes at their feet. Pharaoh turned to sneer at Aaron and me, when suddenly one of the sorcerers gasped and pointed to the ground. Aaron's snake had opened its jaws and one by one it swallowed whole each of the sorcerers' snakes. Then Aaron reached out, picked up his snake by the tail, and it turned back into a staff in his hand.

Pharaoh stood wide-eyed and speechless. I gestured to Aaron to follow me, and together we walked out of the court and left the palace grounds. No one tried to detain us.

Once outside the compound Aaron turned to me. "Why are we leaving? Pharaoh was amazed at Yahweh's miracle! Maybe he was ready to listen to us!"

"No, my brother. Yahweh said that Pharaoh's heart is still unyielding and stubborn. He is not ready to let us leave Egypt. Trust me. Trust Yahweh. We will bring another miracle tomorrow morning."

We returned to the Hebrew camp. The people looked up as we entered, surprised to see us. They wondered why Pharaoh had not had us killed for daring to go back to him again, but they were too spent, too exhausted to do little more than glance in our direction as they returned to their homes to sleep a few hours before they had to rise and resume their thankless labor.

The next morning Aaron and I headed toward the Nile River. Yahweh had instructed me to meet Pharaoh there on the riverbank. We arrived before Pharaoh and stood waiting as he approached. He didn't see us at first, but we stepped toward him as he came to the water's edge.

"You! What are you doing here, disturbing my bathing! Guards!"

"Stop!" Aaron spoke, and the authority in his voice stopped both Pharaoh and his guards in their tracks. "Stop and hear what Yahweh says. We are not speaking on our own, Pharaoh. Yahweh himself has sent us to you, and these are his words."

Pharaoh seemed angry but shaken by our interruption of his morning bath. "What does *Yahweh* have to say to me today?"

"Yahweh says, 'Let my people go and worship me in the desert. Up until now you have not listened to me. You have not let my people leave. You have not believed me, but I will show you that I Am God.' With the staff in my hand, I will strike the waters of the Nile, and the water will be turned into blood! The fish in the Nile will die and the river will stink because of the decaying fish. You will not be able to drink the water, nor bathe in it."

At my command Aaron then raised his staff as Pharaoh and his servants looked on. Aaron struck the water with his staff and droplets of blood splashed out and splattered Pharaoh's robe. As we watched we began to see fish floating belly up to the surface of the now red river. Then we began to hear shouts and screaming coming from all around us the Egyptian people discovered that the ponds, streams, reservoirs, even buckets of water already drawn in their homes had turned into blood.

"Guards!" Pharaoh cried out. "Get my sorcerers at once!"

The sorcerers hurried to the riverbank and gasped at what they saw, rippling red currents, littered with dead fish. Then pots of water were brought from the palace grounds, somehow not yet turned into blood, and once again, the court sorcerers were also able to duplicate the miracle, turning the water in the pots into blood.

Pharaoh turned away from the river and stormed back to the palace. Not long afterwards Pharaoh's servants returned with digging tools and dug along the riverbank to access fresh drinking water that had not been turned into blood. They carried pots of fresh water back to the palace.

All the while, Aaron and I stood by watching. Finally, we stood alone at the riverbank, as everyone had returned to their homes to get away from the stench rising out of the bloody water.

"Moses," Aaron looked to me. "I don't understand? Why does Yahweh allow the evil magicians to duplicate God's miracles? Doesn't he know that our words, his words, are like garbage to Pharaoh when his own wise men can do the very same miracles?"

"Aaron, I don't understand either but come with me."

"Where? Where are we going?"

I did not answer my brother, but nevertheless he followed me away from the stinking river to a place where we could get alone, lay on our faces before Yahweh, and receive his instructions for our next steps.

When we reached a secluded place, a shallow cave on the outskirts of the city, Aaron and I slipped inside. The temperature was several degrees cooler away from the blinding sun. We sat on the stony floor and took some refreshment from a skin of water I'd brought along. Aaron looked terrible, his brow furrowed in worry, his eyes nearly lifeless as he struggled to process our interaction with Pharaoh.

"Aaron, my dear brother." I laid my hand on his arm. "Come, let us seek Yahweh's guidance for our next steps."

Aaron mindlessly followed me as I lay down on the hard floor of the narrow cave. I wasn't sure he could continue with me unless he received some encouragement.

"Aaron, Yahweh is Sovereign. As a servant of Yahweh, I understand and accept that he will not always tell me all that he has planned, or the reasoning behind it."

"Yes, but Moses, at least you have seen Yahweh, or at least a glimpse of him in the fiery bush! And your ears heard his voice. It's not that I don't trust you, my brother, but I'm struggling here. If I could just see him, or hear his voice ..."

Aaron began to weep, his body trembling as he sobbed. I lay next to him, stroking his back as he wept. I shook my head. "Why do I hear your voice, but not my brother?" I prayed silently.

Then I felt Aaron's shoulders tense and heard him breathe deeply, then relax. We lay side by side on the hard cave floor in silence. Then Aaron lifted his face, still wet with tears, and turned to me.

"I heard him!" he whispered.

I offered a silent thanks to Yahweh and waited.

"His voice ... it sounds like Abba, doesn't it?"

I smiled and waited for him to continue.

"He told me ..." Aaron choked with emotion. "He told me he loves me. And he told me to follow you, Moses."

That was all, but that was enough. Together we prayed a prayer taught by our abba, "Blessed are you, Lord our God,

King of the Universe, who brings forth bread from the earth and has kept us alive and preserved us to reach this season!"

Aaron and I stayed in the cave for several hours. Yahweh was there, and we both felt renewed by his presence. Late in the afternoon, I heard Aaron's steady breathing and knew he had fallen asleep. I smiled, thinking of how our ima had rocked him to sleep many times, his little head on her shoulder. Now he was resting in the arms of Yahweh, and I couldn't imagine anything that would rival that place of comfort and satisfaction. My heart was full.

"Yahweh, thank you for hearing my brother's desperate heart, and letting him hear your voice. You are so good, and I love you with all my heart!"

I lay down and waited to hear Yahweh's directions.

"I won't give you any false expectations, Moses," he began. "Pharaoh will let my people leave Egypt, but he will not change his mind easily."

As Aaron slept beside me, Yahweh unfolded his plans to me. Yahweh would bring a series of plagues upon the Egyptian people, each one more devastating than the one before it, until Pharaoh would relent and release the Hebrews from captivity. I woke Aaron afterwards, and we headed to our homes, carefully avoiding the palace area.

There was no respite for Pharaoh. Seven days after the rivers had turned to blood, Yahweh brought forth the next plague. I was surprised that the guards even allowed Aaron and me to enter the courtyard that morning. Apparently, Pharaoh was in a better mood since the blood had finally cleared from the rivers and streams.

Pharaoh turned toward us as we entered the palace. "What do you want now!" he bellowed.

Aaron stepped forward. "Are you ready now to let our people go and worship our God?"

Pharaoh laughed. "Be on your way, you troublemakers! Nothing has changed!"

I knew what Yahweh had planned. "This will not end well for you, O King. Today Egypt will be overrun with frogs!"

"Frogs? You expect to change my mind with frogs?"

"The frogs will invade every home in Egypt, O King. You will find them in your kitchens, in your food containers and ovens, in your beds, crawling over your children as they sleep. From the humblest of homes to the palace, frogs will cover your floors until you cannot move without stepping on them."

As we were driven from the palace grounds, we saw what looked like a carpet of green coming up from the river and spreading until the entire landscape was covered with a twitching, gyrating field of green.

"What is it?" Aaron gasped.

Then as the green flow passed close to our home and veered away, we could see that it was made up of thousands of frogs. I had never seen so many frogs before. We began to hear shouts and screams as the frogs entered the homes of the Egyptians. But not one frog entered the homes of the Hebrews.

Toward sunset, Aaron and I were sitting in our home when we heard frantic banging on our door. Pharaoh's guards stood outside, their eyes wild with fear. One guard was pulling frogs out of his hair, the other knocking them off his face. They watched in amazement as the frogs fell off them and scurried away from Aaron's door.

"You have no frogs in your house?"

"Not a one," Aaron answered.

They stood silent until I finally cleared my throat and asked, "What do you want?"

"Pharaoh sends this message: 'Pray to your God to remove these frogs from me and my people! Then I will release you to worship your God.'"

Aaron's face lit up and turned to me. I slowly shook my head, and his face fell.

We then followed the guards back to the palace, the frogs making way for Aaron and me so that we never stepped on even one frog along the way.

"Pharaoh!" I stepped forward. "We will remove the frogs from your land and your homes. In fact, Yahweh will give you the honor of naming the time you would like this to happen."

Pharaoh seemed to enjoy the fact that he would decide the time for the frogs to leave. The guards and court officials stood silently, slapping at the frogs as they crawled up their legs. The end of this plague could not come soon enough for them.

Pharaoh raised his staff. "Tomorrow!" he stated emphatically. "The frogs must go tomorrow morning!"

"As you wish, O King," I replied. "As you have decided, the frogs will leave you and your homes, your officials, and your people, and will only remain in the Nile. Then, when you see what Yahweh has done, you will know that Yahweh is God. There is no one like him."

Aaron and I left the palace grounds shaking our heads. We heard the murmuring of the guards and officials echoing our thoughts: "Tomorrow? Why would he want to spend another sleepless night with these disgusting frogs?"

Aaron and I went to our home

The following days brought more visits to Pharaoh, more plagues, and more hardening of Pharaoh's heart. But the Hebrews began to take note that all the plagues bypassed our homes. We never found a frog in our kitchens. Our children were not afflicted with lice or boils. Neither the locusts nor the hail even touched our meager gardens. As Pharaoh was brought to his breaking point, I could see hope arising in God's people. And my brother, Aaron clung to the memory of hearing God speak to him and tell him that he loved him. It was enough to carry him through the weeks of waiting to see God's deliverance of his people.

Finally, a plague of darkness so thick you could feel it, covered the land of Egypt. For three days the Egyptians stayed in their homes in utter darkness. Although there was light in the homes of the Hebrews, the light abruptly disappeared within a few steps outside the Hebrew compound.

At the end of the three days of darkness, Yahweh restored light to Egypt and this time, instead of our approaching Pharaoh, he summoned Aaron and me. After refusing once more to let our people go and worship Yahweh in the wilderness, with our families and our livestock, Pharaoh rose from his throne in anger.

"Get out of my sight, Moses! I never want to see your face again, but if I do, that will be the day you die!"

"Just as you say, Pharaoh," I replied. "I will never appear before you again."

Pharaoh was silent, considering my words as Aaron and I left the court. He didn't realize that he had not only ordered two men out of his life, but that we took with us the presence of God that we carried as God's prophets. Pharaoh may not have understood the cold void left behind when we exited his palace, but his silence as we made our way out of the palace grounds assured me that he felt it.

THE FINAL PLAGUE

The Lord woke me early in the morning as the sun rose, beaming warm light through my window. I felt him calling me to get up and go outside to meet him. I quietly dressed and slipped out of the door, trying not to wake anyone else in the house. I hurried to the edge of the field where I could see the mountains in the distance, and stood silently, waiting for Yahweh to speak.

In the silence I sensed a heaviness surrounding me. I could feel the gravity of what Yahweh was about to share with me before he spoke a word.

"Moses!"

"Yes, Lord, I am listening."

"I will bring one final plague on Pharaoh and the land of Egypt. Then Pharaoh will allow you to leave Egypt. And not only will he allow you to leave, but he will drive you out completely. In preparation, you are to instruct the Hebrew people to ask their Egyptian neighbors for articles of silver and gold, and they will comply. Today I am pouring favor over the Hebrew people that will be evident to the Egyptians so that they will freely give their goods to my people when they ask."

The severity of the final plague drove me to my knees as Yahweh spoke clearly to me about what would happen this very night. The firstborn sons of every family would die tonight. I thought of my own firstborn son, Gershom. The evening he was born, my wife, Zipporah and I sat weeping with joy as we watched him sleep. How I loved playing with him, teaching him about Yahweh, showing him how to be a good shepherd to his grandpa, Jethro's flock. The thought of losing him was like a knife wound to my heart, and yet I was now to be part of Yahweh's plan to kill all the firstborn sons of Egypt.

"Oh, Yahweh!" I wept in his presence and then sensed, even felt, the familiar shaking that I knew was Yahweh's weeping.

"Who is this God that weeps over the children of his enemies?" I thought.

"Moses!"

His voice startled me out of my crying, and I raised my wet face toward heaven.

"Moses, do you think you are more compassionate than I am?"

I stood silently before him.

"Moses, who do you think invented compassion? I first was compassionate to your father, Adam, in the marvelous garden called Eden. There I created a life partner for him, your mother, Eve. Then, even though Adam and Eve chose to disobey me in that very garden I had created for them to enjoy, I provided coverings for them, animal skins, and allowed them to go on living, now outside of that garden paradise.

"Moses, you have asked me to show you my face. This is my face, Moses. This is who I am. I take no pleasure at all in the death of the wicked. No, I would much rather that the wicked ones would turn from their sinful ways and live, not die in their sin.

"You yourself have seen my patience, how I sent you time and time again to Pharaoh to try to gain permission for your escape from Egypt. He was not willing, but this final plague, in which Pharaoh himself will experience the loss of his firstborn son, will change his mind and he will drive you out of his land."

I felt as if Yahweh was baring his heart to me, as if he needed me to understand what he was about to do. "Abba, I hear your heart. I know you are a compassionate God who delights to forgive, and that your heart is not to destroy people, even hard-hearted Pharaoh who has treated your people so harshly these many years.

"I know you, my Lord. I have known you since you rescued me from the waters of the Nile in my little basket boat. I trust you, Yahweh. I know that you are good and just. You don't have to explain anything to me. You are God! I am not!"

My eyes were drawn to the sunlight that suddenly came streaming over the hilltop, and I heard Yahweh's voice on the breeze.

"Moses, you are one who I can share my heart with, more than a prophet, more than a teacher. You are my friend."

What is this? Yahweh, Creator of heaven and earth calls me friend?

I bowed my head and worshiped my friend, my God, basking in the warmth of his love and humbled that my God chose to trust me with his heart. Even as I worshiped, I heard God softly speaking to my heart.

"It's not just for you, Moses."

I nodded as I grasped what he was saying. I realized that my calling as a prophet meant more than just speaking the words of God. I was also to represent the heart of God, to call more sons and daughters into the friendship Yahweh had given to me. The sun was fully up when I arose from that place of intimacy to prepare God's people for this final plague.

THE PASSOVER

Aaron had gathered the Hebrew people together so that we could give them Yahweh's instructions regarding the final plague. As I approached the crowd I felt their excitement. For once they were not dreading what we had to say. I heard several conversations as I made my way to the front to address the people.

I heard one man laughing. "I can't believe that they gave me their gold and silver utensils! I wish I had asked for more. It seems like if I'd asked for the moon they would have given it to me, gift wrapped!"

"Yes, I know what you mean. My wife asked her Egyptian mistress for gold and silver cloth and her mistress gave her several yards of each fabric, no questions asked."

"Moses was right this time! The favor of Yahweh was surely on us. Even the slave drivers agreed to lend us their gold and silver!"

I reached the front of the crowd, and Aaron called the people to attention.

"My friends, listen very carefully to the words of your God, Yahweh, Jehovah Jireh. Today marks a new beginning for the people of God. This month will now be the first month of your calendar."

There was some murmuring in the crowd, but Aaron again brought them to order.

I continued. "On the tenth day of this month, from now through eternity, you are to choose a lamb for a sacrifice to Yahweh. It must be pure and spotless, a one-year-old male goat or lamb. Each household should choose its own lamb, for your family. Care for the lamb from the tenth to the fourteenth day of the month. On the fourteenth day you are all to slay your lamb at twilight. Then you are to dip some hyssop in the blood and paint it on the door frames of your houses, on the top frame and side frames of the door. Roast the meat of your sacrifice and have a meal with your family, the roasted lamb, along with bitter herbs, and unleavened bread. If any meat is left over, you must burn it in the fire—keep nothing until morning. And this is how you are to eat this meal: fully dressed, sandals on your feet, walking staff in your hand, ready to flee. This meal is the Lord's Passover meal and is to be a festival you will celebrate every year to remember what Yahweh is now about to do for you this very day.

"Tonight," I continued, "Yahweh will pass through Egypt and strike down every firstborn of men and animals throughout the land."

I heard a collective gasp rise up from the crowd.

"Thus says the Lord! I will bring judgment on the false gods of Egypt. I am the Lord. But fear not, I will pass through the land to destroy the firstborn, but when I will see the blood on your doorposts, I will pass over your homes. No one will die in your households so long as the blood is there as a sign that you belong to me."

Even as I spoke Yahweh's message, I found myself pausing as I spoke the words "when I see the blood." Yahweh was highlighting those words and the words themselves were heavy on my tongue and I found myself repeating them to the Hebrews standing before me. "When I see the blood ..."

The people were silent as I finished delivering Yahweh's instructions. His final words delivered much needed hope to a broken people.

"Obey these instructions as a lasting ordinance for you and your descendants. When you enter the land that the Lord will give you as he promised, observe this ceremony."

I saw the light dawn on their faces as they listened. They heard Yahweh's promise—"*when* you enter." He did not say "*if* you enter," but when, and I could see their eyes widen as they received the promise.

"And when your children ask you, 'What does this ceremony mean to you?' then tell them: 'It is the Lord's Passover sacrifice, to remind us that Yahweh passed over the houses of the Hebrew people when he sent his death angel to kill all the firstborn of Egypt. When he saw the blood, he spared us, his people, and we are alive today to remember and celebrate this Passover meal together!'"

Then a shout rose up from the Hebrews, led by my brother Aaron, and I watched as the people worshiped Yahweh, some on their knees, others jumping up and down with their children, some flat on their faces on the warm sand.

I lifted my head and laughed aloud. "Aaron, they believe us! They believe the words of Yahweh!"

We embraced, laughing, crying, dancing before the Lord. Then Aaron dismissed the crowd to obey Yahweh's instructions. Not long afterwards I heard the bleating of the lambs. Then the scratching of the hyssop branches as the blood was painted on every Hebrew home. I could hear songs of worship coming from many homes, well into the night.

It was still night when I began to hear the sounds of wailing from the Egyptian homes nearby. It wasn't long before people began to stream out of their homes carrying their dead children. The midwives were called to deliver dead firstborn children as the young mothers cried out in anguish. The stench of death rose from the livestock areas. There was not one household in all of Egypt without someone dead.

Then Pharaoh's guards came banging on my door and summoned Aaron and me to the palace.

Pharaoh was standing at the entrance of the courtyard as we arrived.

"Get out!" he screamed. "All of you, get up and leave Egypt. Now! Do not wait until morning. I want you gone now. Take everyone, everything you own and go worship the Lord. Get out now!"

As we turned to leave, we heard Pharaoh's parting words, "And bless me!"

"How can I bless what God has cursed?" I thought as Aaron and I ran away.

We found the people ready when we arrived. They were gathered at the edge of the fenced clearing surrounding the Hebrew homes, cloaks tucked in their belts, children dressed and awake, the gold and silver of the Egyptians in sacks and pockets. Even the livestock were on their feet as if impatient to be on their way. Aaron, always the administrator, walked through the crowd encouraging and delivering last-minute instructions. Without a word I walked to the fence, opened the double gates, and began to walk at a swift pace toward the desert, and away from Egypt. God's people followed and our exodus began in earnest.

THE EXODUS AND JOSEPH'S BONES

Aaron and I watched as our people hurried away from captivity. The women had grabbed whatever food they had on hand so their families would have nourishment along the way. They carried bread dough wrapped in cloth, without yeast, as they had not had time to add it before I called them to leave the compound. Many Egyptian families had gathered outside to watch our departure. They urged us to leave quickly, and even pressed into our hands articles of clothing, silver, and gold as we passed by them.

I heard several Egyptians, their faces in mourning over their firstborn children, urging the Hebrew people to leave quickly. "For otherwise," said one elderly man, "we will all die!"

"Moses." Aaron came alongside me. "I have tried to map out a route for the journey. The shortest route is through Philistine territory."

"Yahweh specifically told me not to go that way, Aaron. Although that route is shorter, Yahweh said we are to follow the desert road towards the Red Sea. He said, 'If they face war in the lands of the Philistines along the way, they might get discouraged and turn around to return to Egypt.'"

Just then my servant Garsher came running past the travelers shouting for my attention. "Moses, Moses! Where do you want the bones?"

Aaron whirled around. "The bones?" he asked. "What bones, Moses?"

I embraced Garsher and smiled. "Thank you, my friend. Keep Joseph at the head of the procession."

Garsher nodded and urging his donkey onward, he moved past the travelers. The donkey pulled an old ox cart carrying a large wooden box.

As the cart went by, there was a hush over the crowd, for they all knew the story of their ancestor, Joseph. Joseph, who had been sold as a slave to Pharaoh. Joseph who never betrayed his God. Joseph who became second in command in the land of his slavery, and who saved the world from starvation in time of worldwide famine. This same Joseph who knew that although he and his family would die in Egypt, that one day Yahweh would deliver his people back to their own land. As he was dying, Joseph made his brothers promise that they would not bury his body in the land of captivity.

"One day" he had told them. "Yahweh will deliver his people from Egypt, and you must promise to carry my bones up with you and bury me in the land of my people, where I buried our father."

It was if the atmosphere became supercharged as the bones of Joseph passed by. Parents began retelling the story of Joseph to their children. Laughter and exclamations of joy erupted as the children of Israel realized that this exodus they were on was that very thing Joseph was talking about as he was dying. I saw the faces of the little ones light up as they watched the coffin roll by.

"This is Joseph? This is what he talked about? This is what God promised?" Whoops of laughter rose up, shouts of praise, and tears of worship.

I wept, laughed, and worshiped with my people as I walked along. "Blessed are you, Lord God, King of the Universe!" I shouted in unison with the crowd. "Blessed are you, Lord our God, King of the Universe, who brings forth bread from the earth and has kept us alive and preserved us all to reach this season!"

CLOUD AND FIRE

I remember as a boy, watching the clouds drift across the sky, looking for the shapes of familiar objects, sheep and angel wings in the various cloud formations. Miriam always saw butterflies, while I was excited to see long straight swords stretching diagonally from heaven to earth. "Look, Miriam! The angels are doing battle in the heavens!"

This morning as I opened my eyes at first light, I saw a pillar of cloud coming up over the horizon. It was huge! It seemed to me that God had grabbed a cloud and stretched it, then twisted it into this massive column that seemed to rise right out of the earth and stretch into the heavens. Even as a gentle breeze blew across the desert, the cloud remained upright, perpendicular to the ground, moving slowly away from our camp.

Then I heard Yahweh speak into my spirit. "Moses!"

"Yes, Lord, I am listening."

"Do you remember Polaris?"

"Yes, of course! It's been a symbol of your guidance, suddenly appearing in the night sky just when I needed it. I smile and worship whenever I see it. It's like a sparkling reminder of your faithfulness!"

"Moses, I am not sending you on this journey alone. I am going with you, ahead of you and behind you. I am both your scout, going ahead into the future to prepare the way, and your protector, your rear guard, healing and protecting you from the trauma of your past."[16]

At this I fell to the ground in worship. "Oh, Yahweh, you are so good, so good! There's no place I can hide from your presence. You surround me, and your people."

"Today I am giving these visible signs of my promise to you, Moses. This pillar of cloud will lead you by day, and a pillar of

---

[16] Psalm 139:6

fire will light the path at night. Teach my people to recognize the signs. I am with you."

As I lay on the ground, I heard the word "Emmanuel" whispered into my spirit. God with us. I thought of the gods of Egypt and the other nations around us. No other god was like Yahweh, who speaks to his people, and surrounds them like a hem encompasses the raw edges of a garment. Then he gives us visible signs of his goodness, just in case we get sidetracked and forget who he is. A pillar of cloud and a tower of fire, Emmanuel.

After a while I began to hear the bleating of the sheep and goats, and the crying babies as they awoke with empty bellies. I stood up and saw the people coming toward me as if I was their source. I smiled and looked toward the steadfast pillar of cloud that had now begun to drift toward the sea. I did not have what the people or the animals needed, but I knew the One who did.

"The eyes of all living things look to you, Yahweh," I prayed aloud. "You open your hand and satisfy the desires of every living thing."[17]

I wept in joy as I heard the voices of my people, from young to old, men and women, little ones still learning to talk, echoing my worship. "You open your hand and satisfy the desires of every living thing!"

"Now gather near, Israel, and learn about Emmanuel."

---

[17] Psalm 45:16

THE RED SEA

We moved slowly across the desert as Yahweh directed. When the pillar of cloud or the tower of fire headed east, we turned east. If it stopped moving, we set up camp for the night. This became our routine over the next few days.

As I sat near the fire one evening, I heard God's voice calling me to walk with him. So I took my staff and wandered a stone's throw from the camp to be alone with Yahweh.

"Do you trust me, Moses?"

"Trust you? Well, of course I trust you, my Lord." Yet even as I spoke I began to tremble inside. Why would he ask me such a question? What is he planning for me that might cause me not to trust him?

"Moses!"

I returned my gaze heavenward and focused again on his voice. "Yes, Lord?"

"Pharaoh has sent his scouts to track your travels. He has once again hardened his heart and is regretting the loss of his slave laborers. He has been told that your company is traveling very slowly, due to the children and young animals and pregnant women, and he has determined that you are just wandering around in circles, lost in the desert."

"But we are not lost, Abba. We are following your lead, so how could we be lost?"

"Moses, I don't want you to be afraid. That is why I am telling you ahead of time what is to come. Even now Pharaoh's army is heading here to recapture my people and bring them back to Egypt."

"But Abba!"

"Moses, do you trust me?"

"Yes. I am afraid. You know it, Lord! I cannot hide my heart from you. But I have seen your burning bush, your pillar of cloud and your tower of fire with my own eyes. Therefore, I choose to trust you!"

"So now gather the people and flee from Pharaoh toward the sea."

I turned and headed back to camp, shouting as I came near the people. "It's time to move. Everyone pack up. Let's go."

But in my mind, I was still questioning Yahweh. "The sea? Abba, if they corner us by the sea, how will we escape?"

PHARAOH'S RETURN

I awoke early the next morning and quickly gazed out of my tent toward the mountains. I stepped outside and turned around, scanning the horizon for the pillar of cloud. Finally, as I turned my face away from the mountains and toward the Red Sea, I saw the pillar rising out of the sand. Looking up, I sought Yahweh's face but heard no new direction.

I called out to the elders of Israel. "Blow the trumpets! It's time to move on."

I watched then as the people heeded my words and began to pack up the encampment, ready to move forward toward the pillar of cloud glowing in the bright morning sun.

A commotion behind me called my attention away from the pillar. Three men on watch duty in the early morning shouted and came running toward me, waving their hands wildly and pointing to what appeared to be a sandstorm on the next bluff.

"The Egyptians!" they shouted as one. "They're coming for us!"

I looked again toward the bluff and realized that Pharaoh's troops and chariots were creating the clouds of sand billowing from the desert as they chased us toward the Red Sea.

I heard the shouts of the men, and the screams of the women and children as fear set in. The men cried out in anger against me. "Moses! Was it because there were no graves in Egypt that you brought us here in the desert to die? Didn't we tell you to leave us alone? If only we hadn't listened to you! It would be better to remain live slaves than to watch our wives and children be slaughtered in the desert. And now we are stuck between the sea and this army intent on our slaughter, with no way to escape."

"No, my friends, this is not the end!" I shouted holding my staff high above my head. "I promise you. Yahweh has not forsaken you."

The people turned eagerly toward me, their mouths hanging open, longing for some evidence that there was still hope.

"Do not be afraid," I shouted.

Several of the men approached me, their faces tight with anxiety. "How can we not be afraid, Moses? What can we do to save ourselves and our families?"

"Do not be afraid," I repeated sternly. "Here is what Yahweh commands: 'Be still. Stand firm and you will see the deliverance the Lord will bring you today.'"

One large man challenged me. "Be still? Not fight back?"

"We can't do nothing, Moses," another countered. "At least we can run, maybe some of us can escape before the Egyptians get to us!"

"No!" I shouted. "You must stand firm. Here is what Yahweh says to you, 'The Egyptians you see today you will never see again. I will fight for you, my people.' The Lord will fight for you. You only need to be still and know that he is God."

I watched as the people quieted, whispered to each other and looked to me for instruction. In my heart I was crying out to Yahweh with every breath I took.

"They still trust me, Yahweh. Tell me what to do."

"Moses!"

Yahweh's urgent voice shook me to the core.

"Moses, why are you crying out to me? Do what I am telling you to do. Tell the Israelites to move on, follow the pillar of cloud."

"But Yahweh, it's leading right into the sea."

Yahweh ignored my remarks and continued. "Raise your staff and stretch out your hand over the sea to divide the water. By your hand you will create a path right through the middle of the sea so that my people can pass through on dry ground. I'm telling you ahead of time that I will continue to harden the hearts of Pharaoh and the Egyptians so that they will follow you right into the sea. Don't be afraid, Moses, because today I will be glorified through Pharaoh and his army, his chariots, and his horseman. Then they will know that I Am the Lord."

Yahweh did not wait for me to act on his words. I heard a gasp from the people and turned to watch the pillar of cloud move steadily around us and come to rest between God's people and the Egyptians. Then I heard one final word from Yahweh, whispered, yet it reverberated throughout my body.

"Goshen."

I stood still and silent for a moment as Yahweh reminded me how with that one word he had separated his people and the Egyptians. There were no flies in our houses, no frogs, no blood saturated water. Our children were passed over by the Angel of Death that slaughtered the firstborn of Egypt. And now yet again, Yahweh had separated his people from the destroyer, by the pillar of his presence.

The pillar remained in its post throughout that night as God's people prepared to flee. On our side of the cloud it was as light as day, while the Egyptians were in utter darkness, unable to even see us through the cover of cloud.

Then, as Yahweh directed, I stretched out my hand and staff over the sea. I heard the rush of a mighty wind as the very breath of Yahweh blew across the sea with a strong east wind and parted the sea. The water rose on either side of a path that was now visible through the water. I could see it churning as it stood up, fish bumping into some unseen barrier that kept them on one or the other side of the path rising from the seabed. All through the night, the wind blew until the path in the midst of the sea was dry.

Then I beckoned the people, and they followed me into the sea, eyes wide as they passed between the walls of water on their right and left. I saw the children reaching out to touch the walls as drops of water rolled from their fingers down their little arms. Their parents grabbed back their hands in terror and hurried on to the other side of the sea. In the last watch of the night when the people of Israel were nearly through the sea to the other side, the Lord lifted the pillar blocking the Egyptians' view. We heard shouts behind us as the Egyptians, at Pharaoh's command entered the dry riverbed in hot pursuit of their runaway slaves.

Anticipating their terror, I continued to repeat the Lord's instructions to our people. "Keep on going. Don't be afraid," I cheered them on. "Be still. Stand firm and you will see Yahweh's hand of deliverance."

As if on cue, Yahweh looked down at the Egyptians from the pillars of cloud and fire and threw them into confusion. We saw wheels come spinning off the chariots. Soldiers leapt from the chariots which were useless without wheels. I heard the commander of the troops shout out, "Run for your lives! Get away from the Israelites. Their God is fighting for them against us."

My heart swelled in worship as I saw the word of the Lord coming to pass in front of my eyes. I prayed that my people saw it, too.

"Moses, now stretch out your hand over the sea and call the waters to flow back and cover your enemies, the Egyptians."

The sun was just rising as I once again stretched out my hand and immediately the walls of water collapsed and rushed over the formerly dry path, drowning the Egyptians, their commanders, and their horsemen. The entire army of Pharaoh that had followed the Israelites into the sea all perished. Not one survived. Just as Yahweh promised God's people would never see them alive again.

I stood with my people on the far side of the sea, watching as the bodies of the Egyptians floated toward the other shore. My eyes filled with tears, and I fell to the sand crying out to Yahweh, "You did it! You saved your people. Thank you, Yahweh. Praise be to Yahweh." Then I heard the voices of the people as they fell in the sand all around me, weeping and laughing as we gave thanks to our God.

"Moses, come on!" I heard my big sister, Miriam, calling out to me. She danced around me as I lay on the sand, then pulled me to my feet, laughing. "Come dance with me, little brother!"

I, in turn, pulled the men around me to their feet and we followed Miriam as she danced and sang before the Lord.

I will sing to the LORD for he is highly exalted,
Both horse and driver he has hurled into the sea.

The LORD is my strength and my defense;
He has become my salvation.
He is my God, and I will praise him,
my father's God, and I will exalt him.
The LORD is a warrior;
The LORD is his name.
Pharaoh's chariots and his army
he has hurled into the sea.
The best of Pharaoh's officers
are drowned in the Red Sea.
The deep waters have covered them;
they sank to the depths like a stone.
Your right hand, LORD,
was majestic in power.
Your right hand, LORD,
shattered the enemy.

In the greatness of your majesty
you threw down those who opposed you.
You unleashed your burning anger;
it consumed them like stubble.
By the blast of your nostrils
the waters piled up.
The surging waters stood up like a wall;
the deep waters congealed in the heart of the sea.
The enemy boasted,
'I will pursue, I will overtake them.
I will divide the spoils;
I will gorge myself on them.
I will draw my sword
and my hand will destroy them.'
But you blew with your breath,
and the sea covered them.
They sank like lead
in the mighty waters.
Who among the gods is like you, LORD?
Who is like you—

majestic in holiness, awesome in glory,
working wonders?

You stretch out your right hand,
and the earth swallows your enemies.
In your unfailing love you will lead
the people you have redeemed.
In your strength you will guide them
to your holy dwelling.
The nations will hear and tremble;
anguish will grip the people of Philistia.
The chiefs of Edom will be terrified,
the leaders of Moab will be seized with trembling,
the people of Canaan will melt away;
terror and dread will fall on them.
By the power of your arm
they will be as still as a stone—
until your people pass by, LORD,
until the people you bought pass by.
You will bring them in and plant them
on the mountain of your inheritance—
the place, LORD, you made for your dwelling,
the sanctuary, Lord, your hands established.

The LORD reigns for ever and ever.[18]

Here I paused in my secret writing spot where I sat in God's overwhelming presence, writing my story.

My pen fell to the ground and I found myself weeping as I recalled the goodness of Yahweh that day by the Red Sea. Then I heard him calling me, as he had called out my name so many times on my journey to my true promised land, my home in heaven.

"Moses!"

"Yes, my Lord?"

"Moses, do you hear?"

"Hear what?" I responded.

"Listen."

---

[18] Exodus 15:1–18

"Is that my sister? I hear my sister, Miriam, singing."

"Yes, come."

And he slipped his arm in mine and together we ran to the Throne Room where my dear sister, Miriam, tambourine in hand was dancing and singing before the King of kings and Lord of lords.

When she saw me, Miriam reached out her hand to me. "Moses, come dance with me and remember the goodness of God!"

I looked to Jesus, and he nodded, and together we skipped into the middle of the dance.

"I will sing unto the Lord for he has triumphed gloriously, the horse and the rider thrown into the sea."

"Yeehah!" Jesus shouted.

Never a dull day here in glory.

Later I returned to my home, so full I could only shake my head in wonder. "Can it get any better than this?" I lay down to sleep and my mind returned to the story I was writing. "Oh, no," I thought. "Tomorrow, after all the glory of the Red Sea miracle, I must write about how my people doubted you once again at the waters of Marah."

Even as I lay in that state between sleep and dreaming, I heard Yahweh's whisper. "But you know the big picture now. You know the end of the story, sitting here in the Promised Land of my glory. You get to look back and remember how I brought you here, every precious memory of my fingerprints on your life. Dream now, my dear friend, and tomorrow continue to write your story."

BITTER WATERS

The next morning, I awoke with joy, remembering how we had sung and danced before Yahweh with all our hearts.

I spied the pillar of cloud beckoning the camp to move out, so I called the people to follow me away from the sea.

"Moses."

I heard his voice in my spirit and responded without uttering a word as I walked through the desert sand. "I am listening."

"Trust me."

I wondered what could happen that day that would challenge my trust, especially after what I had just witnessed the day before. Nevertheless, my heart responded. "I trust you, Abba."

The pillar soon led us into the Desert of Shur. Gone were the few bushes and trees we had seen near the water. This country was barren, dead. Not even a stray acacia tree, only sand as far as the eye could see.

By the third day in Shur, we were desperate for water. Finally, we saw the glisten of water in the distance. Some of the men ran ahead. As I reached the spring, the men were spitting and grumbling.

"The water is bitter!"

"Undrinkable! Now what are we going to do, Moses?"

Even Miriam came and whispered to me. "Moses you've got to get us some water, or we'll all die in the desert."

I felt exhausted from the desert heat and lack of water. Why would the people think I could do anything to find drinkable water in the desert? Was this why Yahweh had reminded me to trust him only three long days ago?

I turned away from the grumbling of my people and toward the manifestation of Yahweh's presence, the ever-present pillar of cloud. In my heart I cried out to the Lord. "I trust you, Yahweh. Show me what to do."

As I stood head bowed before Yahweh's presence, I unconsciously turned my head to the right. I opened my eyes and saw a log lying in the sand. I shook my head in wonder. Not a tree for miles, but here was a log. "Yahweh?"

"Moses, take the log and throw it into the water."

I strode purposely to the log, picked it up, brushing off the sand, and threw it into the spring, then stood by watching the water.

I heard the whispers behind me. "What is he doing now?"

When the log hit the water, it splattered water on one of the young boys standing nearby. He began to lick his lips, and his eyes grew bright as his parched mouth tasted the first water he'd had in days. Then he jumped into the spring and began gulping down large mouthfuls of water.

"No, don't drink that bitter water!" the boy's mother screamed. "You'll die!"

"But Ima, it's delicious." The young boy smiled.

I approached the boy, crouched down beside him and scooped up a handful of the water. I brought it first to my nose and smelled nothing foul, then drank from my cupped hand. "It's sweet now," I told the people. "Come and drink. Yahweh has healed the water."

The people came quietly to the bitter water made sweet, and one by one drank their fill and watered the flocks. The water continued to bubble up and there was enough for everyone.

That evening as we camped around the spring, Yahweh directed me to speak to the people. "I know that those of you who complained today were humbled by Yahweh's provision. You are sorry that you doubted Yahweh would take care of you as he promised to do. Some of you are feeling ashamed and fearful of Yahweh's reaction to your mistrust."

No one said a word as my words hit their mark.

"But Yahweh loves you and has chosen you to be his people. Out of all the peoples of the earth, he has chosen you. Remember Joseph? Remember that he believed the promises of God, that he would one day lead us out of Egypt to a promised land, a land flowing with milk and honey, he called it. Joseph made the people promise that we would carry up his bones when God delivered us out of the hands of the Egyptians. His bones are with us, like a picture, a sign of God's goodness to fulfill his word to us."

The people looked up, some smiling, some with tears on their faces.

"I do not speak these words to shame you. This is not a day of mourning, but a day of promise and provision. The Lord has today made a decree and law for us. He says 'If you listen carefully to my voice and do what is right in my eyes, if you pay attention to my commands and keep all my decrees, I will not bring on you any of the diseases and plagues that I brought on the Egyptians. I am Yahweh Rapha, the Lord who heals.'"

That night as I lay down to sleep on the still warm sand near Marah, I found myself recounting how Yahweh had revealed himself to me over the years. Yahweh constantly showed me more of who he is with every encounter. I had met Yahweh Jireh, the God who provides through the stories my parents recited of my miraculous survival as a baby boy sentenced to death. I'd cowered before a burning bush where I first heard his voice, fearful that I would die because I'd seen his form in the flames. He told me another time that he desired my friendship. My friendship! How amazing. And today I met him as Yahweh Rapha, the God who heals.

"I'm so full, Yahweh! But I'm so hungry. I want to know you. I want to see you. Show me your face, Yahweh. Keep on teaching me who you are. I can't even wrap my mind around how good you are. I love you, Yahweh! With all my heart I love you." And held in his embrace, I drifted off to sleep and dream about my next encounter with a God who called me his friend.

THE DESERT OF SIN

It was the fifteenth day of our second month after leaving Egypt. We were camping in what is known as the Wilderness of Sin. Since we left Marah, we had found oases of water along the route, but little to eat. As I awoke that morning, I could already hear my stomach rumbling in protest, and the people grumbling outside my tent.

"If only we had died by the Lord's hand in Egypt!" one man moaned.

"Yes, in Egypt we worked hard, but we sat around pots of meat and ate all the food we wanted."

I stepped out of my tent, thinking my presence might stop the complaining, but one young father stepped right up to me and shook his fist. "You have brought us into this desert to starve our community to death, Moses!"

I answered not a word to the angry man but turned my eyes toward the pillar of cloud. "Yahweh?" my heart whispered.

I stood silently hearing the words of Yahweh in my spirit for what seemed like a few minutes to me but was closer to an hour's time. I saw and felt the anger of the men standing around me. Then I saw their eyes open wide at the same time that I was experiencing a growing warmth in my face. My furrowed brow relaxed, and I nodded in acceptance of what I was hearing. Their faces changed, too, as their grumbling stopped and they waited to hear Yahweh's words.

"Come near," I beckoned the crowd, "and hear the Word of the Lord."

The people approached me then, but stood back a little, seemingly intimidated by what must have looked like instant sunburn covering my face. I reached up and touched my cheek above my beard and smiled as I felt the warmth on my skin. How could a man draw close to Yahweh and not be impacted. It was like the day I discovered the burning bush. Today there had been no fire, yet my face still reacted to the invisible fire of God's presence.

"Tonight, you will know beyond any doubt that it was Yahweh himself who brought you out of Egypt. And tomorrow morning you will see the glory of the Lord."

I heard gasps and whispers from the crowd.

"Will our faces be burned by his presence, like Moses'?"

"Can we see his glory and live?"

"Let Moses see his glory. That encounter is not for me!"

I cleared my throat to stop the murmurs. "Don't be afraid. Has not Yahweh always provided for you? And who are we, that you should grumble to Aaron and me. We're just men. Aaron, tell them."

Aaron stepped forward, and the people drew closer. "Now listen, Yahweh has heard your grumbling. And he said that tonight, at twilight you will eat meat, and in the morning you will be filled with bread. Then you will know that Yahweh is your God."

While Aaron was still speaking, several men from the crowd began directing the others to look toward the desert. There in the pillar of cloud, they saw brilliant flashes of lightning. Thunder followed, with a loud crack that billowed across the desert until they could hear it no longer. Then the wind began. We heard a shrill whistling as it started and soon had to cover our faces from the sand being funneled into the air by the strong gusts of wind. Peeking out of my cloak I saw a flock of birds approaching the camp. Pummeled by the fierce winds, the birds dropped low, flying just a few feet from the ground.

"Quail!" the men shouted. A little boy reached out his hands and captured the quail that was flying right in front of him. He handed the struggling bird to his mother, who then hurried off to her cooking pot to prepare a meal for her family. All over the camp the quail simply flew right into peoples' outstretched hands. After days of fasting, not one person went to sleep hungry that wonderful night. And we remembered Yahweh's words and knew that tomorrow there would be bread!

MANNA

I awoke the next morning expecting to smell the fragrance of baking bread. I lifted my head and sniffed, but there was nothing. I stepped outside my tent and saw dozens of people standing in their tent entrances waiting, like me, for the promised bread. My stomach rumbled in anticipation.

The desert floor was still damp with dew. I could see steam arising as the water evaporated into the dry desert air. I turned as I heard some children calling out to their parents, "What is it?"

The children had discovered thin flakes, like frost, covering the desert floor after the dew evaporated. I quickly stepped away from my tent and gathered up a handful of the flaky substance. It was white, like coriander seed. I examined the flakes, easily crushing them between my fingers into a fine powder, like flour, I thought. Flour? My spirit prayed, "Is this the bread you promised, Yahweh?"

"Don't eat it!" I heard one mother scolding her boys.

"But it's good, Ima," the little one protested. "It tastes like honey."

I placed a few flakes on my tongue and smiled as the honey flavor exploded in my mouth. "It's safe!" I called out to the parents. As Yahweh whispered his words into my spirit, I gave the people his instructions.

"You have asked, 'What is it?' Yahweh says it is the bread he promised you. Each morning after the dew melts away you will find these flakes on the desert floor. Now quickly, take the children and go gather the flakes. Take as much as you need, at least two quarts for each person in your family. You can eat the flakes or grind them into flour to make cakes of bread or mix with water to make a porridge. I'm sure you'll come up with your own recipes."

Families quickly grabbed whatever containers they could find in their tents and headed out to gather the heavenly flakes.

I gathered enough for my own family and then watched as the others scooped up handfuls of the flakes. The children gave the flakes a silly name, calling it "manna," which means "what is it," and filled their jars and cups with "what is it" until the sun melted the remaining flakes away.

When the families measured out what they'd gathered, they found that those who scooped up great quantities of the manna had exactly two quarts for each person in their tent. One elderly couple couldn't gather as much, but when they measured their manna, it, too, was exactly four quarts, two for each of them, as Yahweh had directed.

"How can that be?" one man complained. "I know I gathered way more than this elderly couple."

I spoke over the murmuring of the people as they measured out their manna. "Here is what Yahweh commands. Take only what you can eat today. Don't try to keep any manna overnight. You don't need to save any because Yahweh promises a new batch every morning."

I smelled manna bread baking over coals as the day went on. There was enough manna for breakfast, lunch, and an evening meal. At each mealtime I led the people to bless Yahweh for his provision.

"Blessed are you, Lord our God, King of the Universe, who brings forth bread from the earth and has kept us alive and preserved us all to reach this season!"

Early the next morning screaming from a nearby tent startled me awake.

"Ew! Maggots!" I heard a woman calling out.

I quickly ran toward the screaming voice. "What's wrong?" I asked.

The woman was standing over a pot of yesterday's manna with a spoon in her hand. Maggots were falling off the spoon onto the tent floor as she screamed out.

"Did you keep some of the manna overnight?" I asked her.

She fell to her knees. "Yes, Moses. I hid some away so we would have enough for breakfast this morning."

I shook my head. "Now toss it out, let the birds eat the spoiled manna and the maggots. Didn't I tell you not to keep any of it until morning?"

I turned to the people who had quickly gathered around the tent. "This is what Yahweh instructs. Do not keep any manna overnight. Now you see why. And if you look around you will see the dew melting away leaving a new supply of manna for today. Now wait with me until the dew is gone and then gather as much manna as you need for today. The manna is new every morning, just like Yahweh's faithfulness to his people. However, Yahweh wants you to know that tomorrow, the day before the Sabbath, you should gather twice as much manna as you need. That way you can honor Yahweh on the Sabbath, resting from all work, but still have bread for the day."

I heard bits and pieces of the conversations going on around me as we gathered our daily bread off the desert floor.

"Only enough for today, son."

"Don't worry, it's new every morning."

An ima and her daughter began to sing, "New every morning, new every morning," and the song soon echoed throughout the camp interspersed with laughter and praise to Yahweh for his goodness.

"Great is your faithfulness, Abba," I whispered. "Great is your faithfulness."

Two days later it seemed the people had forgotten Yahweh's instructions. I rose early and stepped into the warm sunshine of the Sabbath day, only to see several families, jugs in hand, venturing into the desert to gather their daily manna.

Instead of finding "what is it manna" they were saying "Where is it?"

"Back to your tents," I shouted. "How long will you refuse to obey the voice of the Lord? The Sabbath is Yahweh's gift to you. He promised you twice the amount of manna on the sixth day, so you can obey his voice and rest on the Sabbath."

Some of the people were hungry that day, but hopefully they would take Yahweh's words more seriously next week.

I knew Yahweh wanted to speak to me more on this subject, so I went early to my tent that evening and laid down on the tent floor to wait for his voice.

"Moses."

"Here I am, Lord."

"Do you know why the extra manna you gathered on the sixth didn't spoil?"

"No, Lord. Will you tell me?"

"It didn't spoil because I told you it would not."

I was silent before Yahweh, not understanding his explanation.

He continued. "Moses, you can totally rely on my words. My words are always true, always trustworthy, and very powerful. With my words alone I created all that you see around you. Although I don't have to explain my actions to anyone, I am giving to you a full account of creation, what I simply spoke into being in the beginning. Write it all down for future generations to know the supernatural power of my words. I speak things that are not as though they were, 'let there be light,' and daylight breaks into darkness.

"And now I give you my words to speak to the people. Do you think my words are without power when you speak them?"

I lifted my head in surprise. "Are you saying that when people speak your words the words carry the same supernatural power as when you speak?"

"One day that will be so, when I put my Spirit on all those who love me. But that's another topic for another day, my friend."

I sighed. How wonderful to hear him call me friend. I marveled anew each time he said it.

"As for you, Moses, keep speaking my words. Honor every word you hear from my mouth. Receive each command with reverence and expectancy, for I promise you this, every freshly spoken word of God contains within itself the ability to perform itself.[19]

---

[19] Bill Johnson, 2022. Quoting Jack Taylor.
https://www.facebook.com/watch/?v=317613270283792

"If I give you a command, contained within that command is the supernatural provision you need to obey my voice. So shall my word be that goes forth from my mouth. It shall not return to me empty, but will accomplish its purpose, just like the manna that lasted overnight on the sixth day. I invite you, Moses, my friend, to step into the superiority and absolute security of my voice and my words."[20]

I lingered for a time on my tent floor after Yahweh stopped speaking, trying to grasp the meaning of all he'd said to me. I felt privileged to hear his voice, but also fearful of the words I now held in my heart. It was as if the words were burning coals that somehow I was to steward. This assignment seemed impossible, unless what Yahweh had spoken was really true, that the words themselves were impregnated with the ability to complete my assignment.

---

[20] Isaiah 55:12

TESTING AND QUARRELING

Navigating the desert with thousands of men, women and children, plus our livestock was constantly challenging. The joy of receiving bread from heaven faded as we traveled day after day without finding a new water source. Finally, the pillar of cloud led us to make camp at Rephidim. Surely there would be provision there for our thirsty travelers.

As we pitched our tents, several men scouted out the area and returned shouting, "There is no water! We must move on from here."

But Yahweh had directed us to stop in this place, I thought. The murmuring of the people and the whining of the children grew in intensity as the day went on.

"Moses," one man challenged. "Why did you bring us up out of Egypt? So we could die of thirst in the desert?"

"Who am I? Why are you quarreling with me?" I countered. "Your quarrel is with Yahweh himself."

I turned my face to the pillar of cloud dancing in the breeze. "Lord, what am I to do with these people? They are almost ready to stone me!"

"Come here."

I hurried a short walk away from the murmuring crowd.

"Walk on ahead of the people, but don't go alone. Take with you some of the elders of Israel and bring along your staff-the staff you used to part the sea so you could cross over."

I quickly gathered several of the leaders of the people and headed away from camp. As I walked, I heard Yahweh's voice.

"Do you see the large rock to your right?"

I looked up and saw the rock.

"I am here at the rock of Horeb."

My eyes widened and I strained to see Yahweh's form near the rock. Was he going to appear again before me in a burning bush? Was the pillar of his presence going to hover over the rock? But I saw nothing.

"Moses, I am here. Although you cannot see me, I am here. Now take your staff and strike the rock and water will flow from it."

I turned and gazed at the group of men standing with me, making eye contact with each one. Then I approached the rock of Horeb, raised my staff and struck the rock with all my might. I stepped back so the men of Israel could see the rock. I heard their gasps as we watched a tiny crack open where the rock had been struck. Then water began to spurt out of the crack, spraying all of us. After the initial burst of water, it became a steady stream flowing from the rock.

"Go and get your water jugs and fill them up for your families and your livestock," I told the wet faced elders. I heard their shouts of praise as they raced back to their families with the good news.

Later that evening as we sat around our campfires, I told the people the names I had given to this place. "This site will be known as Massah and Meribah. Massah means testing, for you put God to the test when you doubted his promises to you here. Meribah means quarreling. It's what happens when we step away from God's promises. We end up fighting against one another."

The men hung their heads as they recalled the harsh words they had spoken to me and to each other.

I continued. "I heard your questions. You kept asking each other, 'Is the Lord among us or not?' Did you get your answer?"

Joshua, a leader among the people, stood to his feet. "Yes, Moses. We got our answer. We will follow you without quarreling now. Now we know the truth. What other people group has received water from the striking of a rock?"

Joshua then turned to face his fellow Hebrews. One by one the men followed Joshua, standing to their feet. Joshua stood before the group and spoke on behalf of them. "Yes, Moses, the Lord is truly among us. Now we believe."

I looked to Yahweh and sensed that he was standing nearby, listening to the men pledge to follow him. And though he gave me no words to respond to the men, I felt in my spirit that Yahweh knew, as did I, that this would not be the last time on our journey that we would not trust Yahweh.

I sent the men to their tents for the night, relieved that no one in the camp would go to sleep thirsty this night. I sat down again by the fire for a short time of quiet before I joined the others in our tent. The next minute my body was racked with weeping. I held my cloak over my face so as not to disturb the sleeping families. Finally, the tears stopped flowing and I turned my heart to Yahweh.

"What is this, Lord? Where did this weeping come from? I know it's not what I was feeling. I was just enjoying the quiet and sipping the cool and wonderful water you provided from a rock."

I heard his voice. "Moses, ask me what I am feeling."

"Lord, what are you feeling?" I asked.

"I am so filled with love for these people, my people. I know they will fail me again and again, but I love them so dearly that my heart is overflowing into my friend, Moses."

I began to weep again, softly this time. How is it that the Creator of the Universe would share his heart, his tears, with me?

I did not return to my tent that night. The next morning, the watchmen found me stretched out by the fire, with my arms wrapped around my chest as if I was embracing someone. They didn't know that I'd spent the night wrapped in the arms of Yahweh.

I'd learned a valuable lesson the night before, in my sleep. I'd learned that Yahweh's presence was all I needed to complete my assignment. I rose from my sandy bed feeling fully equipped to tackle the next trial, which was right around the corner.

THE AMALEKITES

The pillar of cloud was stationary for several days, allowing the people some precious rest time. The water continued to flow out of the rock I had struck, so we were quite content to stay where we were. I enjoyed listening to the fathers playing with their children and the mothers singing to their babies. Could this be the promised land, I wondered to myself.

Suddenly I heard shouting. Several of the men on watch duty came running toward me. "Moses, we're being attacked!"

Our little respite at Rephidim had come to an end. At once I heard Yahweh's instructions in my mind. Yahweh was sending us into battle against the Amalekites. My first thoughts were of despair. How would this group of former slaves, with no battle experience or training, weary from traveling through the desert, how would we be able to come against the battle-ready troops of Amalek?

"Moses." Yahweh interrupted my spiraling thoughts. "And how could you cross the Red Sea at flood stage? And how could striking a rock bring forth water? Remember, and call the people to remember. This is always how you are to lead my people: First encourage yourself as you recite the testimony of my goodness and provision. Then encourage the people."

The people were already beginning to scatter in fear, but I stepped forward and called them to come near.

"Here is our battle plan. Joshua, choose some of our men and go out to fight our attackers. As you go out to battle, Yahweh has instructed me to stand on top of the hill and hold the staff of God high up in my hands. If the battle seems more than you can handle, just look up here and see the staff that performed miracles against Pharaoh and delivered you out of Egypt. Yahweh will enable you to beat the Amalekites if you don't lose sight of God's staff."

My young leader, Joshua, did not waste a moment, not even to consider his inexperience as a soldier. Just as I was following Yahweh, Joshua was following me. He immediately rallied his men, and they hurried off to fight the enemy. I took my brother, Aaron, and our friend, Hur, and we quickly climbed to the top of the hill overlooking the battlefield. We watched as Joshua and his troops ran toward the enemy soldiers. I thrust my arms into the air, holding high the staff of God.

"Look, Moses!" Hur called out. "Our people are chasing the Amalekites. They're running away from our men."

Then the enemy troops turned back to face the Hebrew army, and we watched the hand-to-hand combat between the soldiers.

Aaron cringed as he watched one of the Hebrew men narrowly miss being impaled by an enemy spear. He turned to me. "Moses, your arm is slipping. You must keep that staff high so the people can see it."

Hur's eyes widened as he realized that the battle seemed to turn in favor of the Amalekites each time my weary arms dropped down. Grabbing Aaron by the arm, Hur dragged him next to me. Then together they rolled a large stone over and motioned for me to sit down. They took up positions on either side of the rock. Aaron lifted my right hand holding the spear, and Hur lifted my left hand. As soon as the spear was raised again, we heard Joshua's voice loud and clear above the fray.

"Attack! For the glory of Yahweh, God of Israel!"

The Hebrews rushed forward again, decimating their enemies.

The battle raged until sunset as the three of us on top of the hill kept our arms raised without faltering, and the soldiers in the field below fought on without growing weary.

Joshua surveyed the battlefield. Every enemy soldier had either died or fled. Then Joshua raised his sword and shouted a roar of victory, and the men responded with roars of their own.

Aaron, Hur, and I dropped our arms and hugged each other, laughing and praising Yahweh.

Then I heard what sounded like thunder behind me. I grabbed Aaron and Hur and turned toward the sound, but they looked at me with confusion in their eyes.

"What is it?" Hur asked. "Is the enemy returning?"

"Didn't you hear that?"

Both men shook their heads. But Aaron grabbed me by the arm. "It's Yahweh, isn't it? What is he saying, Moses?"

"He's ... he's shouting a victory cry in harmony with Joshua!"

Aaron and Hur laughed and began to roar again loudly. They seemed delighted that the God of the Universe would join them in the victory cry.

As we walked back down the hill to join Joshua and his troops, I heard Yahweh's instructions.

"Moses, write this on a scroll. I don't want you and our people to ever forget this day. And make sure that Joshua hears it. I make you this promise. I will completely blot out the memory of Amalek from under heaven."[21]

Then Joshua came running to me and threw his arms around me, spinning me around in a victory dance. After we had danced and laughed together, I took hold of Joshua's arms and looked into his face.

"Joshua, Yahweh spoke to me just now and he told me to make sure that I tell you what he said. He said to me, 'make sure that Joshua hears about it.'"

"He said my name?" Joshua's eyes glistened. "He knows my name?"

"Yes, my son. He told me to make sure you knew that it was Yahweh's power working through you today that won this victory. Yahweh chose you for this very mission, and he is so very pleased with you, Joshua. He also said to tell you that one day he will completely blot out the memory of Amalek from the earth. He will finish what he started today."

Joshua dropped to the ground in worship.

After a while, I took Joshua's hand and pulled him up. He followed me to the edge of the camp and watched as I built an

---

[21] Exodus 17:14

altar to the Lord in the presence of his people. As the fire burned on the altar, I took a scroll and wrote down the words Yahweh had given me earlier. Then I turned and addressed the people.

"Come, draw near and worship with me at the altar which I have named Yahweh Nissi."

I heard the murmurs of the people rippling across the gathering. Joshua spoke for the people. "Moses, we have never known the name, Yahweh Nissi. We know the name of Yahweh, and we know that nissi mean banner or flag, but what is the meaning of Yahweh Nissi?"

"Our God has revealed himself today as Yahweh Nissi, which means the Lord is our banner. The victory you had today in battle was because Yahweh was on your side. He was above you like a banner, showing the enemy that you belong to him, and that is why they lost, and you won. The evidence of Yahweh's presence is visible in the pillar of cloud and the pillar of fire that we see every day. Our enemies see it, too, and are terrified. No other people group travels with their God flying over them like a flag."

Then I told them what had happened on the top of the hill, how Aaron, Hur, and I had together held up the staff of God.

"I want you to understand that what happened today was not because Joshua and his men are such gifted warriors, although they are, but your victory today came about because Yahweh has chosen you as his own."

The people stood silent before me, their faces reflecting what my own heart was feeling. Wonder, that Yahweh would choose us with all our flaws and stubbornness. Delight, because we knew we were loved and chosen by Almighty God. Sorrow, remembering how we had doubted and not trusted this God who proclaimed he was the banner flying over us announcing to all the world that we belong to him.

One by one we dropped to our knees and worshiped Yahweh Nissi at the altar bearing his name.

FAMILY REUNION

I could hardly sleep last night. I had received word through a messenger that my father-in-law, Jethro, was coming and bringing my wife and two sons. I did not regret that I had sent my family away before returning to Egypt to confront Pharaoh nearly one year ago. But I had sorely missed my dear wife, Zipporah and my sons, Gershom and Eliezer. I pictured in my mind the day Yahweh provided Zipporah to me as my wife. I hadn't anticipated such a gift after I had fled Egypt and found refuge and work tending her father's flocks. Then Yahweh had blessed me with my oldest son. I chose to name him Gershom, meaning "stranger."

Zipporah had questioned that name. "Moses, you are no longer a stranger here, and our son is certainly not a stranger, having been born here in my father's house."

"Zipporah," I explained, "Midian is not my home. I will always be a stranger here, even though I have experienced such warm hospitality and honor from my father-in-law, Jethro. Please don't be offended, my wife. Yahweh has put in my heart a yearning for a land, a promised land, where his people will live and thrive. Although I have never seen this land of promise, I know it is my home, and I must never forget it. So I have named my son 'stranger,' Gershom, as a prophetic act. Every time I see the child, call out his name, I remind myself to never become satisfied outside of my promised land."

My second son, Eliezer, was also named prophetically. Eliezer means "God's help." I knew that it was only by the help of Yahweh, my father's God, that I had escaped when I fled from Pharaoh's sword. And that only by Yahweh's help would I be able to return to Egypt and lead my people out of captivity.

Eliezer was just a young child when we started the journey back to Egypt. After a short while I regretted taking my wife and young boys with me on such an uncertain journey, so had sent them back into Jethro's care until it was safe for them.

And now they were on their way to meet me! I rose and prepared to receive my family.

Oh, the tears and kisses that followed as my family entered the camp. I took a whole day and night off from my leadership duties. After the children were asleep, we sat around the fire well into the night. Jethro marveled as I shared story after story of Yahweh's provision for us, the escape from Egypt, passing through the Red Sea to freedom, manna every morning, water from a rock. The next morning Jethro joined me in worship as we presented offerings and sacrifices to Yahweh. Then the elders of Israel joined us, anxious to meet this man who was so dear to me.

The next day I had to resume my duties. Jethro accompanied me. He watched as I took my seat as judge for the people. From morning until evening the people kept coming to seek my help in their disputes, and I was paying for having taken time off to be with my family.

As we returned to our tent that evening Jethro was very quiet.

"Father," I asked. "Is something on your mind? You haven't spoken a word since we left the judgment area."

Jethro turned toward me. "Well, yes, there is something I've been pondering. What is this that you are doing for the people? Why do you alone sit as judge for their disputes?"

"The people come to me when they cannot settle a dispute. They expect me to seek God's will to settle their issues, so that is what I do."

"Moses, how often do you sit as judge? Once a week, twice a month?"

"Pretty much every day," I said.

"May I offer some advice, son?"

"Yes, Father, please share your insights."

"Moses, you have been leading these people for some time now, teaching them the ways of Yahweh. Surely you have some leaders you are raising up that could assist you in your duties. If you don't delegate some of your responsibilities, you will wear yourself out. You can't do this alone."

"Father, you are so right. I have been feeling worn out. How do you suggest I proceed?"

"Teach the leaders Yahweh's decrees and laws, then appoint them as officials over groups of ten, fifty, one hundred, or even one thousand of the people. Let them judge the people's disputes. If a matter is too difficult for your leaders to handle, then they can bring those cases to you. I believe this will make your load lighter, because your leaders—who love and respect you—will share the load of your responsibilities and make it more bearable."

As Jethro shared, I knew in my heart that Yahweh was speaking to me through this man who was so dear to me, the one who had believed in me when I fled from Egypt. Over the next weeks Jethro assisted me in gathering the newly appointed leaders for instruction in the ways of Yahweh. By the time Jethro was ready to kiss his daughter and grandsons goodbye and return to Midian, the new system of judging the disputes of the people was up and running.

With tears in my eyes, I hugged Jethro tightly, then sent him on his way, so much richer for his fatherly insight. No one among my people had even noticed how the stress of leadership was weighing me down.

But Yahweh knew, and he sent someone to show me that I was seen and loved. I heard in my spirit Yahweh's whisper. "I see you, my son. I am El Roi, the God who sees."

THE MOUNTAIN OF GOD

It was three months to the day that we left Egypt that Yahweh's pillar of cloud led us into the Sinai desert. When the pillar stopped moving, we set up camp at the foot of the mountain where Yahweh had first appeared to me in the burning bush.

Zipporah quickly gathered dry grass and started a cooking fire near our tent. I heard her singing softly as she cooked a simple meal for our family. Then our family of four sat near the fire enjoying our simple dinner.

I heard Zipporah speaking to the boys, and their sweet voices telling their mother about what they'd discovered at our new campsite. Gershom pulled a stone from his pocket and held it proudly in his outstretched hand. "Look, Ima, this stone has layers of color, see? It's pink, then brown, then kind of rusty orange."

I heard the children sharing, and Zipporah's comments, but my gaze kept drifting to the mountain towering above us.

"Moses?" Zipporah tugged on my sleeve. "The children want to show you the stones they collected today."

I quickly turned back to the children, commenting briefly on their new treasures, but a few minutes later, I found myself once again gazing at the mountain. I barely noticed when Zipporah called the boys to come into the tent for the night.

"Moses." Zipporah laid her hand on my arm.

"Yes? Do you need help getting the boys to bed?"

Zipporah laughed. "Moses, they are already asleep."

"Oh, I am so sorry, dear wife. It's just that I keep remembering what happened the last time I was on that mountain, the Mountain of God. It's like the mountain is calling me. Yahweh is calling me back to that place where I first saw his face."

"Moses, if Yahweh is calling you, go. We'll be fine. Go and bring back Yahweh's life-giving words to us all."

I hardly slept at all that night and finally rose before dawn to prepare to climb the mountain of God. Would he meet me there again, or was my burning bush experience only a one-time event? As I left my home and turned my face toward the mountain, I heard Yahweh calling to me from the mountain top.

I began to sprint toward the path leading up the mountainside. "I'm coming," I prayed. "I'm coming."

"Moses."

"I am here, my Lord."

"This is what you are to say to my people, the house of Israel, 'You yourselves have seen what I did to Egypt, and how I carried you on eagles' wings and brought you to myself. Now if you obey me fully and keep my covenant, then out of all nations you will be my treasured possession.'"[22]

I smiled at his words. This nation, these people a treasure? Dozens of incidents flooded my mind of how unlike treasure we had been. The grumbling over food, which Yahweh later provided for us when he sent the quail flooding into the camp. Provision which the people immediately forgot when we were faced with a lack of water to drink.

"Moses." Yahweh's voice called me back from my musing. "Yes, Moses I call the people, my people, a treasure. Although the whole earth is mine, this nation I set apart. My people will be for me a kingdom of priests and a holy nation. Moses, the people need to hear these words. They need to hear how I treasure them and choose them out of all the people on the earth. And I choose you, Moses, to deliver my words, but more than my words, to represent my heart to this 'untreasurelike' people. Will you tell them, Moses?"

I hurried down the mountainside, my heart welling up with love for the "treasures" waiting at the foot of the mountain.

The people were huddled around, awaiting Yahweh's next instructions and turned toward the mountain as they saw me slide down the rocky path. I sought out their eyes that were

---

[22] Exodus 19:4–6

fixed on me. I saw fear, and I knew that was not the response that Yahweh wanted from his people. I wanted them to feel what I felt before I went up the mountain, that tugging on my heart to be with him again, that emptiness when I was away from him. I heard once again in my spirit Yahweh's urgent whisper, "Tell them, Moses!"

"Come and hear the word of the Lord," I called out to the crowd. "Don't be afraid. Here is what Yahweh wants you to know. Out of all the people on the earth, Yahweh has chosen you. He said to tell you that you are a treasure to him."

I watched as fear turned to delight in their eyes.

"Yahweh loves you and chose you, and he said to tell you that you will be a kingdom of priests. Do you know what that means?"

A young boy called out, "Priests come close to God, like you, Abba Moses. Does Yahweh want me to come close to him, too?"

"Yes, yes, that is exactly what Yahweh wants, son. He wants relationship with his people."

The boy spoke again. "But I'm afraid of God, Abba Moses. I heard about what he did to the Egyptians, how they drowned in the sea. Yahweh is big and strong and can hurt people."

"Yes, Yahweh is all those things, but I think you still want to come close to Yahweh. Am I right, son?"

The boy hung his head and dug in the sandy soil with his bare toes. Finally, he looked up at me and nodded his head.

Words sprang into my mind that sounded strange to me, along with Yahweh's nudge to "tell them."

"Here is what Yahweh says to you, son, and to all his people: Draw near to me, and I will draw near to you."

I had heard Yahweh's invitation to draw near but had never known it to be an open invitation to his people. I watched the young boy, and the others in the crowd as they considered that the God of the Pillar of Cloud and Pillar of Fire was beckoning them into relationship with him.

I continued to share with the people Yahweh's instructions I'd heard on the mountain. When I had finished, they responded as one, "We will do everything the Lord has said."

I was so full of joy as I returned to the mountain to tell Yahweh that the people had wholeheartedly committed to obey all his instructions. I felt for the first time that the people had grasped what my heart felt each time I was in God's presence.

"Blessed are you, Yahweh, for your transforming words. Your people practically melted in front of me when I told them you called them your treasures."

Instead of responding to my report, Yahweh launched into a new round of instructions. I was confused. I wanted to camp out in the "you are my treasures" frame of mind for a while, but Yahweh had moved on.

"Tell the people to consecrate themselves today and tomorrow, Moses."

I stood silently before Yahweh, noting that his voice had taken on a more serious, even solemn tone.

"I will come to you tomorrow in a dense cloud, Moses. I will speak out loud to you so that the people will hear every word and will know that I have chosen you to lead them. When they hear me speaking to you, they will put their trust in you."

Still confused, I nodded, acknowledging Yahweh's words.

"You must warn the people to stay back from the mountain, Moses. Put markers, boundaries around the mountain so they keep their distance. Tell them to be careful not to go up on the mountain or even step up as if to climb the mountain with you. If anyone, man or beast touches the mountain you must stone that person or animal to death."

I trembled and shook my head in confusion. "But Yahweh, you said you wanted your people to be priests. I am confused. How can they be a nation of priests—your words, not mine— if you don't allow them to come near to you?"

Yahweh was silent for a moment, and I feared I had overstepped my own boundaries with Almighty God by my questioning. Finally, I heard his soft whisper. "Moses, you are my friend."

"And I am so humbled, so grateful to be your friend, Yahweh. Truly you are my closest friend. You know me inside and out and still welcome me to draw near to you, as broken as I am. I want to be a friend, a confidant to you, as well."

"Moses, you can totally rely on every word I speak to you, even when you do not understand. And you are welcome to bring your questions and confusion to me. I may not always answer for reasons that you may not understand at the time. But I want to assure you that you can trust me. I do love you, and I do call you my treasure and it is truly my desire to make these people who are my people into a kingdom of priests. In fact, I already see them as such, even before they begin to function as priests. I call this mystery 'now and not yet.'"

I bowed to the ground. "Yahweh, I do not understand 'now and not yet.'"

"Moses, do you remember when your father-in-law, Jethro first promised you his daughter, Zipporah as your wife?"

"Ah, yes! What a wonderful surprise that was." I sighed as I remembered that night around Jethro's table.

"You experienced the thrill of being engaged to a beautiful woman, and you felt instantly connected into a new family after being exiled from your own family back in Egypt. Your identity was changed from visitor, outsider to son, husband and no doubt, father. All this while you sat in Jethro's kitchen, when nothing had yet changed. You had not even consummated your marriage but were already dreaming of what was to come out of your union with Jethro's lovely daughter. You were experiencing 'now and not yet.' You embraced the 'now' promise right then and there, before the 'not yet' of your wedding night."

I was silent as Yahweh described the intimate thoughts of my heart that night when I became betrothed to my wife.

"This day I am sharing the intimate thoughts of *my* heart with you, Moses, because you are my friend. Today I am betrothing myself to you and to this people. And although the wedding night is still to come, when all the people will come to me as priests in intimate connection with their God, today I am rejoicing in the not yet that is to come and sharing my joy with my friend."

"Would it be alright if I think on this concept some more, Yahweh? I feel so humbled that you would bare your heart to me, but I confess I still do not understand how you can call the people a kingdom of priests and then forbid them to even set a foot on the mountain slope, the very slope where I am permitted and invited to climb into your presence."

"Trust me, my son, and take all the time you need."

I felt strangely comforted, even as I descended the mountain later that day and warned the people, the very people Yahweh called his "not yet" kingdom of priests. They were terrified, of course, when on the morning of the third day they awoke to the rumble of thunder and flashes of lightning surrounding a mountain completely obscured by thick smoke. Parents comforted their shaking children as they watched black clouds billow up from the mountain like smoke from a blazing furnace. The entire mountain shook. Then we heard a trumpet blast coming out of the smoke. The children covered their ears and cowered in their mothers' arms as the trumpet roared louder and louder.

I heard Yahweh's voice and answered, "Here I am, Lord."

"Come up to me, Moses!" Yahweh's voice thundered from the mountaintop.

I watched as the people fell to the ground, speechless, some whimpering in fear.

"Tell the people to stay back and not force their way to follow you up the mountain, Moses. If they do so, they will surely die."

"Now and not yet?" I thought as I began to climb the mountain. My body trembled with the same terror that gripped the people now lying prostrate in the shadow of the smoking mountain. It was as if Yahweh's heart was calling silently to mine, calling me into the "not yet" he had promised his people. I marveled even as I trembled that despite my fear, I was so drawn to this terrible and wonderful God. My heart made the choice that the risk of stepping into the blinding smoke, lightening crashing all around me, was worth encountering the heart of Yahweh.

MOSES ON THE MOUNTAIN

Hours turned into days, then days into weeks as Yahweh gave me detailed instructions for his people, including what became known as the Ten Commandments. He shared his plans for a Tabernacle for us to build that would host his presence, and the articles that we should make and place in the Tabernacle. The focal piece would be a wooden chest, which Yahweh called the "ark of the covenant." It was to be constructed according to the specific dimensions Yahweh gave me, built out of acacia wood and overlaid with pure gold inside and out. We were to place rings at each corner of the ark, so that acacia wood poles also overlaid with gold, could be inserted into the rings to transport the ark whenever the Pillar of Cloud beckoned us to move.

On the mountain Yahweh told me that his people would inhabit the entire land before us, from the Red Sea to the Mediterranean Sea, so we would constantly need to pack up and relocate the Tabernacle as we journeyed on to the Promised Land.

In each place we traveled we were to set up the Tabernacle tent as the central point and place every gold overlaid piece of furniture in its place inside the tent. Yahweh gave me instructions about altars and offerings to atone for our sins. He described the function of the priests who would serve in the Tabernacle, with my brother, Aaron, as the head priest, and the specific garments they were to wear while serving.

Yahweh mentioned by name two men he had chosen to create the artistic designs he planned for the Tabernacle. I knew that Bezalel and Oholiab would be ecstatic that Yahweh had handpicked them to decorate the place where Yahweh's presence would rest.

Then Yahweh gave me two tablets of stone on which he had engraved his instructions. "Tomorrow you will deliver my written words to my people."

I woke early on my fortieth day on the mountain and breathed deeply in the cool, fresh air. I gave little thought to my family. I had not seen my wife or children in over a month, nor the rest of the Hebrew people that I was supposed to be leading. Every day since Yahweh called me to the top of the mountain I had spent listening to his teaching, writing down his words, and drinking in his presence.

As I waited for his voice on the fortieth day, I mused aloud. "Is it possible for a man to become addicted to the presence of God?" A delightful addiction that would be!

Then Yahweh burst into my hearing with a terrible announcement. "Moses, quickly, go down the mountain. The people, your people whom you led out of Egypt have forgotten me and become corrupt."

"What? How? How can that be? After all they've seen, all they've experienced! How can that be?"

"Go down and see for yourself, Moses. The people are now bowing down to an idol, a golden cow fashioned for them by your brother, Aaron."

I could not even form words to respond to Yahweh. My mind swirled with confusion. "Aaron heard your voice, like I did," I thought. "How could he now worship a metal statue he made with his own hands?"

As if Yahweh heard my thoughts he responded. "Even now Aaron is presenting animal sacrifices to his new god."

I fell to the ground weeping even as the air around me became thick with smoke. I lifted my head to see what was burning but realized what I was sensing was the anger of the Almighty.

"Yahweh?" I ventured.

"Leave me alone, Moses, so my anger may burn against these ungrateful people."

"But Yahweh, they are your people."

"I will destroy them, Moses, but I will create from you a new nation that follows me."

I rose from the ground and faced the billowing cloud of smoke. The very earth beneath me trembled under the anger of the Lord.

"Yahweh, I know this is a terrible thing, a senseless act that my brother has done and the people following him. But Yahweh, why should your anger burn against your people, the very people you rescued from Egypt with your great power and mighty hand? What will the Egyptians say when they hear that you slaughtered your people? Did the God of the earth bring his people out of bondage only to kill them in the mountains?"

Yahweh said nothing, but the smoke of his anger rose higher and higher in the morning sky around me.

I knelt before the Lord. I knew what it felt like to be surrounded by God's presence. I knew the longing I experienced when I had to leave that presence to lead the people. But what Yahweh was promising was like I imagined Hades would be, the absence of his presence, utter darkness with no hope of light, the end of hope, the end of life.

"Oh, Yahweh, I beseech you, turn your anger away from your people. Don't abandon them. If you no longer watch over them, they will wither and die like a wildflower in parched ground."

Yahweh still said nothing.

I was silent for several minutes. "Remember?"

I felt him turn toward me.

"Yahweh, remember your sons, Abraham, Isaac, and Jacob, how you swore to them by your own self? You promised you would make their descendants—these wayward people—as numerous as the stars in the sky. You promised that they would own the land around this mountain, that this land I stand on, this mountain, would be their inheritance forever."

The rumbling abruptly stopped, and I felt a stiff breeze blowing away the dark smoke.

"I do not condone what my people have done, Moses."

His voice was harsh, but my heart leapt inside me when I heard Yahweh call Aaron and the others "my people."

I grabbed the two stone tablets of the Testimony which Yahweh had given me, inscribed by the very hand of God, and hurried down the mountain then, dreading what I would find at the bottom.

Joshua was waiting a short distance away and joined me on my descent. He said nothing, no doubt noting the harsh look on my face. After a short while we heard shouting coming from the foot of the mountain.

"Moses, it sounds like war in the camp!" Joshua warned.

I shook my head in anger. "No, Joshua. It's not war. It's not the sound of victory in the camp, nor is it the sound of defeat. Listen! The people are singing."

"Oh, then there's no need to worry, right?" Joshua asked.

My face told him no, and he followed me toward the music.

THE GOLDEN CALF

I could hardly believe my eyes. I marched into the camp, still clutching the stone tablets of the Testimony. The people were dancing and singing around an altar, but when they saw me and Joshua enter the crowd the music stopped abruptly. There was my own brother, Aaron, kneeling before a glistening, golden calf.

Filled with anger, I threw the stone tablets down where they crumbled into pieces. Aaron leapt to his feet and tried to stand in front of me as I headed straight to that despicable idol, the object of their worship. I pushed him aside, grabbed the golden calf off the pole, and threw it to the ground. I crushed it under my feet, then threw it into the fire on the altar.

Aaron stood by, trembling, not saying a word.

When the fire had gone out, I lifted the scorched "god" out of the ashes and ground it into powder with a sizable rock. I sprinkled the powder into a large water bucket and forced the people to drink it. Then I turned to Aaron.

"Aaron, how could you? After all you've seen, after you heard the voice of Yahweh in your own ears? How did these people force you to lead them into this sin of idol worship?"

Aaron's voice shook as he whispered, "Moses, you know what these people are like. You remember how they doubted you so many times both in Egypt, and even as we entered the land Yahweh promised us. You had been gone so long on the mountain, we were not even sure you were still alive. So the people demanded that I make them a new god. I was afraid for my life, so I did what they asked. I collected their gold jewelry, most of it spoils from when Yahweh led us out of Egypt. It was almost miraculous. When I threw the jewelry and other golden items into the melting pot, out came this calf shaped figure. I touched it up a bit to make it look more like a cow, but it felt to me like this calf divinely appeared out of the molten gold. I guess I started believing it was more than just metal."

The people were running wild by this point, some very angry with me for destroying their new god, some still choking on the water I'd made them drink.

I stepped away from Aaron and addressed the crowd. "You get to choose!" I shouted. "You can follow the 'god' I destroyed before your eyes, or you can follow Yahweh. Those who choose Yahweh, come stand with me."

The crowd separated and the Levites were the first to rally around me and Aaron. Then the rest of the people chose their sides. I was relieved to see that most of the people had repented from worshiping an idol and had joined God's people.

I addressed the ones standing with me and Aaron. "Now here is what the Lord, the God of Israel commands. Each man is to strap a sword to his side. Now go through the camp and kill both your friends and your brothers, anyone who is not on the Lord's side."

Swords in their hands and tears on their faces, the Levites led the people to attack all those who had not returned to the Lord throughout the camp. Over three thousand people died that day, but there was no victory song in the camp that night, only weeping.

I heard the surviving crowd murmuring the next morning as I called them together. I saw fear on their faces and Yahweh opened my ears to hear their thoughts. "We are no different than our brothers who we killed. We, too, left Yahweh and worshiped an idol. Will we be punished as our brothers?"

What they didn't know was that I had already interceded for them up on the mountain the day before. When Yahweh spoke of destroying them and building a new nation out of my descendants, I had asked him to remember. Remember your promises, I had said.

I answered the fearful thoughts of my people. "Today you are set apart to the Lord. You were against your own people, some of you killed your own family members, as you took your stand on the side of the Lord who brought you up out of the land of Egypt with signs and miracles. Today Yahweh calls you blessed.

"Still you, too, have sinned against the Lord in a serious way. But do not fear. I will go back up the mountain and make atonement for your sin."

The people watched in silence, many still weeping over yesterday's awful events, as I turned and climbed the mountain of God to intercede once again for my people.

The smoke had cleared around the peak as I approached Yahweh.

"Moses?" he asked.

At the sound of his voice, now devoid of the anger I had heard days earlier, I fell to the ground weeping.

"Yahweh, I don't have any excuse to give you. What the people did, what my people did is inexcusable. They made themselves gods of gold; they chose worthless idols instead of you. Please forgive them, Yahweh."

Yahweh did not speak. I feared that the sin of my people was too great to forgive. Were they all to die in the wilderness because of their sin?

"My Lord, if you will not forgive their sin, if someone has to die to atone for them, then let it be me. Blot me out of the book you have written but let my people live."

Then Yahweh answered me. "The one who sins against me I will blot out of my book, but you, my son, will live. Now go, return to the people and lead them to the place I told you, your promised land. And before you ask, yes, Moses, my angel will go before you as before."

I wept harder, my shoulders heaving on the stony ground until I felt the pressure of a hand on my back, then the whisper of his voice.

"I remember. You asked me to remember, Moses, but I want you to know that when I remember, I act. I will always remember what you offered to do for your people today. You asked me to put their sin, their consequences on you. You offered to die for them, so they don't have to die. I want you to know, Moses that I put that fierce love inside of you, just as I put my very words inside your mouth, because it is the same love I have for our people. And one day ..."

"One day, my Lord?"

"One day I will remember, and yes, one day I will act, and all the world will encounter my fierce love.

"Yet I tell you, Moses, there will be consequences for my peoples' sin."

THE TENT OF MEETING

It was with much sadness that I brought the word of the Lord to the people after I came down from the mountain again.

"Yahweh is about to lead us out of this camp and on to our next destination. He promises to send his angel before us to drive out the inhabitants of the land ahead of us. He describes the land as a place flowing with milk and honey."

"That is a good thing, Moses, is it not?" Joshua asked. "Why is your face downcast?"

I continued to address the crowd.

"Yes, God is leading us into the land he promised us, but he has instructed me to tell you this: 'I will send my angel to lead you, but I myself will not go with you, Because you are such a stiff-necked people, I might destroy you along the way.'"

When the people heard Yahweh's words they began to mourn. They took off any jewelry or ornamental clothing they were wearing. When the children asked their parents why they were in mourning they said, "It's because Yahweh will not be with us anymore. He said that if he were to go with us, even for a moment, he might destroy us."

"We can't go on without Yahweh, can we?" the children began to cry.

"No, we can't, and we won't. Moses told us to wait here until Yahweh decides what to do with us."

The somber group watched as I approached the Tent of Meeting pitched just outside the camp.

I had instituted the tent at Yahweh's direction. Whenever one of the people had questions, they could go to that tent and share their questions with me. Then I alone would enter the tent to meet with Yahweh. It was always exciting to see the Pillar of Cloud that lead us daily on our journey slowly drift across the camp and fill up the Tent of Meeting. Each family stood at the entrances of their own tents and worshiped whenever I entered the Tent of Meeting. There the Lord would speak to me face to face, as a man speaks with his friend.

I saw the people clasping their hands in prayer as I walked toward the Tent. I knew they were praying that I would meet with Yahweh and bring them words of hope when I returned to the camp. I heard their collective gasp as once again the cloud of Yahweh's presence enveloped the Tent. I stepped in and immediately felt the coolness of the mist inside the cloud. I sighed and closed my eyes. Although it had only been a few days ago that I had been in Yahweh's presence on the mountain, I opened my mouth and began to gulp in his refreshing presence as if I just couldn't get enough.

Finally, my breathing slowed, I opened my eyes and approached the source of the light at the front of the tent. Yahweh seemed to know I had something weighing on my mind and waited for me to speak.

"Yahweh, you have been telling me to lead these people, but that you won't be going with us anymore."

He did not answer.

"Yahweh, you have not let me know who you will send with me to take your place. Surely, I cannot take my people to their Promised Land without a guide.

"Yahweh, you have told that that you know me by name and that you have found favor with me, yes? So if this is true, and you are truly pleased with me, teach me your ways. You know me, but I want to, I need to know you so that I may continue to please you and find favor with you. Yahweh, I ask you once again to remember that this nation is your people."

Finally, Yahweh spoke, and my heart began to pound inside me at his words. "My Presence will go with you, and I will give you rest."

I rose up then and felt my voice cracking as I cried out to Yahweh. "If your Presence does not go with us, then don't even send us. We won't go without you, Yahweh. If you're not going, we're not going. Don't you see that no one will know that we are your people unless you go with us? What will distinguish us from all the other people of the world if you no longer go with us on our journey?”

“Moses.” Yahweh’s abruptness startled me out of my rambling. “I will do the very thing you are asking me, because I am so very pleased with you, and I know you by name.”

I fell to the ground again, consumed by weeping. “Oh, God!” I croaked through my tears. “He, Yahweh, Lord of the Universe is pleased with me. The Great Elohim knows the man, Moses, by name. Oh, God!”

After a time, I felt Yahweh lifting me off the ground.

“Moses, what is your heart longing for right now?”

I blurted out the first thoughts that came to mind. “I want you to lead my people to the Promised Land.”

“No, Moses, ask your heart what it is longing for.”

I lay my hand over my heart. “Heart,” I whispered. “What are you longing for?”

My heart cried out, “Yahweh, show me your glory! That’s what my heart is longing for.”

“This I will do for you, Moses. I will cause all my goodness to pass in front of you, and you will hear my voice proclaiming my name, The Lord. But no one can see my face and live. So here is what I will do. There is a place I will bring you, up on the mountain, in the cleft of a rock. I will put you there and cover you with my hand until I have passed by.”

“When, my Lord? Shall I get ready now?”

But Yahweh spoke no further. So I tucked his promise into my longing heart and left the Tent of Meeting to encourage my people that God was not sending someone else to lead us into the Promised Land after all. His presence would go with us. I rushed back into the camp with this wonderful announcement.

A BLESSING FOR THE PEOPLE

The days and months passed quickly. I frequently spent extended times on the mountain receiving Yahweh's instructions. Each time I returned from the mountain I shared God's words with the people. We built the Tabernacle according to Yahweh's specific instructions. The priests were dressed as Yahweh commanded and ordained into service. Sacrifices were made to atone for the sins of the people, as Yahweh directed. We used Yahweh's rules for business, marriage, parenting, and relationships.

I stood back one morning and watched the people going about their chores, doing life, honoring the Lord and his commandments, and was filled with joy. Then I felt the warmth of Yahweh's presence seeping through my body.

"Moses, do you see what I see?" Yahweh asked me in a sing-song voice.

I smiled and sang back to him, "Do you see what I see, Abba?"

"I see a people following my ways. I am filled with joy, and I see that you are feeling what I am feeling as you gaze on our people. So I want to give you a special blessing to give them."

I waited expectantly. I had scolded the people so often when they went astray, even to the point of separating out the disobedient and calling for their stoning. Now Yahweh was inviting me to bless the people. Would the blessing be rain for our crops? More children born? The defeat of our enemies?

"Moses," Yahweh interrupted my thoughts. "Tell Aaron and his sons, this is how you are to bless the Israelites. Say to them: The Lord bless you and keep you; The Lord make his face shine upon you and be gracious to you; The Lord turn his face toward you and give you peace. With the declaration of this blessing, you will put my name on the Israelites, and I will bless them."[23]

I was silent at first before the Lord. The reward Yahweh was offering to his people was not a tangible prize. I considered his words of blessing.

First, the words were to be spoken by a priest, one who heard from and then spoke the very words of Yahweh, and to be received as such by the people. Yahweh blesses you and keeps you. He both sustains you and keeps you safe. I thought of my young wife, suckling my first born. She gave him life, sustained him with the milk of her breasts, and kept him safe in her arms.

I felt Yahweh nodding as he listened to my thoughts.

Next the priest was instructed to declare that Yahweh would make his face shine upon them. I knew what it was like to displease my own father, both my birth father, Amram as well as my surrogate parent, Pharaoh. I remembered the sadness in Amram's eyes when I disobeyed, and the anger in Pharaoh's when I killed an Egyptian and had to flee for my life. But now Yahweh was promising that his face would shine upon his people resulting in grace, the receiving of gifts not earned, but bestowed on his people out of his goodness. I had loved returning to my Hebrew home where the faces of my siblings, Miriam and Aaron, and my parents, Jocabed and Amram, would light up as they gazed on me. Not because of anything I'd done or not done, but just because they adored me. I had felt Yahweh's eyes on me with the same affection, and now Yahweh wanted to shine his face in adoration on the people he had sent me to lead.

How often I had craved to see the face of God, to look into his eyes the way I gazed into my sons' eyes. And I knew my heart's desire echoed the desire of the people I led. I had watched their yearning eyes each time I entered the Tent of Meeting, and when I emerged later, my face was shining. I saw the fear reflected in their eyes, yes, but also the longing of their hearts to enter into greater intimacy with Yahweh.

---

[23] Numbers 6:24–26

"Yes, Moses, I desire to turn my face toward my people. And when I do, they will experience my shalom, the utter sense of complete fulfillment—nothing missing, nothing lacking. Now tell Aaron and his sons to bless my people with my words. In so doing they will put my name on my people, and I will bless them."

"Yahweh? What will it look like when the people receive this blessing? Will they never doubt you again when they realize that you will keep them? Will they never act out because they feel abandoned when they recognize that your face is turned toward them, shining on them? Will their faces glow in the brightness of your presence?"

"One day, my son. Your job is to deliver the blessing not once, but over and over again. And each time you recite my words, you are to revel in the wonder of my promises. You may not always see what you are declaring but remember what I've told you. Every word I speak is pregnant with the ability to perform itself. Your job is not to bring about the blessing, only to deliver it."

At once I felt a gust of hot wind that knocked me to the ground. Just as I covered my head to deflect the intense heat it suddenly lifted.

"Bless, as you have been blessed. I will ignite the blessing."

A TIME OF REST AND PREPARATION

Camping in the Sinai Desert had been a time of rest and equipping for people of God. I had received and delivered Yahweh's instructions and commandments. We had built and furnished according to his specifications the wonderful Tent of Meeting where God's presence rested. I marveled at the genius of Yahweh's specific instructions to make the tent and its furnishings fully portable. Just knowing that our Tabernacle was going to accompany us on the journey created a restlessness in my spirit.

"We're ready, Abba," I prayed. "We're ready to move on to the land you promised."

But all Yahweh would say whenever he caught me pacing around the camp was "Soon, very soon."

Then early on the twentieth day of the second month of our second year out of Egypt, the cloud lifted from above the Tabernacle, and we knew it was time. The trumpets were blown to gather the leaders, but the delight on their faces reflected that they were well aware it was time to leave this place. They hurried back to their groups, and we began the process of packing up our huge camp.

Finally, we were ready, and I heard the children squealing with excitement as they pointed to the cloud that had lifted off the Tabernacle. We watched as the cloud formed into a tall pillar that began to drift ahead of the camp.

"So it begins," I thought. I felt no dread although I had no map or travel plans. I lifted my head and smiled at Yahweh. "All that matters is that you are going with us."

The tribes were in place, leaders from each tribe in command of their people. As one they looked to me, and I in turn looked to Yahweh.

"Rise up, O Lord!" I shouted. "May your enemies be scattered; may your foes flee before you."

And we were off. The cloud led us for three days as we journeyed away from the mountain. The Ark of the Covenant was positioned at the front of our caravan, carried on its poles by Aaron and the other priests, as Yahweh had commanded.

After three days the pillar of cloud paused, standing ramrod straight in the sky, and it was time to stop and set up camp. I watched as the young mothers, still holding sleeping infants, practically collapsed into their tents.

"How good of Yahweh to have us travel in short bursts," I thought.

Then I prayed aloud before the people. "Return, O Lord, to the countless thousands of Israel."

And so it was that each time the cloud lifted, and we moved on that I would pray those same prayers. "Rise up" and "Return O Lord" became the prayers on every heart as we broke and set up camp in response to the moving cloud of God's presence.

I lay in my tent that night, Zipporah and the boys sleeping beside me, remembering briefly when Yahweh had threatened that he would not go with us in our travels. I shook my head thinking of the fear that had risen up in me until I blurted out "If you're not going, then I'm not going either." I smiled, knowing that Yahweh was smiling too.

"You were pretty desperate, Moses," he whispered to my heart.

"You bet I was, Yahweh. And still am. Once I met you, once I encountered you and heard your voice, it was all over for me. I love you, Abba, and I don't ever want to do life without you."

"Remember who initiated this relationship?" Yahweh asked. "I chose you to lead this people. I intentionally gave you two names, Jekuthiel meaning hope, and Moses, pulled from the waters. So I rescued you so that you could be a source of hope to my people."

I lay on my side, watching the chests of my sons rise and fall as they slept, hearing Yahweh's voice in the sound of their every breath. Yah, breathing in. Weh, breathing out.

"Oh, how good you are, Yahweh! You are an Abba to me, delighting in my every breath, loving me like I adore my sons. You are the air I breathe, as I whisper your name with my every breath."

I fell asleep sometime after that, cradling the boys I loved, as we were all cradled in the arms of Yahweh.

FIRE AND QUAIL

The next morning, I woke slowly, remembering the sweetness of Yahweh's presence, but something was nagging at me, pulling me awake more quickly than I wanted to. Suddenly I realized that the nagging sensation calling to me was actually the smell of smoke, and I sat up and looked around my tent to find out what was burning. Finding nothing amiss, I hurried outside where I saw a swatch of fire along the outer perimeter of the camp. I ran toward the blaze and found several tents already scorched to the ground, along with their inhabitants trapped inside.

There was no water available to douse the flames in our desert camp, only the jugs we had brought along for drinking, washing, and cooking. As nearby tents began to smoke, I realized that the fire was only in its beginning stages, and we needed to wake the people to flee and move away from the flames threatening to engulf them.

"Moses!" Yahweh's voice broke through my anxious thoughts.

Choking on the thickening smoke, I turned my face toward the Mountain of God and waited for his voice.

"Moses, I am weary of the complaining of the people over the hardships they've been facing. They do not look to me for provision, even though I have provided for them time after time these two years in the wilderness."

In the background I heard the cries of the people, the squealing of the frightened children as the fire from heaven leapt along the ground consuming as it burned.

"Yahweh!" I cried out. "I come to you on behalf of these people I love and you love. Yahweh, forgive us for not trusting you yet again. I repent on behalf of these ones and ask you to quench this fire and rescue your people, called by your name."

I heard the weeping of the people after that, like waves of wailing ripping across the camp, and felt Yahweh's heart yearning for his people. Then the wind ceased. The people hurried to throw sand on the smoldering tents, and the fire died down and stopped spreading.

"Taberah," Yahweh spoke again. "Name this place Taberah."

Then I saw the people rise from the sand as we watched the pillar of cloud rise to lead us away from this place. They turned as one and looked toward me, waiting for the familiar call to "rise up" to usher us away from this awful place of burning

I knew I had to explain to the people about Taberah, before we could follow the cloud away from the smoking and destruction they had witnessed.

"Come." I beckoned the elders to join me. "Yahweh has heard your cursing, your complaining."

I saw the men look to one another and begin to accuse each other for cursing God. I heard one man defending himself, "I never uttered one word."

"Oh, but your face said it all!" another retorted.

"Enough!" I shouted. "Yes, even the unspoken words of your heart were heard by the Most High God. He sent his holy fire to burn and consume the camp, but I have prayed for you, and Yahweh again pulled back his hand. Now it is time to move on from this place of burning that Yahweh has named Taberah. May we never encounter Taberah again. Now break camp."

After the tents had been packed up for travel, the people again gathered and looked to me, waiting for the words of hope and promise of Yahweh's continued care for us, his people, even after we had again angered him with our unbelief.

I stood before them, waiting for Yahweh's voice. I did not hear him speak, only heard his deep intake of breath, and felt the nodding of his head as the pillar of cloud wavered in the bright sun.

"Rise up, O Lord!" I shouted. "May your enemies be scattered; may your foes flee before you."

It seemed like the whole camp had been holding their breath, waiting to see if Yahweh would allow us to hear those words again, then collectively released their breath as I shouted. And we eagerly moved away from Taberah.

Yahweh continued to sustain us with manna as we traveled through the desert, but not long into this next leg of our journey, the people began to complain again.

"We are sick to death of this manna," they wailed.

The young children, many of whom had never known any other food than the manna we gathered every morning, grew frightened by their parents' wailing.

I saw young Jaram sniffling as he stood by the cooking fire outside his tent listening to his parents' angry complaints. He tugged at his ima's dress. "What's wrong, Ima? Didn't I collect enough manna for breakfast?"

"No, no, Jaram, it's not your fault. We have plenty of this tasteless manna for breakfast, and lunch, and dinner."

Jaram's abba pushed his plate away in disgust. "If only we had some meat to eat," he muttered. "Oh, that wonderful salty fish we ate in Egypt at no cost, and the onions and garlic. I can't eat another bite of this manna."

"What's fish, Abba?" Jaram asked timidly. But his father only shook his head in silent anger.

The complaining which started out as muttering, words whispered inside a few tents, slowly erupted until it seemed the whole community was involved. I watched the men gather in groups and then felt their anger as they turned as one to stare at me.

As if all of this was my fault.

I stood outside my tent feeling the anger rising all around me. Suddenly I realized that the anger was also above and within me. Yahweh was angry, too, and so was I.

"Yahweh, why have you brought this distress on me? You called me your friend, so what have I done that displeased you that you would put the burden of this miserable people on my shoulders?"

Yahweh was silent, so I continued. "How is this my problem? I didn't birth these people, so why do you ask me to carry them in my arms like a woman carries her infant. Do you expect me to carry them all in my arms all the way to the promised land?"

I was weeping by now, and I could sense the distress of the Israelites as they watched their leader break down.

"Yahweh, answer me! Where can I get meat for these thousands of people? I can't provide for them. This burden is too heavy for me to carry. If this is how you are going to treat me, then just put me out of my misery. Put me to death right now, like you did to Pharaoh and the Egyptians. If I have found favor in your sight, do me this kindness by striking me dead. Do not let me face my own failure and ruin."

And I, the one Yahweh chose to lead his people, fell to the ground, my body heaving with loud sobs muffled only by the sand on which I lay.

I lay there for some time as the sun rose to full height, brightening the skies above me. I felt the rays of sunlight now warming me like the breath of God upon me, and then he spoke.

"Moses, my friend. Yes, you are my friend. Here is what you are to do. Bring me seventy of Israel's leaders, ones that have proved themselves faithful to you and the people. Come together to the Tent of Meeting. I will meet you there and speak with you as before. And Moses, hear me, I will take of my Spirit that is on you, and I will put my Spirit on the seventy leaders that you trust. I will take the burden of the people that you are struggling to carry and place it on these seventy. These leaders will love my people as you do and help you carry them from now on so you don't have to do it alone."

I looked around me, already starting a mental list of those leaders that could be part of the seventy Yahweh was raising to support me and our people. Would seventy of us, seventy-two along with Aaron and myself, be able to carry the thousands of men, women, and children across this unyielding desert?

Yahweh spoke again. "Now tell the people to rededicate themselves to follow me, in preparation for the surprise I have planned for them tomorrow. Tell them that I heard their wailing for meat, cursing the day they left Egypt. I will give them meat, and they will eat. They will eat it not just tomorrow, or the day after, or a week, but for a month until they are sick and tired of meat, because they did not honor me as their provider."

I stood from the ground and shook my head in frustration. "Yahweh, what you are saying is ridiculous. Here I am standing before more than six hundred thousand men, women, and children, and you say you're going to give them meat to eat for a month, so much meat they'll be sick of it. How can you say this? If we slaughtered all our livestock today, there would not be enough meat to eat for six hundred thousand hungry mouths for an entire month. If we somehow were able to catch all the fish in the nearest sea, that would not be enough for such a large group for a month."

I trembled at the sound of my own defiant words. It sounded in my own ears like any one of my people as they shook their fists at Yahweh and wished they had never heeded his call to leave their bondage in Egypt. How could Yahweh choose one such as me to lead his people when I myself doubted his words. Surely, he will strike me dead and raise up another leader in my place. I fell once more to the ground, this time in shame. I knew he chose me for this mission. I had seen him in the burning bush. I had watched water bubble out of a dry rock. I had marveled as pestilence and plagues devastated Pharaoh and the people of Egypt but never dared set foot in the camp of the Israelites. But now, I had spoken out loud in doubt and anger. I was not fit or worthy to lead God's people another step in this journey to a Promised Land.

I felt a strong breeze come sweeping across the land and then Yahweh pulling me to my feet. It was as if the wind was the breath of his Spirit refilling me. Could it be that Yahweh would still call me friend, would still allow me to complete this mission? Then I heard his gentle voice.

"Moses, is my arm too short? Is there anything I cannot do? Haven't you learned that by now, my son? You will now see if what I have promised will come true or not. Trust me."

I nodded my head, still too ashamed to lift my face toward him, although his voice was not harsh, but gentle. I gathered the people and told them what Yahweh said.

"You will have meat to eat very soon" I told them.

Then I watched as various men, trusted and faithful leaders, left their families standing at the entrance to their tents and began to gather at the Tent of Meeting until a group of seventy leaders stood shoulder to shoulder looking toward me. Yahweh had chosen the seventy to help me, I realized, and yes, there were Joshua and Caleb, Beniah, Jared, and others that had sprung to mind when I started my own mental list. I smiled and raised my face at last to Yahweh.

"Thank you, Abba," I whispered as I strode quickly across the compound to join the seventy elders at the Tent of Meeting.

A gust of wind blew through the camp and the cloud of Yahweh's presence appeared in the sky and slowly dropped down to cover us. I felt his breath fill my lungs to nearly bursting. Then I exhaled and felt the rush of God's Spirit pour out of my mouth and enter the lungs of each of the seventy elders. I watched them breathing deeply of his Spirit, gulping in the sweetness of his presence in the cloud.

"Now they know." I smiled to myself. "Now they know your voice, your words, and they'll never be the same."

Slowly the seventy began to speak, first somewhat timidly, and then as they realized that they were speaking the words Yahweh was communicating to their hearts, they began to raise their voices, laughing, crying, singing the words of the Most High God.

Joshua's wife went running to him as he stood with the seventy elders and whispered something in this ear. Then Joshua turned to me and relayed the message from his wife.

"Moses, my wife has brought word that two of the seventy who were not at the Tent of Meeting but had stayed behind in the camp, Eldad and Medad, also received the impartation of

God's Spirit and began to prophesy, but they are not here with us. Make them stop, Moses!"

I wrapped my arm around my young friend. "Son, are you jealous for my sake? I wish—"

My voice cracked, and I began to sob so violently that Joshua grabbed my shoulders and looked into my face. "What's wrong, Abba Moses? What do you wish? Do you want me to go and force Eldad and Medad to shut up?"

I wiped my face and cleared my throat. "No, no, Joshua. It's all good. Yahweh chose Eldad and Medad and placed his Spirit on them even though they stayed by their young families. It's just that as I began to speak what was on my heart, 'I wish,' that I realized it was Yahweh speaking, not just the cry of my own heart, but the very heart of God for all his people, from the little ones to the ones bowed down with age. Yahweh said, 'I wish that all of the Lord's people were prophets and that the Lord would put his Spirit on every one of them.'"

I turned to address all the elders. "Today you have experienced what few people do. You have heard Yahweh's voice and had the privilege of sharing those golden words through your own mouths."

And as if that experience was not enough in itself to equip God's people to keep going, shortly after we returned to camp a strong wind went out from Yahweh and drove quail in from the sea. The wind was so strong that the quail were forced to fly just a few feet above the ground, about a day's walk all around the camp. The people shouted out in joy at the prospect of eating meat again. All that day and the next the people spent catching the quail in midair. They feasted and prepared some of the meat for drying to preserve it for days to come.

In the midst of the rejoicing in the camp some people ate the quail with no gratitude and no repentance for how they had doubted Yahweh's provision. Some of those people never enjoyed the nourishment from the meat, for as they chewed the quail, before they even swallowed any of it, God's anger broke out, and he struck them with a severe plague.

We named the place Kibroth Hattaavah, graves of lust. There we gathered meat provided by the Lord Yahweh, and there we buried the ones who would never be satisfied.

BETRAYAL BY FAMILY

I was relieved to leave behind the graves of lust at Kibroth Hattaavah. My soul and my body were so tired of conflict. The Pillar of Cloud led us to Hazeroth and then stopped to allow us to rest and set up camp. As soon as my tent was set up, I fell onto my sleeping cot and was asleep almost immediately. Zipporah stayed awake a bit longer and turned away the ones who approached our tent so as not to disturb my much needed rest.

I awoke the next morning to the chirping of birds and the sound of loud whispering just outside my tent. I heard Zipporah's melodic voice and a male voice in what sounded like a heated discussion. I made my way outside and found my close friend, one of my trusted leaders, Joshua, his hands waving about as he gestured anxiously to Zipporah.

"My friend," I interrupted. "I'm awake. What's going on?"

"Moses, maybe it's nothing," Joshua began apologetically, "but I've been hearing two people speaking some harsh words against you for the past few days as I monitored the people on our way to Hazeroth. I thought it might blow over when we stopped and set up camp here, but when I arose at first light, I found these two individuals had already gathered and you were still the topic of their arguments."

"So, it's not a large group speaking against me, Joshua? Just a few people? Let's not get excited. Maybe it will blow over after these two get some rest."

Joshua was silent for a moment, then looked directly into my eyes. "I have a feeling this will not blow over, Moses. These few people are very influential."

"Joshua, who are these two people you're talking about?"

Zipporah interrupted our conversation just then to announce that my brother, Aaron, and sister, Miriam, were headed toward our tent. "They look upset, Moses," she added.

I turned to Joshua and before I could ask a question, Joshua nodded his head vigorously and gestured toward Aaron and Miriam as they hurried toward me.

"Good morning, brother and sister," I called out.

"Save your greetings, old man," Miriam called out with a sneer. "Who do you think you are? You think you're someone special, better than any of us. You didn't even marry someone from our people, yet you think that God only speaks through you, and none of us has anything to say."

Aaron stood by Miriam but did not speak. It reminded me of the time he had stood by the people when they decided they needed a god made out of gold since I was gone so long on the Mountain of God. Here he was again, going along with another person's bad decision, this time our sister, Miriam.

Miriam marched right up to me until we stood practically nose to nose. "You think that God only speaks through you, but hasn't he also spoken though me and Aaron?"

My heart was filled with sorrow at her words. What could I say to her? Should I remind her of when she danced and led us all in worship of the God who drowned our enemies, the Egyptians, in the Red Sea? Should I remind Aaron of our wonderful reunion in the desert, when Yahweh told him to come and meet me there. We have history together serving our God. How can they betray me like this?

"Moses!" Yahweh broke into my thoughts. I lifted my face toward the Mountain of God visible in the distance.

"Moses, you are a humble man, more humble than anyone on the face of the earth. I know you will not defend yourself, but I will."

Yahweh's voice came audibly then booming from above us. "Moses, Aaron and Miriam, Come out to the Tent of Meeting, all three of you."

Without hesitation I turned and headed to the Tent of Meeting on the outskirts of the camp. Aaron and Miriam followed at a short distance until they stood beside me outside the tent. Then the Pillar of God's presence came and stood before us.

I heard Miriam whisper to Aaron, "See, all three of us heard Yahweh's voice, and now the Pillar of Presence has come to all of us, not just to Moses." She folded her arms defiantly and turned to me to defend her and Aaron's position.

But before Miriam could utter a word, Yahweh spoke again. "Aaron, Miriam, come here."

"See!" Miriam whispered to Aaron. "He's setting us apart, leaving Moses behind."

I fell to the ground and began to weep. I knew Yahweh's voice and recognized the serious tone of his voice. I felt the earth trembling under my feet and knew it was shaking from the anger of the Most High God.

Through my tears I saw Aaron shaking and Miriam's eyes widened with fear.

"Listen to my word!" Yahweh bellowed from above the cloud.

Both of my siblings fell to the ground. Then they disappeared as the cloud of Yahweh's presence covered them.

Yahweh continued. "When a prophet of the Lord is among you, I reveal myself to him in visions, I speak to him in dreams. But this is not true of my servant, Moses; he is faithful in all my house. With him I speak face to face, clearly and not in riddles; he sees the form of the Lord."[24]

The volume of Yahweh's voice had increased as he spoke each phrase until he finally shouted, "Why then were you not afraid to speak against my servant Moses?"

A crowd had gathered by now, and we heard Miriam and Aaron crying out in anguish from within the cloud of Yahweh's presence.

Then suddenly the cloud of his Presence lifted from above the tent, and I heard a collective gasp from the people watching. Miriam was standing there as white as snow. Leprosy appeared on every exposed inch of her skin from her head to her feet. Then Aaron rose from where he was cowering on the ground and turned toward Miriam.

---

[24] Numbers 12:6–8

"No! No, Moses, please my lord, do not hold against your sister this sin we have so foolishly committed against you. Do not let her flesh be eaten away and her life taken."

The people looked to me, as if I held the keys to life and death. Then I realized that Yahweh was also looking to me, waiting on me.

"Yahweh," I cried out in anguish. "This is my sister, Lord. Please do not hold this sin against her. O God, please heal her!"

The ground ceased trembling, and I heard Yahweh's reply. "If her father had spit in her face, would she not have been in disgrace for seven days, according to the Law I gave you on the mountain? Confine Miriam outside the camp for seven days as you would do for anyone unclean. I will heal her, because you have asked me to do so. But she will suffer this disgrace before all the people, even as she challenged your leadership before all the people."

So Miriam was placed in confinement outside the camp. No one approached her except to push a plate of food near her confinement area several times a day. I, too, took my turn to deliver her food and heard her weeping on and off as I sat a distance away waiting for her to take the food.

That first evening I lay awake as Zipporah slept beside me. I saw a shaft of light shining under the tent flap and slowly slipped outside and found Polaris in the sky.

"Moses," Yahweh spoke softly. "What do you want to ask me?"

I smiled. He always knew, knew when my heart was troubled, when I had questions on my mind.

"Leprosy is often a death sentence, Abba."

"Yes, Moses. Do you question my sense of justice, my son?"

"No, I do not. But you promised me that you will heal my big sister. She will not die."

"Yes, that is my mercy."

"So I am confused. I do not understand how justice and mercy can be meted out in the same instance."

"Yes, that is a hard concept. Moses, do you trust me?"

"Yes, yes, Abba, I do trust you. I know you, know your character. I saw your goodness pass before me on the mountain. You are just, and good. I'm just not used to seeing your justice and your mercy manifest at the same time."

"Moses, one day you will understand this truth, mercy triumphs over judgment."

"Surely, I have already seen this truth played out in your dealings with this fickle people we lead, and even with this fickle leader you have chosen. You are nothing like the gods of the foreign people around us. The people grovel in fear of displeasing these gods who are not gods at all. They spend their lives trying to appease the anger of their gods."

"And I am different, how?" Yahweh quizzed me.

"You are a God who loves his people, who lays down laws and practices to both teach and protect. You are a God who promises good things, a Promised Land to a people who fail you time and time again. You are a God who delights to forgive. You are a God of Mercy that triumphs over judgment."

I felt his smile then. And more than that, I felt his friendship. How wonderful it is to be known by someone, known and loved and trusted. Yahweh was my safe place, my rock, my refuge. But more amazing was that the Eternal Elohim somehow valued my friendship toward him, that my knowing him gave him pleasure, that I was a resting place for him, as he was to me. I returned then to my bed and slept soundly until morning.

SCOUTING OUT THE PROMISED LAND

After Miriam was healed and restored to our camp, Yahweh led us into the desert of Paran. I awoke the first morning in Paran and bolted upright. I quickly dressed and headed outside until I was stopped by the sleepy voice of my wife.

"Moses, where are you going in such a hurry? The sun is barely up. We just set up camp last night. I think everyone is going to take their time getting up this morning."

I just stood there, listening to Zipporah and realizing that I had no idea where I was going in such a hurry. From the moment I opened my eyes I had this feeling that there was something I needed to attend to right away. I had this deep sense of anticipation, but as I searched my mind, I could not think of a single reason to be anticipating anything.

"Moses?" Zipporah continued, but by then I had left the tent to inquire of Yahweh.

These feelings of expectation, anticipation were not mine, so I turned to Yahweh. But before I could utter a word, he spoke.

"Moses, can you feel it?"

"I feel something, Abba, but I don't understand what it is."

"Moses, as my prophet and friend, you are sensing what I am feeling this morning, and I am excited."

"Lord, tell me more."

"You're almost there, Moses. Smell that?"

I looked all around me and took a deep breath through my nose but only inhaled the warm air radiating off the desert sand.

"Moses, the Promised Land is near, so near I can smell it. I want you to experience it, too, so you can encourage the people to fully commit themselves to move forward to that place they've been hearing about since you showed up in the

Egyptian prison camp. Now call the leaders of the tribes and form a scouting party to go up into the land of Canaan."

Now I was excited, too. I gathered the leaders of the community and chose a man from each of the twelve tribes of Israel to join the scouting party. Finally the twelve young men stood before us: Shamma from the tribe of Reuben, Shaphat from the tribe of Simeon, Caleb from the tribe of Judah, Igal from the tribe of Issachar, Hoshea from the tribe of Ephraim, Palti from the tribe of Benjamin, Gaddiel from the tribe of Zebulon, Ammiel from the tribe of Dan, Sethur from the tribe of Asher, Nabhi from the tribe of Naphali, and Geul from the tribe of Gad.

The young men stood shoulder to shoulder with their eyes on me, waiting for their orders.

"Yahweh has chosen each of you for this special mission, my sons. Your job? Explore the land before us, the land of Canaan. See what the land looks like. Are there trees? Mountains? Take note of the people, are they strong or weak, few or many? What are the towns like, walled or un-walled? See what the soil is like. Is it fertile or poor? Do your best to bring back some of the crops of the land."

As the scouting party scattered to gather provisions for the journey, one of the men, my close friend, Hoshea stayed behind and drew near to me.

"Moses, thank you for this opportunity to explore the Promised Land. What an honor it is to serve you and Yahweh in this mission."

I drew Hoshea close to me and hugged him. He was like a son to me. Then I heard Yahweh speaking in my spirit and knew the words were for this young man.

"Hoshea, as you know, your name means salvation. But I want you to know that today Yahweh calls you Joshua, which means Yahweh is salvation. Many challenges will be coming your way, son. You will need to remember in those challenges that Yahweh is your salvation. He carries the answers to each and every problem you may face. You are a leader, Joshua, and many will look to Hoshea for salvation, but there is no salvation in any man. Your new name, Joshua, will remind you that Yahweh is your salvation and the salvation of your people. Always point the people to Yahweh, my son, and you, and they, will be saved."

The people gathered at the edge of the camp as the twelve scouts disappeared over a hill on their way to Canaan.

No one knew how long they would be gone. So we settled into the campsite to wait as long as it took for the men to return.

As the days passed, I often caught myself gazing down the route the men took when they departed camp and saw others doing the same. Those twelve men were brothers, sons, even some young fathers, and each day we prayed for their safety and success on their mission.

Finally, over a month had passed and the scouting party still had not returned. One morning Zipporah caught me gazing down the road and sighing in frustration when there was still no sign of our men.

"Now you know how I felt when you were up on that mountain for forty days, Moses. Come and have some breakfast. They'll be back before you know it."

"And hopefully with good news," I muttered, entering my tent.

Ten days later the shouts of the children told me our scouting party had returned. I hurried down the road to meet the twelve dusty and dirty travelers.

"Look, Abba Moses!" Nahbi shouted. "Here is a cluster of grapes that Sethur and I cut down in the Valley of Eschol."

The grape cluster was so huge that the men had tied it to the middle of a tree branch, each man carrying one end of the branch to bear the weight of the fruit.

"And try these pomegranates and figs!" Joshua called out.

The people were cheering as they drew near to hear the scouts' report of the land.

Joshua spoke up first in a loud voice so all could hear.

"Abba Moses, the Promised Land is everything Yahweh promised, truly flowing with milk and honey. Come taste the fruit of the land."

But some of the others spoke up after Joshua gave his account.

"Yes, the fruit and crops were amazing, but the people who live there are very powerful. They live in large, fortified cities."

"And we saw the Nephilim, descendants of Anak—giants!" Gaddiel gestured wildly over his head to show how greatly the Nephilim towered over him.

By now the excitement of the people had waned as they heard the frightening report of the enemies they would face if they ventured to take land in Canaan.

Caleb stepped up next. "We should go up and take possession of the land as God is showing us to do. We can do it. We can certainly beat them with Yahweh on our side."

"Yes." Joshua joined Caleb. "If God has given us this assignment, he will enable us to do it. Remember how Yahweh has been with us every step of way since we left Egypt. He won't fail us now."

But the other ten scouts banded together and took turns giving negative reports. "We can't attack these people," they warned the now trembling people. "These people are stronger than we are, and Canaan is a wild territory that devours the people trying to tame it. All the people of Canaan are giants, towering over us. We felt like grasshoppers in their presence, like they could just stomp us out with their sandals."

I disbursed the crowd after that. The day had begun in excitement and anticipation but now ended in dread and confusion.

That night I listened as the whole community grumbled against Aaron and me. One man's voice rose louder than the others.

"If only we had died in Egypt or in the desert! Why, oh why, is the Lord bringing us to the 'promised land' only to let us fall by the sword of the Canaanites? We will die here, and our wives and our children will be kidnapped and taken as plunder."

I heard another man pick up the dialogue. "Wouldn't it be better for us to go back to Egypt?"

"Yes! But not with these guides. Let Moses and Aaron die in the wilderness. We will choose a new leader and return to Egypt."

I grabbed Aaron's arm and led him out to the front of the angry mob calling for our death, and we fell together face down in front of the people we had been leading.

I heard Joshua and Caleb call out to the crowd and watched from my place on the sand. They tore their clothes and wept aloud.

"Listen, my brothers," Joshua begged the people. "The land we passed through and explored is wonderful beyond our expectations. If the Lord Yahweh is pleased with us, he will lead us into that land, a land flowing with milk and honey, and he will give us that land. Only do not rebel against the Lord. And do not be afraid of the people of Canaan. We will swallow them up. Their protection is gone, but the Lord is with us. Do not be afraid of them."

The ten scouts mocked Joshua and Caleb. "You're out of your minds. There's no way we can take the Canaanites. You're leading the people into a death march."

"Let's stone these deceivers, and Moses and Aaron as well!"

I felt Aaron trembling as he lay before me. Then I heard a collective gasp from the people who had already begun to gather large stones. I raised my head and saw that the glory of the Lord had appeared at the Tent of Meeting in full view of all the Israelites. They fell back, dropping their stones as they fled from the Glory Cloud rising higher and higher in the desert heat.

"Moses!" I heard the Lord and felt the heat of his great anger. "How long will these people treat me with contempt?" he said.

I sensed impending doom for my people. "No, my Lord, it is me and Aaron they are rebelling against," I pleaded.

"Moses, do not make excuses for this people. How long will they refuse to believe in me, in spite of all the miraculous signs I have performed among them from the day they escaped slavery in Egypt to this day. Manna every day. Water from a rock. A Pillar of Cloud by day and a Pillar of Fire by night, visible signs that have led them every step of the way."

I waited silently as Yahweh continued.

"I have made up my mind, Moses. I will strike them all with a plague and destroy them. But I will make of you a new nation, greater and stronger than this pitiful people."

After Yahweh uttered his promise of condemnation it was as if the whole world paused. No wind blew. The people who had scattered were completely silent as if struck dumb. Even the birds stopped chirping from within the desert shrubs. But words were burning inside of me. Yahweh had given me an assignment, to lead these people to the land of promise, and I could not, would not give up on these people. In my heart I knew that Yahweh still loved them, too.

I bowed low to the ground. "Yahweh. If you destroy your people, the Egyptians will hear about it. By your power you brought these people up from among them. The Egyptians will then tell the people of Canaan about it. They already heard that you, O Lord, are with these people and that you, O Lord, have been seen face to face, that your cloud stays by them, and that you go before them in a pillar of cloud by day and a pillar of fire by night. If you kill all your people at the same time the nations who have heard this report about you will say, 'The Lord wasn't able to bring these people into the land he promised them on oath, so he slaughtered them here in the desert.'

"Now may the Lord's strength be displayed, just as you have declared. This is who you are, Abba!" I was weeping loudly now as I continued. "As you yourself taught me, the Lord is slow to anger, abounding in love and forgiving sin and rebellion. Yet he does not leave the guilty unpunished; he punishes the children for the sin of their fathers to the third and fourth generation. In accordance with your great love for these people, O Yahweh, forgive the sin of your people, just as you have pardoned them again and again from the time they left Egypt until now."[25]

It was as if the earth had been holding its breath while Yahweh lashed out his anger. Then suddenly the stillness ceased and once again I heard the birds, the weeping of the frightened children, and I felt a dry desert wind cooling my hot face.

Yahweh's voice was different when he spoke again. "Moses, I have forgiven them, as you asked. Nevertheless, as surely as I live and as surely as the glory of the Lord fills the earth, not one of the men who saw my glory and the miracles I performed in Egypt and in the desert but who disobeyed me and tested me ten times. Not one of them will ever see the land I promised on oath to their fathers. Not one who has treated me with contempt will ever see it. But because my servants, Caleb and Joshua, who have a different spirit within them and who follow me wholeheartedly, these two and their descendants will inherit my Promised Land. I will bring them back into the land they explored, and they and their descendants will inherit it. Now turn away from Canaan and head back out into the desert.

With a heavy heart, I delivered Yahweh's words to the cowering Israelites. They were weeping aloud as they grasped the consequences of their rebellion.

"As surely as I live, declares the Lord, I will do the very things I heard you say: In this desert your bodies will fall-every one of you twenty years old or more who was counted in the census and who has grumbled against me. Not one of you will enter the land I swore with uplifted hand to make your home, except Caleb son of Jespunneh and Joshua son of Nun. As for your children that you said would be taken as plunder, I will bring them in to enjoy the land you have rejected. But you ... your bodes will fall in the desert. For forty years, one year for each of the forty days you explored the land, you will suffer for your sins and know what it is like to have me against

---

[25] Numbers 14

you. I, the Lord, have spoken, and I will surely do these things to this whole wicked community, which has banded together against me. They will meet their end in this desert; here they will die."[26]

Only sobbing was heard as the people stood huddled together in fear. My heart grieved for them. I couldn't imagine feeling as separated from Yahweh as they must have felt right then.

Then loud coughing interrupted our grieving. It was coming from the ten scouts standing off to the side. We watched in horror as one by one the ten young men gasped for breath in between violent coughing spasms and then fell dead to the ground.

There was weeping throughout the camp all night long. I wept, too, over these young men I had chosen as scouts. "Perhaps I chose unwisely," I wondered. "Where else have I made decisions that hurt my people?"

"Moses," Yahweh interrupted my thoughts yet again. "It's not about you. Stop making it about you and be the leader I have called you to be. Remember, I chose you, and I did not choose unwisely. Do you not understand that it's because you stood in intercession for these thousands of people that they are not all dead in the sand tonight?"

I lifted my head, suddenly grasping this amazing thing Yahweh was saying to me.

"Abba, so you never intended to kill these people and make a new nation out of me and my seed?"

"Oh, yes I did," Yahweh answered firmly. "I am not a man that I should lie."

I bowed my head, rebuked.

"But Moses," Yahweh continued. "I knew that you as a leader and shepherd would never forsake your flock. I knew that you would intercede for your sheep. I was counting on it, counting on you to stand in the gap for the people and plead for their forgiveness. Moses, do you know that I love how we, you and I, lead the people? I chose you, Moses. I saw a father's

---

[26] Numbers 14:28–35

heart in you and knew you would be the one to co-lead these exasperating people. I knew you wouldn't give up on them, and I already knew I would pardon each one when you asked me to. You know me, Moses, and I am so pleased with you that you know me well enough to ask me to pardon these people."

I had no words to respond. I shook my head in wonder of it all, that somehow this stuttering and meek man brought pleasure to the King of the Universe.

The next morning, I awoke to the sounds of troops marching. I ran outside, past my sleeping family and found that men had rallied and were heading toward the high hill country to go into the Promised Land.

"Stop!" I shouted. "Why are you disobeying the Lord's command? This will not succeed. Do not go up, because the Lord is not with you in this, and you will be defeated by your enemies."

But the men just pushed me aside and made their way into Canaanite territory although neither I nor the Ark of the Lord's covenant went with them. On the other side of the hill, they encountered Amalekite and Canaanite soldiers who attacked them and beat them down all the way to Hormah.

Later that day we sorrowfully packed up camp and set out toward the desert along the route to the Red Sea, as Yahweh directed. We left behind the first of the group of men twenty years old and older who had already died, as Yahweh had warned, including the ten scouts.

PREPARING FOR LIFE
IN THE PROMISED LAND

As we traveled, Yahweh began to reveal to me his instructions for life once we reached the land of promise. I knew he had said we would not reach that land for another forty years, which felt like a lifetime. It was strangely comforting to me to hear Yahweh speak of offerings and commands to be followed once we reached there. It was as if he was reciting the proverb, "Hope deferred makes the heart sick, but a longing fulfilled is a tree of life."[27] Our hopes had surely died in the desert, but Yahweh stirred up a longing that we thought had died there, too.

As Yahweh continued to share his instructions, I in turn shared them with the people. I watched as the weight of his words fell on their weary hearts.

"Yes," I encouraged them. "You get it! Yahweh has not given up on you. You are still his chosen people to inhabit his Promised Land. And yes, we will get there, so let's listen intently to his words and prepare ourselves to obey Yahweh in all things."

"So much to remember." I shook my head as I wrote down another dozen or so rules Yahweh had given to me as I slept.

"Moses?"

"Yes, Abba?"

"Zipporah has made something for you. It's a surprise, but she doesn't know that I put it in her heart to make it for you."

"So it will be a gift from you and my wife." I smiled.

I returned to my tent then, hoping Zipporah would give me my gift right away.

---

[27] Proverbs 13:12

"Moses, I have a surprise for you! But wait, you look like you already know about it. Did you snoop in my sewing bag? Did the boys tell you?"

"No, sweet wife. I don't know what the surprise is, but Yahweh told me that you had one for me, and that he put it in your heart to make it for me." I laughed.

"Oh, how wonderful!" Tears sprang into Zipporah's eyes. She handed me a small package wrapped in a linen cloth. I unfolded the linen to find two bright blue tassels.

Tears filled my eyes then as Yahweh spoke into my spirit.

"Yahweh says"—I stopped to wipe my eyes—"I heard you, Moses, wondering how you could remember all the instructions I've been giving you and the people. So, Zipporah and I give you these tassels. Throughout the generations to come you are to make tassels on the corners of your garment, with a blue cord on each tassel. You will have these tassels to look at and so you will remember all the commands of the Lord, that you may obey them and not prostitute yourselves by going after the lusts of your own hearts and eyes. Then you will remember to obey all my commands and will be consecrated to your God. I am the Lord your God who brought you out of Egypt to be your God. I am the Lord your God."

Zipporah ran into my arms, and we wept before the Lord who knew us, knew we were but flesh, people who forgot and made foolish choices. It was as if he said, "Look, here is a token to remind you of who you are, and whose you are."

Zipporah later instructed the young ladies in making hundreds of the silky blue tassels. I recited the words Yahweh had spoken about the tassels as they were handed out to each of our men.

"Never forget," I told them. "Yahweh chose you. He is your God."

BETWEEN THE LIVING AND THE DEAD

The Levites served in the Tabernacle that was set up each time we camped, another visible sign of Yahweh's continued presence among us. But even the Tabernacle of God's presence was not immune from conflict. What began as rumors and complaints among some of the Levites eventually erupted one afternoon into a violent rebellion. Korah, son of Kohath and certain Reubenites, Dathan and Abiram, sons of Eliab became insolent and challenged my authority. Accompanied by a group of about two hundred and fifty influential Israelite leaders, members of the leadership council, they cornered Aaron and me outside the Tabernacle.

"You two have gone too far!" Korah shouted. "We are all Levites, holy to the Lord. Isn't Yahweh with each of us? Why then do you elevate yourselves above the Lord's assembly?"

"Not again," I thought, falling facedown. "I can't, Yahweh, I just can't."

Then Yahweh lifted me up. "Moses, this is not your fight."

I rose and turned to Korah and the men at this side. "Let the Lord decide. Tomorrow morning the Lord will show you who belongs to him and who is holy. You, Korah, and all your followers are to do this: take censers and tomorrow we will gather here at the Tabernacle. You will put fire and incense in your censers before the Lord. And the Lord will choose the ones who are holy.

"You are already recognized by our people," I implored the angry Levites. "Isn't it enough that the God of Israel has separated you Levites from the rest of the community and brought you near himself to do the work of the Lord's Tabernacle and to minister to the community? Now you're trying to get the priesthood, too?"

Dathan and Abiram stepped out from the crowd around Korah. "We won't come to your contest, Moses! Isn't it enough that you brought us out of a land flowing with milk and honey to kill us in this desert? And now you want to lord it over us? You wooed us out of Egypt with promises of our own land flowing with milk and honey, but you have given us nothing but miles and miles of this barren desert."

I didn't trust myself to speak at that point, so I turned my face to Yahweh. "When did I lord anything over these men?" I asked in my spirit. "I've never taken so much as a donkey from their hands, nor have I wronged any of them. Do not accept their offering, O Lord."

I turned once more and faced the crowd. "You will appear here tomorrow, all two hundred and fifty of you, and Aaron and I will appear. Each of you will bring your censor filled with incense, as will Araon and I."

The next morning each man took his censer and filled it with incense and fire and stood at the entrance to the tent.

Suddenly the glory cloud of God's presence rose up before us, and I heard Yahweh's voice in my spirit. "Moses, you and Aaron are to separate yourselves from Korah and the Levites so I can put an end to them at once." I took Aaron's arm and pulled him with me, and we fell to the ground some distance away.

In my spirit I cried out to Yahweh, "O God, God of the spirits of all mankind, will you be angry with the entire assembly when only one man sins?"

I heard Yahweh's response and called out to the people, "Move away from the tents of Korah, Dathan, and Abiram."

Then I got up and approached Korah and his men. I realized that I was not alone. Aaron and the elders were standing with me.

I turned and spoke to those following me. "Yahweh says 'Move away from these wicked men. Don't even touch anything belonging to them or you will be swept away with them.'"

The people quickly separated themselves from Korah, Dathan, and Abiram. The three now stood alone outside their tents with only their wives and children.

"This is how you will know that the Lord has sent me to do all these things and that it was not my idea. If these people die a natural death, then the Lord has not sent me. But if the earth opens up its mouth and swallows them with everything and everyone who belongs to them, and they are buried alive, then you will know that these men have treated the Lord with contempt."

The echo of my voice had barely faded before the ground began to rumble from deep beneath the sand. A huge chasm suddenly opened up and all of Korah's, Dathan's, and Abiram's households and belongings fell into the gap and the earth closed up over them.

Screams pierced the now still air. "Run for your lives! The earth is going to swallow us, too!" the people shouted, running away in all directions.

Then fire came out from the cloud of Yahweh's presence and consumed the rest of the two hundred and fifty followers of Korah.

The Lord instructed the priests to gather the discarded censers of the fallen from among the ashes of their remains. They were to hammer out the bronze censers into sheets of bronze to overlay the altar.

I watched as the priests sifted through the ashes, the stench of burned flesh assaulting my senses, and I wondered why Yahweh wanted us to save those misused censers. In my spirit I heard his answers.

"Moses, the censers were holy, dedicated to me. They were misused by the Levites who sinned at the cost of their lives, but the censers remain holy, now purified by fire. They are mine. Now overlay my altar with them as a sign of remembrance that only my priests, descendants of Aaron may approach my altar to burn incense."

Another crowd gathered outside the tent as the priests were completing their assignment at the altar. I turned to face them.

"You have killed the Lord's people!" they shouted.

Suddenly the Glory Cloud of Yahweh's presence descended over the Tabernacle. I heard the Lord's angry whisper. "Moses, you and Aaron get away from these people so I can put an end to them once and for all!"

I shouted to Aaron, "Quickly, take your censer and fill it with incense and fire from Yahweh's altar. Then run to the people and make atonement for them!"

Aaron's face was distorted at first as he considered what I was asking him to do. I could imagine his reasoning as he was directed to run toward the ones calling for his removal, when everything inside him was telling him to get as far away from them as possible. He stopped and turned toward the angry crowd and gasped in horror. I turned, too, and saw that a plague had already begun. People were clawing at their throats, gasping for air, and some had already dropped to the ground.

So we ran with our incense into the midst of the screaming plague-stricken crowd. Aaron offered the incense and made atonement for the people. He stood between the living and the dead, and the plague stopped. However, in that brief amount of time nearly fifteen thousand of our people had died, in addition to those taken with Korah and his followers.

The wailing never stopped the whole night long. Some people camped outside the Tent of Meeting, too fearful to return to their tents.

In my tent, I cried out to Yahweh. "Mercy, mercy. You did it again, Abba! You said you would destroy all the people, but you allowed my brother and me to once again plead for their forgiveness, and they are alive this morning. I don't know how long I can take this extreme emotional stress, Yahweh, watching my people being swallowed up by an earthquake, burned alive by your fire, overtaken by plague that strangles the very life out of them. And then watching the plague suddenly stop and recede, people nearly suffocated taking deep breaths again."

"Remember what I told you, Moses? I choose the ones to come near to me. I am here, now come."

I collapsed then onto my bed and wept until I was totally drained, then lay in the physical awareness of Jehovah's embrace until morning. Then puffy faced, but held, I rose to deliver his words once again.

I heard Yahweh's voice as I left my home and headed to the Tent of Meeting.

"Moses, I know that you are a humble man and would rather walk away than defend yourself when the people challenge your authority."

I nodded in agreement. I was still reeling from the Levites' accusations and had no strength within me for another challenge.

"I will deal with them myself," Yahweh continued. "Tell Aaron and the leaders of each of the tribes to find and bring me a staff cut from one of the trees growing on the side of the mountain. Each leader is to write their name on their staff and turn it over to you."

I delivered Yahweh's instructions to the tribal leaders, and they scattered to harvest their staffs, stripped them of leaves, and brought them to me at the Tent of Meeting. I could see the leaders comparing their staffs to see whose was longer, smoother, stronger than their co-leaders.

That evening, in their presence, I entered the Tent and placed the staffs side by side before the Lord, as he had told me to do.

I heard the leaders whispering among themselves. "What's this all about? I spent the better part of the day choosing the sturdiest and straightest branch I could find, and now we're just going to leave them all here in the Tent of Meeting?"

I could not answer their questions. Yahweh had not yet explained to me what this exercise of the staffs was all about. So I left the Tent of Meeting and went home to my family for the night.

The next morning Yahweh's voice roused me from my sleep. "Moses, get up and go to the Tent of Meeting. I will meet you there."

I smiled and shrugged off my sleepiness. If Yahweh asked me to climb a tree or jump into a well, with the promise that he would meet me there, I would do it. "You know I would go anywhere you ask just so long as you promise to meet me there," I prayed as I hurried to the tent. The people saw me heading for the tent and began to follow me across the compound.

Nearly there, my senses were assaulted with the sweet fragrance of almond blossoms wafting out of the Tent of Meeting. I hurried inside and found the twelve staffs lying where I'd placed them the day before. Eleven of the staffs were the same bare, smooth branches, but the almond tree branch that bore my brother's name had almond leaves sprouting out the top. I lifted it up for a closer look and saw that the staff had not only sprouted, budded, and blossomed, but there were ripe almonds ready to be harvested.

I gathered up all twelve staffs and went outside the Tent where the people waited for me.

I gave each of the leaders the staff bearing their name and then laid the almond laden branch in the arms of my brother, Aaron. I heard gasps all around, but no one said a word.

"Yahweh has spoken today. These are his words to the people of Israel. Aaron's staff shall remain in the tent to remind any who challenge my leaders. This will put an end to their grumbling against me, so they will not die."

My heart thrilled to receive this visible token from Yahweh, something we could look at and touch and remember his words.

"Thank you, Abba," I breathed a prayer. "You know we are but dust, so you give us signs and wonders to confirm your words. I am humbled and so thankful."

I could see Aaron weeping silently and knew he was feeling the same.

But somehow the other tribal leaders did not take comfort in Yahweh's visible sign. They began to cry out, "But we will die, we are all lost," they wailed. "Now if anyone of us even approaches the tabernacle of the Lord, we will die. Now we're all going to die."

I looked at Aaron, and he shook his head in disbelief.

"Oh, Yahweh, if only they knew you as I do," I prayed.

"Show them, my son. Show them."

WATER FROM THE ROCK

I continued to instruct the Levites and priests as Yahweh directed as we traveled. Finally, in the first month we reached the Desert of Zin and set up camp in Kadesh. There my sister, Miriam, became very sick and died. Aaron and I buried her in Kadesh, and the community mourned her passing for several days.

Kadesh was a barren place. Nothing grew in the dry sand, and we could not locate a source of water. It wasn't long before the people gathered before Aaron and me and challenged us again.

"We should have died with our brothers before the Lord. At least that would have been quicker than dying of thirst and watching our children die of thirst. Why did you bring us here, so we and our livestock could perish in the sand? This is a terrible place. There is nothing to eat, no grain or figs or fruit, and there is no water."

I heard Yahweh calling me to the Tent of Meeting. I grabbed Aaron's arm and led him to the tent entrance. We fell facedown before the Lord, and he responded immediately as the cloud of his glory settled around us.

"Both of you take Aaron's staff and go and gather the people around that great rock near the tent," Yahweh commanded. "You are to speak the words I give you to that rock in front of all Israel, and it will pour out water."

"Oh," I thought. "We've done this before. Yahweh saved us once before by bringing water out of a rock. Don't they remember?"

I shook my head in anger. Grabbing Aaron's staff and pulling Aaron along by his sleeve I ran to the rock.

"Listen, you rebels, do I have to make water flow from a rock to satisfy you?" I glared at the people who were now cowering before me as I released my anger and frustration on them.

I turned to Aaron, then drew back my arm and smashed the staff onto the rock with all my strength. The sound of the wood striking the massive rock reverberated across the camp. Then we watched as water burst from the rock, gushing out on the desert floor.

The people rushed to fill bowls and jugs with the fresh water for their families and animals, then retreated to their tents. I stood watching the crowd disburse, my arms folded angrily across my chest.

Then Aaron and I were left alone at the rock, where water continued to trickle down.

Aaron turned to face me but backed away slowly as he saw my angry stance.

Finally, Aaron spoke softly. "Moses, isn't this a good thing? Just like the staff when it bore almonds overnight, a visible sign of God's word? Why are you so angry?"

I shook my head. Why was I so angry? Why wasn't I thanking Yahweh for providing once again? Something was wrong. I suddenly realized that I was alone with my thoughts. Yahweh was not speaking to me.

"Yahweh, where are you?" I cried out, desperate for his presence to return.

"Moses, what have you done?"

"What? What have I done? I did what you told me to do to make water flow from the rock."

"Moses, what did I tell you to do?"

I stopped and rehearsed the words Yahweh had said to me. It wasn't the same as the first rock that released water. He had told me to strike that rock. This time he told me to speak to the rock.

"I needed you to trust me and do what I told you to do, not rely on the power of your anger as if I needed the might of your blow to bring water out of the rock."

I sunk to the ground. Aaron quickly followed.

"Moses, you did not trust in me enough to honor me as holy in the sight of all Israel by obeying my exact instructions to you. You added anger and the strength of your own arm to my instructions, as if the very words I gave you to speak were not powerful enough without your might added to the mix. I still brought forth the water, because your people are my people, and I promised to never forsake you, but you and Aaron will not bring this community into the land I am giving them."

Aaron left me there, weeping before the Lord. He ran to my tent, and soon my beloved Zipporah crouched down alongside me. "Moses, get up, come home."

"No," I gasped out between my sobs. "He is my friend; I will not leave him until he speaks to me. Tho he slay me, yet will I trust him."

I lay before the Lord the entire night as darkness crept over the camp. And Yahweh came, his glory cloud slowly covering me.

"Will you choose someone else to lead the people?" I asked.

"No, I still choose you, Moses. I see your heart. I know you are grieving. But what are you grieving, the fact that you will not enter the Promised Land?"

"No, my Lord. You know my heart. I am grieving that I disappointed my friend. Please forgive me for hurting your heart, Yahweh."

Then Yahweh wrapped me in the cloud of his glory. I felt waves of liquid love causing my body to heave in spasms as I lay there on the sand. Then shalom enveloped me, unexplainable peace, nothing missing, nothing lacking. I raised my head and took deep breaths of Yahweh's shalom.

I lay spent before the Tabernacle until nearly dawn. Then Yahweh's whisper broke the stillness of the night. "Go home now. Zipporah is worried and hasn't slept a wink waiting for your return. And yes, I will go with you."

New tears sprang into my eyes. He remembered that I had refused to go anywhere without him, and his words echoed the promise I'd made to him earlier, that I'd go anywhere as long as he promised to meet me there. I couldn't think anymore about the consequences of my actions, and his declaration that I would not lead the people into the land of promise. I could only draw near to him and choose to follow him tonight, tomorrow, one minute at a time, and leave the future, my future in the hands of the one who called me his friend.

ENCOUNTER WITH THE EDOMITES

The pillar of cloud wavered in the early morning sun and slowly began to drift away from Kadesh. I was not unhappy leaving this place of disappointment. I sought Yahweh's directions as we packed up the camp.

"Head toward the people of Edom, your brothers," Yahweh advised.

I lifted my eyes to gaze at the rolling hills of Seir, the land Yahweh had given to Jacob's twin brother, Esau. Our families had separated long ago, before Israel's descendants became slaves in Egypt.

I remembered the stories my family recited about Jacob's first meeting with Esau as he returned from his brief self-imposed exile in Haran. He feared for his life and the lives of his wives and children after his deceitful theft of the first-born birthright from his brother, Esau.

I wondered to myself if Esau's descendants, the Edomites still bore a grudge against the people of Israel. Yahweh had warned me that he had given Esau the land of Mount Seir as his possession. Mount Seir was not to be part of our "promised land," so I knew we were not to try to take any territory from them. But we did need to pass through their land to get to the territory on the other side.

I sent messengers ahead to the king of Edom seeking permission to pass through their country, appealing to our blood connection. A troop of soldiers came out to meet my messengers, swords at their sides. My servant, Abisha, shared later how he had bowed low to the ground, then stepped out from the others to deliver my words.

"This is what your brother, Israel, says. Surely you have heard of the hardships of your brother, how we were exiled in

Egypt, mistreated and enslaved for many years. We cried out to the Lord, and he sent his angel to lead us out of captivity."

The king stood stone-faced, giving no sign of his reaction.

Abisha continued. "Now we stand at Kadesh, a town on the edge of your territory. Please allow us to pass through your land. We will avoid trampling any fields or vineyard and will not take any water from your wells. We will follow the main road and not turn to the right or left until we have passed through your borders."

Then Edom shouted his response. "No!"

Abisha spoke up to assure the king that we honored their God-given ownership of the land of Edom, but the king cut him right off.

"You may not pass through our land. If you as much as set a foot on this land, we will march out and attack you with our swords."

As he spoke, a large contingent of armed soldiers came out of the camp and stood behind their king. Abisha and the others then turned, without a word, and returned to our camp.

I watched Abisha and the others enter the camp. I could sense their frustration as they approached me near the Tent of Meeting.

"He said no, Moses," Abisha complained bitterly. "He wouldn't listen to my explanation that we weren't interested in taking their land, just called his troops and they stood in front of us to block our way. Should we attack? I know we can take them!"

"No, Abisha. Yahweh gave them their land, and they have the right to turn us away. We will have to travel around Mount Seir."

Abisha was angry. The people were angry.

I looked out over our disgruntled company and heard Yahweh's voice.

"Moses, this delay, about a day's journey, is unfortunate, but there is a lesson to receive that you and my people will need to remember for centuries to come."

I was surprised at Yahweh's words. I thought it was just an old relationship problem coming back to haunt us and keep us from moving forward. I waited for Yahweh to continue.

"One day Israel will be in this same position as Edom was today. Enemies will surround them, try to make treaties and take their land. I gave Edom their land, the land surrounding Mount Seir. I want you to understand that the gifts I give are without revocation. Just as I did not allow you to illegally infiltrate Edom's land, so I will defend Israel when any other nation comes to trespass on their land, from now through centuries to come."

I relayed Yahweh's promise to the people. As they received his truth, I saw the anger fade from their faces, and they nodded in understanding of the faithfulness of our God.

We left the borders of Edom and traveled to Mount Hor, on the edge of Edom. There Yahweh called Aaron and me to scale the mountain as the people set up camp.

My brother and I stood on the mountain top waiting for Yahweh's words. There was a strange stillness surrounding us. Then Yahweh's somber voice broke the silence.

"Aaron will die here, on this mountain. He will not enter the Promised Land because both of you dishonored me at the waters of Meribah."

My eyes filled with tears, and I grabbed my brother and held him close to my heart.

"Moses, call your nephew, Eleazar, Aaron's son to join us on the mountain."

I left Aaron standing before the Lord and went down the mountain. "Eleazar, come with me. Yahweh is calling for you to take your father's place as priest."

Eleazar fell to the ground and cried out in distress. "Is my father still alive?"

"Yes, my son, but he will pass away on the mountaintop. Come up with me."

All of Israel watched as I led Eleazar up the mountain path. Eleazar ran to his father, and they wept in each other's arms.

"Abba," Eleazar sobbed. "How can I lose you? How can I be a priest for these people without your guidance?"

Aaron's voice was weak as he answered. "Yahweh will be with you, son. And Uncle Moses will help you to hear Yahweh's voice."

I removed the priestly garments from my brother and put them on Eleazar. Aaron was visibly trembling so Eleazar and I held his arms and walked him to a nearby flat rock where he could recline. Then we sat alongside this man of God, each of us holding one of his hands, as he breathed his last. We wept together for some time, then buried Aaron on the mountain top. Then Yahweh called us to return to the people.[28]

When the camp saw that Aaron was not with us, cries of sorrow and mourning erupted. We honored and mourned Aaron for thirty days.

---

[28] Numbers 20:22–28

HORMAH

Still reeling from Aaron's passing, we broke camp and continued to skirt along the outer borders of Edom. Several scouts went on ahead. Coming upon a clearing they ran right into a contingent of troops led by the Canaanite king of Arad. The Canaanites quickly encircled the scouts and captured them, but one man following close behind saw the incident and sprinted back to the people.

"Moses, the king of Arad has captured the scouts!"

The men of the camp came running. One leader spoke up. "Shall we attack this army that has kidnapped our young men? What does the Lord say? We are ready. If Yahweh will deliver these people into our hands, we will totally destroy their cities!"

I heard Yahweh's voice then, just a whisper. "I hear your plea for your young men. I will deliver the Canaanite army into your hands."

Our troops rose up and ran to the waiting Canaanite army. They totally destroyed the enemy army and all their towns, and named the place Hormah, which means destruction.

Buoyed on by our success in battle, we continued our journey around Edom, along the route to the Red Sea. They expected more victories, but instead traveled on day after day, in the dry desert heat, with no end in sight.

"We should have forced Edom to let us pass!" some people complained.

"Look what we did to Arad! Why did we let Edom have their way and keep us going around their land in this miserable heat?"

I heard their grumbling and knew Yahweh was listening, too. Finally, the men of the camp approached me directly.

"Where are you leading us, Moses? To die here in the desert? We have no water, no food. We should have died with Aaron."

I could feel Yahweh's anger. Then I heard the screams of my people.

"Moses, venomous snakes are crawling into the camp! Look, my daughter was bit and she's dying."

"My mother and father were both bit and died within minutes."

The leaders ran to me, some carrying the dead bodies of their children. "We have sinned against the Lord when we spoke against the Lord and against you, Moses. Please pray for us that Yahweh will remove the snakes."

I fell on my face before the Lord. "Yahweh, my people are dying. Yahweh, forgive us, save your people. Remove the snakes, just as you kept us safe in the land of Goshen back in Egypt."

I heard Yahweh's instructions. "Here is what you must do. Make a snake out of bronze and put it on a pole."

I shook my head in confusion. Yahweh gave no mention of the people dying from the snake bites as their cries filled the air. I called for the craftsmen of the camp, workers in bronze, and gave them Yahweh's assignment. How long would it take to sculpt a metal snake? And how would this help my people as they continued to get bitten and die?

Finally, the bronze snake was finished and erected on a pole. People lay dying all around the camp. I lifted up the snake as Yahweh directed and walked through the camp calling to the people.

"Look! Set your eyes on the snake."

A listless grandfather opened his eyes as he lay dying outside his tent.

"You, sir, look at the snake," I called out to him.

I heard a young man who stood next to the dying man, grumbling in frustration. "Why should he look at your sculpture?"

The older man turned his face upwards and saw the snake on the pole. Suddenly he sat upright and began gulping fresh air into his lungs. Then he got to his feet and ran alongside me shouting to the sick and dying. "Do what Yahweh says. Look to the snake and live."

We buried our dead and mourned there on the borders of Edom for several more days. The snakes were gone, and everyone who looked to the snake on the pole had recovered.

I withdrew to the mountainside as the camp recovered, needing some time alone with Yahweh.

Yahweh initiated the conversation. "Tell me what you are thinking, Moses."

"I don't know what to think, Yahweh. I understand that you allowed the snakes to enter the camp because of the peoples' rebellion. But I prayed for the people, and they repented, yet the snakes continued to bite, and people continued to die."

I broke out weeping and could not speak for some time. Yahweh's presence came and enveloped me as I wept.

"So many died ..."

"Yes."

"Some innocent ones, children, who had nothing to do with the grumbling. I don't understand, Yahweh."

"Come near, my son."

"I'm here."

"No, come closer."

I realized that in my confusion and sorrow I had been holding back a part of my heart from Yahweh. I collapsed on the ground and sobbed until I was spent.

"I'm here, Lord."

"Now look to me, Moses, just as you asked the people to do with the bronze snake. Look to me when you are desperate, when you are angry, when you are confused, when you don't understand how a piece of crafted bronze could heal a venomous snake bite."

"Those who look to me are radiant; they will never be put to shame."[29]

"I still don't understand."

---

[29] Psalm 34:5

"One day you will. Can you trust me for now until that day comes?"

"Yes, I trust you, Abba, even when I cannot understand. Only don't ever leave me. Remember, I don't want to go anywhere unless you're coming with me."

"I remember. Come, it's time to move on from this place. I have refreshment for you just up the road in Beer. Tell the people."

True to his word, Yahweh led us to an overflowing well in Beer. The people rejoiced. The children splashed about in the icy water. I watched nearby, with a cup of water in my hand as they frolicked and sang, "Spring up, O well! Sing about it!"

I lifted my eyes, as if to see if Yahweh was also watching the fun. Then I felt Yahweh right beside me, smiling and sharing his peoples' joy.

SIHON AND OG

We were not permitted to go to battle with our relatives, the Edomites, but I was confused when we approached the land of the Amorites, who were not our ancestors, that Yahweh gave us similar instructions.

I sent messengers ahead of our company to seek permission from Sihon, king of the Amorites, to pass through his land. Again, our messengers assured the king that we did not wish to take anything from him or his people, just to travel through to the other side.

Sihon denied our entry, and we retreated. I gathered my elders to plot a route around Amorite territory, but army scouts came rushing in with a change in plans.

"King Sihon has mustered his entire army and is even now marching into the desert toward our camp!"

I knew that Amorite territory was part of what Yahweh had shown me to be our Promised Land. He had told our father, Abraham that after four hundred years of captivity in Egypt our people would return to Canaan and conquer the Amorites, but that the iniquity of the Amorites was not yet complete at that time.[30]

"Is it time?" I prayed silently. "Have these people reached a level of evil that they can no longer recover from?" Even as I prayed, I shuddered to think that someone could sink to such a state that they no longer could recover and be in relationship with God. "Please, Lord, don't let me ever fall out of your hands."

He did not answer except that I felt a wind blowing at my back, pushing me toward my awaiting soldiers.

"Is this the time when we will begin to possess the land of promise?" I prayed as we marched out to meet our enemies.

---

[30] Genesis 15:13–16

The Amorite army breached our camp at Jahaz, but Yahweh's people fought valiantly, put the king to the sword, and took over a large portion of Amorite territory. All their cities were now occupied with Israelites, including the city of Heshbon where the king had resided.

From Heshbon, I sent spies to Jazer, and we proceeded to drive out all the Amorites living there. The Israelites then turned toward Bashan, only to learn that King Og of Bashon and his entire army were marching toward them.

My troops turned to me for guidance. They knew the reputation of Og.

Og was one of the giants that had stymied our spies forty years ago. A huge man, over twelve feet high, he led a fierce army of accomplished soldiers.

I stepped up in front of my troops and told them exactly what Yahweh had spoken to my heart. "The Lord Yahweh says 'Do not be afraid of Og. Today I am handing him over to you along with all his troops and his land. Do to him what you did to King Sihon.'"

A battle cry instantly arose from my troops, and they rose as one and ran toward their enemies. Armed with their meager weapons and the promise of Yahweh they struck down every last soldier, including King Og and his sons. Not one survived. Then we entered Bashan and located the royal quarters. One of my men pulled me along to Og's personal chambers. I gasped as I saw a huge bed made of iron, at least thirteen and a half feet long! I fell to my knees and worshiped the God of Angel Armies who had delivered this giant into our hands that very day.

And Israel took over Bashan and all the towns surrounding it, adding to our territory in the Promised Land.

BEHIND THE SCENES

Our reputation as a conquering army was growing with each battle. I did not know it at the time, but Balak, the King of Moab was terrified that we would turn our sights on Moab next. Especially since we were now encamped in his backyard, the plains of Moab along the Jordan River, just across from Jericho.

Balak did not, however, muster his large troops. Instead, he tried a different strategy. Neither I nor the Israelites were even aware of Balak's strategy, cr its failure until sometime later when I awoke one Sabbath morning from a long night of intense dreaming.

"Moses," Yahweh called to me as I slept.

"Yes, Lord?"

"Do you think that hearing my voice changes a person forever?"

I didn't hesitate in my response. "Yes, my Lord, it's like you told me once, how all the kings of the earth will one day rise up and give you thanks when they hear your voice, as I do."

Yahweh smiled in pleasure that I remembered what he'd taught me.

"Yet not everyone is changed when they have the privilege of hearing me speak."

Then, in my dream, Yahweh told me the story of a prophet named Balaam who had threatened our people as we camped unaware by the plains of Moab.

"Balaam was a sorcerer who was occasionally hired by local leaders to cast spells and divination against their enemies. A lover of money and fine things, Balaam delivered curses to the highest bidder. Even though Balaam did not worship me, he was well aware of my authority over all other spirits.

"While you were camped along the Jordan River, Balak, king of Moab sent princes to Balaam to hire him to curse Israel in exchange for gold and jewels. Balaam was more than willing to comply, but my spirit created such an uneasiness in his spirit that he did not immediately agree to curse Israel. Balaam asked the messengers to stay with him overnight while he inquired of me as to whether or not to curse you. But before Balaam even began to pray I spoke to him.

"What are you doing here, Balaam?" Yahweh had asked him. "Who are these men sleeping in your camp?"

In my dream, a trembling Balaam told Yahweh what Balak had requested. "He told me about this nation that came from Egypt that had multiplied and now covered the land and threatened Moab's existence. He asked me to put a spell on them so his armies could defeat the people called Israel."

I now groaned in my sleep. I realized that what Yahweh was describing to me actually took place while my people lay camped out on the plains below the mountain where Balaam met with the princes.

Yahweh continued. "I told Balaam in no uncertain terms he was not to go with these princes to curse my people."

I released the breath I hadn't known I was holding.

Yahweh continued. "Balaam sent the princes away the next morning. 'Go back to your own country,' he said. 'Yahweh has refused to let me go with you.'

"But Balak was not dissuaded so easily. More princes were sent to Balaam, promising an even greater payment to do the king's bidding.

"At first Balaam stood his ground. 'Even if Balak gave me his palace filled with silver and gold I could not do anything great or small to go beyond the command of the Lord my God.'

"But Balaam was plotting in his mind how he could manipulate me and get his way. 'Let me pray about it again,' he told the princes. 'Maybe God will change his mind. Stay overnight and I will see what he says to me.'"

I could hardly believe that all this wrangling was going on while we camped unknowingly in the valley below.

"This time I told Balaam he could go with the princes, but he was only to speak what I told him to say. He put on a noncommittal face, but I knew that in his mind he was already spending the treasure the princes had promised him.

"Balaam saddled his donkey and followed the Moabite princes. I was very angry with him for speaking out of both sides of his mouth, thinking that I, Yahweh, was ignorant of his deceitfulness.

"As Balaam's donkey plodded along the mountain path, I stationed an angel of the Lord holding a large sword directly in his path. Balaam didn't see the angel, nor did his servants, but I opened the eyes of the donkey to see the danger in the road. Immediately the donkey veered off the road into a field and stopped."

In my dream I saw Balaam fall off the donkey, grab a large stick, and begin beating the beast until it bleated in distress. Then Balaam's servants pushed and pulled until the donkey returned to the road. Balaam mounted again and they headed into a narrow path between two vineyards, with stone walls on either side of the path. The Angel of the Lord again appeared, sword drawn, and the donkey lunged to the side, scraping Balaam's foot against the rough wall.

Still holding the stick, Balaam beat the donkey once more until it finally started moving again. They came to a very narrow place in the path where there was no room for the donkey to turn around. The Angel stood right in front of them. So the donkey simply lay down in the path and Balaam again tumbled to the ground.

At that point, Zipporah told me later, I actually laughed out loud in my sleep. Until Balaam began to beat the poor donkey incessantly until stripes of blood flowed down his side.

Then in my dream, I heard a strange but plaintive wailing and listened as the donkey's bleating turned into words. "Why are you beating me, master?" it wailed. "Have I ever done anything like this to you before? Haven't I always taken you wherever you wanted to go?"

Then Yahweh opened Balaam's eyes so he, too, could see the angry Angel of the Lord standing right in front of him, sword raised as if to strike. Balaam immediately fell on his face before the Angel.

"I swear to you," the Angel said. "If your donkey had not turned away from me these three times you would be dead on the road. Your path, Balaam is a reckless one before me, the Lord of all the earth."

Then Balaam confessed his deceit. "I won't go with the princes if you are not pleased, my Lord."

"You may go with them," Yahweh told him sternly. "But only speak what I tell you."

A sobered Balaam and his donkey continued without further incident until they reached Balak, king of Moab who was waiting impatiently for their arrival. "Didn't I tell you this assignment was urgent?" he scolded Balaam. "Why didn't you come sooner? Don't you know what treasures I have for you?"

Balaam did not explain what had happened along the way, allowing Balak to see his injured donkey and make his own judgments. "Well, I'm here now, Balak, but I'm telling you up front. I come as a prophet of God. I can only speak what God puts in my mouth."

Then Balak proceeded to lead Balaam to a barren height overlooking the Israeli troops in the valley below. Balak preceded this meeting by sacrificing sheep and cattle to his gods. Then he led Balaam to the edge of the mountaintop.

"Look, Prophet. There they are, the people called Israel."

Balaam followed with his eyes and saw God's people outside their tents, just starting their day.

"Those are the people I need you to curse. Once you've cursed them, then you get paid."

Balaam wet his lips anxiously. Would Yahweh allow him to speak a curse over the people? Not hearing any instructions from Yahweh, Balaam bought some time. He called for seven altars to be erected. Then he instructed the princes to bring him seven bulls and seven rams. Balak joined Balaam in sacrificing one bull and one ram on each of the seven altars. Then Balak turned and looked to Balaam to deliver the word curse he had bargained for.

"Stay with your offering, Balak, and let me go aside and inquire of the Lord. Maybe he's ready to deliver your curse now."

My dream was interrupted by a loud belly laugh. I looked about for the source of the outburst and found it was Yahweh himself. He was clutching his side as he sputtered out "as if the slaughter of fourteen animals would somehow butter me up enough to curse my people!"

Although I found myself very uncomfortable with the unspoken tension coursing through the dream, Yahweh seemed to think it was laughable. I looked at him, and he just nodded, as if to say, just wait.

Balaam returned from a short time of prayer.

Balak stood up and turned to him. "Well?"

"The Lord gave me a message to deliver to you, Balak," he began. He closed his eyes and began to hum. Then he sang out an oracle, a story straight from the mouth of Yahweh:

> "Balak brought me from Aram,
> the King of Moab from the eastern mountains.
> 'Come,' he said, 'curse Jacob for me;
> come, denounce Israel.'
> How can I curse
> those whom God has not cursed?
> How can I denounce
> those whom the Lord has not denounced?
> From the rocky peaks I see them,
> from the heights I view them.
> I see a people who live apart
> and do not consider themselves one of the nations.
> Who can count the dust of Jacob,
> or number the fourth part of Israel?
> Let me die the death of the righteous,
> and may my end be like theirs!"[31]

When the last note of the song faded, Balak shouted, "Shut up, Prophet! What have you done? I brought you to curse my enemies, but you've done nothing but bless them!"

---

[31] Numbers 23:7–10

Balaam hung his head, thinking of the treasure that he would not be receiving. "I told you that I must only speak what the Lord puts in my mouth."

Balak wasn't giving up so easy. "Come on, let's go to another lookout where you'll get a different view of the people. Then you can curse them."

Balaam listened briefly, heard nothing from the Lord, so he agreed to follow Balak to the next overlook, the field of Zophim at the top of Mount Pisgah. There he and Balak repeated the building of seven altars, and the sacrifice of another seven rams and seven bulls. Then Balaam stepped aside to inquire of the Lord.

This time Balaam returned more quickly to the altar where Balak was waiting.

"Perhaps the speediness of his return means a more favorable outcome this time," Balak thought.

Once again, Balaam closed his eyes and sang out another oracle from the Lord:

> "Arise, Balak, and listen;
> hear me, son of Zippor.
> God is not a man that he should lie,
> nor a son of man that he should change
> his mind.
> Does he speak and then not act?
> Does he promise and not fulfill?
> I have received a command to bless;
> he has blessed, and I cannot change it.
>
> "No misfortune is seen in Jacob,
> no misery observed in Israel.
> The LORD their God is with them;
> the shout of the King is among them.
> God brought them out of Egypt;
> they have the strength of a wild ox.
> There is no sorcery against Jacob,
> no divination against Israel.
> It will now be said of Jacob
> and of Israel, See what God has done!
> The people rise like a lioness;

they rouse themselves like a lion
that does not rest till he devours his prey
and drinks the blood of his victims."[32]

Balak was furious. "If you can't curse them, at least do not bless them!" he shouted.

Balaam only shook his head. "I have to speak what he puts in my mouth. I can do no more and no less."

Still Balak persisted. "Let's try one more place. Maybe your God will allow you to curse them from there."

Balaam followed Balak to the top of Peor, overlooking the wasteland.

"Surely in this desolate place that is already cursed in drought, surely here he will permit you to deliver a curse."

They repeated the seven-fold offerings on seven new altars in the third location. This time Balaam did not attempt to step away and revert to his familiar ways of manipulation and sorcery to conjure up a curse on Israel. God's words were already coursing through his chest and erupting through his open mouth. In fact, Balaam seemed bewildered as if the words coming out of his mouth surprised even himself. He knew without a doubt that the very Spirit of God was speaking the oracle that came forth.

"The oracle of Balaam, son of Beor,
the oracle of one whose eye sees clearly,
the oracle of one who hears the words of God,
who sees a vision from the Almighty,
who falls prostrate, and whose eyes are opened.
How beautiful are your tents, O Jacob,
your dwelling places, O Israel!
Like valleys they spread out,
like gardens beside a river,
like aloes planted by the Lord,
like cedars beside the waters.
Water will flow from their buckets;
their seed will have abundant water.
Their king will be greater than Agag;

---

[32] Numbers 23:18–24

their kingdom will be exalted.
God brought them out of Egypt;
they have the strength of a wild ox,
they devour hostile nations
and break their bones in pieces;
with their arrows they pierce them.
Like a lion they crouch and lie down,
like a lioness—who dares to rouse them?
May those who bless you be blessed
and those who curse you be cursed!"[33]

Balak clapped his hands loudly. "Stop, stop! I called you to curse my enemies, but you have blessed them instead, three times. Go, leave and return to your home. You will not receive one penny of the treasure I had planned for you. Your God is to blame for that."

Balaam stepped out from the men that were pushing him away from their angry king. "I told you from the first time you summoned me that I could not, would not speak anything of my own accord, good or bad, to go beyond what Yahweh commanded. Even if you emptied the treasures of your palace, the silver and the gold, I cannot speak unless I speak his words."

Balak shook himself as if to remove the taint of Balaam's words, but Balaam called out to him as he fled my voice.

"Now hear what this people will do to your people in the days to come:

> "The oracle of Balaam, son of Beor,
> the oracle of one whose eye sees clearly,
> the oracle of one who hears the words of God,
> who has knowledge from the Most High,
> who sees a vision from the Almighty,
> who falls prostrate, and whose eyes are opened.
> I see him, but not now;
> I behold him, but not near.
> A star will come out of Jacob;
> A scepter will rise out of Israel.

---

[33] Numbers 24:3–9

He will crush the foreheads of Moab,
the skulls of all the sons of Sheth.
Edom will be conquered,
but Israel will grow strong.
A ruler will come out of Jacob
and destroy the survivors of the city."[34]

"Moses, Moses, wake up!" I felt Zipporah shaking me gently. "Are you weeping in your sleep, my husband?"

I opened my eyes and laughed out loud, startling my frightened wife. "No, no, it's all good, sweet wife. I am not weeping. I am laughing and Yahweh is laughing with me. Let me tell you about my dream."

I shared every vivid detail of what Yahweh had shown me in my sleep.

"So you see, Zipporah, this is what Yahweh does while we sleep. He protects us from curses and blesses us instead. He wins our battles as we rest in his goodness. Surely, he who watches over Israel does not slumber and does not sleep, blessed be his name forever."

I was careful to write down every word of the Oracles of Balaam. I knew they held prophecies and words of encouragement not just for me, but for generations to come.

Then I rested once more in Yahweh's care.

---

[34] Numbers 24:15–19

BALAAM'S REVENGE

I did not share with the people my dream of Yahweh thwarting Balak's curses against Israel, although I did share with some of the elders the oracles I had written down at Yahweh's request.

Yahweh had not directed us to move from Shittim, so we continued to camp on the edge of Moab. The land was flat and easy to traverse, and Yahweh had already provided a water source. Even though we all knew Yahweh had other lands for us to conquer as we took the promised land as our own, the people were content to stay right where they were.

We were not aware that Balaam was still plotting his sorcery against us as we camped in that place so near to our enemy. If he could not manage to curse us with his words, he found another way to breach the Israelite stronghold. At his suggestion, Balak assigned some of the young, beautiful Moabite ladies to visit the Israelite encampment. At first, they came with gifts and offered to sell us fresh fruit and grains from their fields. As the people became accustomed to their visits, the ladies came more frequently and instead of just bartering with the women of the camp, they began to approach the Israeli men.

Zipporah cautioned me one day as we ate some of the delicious grapes the Moabites had sold to us that morning. "Moses, have you noticed that the Moabite women no longer approach the women of our camp when they come to sell their goods?"

"No, I had not noticed. Are you sure about this?"

"Yes, I am very sure." Zipporah stood up from her seat in the tent. "And I have also noticed that the Moabite women are wearing less clothing each time they visit."

"Well, it is very hot."

"Moses!" Zipporah voice became stern. "I have seen our men following every movement of these women with their eyes. And I know for a fact that Shemiah's husband, Jedah and her brother with him, followed two Moabite seductresses out of the camp last night, and as of this morning, Shemiah is still weeping alone in her tent! Open your eyes, Moses!"

I fell to my knees. How could I have allowed this evil to happen right in front of my eyes? Had my eyes also been following the movements of these unclothed temptresses?

Then Yahweh spoke to my spirit.

"What Zipporah has told you is true, Moses. Not only these two men have been seduced, but other men are also missing. They have committed sexual immorality with these women and have also joined them in sacrificing to the gods of Baal. Even now another plague is coming over the camp and people are dying."

I was shaking as I realized that our camp had been infiltrated by the enemy so easily right in front of my face. I myself had not wanted to see the harm in the visits of the women, and had enjoyed the fruit of their land, and yes, the beauty of their appearance.

"Moses!" Yahweh interrupted my thoughts. "Moses, I forgive you. We can process this later, together, but now I need you to take action."

"Yes, Lord, I am ready."

"Call the leaders of the camp to surrender all those men who have joined in worship of the Baal of Peor."

It took several hours to gather the men who had been seduced into idolatry as they slowly returned to camp. Finally, the leaders announced that every guilty man was now accounted for, standing shoulder to shoulder in the heat of the noonday sun. Their faces were hard, angry. And the whimpers of their wives and families, now apart from them, were heard from the crowd standing at a distance.

Then I called out to the ones I had appointed as judges over the people. "Each of you must put to death those of your clans who have sacrificed to the false gods of the Moabites."

I watched as the judges received my words and saw the anguish in their eyes as they considered killing their own brothers, fathers, and children. Quiet weeping began sweeping the crowd in waves, from the judges to the men and women surrounding the guilty ones.

Then, before anyone drew a sword to carry out Yahweh's command, an Israeli man named Zimri, son of Salu, defiantly broke away from the group condemned to die. The people gasped but did nothing as he marched to the outskirts of the camp and brought out a scantily clad Midianite woman.

"Come, Cozbi, daughter of Zur," he declared loudly, and he pulled her into his tent, in full view of our camp, and right in front of the tent of Yahweh's presence.

Phinehas, a priest in Aaron's family, watched the scene unfold as he stood in the entrance to the tent. Then he screamed something unintelligible, grabbed a spear, and ran right into the tent. Phinehas drove the spear right through the body of the man, and into the body of the Midianite below him and they both died.

At the very moment the spear entered their bodies, the plague lifted off the camp. I saw a cloud of what looked like black ashes rise up from the camp and blow away toward the desert. Twenty-four hundred people had perished from the plague.

Yahweh spoke as I watched the death cloud dissipate in the wind. "Phinehas, son of Eleazer, son of Aaron, has stood as a priest between the living and the dead and turned my anger away from my people. Today Phinehas was a champion for my honor, so that I did not need to carry out the death sentence on my people."

I knew these words were not for me. I had been paralyzed, but young Phinehas had stood up for the honor of Yahweh which was being challenged by the wayward men of our camp.

"Phinehas, this is what Yahweh says to you," I called out so that all could hear. "I am making a covenant of peace with you, Phinehas. You are your descendants will always be my priests, for you were zealous for my honor and made atonement for the people. You have honored Yahweh, and now he honors you."

The people cheered and wept as Phinehas bowed low before the Lord.

Then I disbursed the crowd to go and bury the dead and cleanse the camp from anything leftover from the Moabite people.

I entered the Tent of Meeting and embraced my weeping, great nephew, Phinehas. "I am so proud of you, son. You did what every man among us should have done. Your grandpa, Aaron, would have been so proud."

Then I walked to the front of the tent, in view of the Ark of God's Presence, and waited.

"Moses, you have questions for me?"

"I don't know where to start."

"Let's start with Phinehas."

"Okay."

"Do you remember when I called you to go and set my people free from Pharaoh?"

"Yes."

"And you were arguing with me that you couldn't do what I asked you, that you needed someone to go with you? Remember? And who did I send?"

"My brother, Aaron."

"Yes, Aaron, who I appointed as a priest over my people, and the grandfather of my priest, Phinehas, who stood in the place of mediator today between life and death and interceded for Israel. Although your brother Aaron has died, I have not left my people without a man of my honor, my choosing to stand in the gap for my people.

"You were not the man of my choosing to slay Zimri and Cozbi. My priest was chosen for this assignment. Today Phinehas was your priest as well as priest over my people. Today he upheld the honor and righteousness of Yahweh on your behalf. And I will never be without a witness on this earth for my eyes are always searching for the ones who are faithful to me, so that I may strengthen them to minister on my behalf."

His voice was without condemnation, just as he never condemned me for needing my brother, Aaron, before I could fulfill my assignment.

"I do not condemn you for being a man, Moses. I know that you need a priest, too. That is why I brought your brother to join you. And why Phinehas came to the forefront today."

I felt exposed before the Lord. And yet safe. He knew me, knew my strengths and my weaknesses, yet he loved me and chose me to lead his people.

"That is the reason that one day all the kings of the earth will rise up and give you thanks, Yahweh," I exclaimed.

"What is the reason?" he asked.

"Because they will know that you know them, all their strengths and weaknesses, and that you love them and have chosen them for your assignment. Yahweh, knowing you is truly everything to me, and being known by you, known, understood and valued for who I am, that I can't even put into words. But when the kings of the earth enter into this kind of relationship with Yahweh, the God of the Universe, they'll be with me, on their faces before you, laughing, weeping, overwhelmed and overcome by your goodness."

I lay for sometime in his presence, late into the evening before Phinehas nudged me. "Zipporah is asking for you, my lord."

I rose and glanced at the Ark before turning to leave the tent for the evening.

"One day," I heard as I walked away from the tent. I stopped and waited for him to finish the thought but heard nothing until I started walking again. "One day, you'll never have to walk away."

MAKING PREPARATIONS FOR MY DEPARTURE

I didn't realize it at the time, or maybe I did, but pushed the thought right out of my brain. I knew Yahweh had told me that I would not enter the promised land with my people. Nevertheless, I began to make preparations for how we would take on the battles before us, not knowing if I would still be around to lead the people.

At Yahweh's direction I counted the people. There were 601,730 men of fighting age. Yahweh reminded me that none of those six hundred thousand plus men were counted in the previous census we'd taken in the Desert of Sinai. Yahweh had told us that none of those in the original census would be alive to enter the Promised Land because they had refused to obey Yahweh after the unfavorable report from the spies some forty years ago. None except two men, Caleb and Joshua, were alive from the previous generation, just as Yahweh had spoken.

We traveled on and camped near the Abarim range of mountains. As I gazed upward at the mountain peaks, I heard Yahweh calling me. "Come up here, Moses and see the Promised Land!"

"I can see it from up there?" I wondered and hurried to grab a skin of water and my staff out of my tent.

When I reached the mountaintop, Yahweh's presence surrounded me. "Come and look, Moses. Here is the land I am giving to my people."

I gazed across the mountaintop and turned around to survey all the land to the east and west, north and south, that lay sprawled out around the Abarim peaks.

"All of this?" I asked.

"Yes, all of it."

"Wow, it's wonderful. I see bodies of water, hills, mountains, deserts, and valleys, every type of terrain."

"I told you it would be wonderful, Moses." Yahweh's voice portrayed the smile I imagined on his face. "It's a land flowing with milk and honey, just as I promised."

I gulped the cool mountain air as I stood gazing over the land of promise.

"Moses, you will only see the land with your eyes. You will not enter it, as I told you when you did not obey me at the waters of Meribah. Soon you will die, as Aaron died in my presence.

"Yahweh?"

"Yes, my son?"

"Please, my Lord, may the Lord, the God of the spirits of all mankind, appoint a man of your choice to take my place, to lead this community, to go with them, to lead them out and bring them in so they're not like sheep who have lost their shepherd."

"Yes, Moses, with all my heart, yes. You have truly been a shepherd to this people, the people of my heart. The ones I love you have loved. And even now, when a lesser man would grieve his imminent departure, you instead have not begged me to change my mind, but only to make sure that the people you love continue to be led by a good shepherd."

I wept in his presence. "Am I crazy, staring into my own death with no terror?"

"No, my son. You already told me the one thing you are terrified of is of me not going with you. And I've already addressed that with you, haven't I?"

I nodded as I wept, remembering my petition to him. "I'll go anywhere, as you long as you are going, only never leave me."

"Now, arise, and go down the mountain. Take your general, Joshua, son of Nun, a man in whom my Spirit already rests, and commission him as leader in your place, but not just with your words. Lay your hand on him. Impart to him everything you have received from me. Have him stand before Eleazer, the priest and the entire assembly and commission him to take your place of leadership over the people. Give him some of your authority immediately so the people will obey him as they obey you. Eleazer will be his priest. He will inquire of me on Joshua's behalf so Joshua will know how to lead the people on the journey into the Promised Land.

That very afternoon I did all that Yahweh had commanded. I stood behind Joshua, the son of my heart, and felt Yahweh in turn standing behind me. My hands grew hot on Joshua's shoulders, and we both trembled as Yahweh's presence flowed from me into my successor.

The next days I spent training Joshua, and teaching the Israelites the lessons Yahweh had given me for life in the Promised Land. I instructed them regarding offerings to make to the Lord, feasts to celebrate and remember God's goodness, celebrating the Passover every year so they would never forget where they came from and who brought them into the Promised Land.

I was often flustered, knowing my time of death was rapidly approaching and trying to think of everything I needed to do to equip my successor and my people to follow Yahweh after I was gone. I lay awake one night and finally got up and left the tent to stare into the night sky.

I heard a noise behind me and then Zipporah came and stood with me gazing at the stars.

"Isn't that your star, Moses?" Zipporah pointed to the north.

"Yes, yes, it is, my dear. Polaris, my old friend." I smiled.

"Moses, I think Yahweh is speaking to you through your 'old friend' tonight."

"Oh, you think so." I laughed, thinking of the many times I had told Zipporah what Yahweh was speaking, only to have the tables turned on me.

"Yes, I do." Zipporah locked her arm through mine. "Yahweh doesn't want you losing sleep over worrying."

I knew in my spirit that my wife was spot on. Not only had he arranged for me to see Polaris, the star of navigation that pointed the way for anyone needing direction, but he had also awakened my wife, who loved me. She always pointed me in the right direction, directly back to Yahweh.

Then Yahweh joined the conversation. "Listen to your wife," was all he said, with a chuckle. I didn't tell Zipporah this. No need for her to get a swelled head. But I followed her back into the tent and slept through the night, Polaris' light shining on me all the while through the open tent flap.

I heard Yahweh the next morning, before I'd even opened my eyes.

"Now that you've slept well, thanks to your lovely wife," he quipped, "How would you like to start taking some of the Promised Land on this side of the Jordan?"

I jumped up and hurried to my general, Joshua, to give him Yahweh's battle plans.

"Yahweh said it's time for us to avenge ourselves against the Midianites," I told Joshua. What I did not tell him was that this excursion would be my last. Yahweh had told me I would be gathered to my people after we took Midian.

At Yahweh's instruction Joshua and I mustered one thousand people from each of the twelve tribes of Israel, a fighting force of twelve thousand men. Phinehas, the priest went with them, carrying holy articles of God's presence from the Tent of Meeting and trumpets to signal the troops in battle.

The Israelite soldiers killed every Midianite man, including the five kings of Midian. They also killed the sorcerer, Balaam, who was embedded with the enemy army. They took all the women captive, along with all the Midianite's livestock and treasures, and brought them to me at the camp.

I watched the women being paraded before the camp and called out to the leaders of the troops.

"Have you allowed all the women to live? They were the ones who followed Balaam's advice and led you away from the Lord at Peor and caused a plague that killed twenty-four thousand of your people. Now then, all women who have slept with a man must be killed, along with all boys. Only the virgin daughters may live."

So the troops slaughtered the women and boys as I commanded.

"Now all of you who have blood on your hands must purify yourselves and remain outside the camp for seven days."

The commanders brought back the statistics of the battle to Joshua and me the next day. Every Midianite male had been slain. Thirty-two thousand virgin women were taken as plunder along with hundreds of thousands of sheep and thousands of cattle and donkeys. Not one Israeli soldier had died in battle.

"Only Yahweh," I whispered to Joshua. He nodded and we walked together to the Tent of Meeting to worship.

As we rested the next day from the battle, leaders from the tribe of Reuben and Gad approached Joshua and me. They bowed in honor, and I invited them to join us and speak their minds.

"As you know, our people have very large herds and flocks. During the battle against the Midianites, we saw that the land of Midian which we have taken is very suitable grazing land. Please, if it pleases the Lord, make this land our inheritance in the Promised Land."

"What?" I shouted, rising to my feet. "Are you telling me that you want to now settle in this land which all twelve tribes of Israel have taken, and let the other ten tribes do all the fighting to conquer the rest of the land? Oh no, you don't. If you separate yourselves from going up with us to take the rest of the land, you will discourage the people to go forward in conquering the rest of the Promised Land, just like your fathers did forty years ago, and you will bring Yahweh's anger against his people again. Not on my watch! I won't let that happen again."

I began to summon Joshua to arrest the leaders of Reuben and Gad on the spot.

"No, my Lord!" The leaders fell to the ground. "No, my Lord, we are not deserting our fellow Israelites. We only want to build pens for our flocks, and cities for our families to live in. Then we will go with our fellow soldiers to battle in Canaan on the other side of the Jordan and take the rest of the land Yahweh promised. We will not forsake our brothers."

Satisfied, I declared that the land called Gilead on this side of the Jordan River would belong to the Gadites and Reubenites and the half tribe of Manasseh, son of Joseph.

As the leaders returned to their tents I sat back and realized that I was watching the Promised Land come into being right before my eyes. We had failed miserably forty years earlier, but it seemed that all Israel was in agreement this time. My heart swelled in pride as I surveyed the fighting men from all twelve tribes of Israel who stood before me waiting for their next instructions.

There on the plains of what had been Moab, across the river from Jericho, Yahweh gave me his plans for the battles to come after my death. I stood and relayed all his words to the troops.

"Yahweh says, 'When you cross the Jordan River into Canaan, you must drive out all the inhabitants of the land. Destroy every idol, every carved image, even those made of gold and precious metals. Demolish every place of idol worship. Let nothing remain.' You are to take possession of the land and live in it. Distribute the land to the tribes according to their size and needs.

"'I warn you,' says Yahweh, 'if you do not drive out the inhabitants of the land, but allow them to remain, they will become barbs in your eyes and thorns in your sides. They will turn you away from following me, and then I will do to you what I did to them.'"

The troops shouted their response. "We will obey the voice of the Lord."

Over the next days I often asked Joshua to gather the people. Yahweh had reminded me of how my parents would tell me my story over and over again as I was growing up. How Yahweh had rescued me after my birth when the infant boys were supposed to be killed. Then again how he had spared my life by setting me in a little boat in the Nile River. Each story of Yahweh's faithfulness reminded me of my identity and my part in his story. So when Yahweh announced one morning that it was story time, I assumed he wanted me to tell my children about my life.

"No, Moses, tell my people their story. Start from the beginning. Let them see my hand on their lives from their time of slavery in Egypt, until today as they stand on the boundaries of the Promised Land. Tell them."

So I stood before my people and told them their story. None of these people remembered Egypt, except for Joshua and Caleb. They needed to remember where they came from, and how they got here. So I described our lives in Egypt, the poverty and mistreatment we suffered from our Egyptian slave masters. I told them how Yahweh had heard his people crying and sent Aaron and me to lead them out of slavery.

Even the little ones whooped and cheered as we relived the crossing of the Red Sea and how our enemies drowned when they tried to follow us.

I heard weeping as I reminded them of their fathers who had disobeyed God and refused to go up to the Promised Land.

"What should have been a two-week journey became a forty-year journey as we wandered around in the desert. Not one person from that generation lived to see the Promised Land, except for Joshua and Caleb. All our ancestors died in the desert and did not see the promise of the land we are now standing on, which is now the possession of the Israeli tribes of Reuben, Gad and the half tribe of Manasseh.

"And I, too, disobeyed the voice of Yahweh, at the waters of Meribah. So I will not be going with you across the Jordan into Canaan."

At this, the people wept aloud.

"It's okay," I called out. "I'm okay. I wanted to let you know that I pleaded with the Lord about it. The Lord called me up to Mount Pisgah and showed me the Promised Land from there. I stood there on the mountaintop turning in circles, surveying the land of our promise. I was so excited. I so wanted to be with you all when we took the land. But Yahweh said no. 'You will see with your eyes from this mountaintop, but you will not cross the Jordan,' he told me. But he called me to commission Joshua to lead you. He said, 'Joshua will lead this people across and will lead them into their inheritance of the land you see before you.'

"Every word of Yahweh is sure." I cleared my throat loudly to get everyone's attention. "Every word of Yahweh is sure. That means whatever Yahweh says will come to pass. He is not a man, that he should lie, or change his mind. He called you his people. He called this land your land. So you are, so it is, and it shall ever be so, because he spoke it.

"I am going to give you many more lectures before I go up the mountain one last time. Yahweh wants you to succeed in all you do, so he is giving me messages for you by which a man will live, if he follows them.

"But if you cannot remember everything, I will also write it down for you so you can read it and remember.

"Still, if you remember anything I've said today and in the days to come, let it be that Yahweh's word is true and trustworthy. I've banked my life on it, and I encourage you to do the same. It's a safe place.

"Be careful, my children, watch yourselves closely so that you do not forget the things your eyes have seen, or the words I've spoken to you. Teach them to your children, and your grandchildren. Don't make any false gods for yourselves, like the ones in the nations God is driving out before you. As for you, the Lord took you and brought you up out of the furnace of Egypt to be the people of his inheritance, as you are today. You belong to Yahweh. He calls you his people. Never forget that he chose you out of all the peoples of the earth to be his own."[35]

I found myself desperately pleading with the people as my time with them drew to a close.

"Never before from the day Yahweh created the earth has any other people heard the voice of God speaking to them out of fire. No god has ever rescued a people and taken them out of another nation and given them a Promised Land. No other

---

[35] Deuteronomy 4:20

people received bread from heaven, pillars of cloud and fire to lead them, water from a rock not once, but twice. You and your fathers experienced these God encounters for one reason, that you would know that the Lord is God; besides him there is no other. Now follow this God, keep his commands which I am giving you again this day and I promise you, if you do, it will go well with you and your children after you for the rest of your lives.[36]

"Hear, O Israel: The Lord our God, the Lord is one. Love the Lord your God with all your heart and with all your soul and with all your strength. Tell your children, teach them to love Yahweh. Talk about Yahweh, tell them these stories when you sit home, or when you walk along the roadside, when you sit down and when you get up. Do whatever you have to do to remember and to remind your children. Tie them as symbols on your foreheads; write them on the door frames of your houses and on your gates so they stare you in the face and remind you that you belong to the Lord. Whatever you do, don't forget. I love you, and Yahweh loves you. Never forget, even when life is hard. When your babies get sick. When you suffer persecution from people who hate Yahweh."

I was weeping by now, so wishing I could go along on the hard journey before the people. But I felt Yahweh's presence standing behind me.

"Listen, what I'm telling you is not too difficult for you or beyond your understanding. It's not far away up in heaven so you have to wonder who is going to go up there and get it for you. It's not on the other side of the sea so you need to hire a boat and cross the ocean to bring it back. No, the word is right here. It's in your mouth and in your heart so you may obey it.[37]

"Look, I'm setting before you today a choice you have to make. Will you choose life and prosperity, or death and destruction? If you love the Lord your God and follow his commands and decrees and don't worship other false idols you will live and increase in the land Yahweh is giving you. But

---

[36] Ibid.
[37] Deuteronomy 30:11–19

if your heart turns away from Yahweh and you start worshiping other gods, destruction is your lot.

"This day I call heaven and earth as witnesses against you that I have set before you life and death, blessings and curses. Now choose life!

"I'm now one hundred and twenty years old. I am no longer able to lead you. Yahweh has told me that I will not cross the Jordan with you."

Again, the people began to weep, and when the children heard their parents weeping, they began to cry as well.

"Shhhh. Wait. Even though I will not go with you, Yahweh himself will cross over the Jordan ahead of you. He will destroy the nations before you. And here is Joshua. Yahweh says that his servant, Joshua will cross over the Jordan ahead of you. Joshua, come."

Joshua came forward and I laid my hands on his shoulders. "Be strong and courageous, my son. Yahweh himself will go with you wherever you go. Don't be afraid; don't be discouraged."

The people rallied and stood to their feet clapping for Joshua.

I spent many nights writing down the words of instruction Yahweh was pouring into me, and I was pouring out to the people each day. I loved every minute of it. And then, one night, he said, "It's time."

Not everyone is told the day they're going to die. But not everyone walks around knowing that Yahweh will never leave them. I knew that even in death, he had promised to never leave me. Joshua and I came and stood at the Tent of Meeting as Yahweh instructed us. The Pillar of Cloud came and surrounded us both.

"You're going to pass away soon, Moses."

"I know. I'm ready, my Lord."

"My son, I regret to tell you that these people will not always follow me after you leave; they are going to forsake me and suffer much because of it. So I have one last assignment for you. Teach our people this song I will give you and it will be a witness after you have died. When they sing it in years to come, they will remember and return to me."

I grieved at Yahweh's words, but I had already witnessed that what he said was true. The people had been so quick to turn away from Yahweh time and time again on our way to the Promised Land.

I sat inside the Tent of Meeting the next day and wrote the song. The people were waiting when I came out. They followed me around like a puppy those days, not knowing when I would pass away.

"Yahweh is singing over you," I said. Then I closed my eyes and began to sing Yahweh's song over the people.

> "Listen, you heavens, and I will speak;
> hear, you earth, the words of my mouth.
> Let my teaching fall like rain
> and my words descend like dew,
> like showers on new grass,
> like abundant rain on tender plants.
>
> I will proclaim the name of the LORD.
> Oh, praise the greatness of our God!
> He is the Rock, his works are perfect,
> and all his ways are just.
> A faithful God who does no wrong,
> upright and just is he.
>
> They are corrupt and not his children;
> to their shame they are a warped and crooked
> generation.
> Is this the way you repay the LORD,
> you foolish and unwise people?
> Is he not your Father, your Creator,
> who made you and formed you?
>
> Remember the days of old;
> consider the generations long past.
> Ask your father and he will tell you,
> your elders, and they will explain to you.
> When the Most High gave the nations their

inheritance,
when he divided all mankind,
he set up boundaries for the peoples
according to the number of the sons of Israel.
For the LORD's portion is his people,
Jacob his allotted inheritance.

In a desert land he found him,
in a barren and howling waste.
He shielded him and cared for him;
he guarded him as the apple of his eye,
like an eagle that stirs up its nest
and hovers over its young,
that spreads its wings to catch them
and carries them aloft.
The LORD alone led him;
no foreign god was with him.

He made him ride on the heights of the land
and fed him with the fruit of the fields.
He nourished him with honey from the rock,
and with oil from the flinty crag,
with curds and milk from herd and flock
and with fattened lambs and goats,
with choice rams of Bashan
and the finest kernels of wheat.
You drank the foaming blood of the grape.

Jeshurun grew fat and kicked;
filled with food, they became heavy and sleek.
They abandoned the God who made them
and rejected the Rock their Savior.
They made him jealous with their foreign gods
and angered him with their detestable idols.
They sacrificed to false gods, which are not God—
gods they had not known,
gods that recently appeared,
gods your ancestors did not fear.
You deserted the Rock, who fathered you;
you forgot the God who gave you birth.

The LORD saw this and rejected them
because he was angered by his sons and daughters.
"I will hide my face from them," he said,
"and see what their end will be;
for they are a perverse generation,
children who are unfaithful.
They made me jealous by what is no god
and angered me with their worthless idols.
I will make them envious by those who are not a
people;
I will make them angry by a nation that has no
understanding.
For a fire will be kindled by my wrath,
one that burns down to the realm of the dead below.
It will devour the earth and its harvests
and set afire the foundations of the mountains.

"I will heap calamities on them
and spend my arrows against them.
 I will send wasting famine against them,
consuming pestilence and deadly plague;
I will send against them the fangs of wild beasts,
the venom of vipers that glide in the dust.
In the street the sword will make them childless;
in their homes terror will reign.
The young men and young women will perish,
the infants and those with gray hair.
I said I would scatter them
and erase their name from human memory,
but I dreaded the taunt of the enemy,
lest the adversary misunderstand
and say, 'Our hand has triumphed;
the LORD has not done all this.'"

They are a nation without sense,
there is no discernment in them.
If only they were wise and would understand this
and discern what their end will be!
How could one man chase a thousand,
or two put ten thousand to flight,
unless their Rock had sold them,

unless the LORD had given them up?
For their rock is not like our Rock,
as even our enemies concede.
Their vine comes from the vine of Sodom
and from the fields of Gomorrah.
Their grapes are filled with poison,
and their clusters with bitterness.
Their wine is the venom of serpents,
the deadly poison of cobras.

"Have I not kept this in reserve
and sealed it in my vaults?
It is mine to avenge, I will repay.
In due time their foot will slip;
their day of disaster is near
and their doom rushes upon them."

The LORD will vindicate his people
and relent concerning his servants
when he sees their strength is gone
and no one is left, slave or free.
He will say: "Now where are their gods,
the rock they took refuge in,
the gods who ate the fat of their sacrifices
and drank the wine of their drink offerings?
Let them rise up to help you!
Let them give you shelter!

"See now that I myself am he!
There is no god besides me.
I put to death and I bring to life,
I have wounded and I will heal,
and no one can deliver out of my hand.
I lift my hand to heaven and solemnly swear:
As surely as I live forever,
when I sharpen my flashing sword
and my hand grasps it in judgment,
I will take vengeance on my adversaries
and repay those who hate me.
I will make my arrows drunk with blood,
while my sword devours flesh:

the blood of the slain and the captives,
the heads of the enemy leaders."

Rejoice, you nations, with his people,
for he will avenge the blood of his servants;
he will take vengeance on his enemies
and make atonement for his land and people."[38]

Then I blessed each of the twelve tribes of Israel with the words Yahweh spoke into my spirit. I watched the peoples' faces as they listened and received the blessings as if spoken directly from Yahweh's mouth.

"Reuben." The tribe rose as one from the sand and set their eyes on my face. I could see tears forming in their eyes and I knew exactly what they were feeling. I had felt it, too, every time Yahweh spoke my name.

"Yes." I smiled through my tears. "Yes, Reuben, he knows your name. He knows who you are, and he has great plans for you to live and not die."

"Judah." I waited for every eye to focus on me and spoke Yahweh's blessing. "You are a defender of my people, Judah, and I will defend you.

"Levi, my priest, you have faithfully watched over my words and instructed my people. I am pleased with you, Levi.

"Ah, little Benjamin. The beloved of the Lord rests secure in him for he shields him all day long. And the one the Lord loves, Benjamin, rests secure between his shoulders.

"Joseph, prince among his brothers, may the favor of him who dwelt in the burning bush be upon you and your sons, Ephraim and Manasseh.

"You, Zebulin, and Issachar, you will feast on the abundance of the seas and on the treasures hidden in the sand."

"Gad, blessed is he who enlarges God's domain.

"Dan, the cub of the lion!

"Naphtali, abounding with my favor, full of my blessing.

"Asher, most blessed of the sons of Israel, your strength will equal your days."

---

[38] Deuteronomy 32:1–43

The peoples' faces beamed under the blessings.

Then I released one final blessing on all the tribes.

"Blessed are you, O Israel! Who is like you, a people saved by the Lord? He is your shield and helper and your glorious sword. Your enemies will cower before you, and you will trample down their high places."

Yahweh woke me early the next morning while the camp was still silent. I knew it would be my last time climbing the mountain to hear his voice. I took my staff and silently slipped out of my tent to climb Mt. Nebo.

"Welcome, my friend!" Yahweh's voice greeted me as I reached the pinnacle.

I stood and breathed deeply of Yahweh's presence and the sweet mountain air.

"Come and look, Moses. This is it. This is the land of promise, from Gilead to Dan, all of Naphtali, the territory of Ephraim and Manasseh, all the land of Judah as far as the western sea, the Negev, the whole region from the Valley of Jericho across the river, Jericho and as far as Zoar."

I stood and turned as Yahweh pointed out the places he named.

"This is the land I promised to Abraham, Isaac, and Jacob. I have let you see it now with your own eyes, although you will not cross over into it with your people."

I closed my eyes, satisfied to see the land with my own eyes, and to be standing here on this mountain top with my God and my friend.

"Moses."

I opened my eyes and discovered I was no longer standing on a rocky mountain ledge but was in a green pasture with wildflowers swaying in a gentle breeze all around me. And coming toward me was a man who looked vaguely familiar.

"Moses."

I knew that voice.

"Yahweh!" I rushed into arms of the one whose voice I had known since the time he called my name out of a burning bush. I had felt these arms around me before. It was a safe and familiar place. I reached out my hand and touched his face, traced the contours of his cheeks, and finally rested my head on his shoulder. I stood there, just breathing it all in.

"Is this what it's like to die?" I wondered.

"It is for every child of mine," Yahweh responded to my unspoken words. "To be absent from the body is to be present with me. You merely close your eyes in one realm, and open them in another."[39]

I sighed and relaxed in Yahweh's embrace.

"This is it." I thought. "I feel ... I feel completely satisfied, completely fulfilled. I need nothing more. This is what I've lived my whole life for."

After a while my thoughts returned to my people who would never see me return from Mt. Nebo.

"Yahweh? What about the people?"

"I have buried your body, Moses, up on the mountaintop. Even now the people are mourning for you, honoring you."

"Will you bless them, Abba? Will you remind them of everything I taught them?"

"Yes, I will, my son. And from time to time, I will allow you a glimpse of where I'm taking the people so you can continue to pray for them and bless them from here."

"Now come, there are some people who are very anxious to see you."

I heard the sound of people running through the field and saw two men and two ladies bounding over the tall grass.

"Abba, Ima, Aaron, Miriam!"

My family encircled me, surrounding me in their arms as we wept tears of joy at our reunion. I looked up at Yahweh whose face shone even as tears slipped from the kindest eyes I had ever seen. Then he skipped over to our group hug and wrapped his arms around us all.

"Moses sandwich!" he shouted, and we all laughed and cried and worshiped in the place we knew was home.

---

[39] 2 Corinthians 5:8

ACKNOWLEDGMENTS

So many people have poured into my life and encouraged me to write this book.

I first want to thank my personal cheerleader, my husband, Jimmy. Jimmy is not a reader, except for technical writing, art books, glass-blowing techniques, and the like. So, after most writing sessions I would carry my laptop into the kitchen and read aloud to Jimmy. He offered encouragement, suggestions, and even sat and wept with me a few times over the lessons learned by the prophets. Special thanks to Jimmy for partnering with me and painting the incredible portrait of Elijah that graces my book cover.

Several years ago, as God was developing in me the inspiration for this book, but it was still in the dreaming stages, a young man at church called out a prophetic word during the worship service. My dear friend and son from another mother, Michael Giordano told me that Father God had a book for me to write and confirmed what was already in my heart. Thank you, Michael. That word was like a firecracker in me. I love you, buddy.

My Monday night sewing group was always game to have me read aloud to them as they worked on their quilting and crochet projects around my kitchen table. Thank you, my dear friends for your love and encouragement!

My baby sister, Roberta Brosius, already a published author herself, helped with the initial reading and editing. Although I greatly appreciated and relied on her amazing grammatical skills, what thrilled my heart the most was when she told me that she caught the intimacy theme running through the book. That was enough, to know that somehow, I had effectively communicated the greatest value of my life through the pages of my book. Thank you, dear sister!

A big thank you to my dear friend, Carolyn Malinowski who not only proofread and listed corrections for me to fix, but she also took the time to tell me over and over again as she read through each chapter how much she was enjoying the stories.

My dear friends and mentors, Richard and Darlene Tittle have loved me and prayed for me for many years. They encouraged me to use my voice when they invited me several times to speak at their Vineyard church. They also encouraged me to read aloud to them during our visits and let me know how my stories had blessed them.

Thank you also to my wonderful friends, Dottie & Joe Scalzo who have become best buddies to Jimmy and me. They provided much encouragement to me as I wrote this book.

My gratitude to so many sweet friends who dreamed with me over this book:

My bestie, Patricia "Grammie" Lorentzen who always believed in me, now cheering me on from heaven; My long-time faithful friend and partner in crime as we raised our kids together, Ruth Clarke; My delightful new friend, Lisa Perna whose child-like enthusiasm spurred me on to the finish line. Lisa showcased my short stories on her daily podcast on several occasions, wrote the forward for this book, and shared my joy all along the way; The ladies at our Women of Hope study group who shared their dreams and then dreamed along with me about this book before I even started writing it! May Daddy bring your every dream to fruition!

My church family at Shore Life Church who kept asking when the book would be ready.

I don't know if he'll ever hear about my mention of his name, but I have to include a special thank you to my favorite pastor, Bill Johnson from Bethel Church in Redding, CA. I've visited your amazing church several times, Bill, and devoured your books and devotionals. I grabbed onto the concept you shared several times in your sermons and books, how Old Testament characters were able to reach into the future because of their hunger for more intimacy with God and pull into their time the eternal promises of God that were not yet known in their lifetime. One such example was the night and day worship experience that King David started during his reign. In Bill's words, "David reached into the future and pulled New Testament promises into his day." I can only hope that I communicated that amazing concept as clearly as you, Bill Johnson. Although we've never met, I consider you a spiritual papa and I thank you for releasing what Daddy shares with you in the secret place.

And thank you, Daddy, Father God, for that night, May 9, 1966, when you came to live inside of me. I can't, nor do I want to, imagine life without your presence surrounding me and your voice leading me. Your written Word is my lifeline, and your still small voice inside is my anchor. I love you always. Tell Grammie to save the seat next to you in the Throne Room for me. It's okay if we have to squeeze to fit us all in. Just so long as I can be close to you, that will be heaven to me.

Love, Taffy

ABOUT THE AUTHOR

Taffy Spaloss lives in Ocean County, New Jersey, with her husband, Jimmy, of over fifty years. She has five grown children, two of whom now live with Jesus, and fourteen amazing grandchildren. Taffy loves to read, write, quilt, and release the Father's heart wherever she goes. The self-proclaimed theme of her life is intimacy with God, and if you hang out with her enough, don't be surprised if she grabs you by the hand or wraps her arms around you and brings you along. After all, she says, Daddy always has room at his table for another son or daughter.

For more intimate moments with Daddy, you are also invited to visit Taffy's blog, *Kisses from the Father* at taffyspaloss.blogspot.com.

See you in the Throne Room!

Taffy